Nethermost Regained

Written & illustrated by

Nancy Guild Bendall

Meade House Press
Toronto, Canada

Dedication

This book is dedicated to the memory of

Tony White

"The comfort of having a friend may be taken away,
but not that of having had one."
(Seneca the Younger)

for readers 15 years and older

Meade House Press
20010 Main Street
Alton, ON, Canada
L7K 0C2

ISBN: 978-0-9939049-9-8
(greyscale version)

"We don't create a fantasy world to escape reality.
We create it to be able to stay."

(<u>What It Is</u> — Lynda Barry)

Cait and Rhue's Direct Family Tree

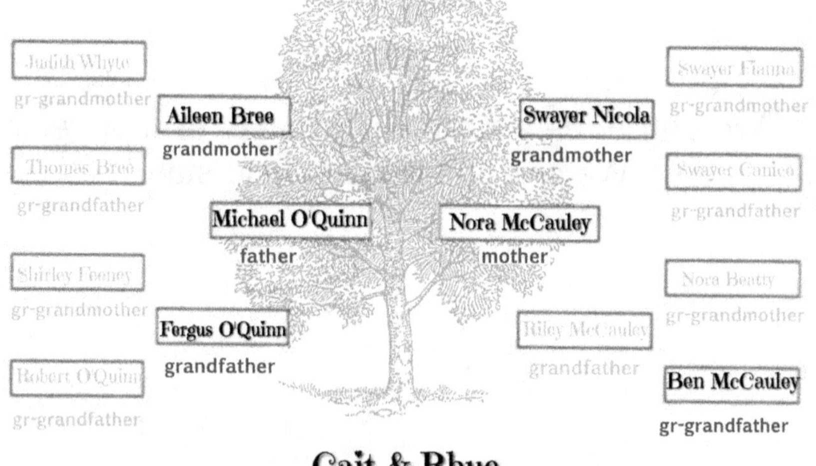

Cait & Rhue

Nethermost Regained

Table of Contents

The Illustrations …

Shin's Oil Paintings

Chapter 3: "I'd been watching the lone dog parked outside the shop for hours on the day of that late February snow squall."

Chapter 8: "My father and mother both held the same political office, that of Chief Counsels to the two Swayers of Nethermost, Her Grace Fianna, and His Grace Canice, regals of the first bloodline, sovereigns of Nethermost."

Chapter 11: "These were hardest to bear — especially the portrayal of citizens of all species being caught at the point of gilding and, for all I knew, frozen for all time. "Please! Stop!" I whimpered, shocked and horrified by the fear and loathing on their frozen gold faces. "How could you bear to paint such images?" It was one thing to hear carefully worded summations of hardship and battle, quite another to witness them."

Chapter 15: "The little settlement we constructed was impressive, if compact. We set up two, no pegs required tents, lining their floors with animal skins, and stacking one corner 10 cm. deep with pelts as a bed for Ol'Ben."

Chapter 19: "The scene was dark and obscured, an indoor setting, a couple of characters in odd dress — streaky because … "It's moving," I said, "the paint and the figures … moving," The action was incomplete and undefined, seconds only in length, repeating on a loop."

Chapter 31: "From my position on the veranda I witnessed the bustle of everyday life in Carrickbeg. The produce stalls were open for business and people were lined up for such items as bread, milk, fresh fruits and vegetables. It seemed that a barter system was in place — I saw little money change hands. It was more a matter of people exchanging one product for another"

Chapter 32: "Zee led me along a path to the edge of the settlement where the view opened up into an explosion of pure paradise. The colour of day in this land was somehow different — like the pinkish tones of an early dawn without the glare of a fireball sun — which made the sky the first thing I noticed. The effect was created by a single shaft of light shining down, energizing the vitreous crystal ceiling and diffused by large white crystal disks scattered about the fields."

Chapter 33: "… a larger than life character who could only have been Peadar, dressed in what looked like an old coronation cloak over satin undergarments, fat and bald from years of debauchery …"

Chapter 34: "It was a painting of course, a prevision, a prediction of what would be. It was Rhue on her dapple grey horse, dressed all in leathers, with a tooled breastplate. She wore her hair wild like mine now and her face was determined and vibrant. In one hand, she held the horse's reins, but in the other, she brandished a handsome sword. By her side, riding his fancy white steed, was Keane in similar leathers. The bond between them was obvious, their determination mutual. In the prevision action loop she was flourishing the sword, while he looked intent upon her with admiration in his eyes."

Chapter 42: "… flower petals dotted the path leading to the water, orchids floating on its surface, jouncing in the drizzle of the waterfall, a scent of jasmine in the air. At the bijou shoreline, a wooden folding table had been set, laden with food dainties that could only have been the handiwork of Shin. A freshly brewed teapot leaked steam into the still air, and my mother's hand selected companion sat at the table."

Aileen's Graphite Portraiture

Chapter 1: "She looked so travel weary — short sculpted auburn hair now tousled, beautiful violet blue eyes now puffy, tastefully applied makeup now smudged, clothes slightly untucked."

Chapter 2: "His entire body was shaped more or less like a lowercase *b*. He had a small egg shaped bald head with only four or five white hairs right on top that stood on end and breezed about each time the shop door opened. His well worn clothes never varied, taking on the look of some sort of weird uniform — polyester, wrinkle free shirts in faded pastels to cover his sunken chest, buttoned to the neck and tucked under his flaccid chin. In old age his weight had settled into his midriff which he then bifurcated mid belly with a worn leather belt that he used to hold his threadbare trousers in place. The bagginess of the trousers camouflaged his lower bits — where his belly joined up with his stubby white legs and thin ankles."

Chapter 4: "In stature, she was the size of a five year old, but she bore the demeanour of a queen. Her clothes had simple lines, skirts draped to mid calf length covering fitted leggings, fashioned of shimmering taffetas rich with colour. Beneath this sumptuous fabric, her thin legs looked mismatched, the explanation for her walking stick. It was impossible for me to decide how old, or how young, she actually was. She seemed ageless, with the wispy white hair of the aged, the smooth skin of the young, the textured eyes of the experienced."

Chapter 5: "This assistant's name was Loo Blakely, a nice sort of guy, born and bred in the village, who I'd known more or less all my life — handsome and keen, if a bit too full of himself. He had strong balanced facial features framed by dark blonde hair that was forever falling onto his forehead, and that he kept swooshing back unconsciously with his fingers a couple of hundred times a day. His well developed muscles strained the fabric of all his shirts in interesting places and left no room for the imagination in his tight fitting jeans."

Chapter 18: "… With my exact same face, but more confident, more muscular, with long reddish hair plaited into braids, clothed in a khaki jumpsuit, belted at the waist, with a holstered dagger looped in. Her boots were no nonsense too — weathered but well polished, clunky and sensible. She was a warrior, from top to toe, and she was, by any measure, fiercer than me."

Chapter 20: "In their features I saw many parts of both my father and my aunt. Aileen, for instance, was the obvious suspect for my aunt's auburn hair and violet eyes, although her auburn was now streaked with grey, her violet eyes framed with character lines."

Chapter 22: "He appeared on our stoop the day after Ol'Ben moved in, dressed in a super sized version of the khaki jumpsuit that Rhue always wore. He was big featured to be sure, with a strong, bold nose, trim beard over a long jaw, dark fuzzy hair and deep brown eyes that darted about the room constantly. Under the tight fitting uniform you could appreciate his well toned muscles, and where the uniform ended, a shocking amount of body hair began. Ol'Ben stared up at his six and a half foot frame for a good two minutes, before sputtering, "Mánús, my dear fellow!"

Chapter 23: "My father's dark colouring came from his father to be sure, whose black hair and sooty eyes were similarly salted with age. At a guess, they were in their sixties, lean, alert, and full of joy at the sight of Rhue and me entering the room."

Chapter 35: "The woman before me gasped, blinking to adjust to the sudden light — bloodshot eyes, their sockets smudged — a woman clearly overstretched with fatigue. But beauty was hiding within, beneath that white pallor and limp hair; and something else besides — strength, courage, defiance — those admirable features I saw in my sister."

Foreword

I am proud to say that I have known Nancy Guild Bendall for over 4 decades and even more proud of the legacy she is creating through her written word and extensive body of artwork that covers several mediums and genres. Nancy and I began our literary journey at university and even though my graduate studies have taken me in a different direction, I am so happy that we have reconnected at this point in our lives to celebrate her accomplishments.

Nancy is a magical storyteller, a true logophile, and an incredibly talented artist. In her most recent book, she has woven her two passions into a beautifully annotated tale of family love, heroism and the triumph of good over evil. In a world where fantasy is often used as a platform for extreme violence and blood shed, Nancy has distanced herself from this clutter with a story for all generations; a story that is relevant with its message of hope; a story that can be enjoyed as either 'read aloud' or 'in private'; a story that can be enjoyed again and again.

The characters follow an arduous journey from the small town of Alta, somewhere in rural Ontario, to Nethermost, an enchanted land located in middle earth somewhere beneath the northern Canadian wilderness. After almost 19 years apart, the journey to the subterranean realm reunites one of the heroines, Cait, with her family in a quest to regain the throne that had been clutched from her grandparents some 40 years before by an evilly ambitious relative. What ensues is a cleverly crafted mission to regain Nethermost and the palace. The cast of characters includes citizens from Nethermost Gate and Carrickbeg — elves, fairies, dwarves, heroic warriors and a troop of characters loyal to the old régime. The tale is full of magic, betrayal, intrigue, heroism and amazing plot twists.

Character development is an integral part of Nancy's craft. The characters are not only interesting and complex, they are believable. We quickly align our own experiences with theirs. Through these characters, the reader is opened to a view of the world that celebrates good over evil. The characters in Nethermost Regained challenge the reader to submerge themselves in a world of fantasy and fiction where they can either celebrate or question their own values. In the end, a belief in family and the power of 'the cause' become the motivation to act. The reader will enjoy the optimism, determination and sincerity of these intriguing characters.

The pace within a story is very important to me. I was happy to find there were no excessive descriptive passages that had nothing to do with either the theme or plot of the story. Every chapter has been beautifully crafted to be relevant and advance the plot and character development. As a result, the story is engaging; holding the reader's attention until the very end. A young adult audience will not want to put this book down. Nethermost Regained will spark mid teen and adult readers' imaginations and encourage the all important 'reading for pleasure'. According to Alan Gibbons, an award winning author and organizer of the Campaign for the Book, those "… who read regularly and for fun open up new worlds. They embark on journeys. They step into other people's shoes and walk around in them …"

One cannot review this book without acknowledging the exceptional drawings (31 in all) that Nancy has personally created for the publication. With her intimate insight into each character, she has created digital portraits and paintings that add 3 dimensional clarity to the story of Nethermost Regained. I am particularly fond of the portrait of Mánús. It perfectly depicts his magical qualities and visually supports his role in the story. In Nancy's own words, "A great photographer can capture a moment at its most exquisite — a great artist can interpret that moment." Her interpretation of specific moments is magical and through the lens of her artwork we gain a deeper connection to Nethermost and the men and women who make it special.

In closing, <u>Nethermost Regained</u> is a 'must read' for readers of all ages. This is a book that can be savored slowly alone or together, or read quickly in an afternoon. Whatever your motivation … enjoy the experience. Let yourself be submerged in the magical world of Nethermost. The ride is certainly worth it.

Paul McElhone, PhD
Former Dean
Mihalcheon School of Management
Concordia University of Edmonton
Senior Consultant, McElhone Consulting

Chapter 1: Raised in Captivity

"Where is Nethermost?" I asked, sitting across from her again in that parlour the following Sunday.

"Ah, now that is the question isn't it Cait … Where? And it is also the key to opening the doors to 'why' and 'how' as well. It is a difficult question, so I will answer as clearly as I can. Shut your eyes, if you will, and imagine going on a journey … a very, very long journey along a rigid, unforgiving, northbound path, for days and days — and days — until you feel that you cannot bear taking a step further. There!" she exclaimed, "There is Nethermost!"

Nethermost Regained

*****

I was never bullied, or even disliked — I was ignored.

My name is Cait O'Quinn. I've always felt grateful to whoever named me, that they gave me such a pretty name. Whenever I put name to paper, I would add plenty of flourishes so that my signature looked extra fancy. I wanted my signature to make the statement I never could.

I remember in high school, tenth grade it was, this cool Irish girl named Sían O'Brien, who was not so much a friend as she was an acquaintance, sharing a giggle with me beside our lockers between classes one day, declaring that with names such as hers and mine, it was obvious that we'd both come straight off the boat from Ireland, from where the fields of shamrocks were the kind of rich green only a Kelly could have painted, whatever that meant. But she made it sound exotic and for a heartbeat I felt included in her cool club, that is until I opened my fool mouth and spoiled it all by confessing that I wouldn't know where I was born.

I wouldn't know for the stupid, sad reason that I didn't even know my own parents! Not that I was an orphan. I was not an orphan, exactly. But I didn't live with my parents either, and I didn't know why, and I didn't know where they lived even, nor had I had ever met them — that I could remember. Hell, I couldn't know for sure if O'Quinn was my real last name. I was, however, told that my real parents' first names were Michael and Nora. They sound Irish — right?

The only reason I knew that I was not an orphan was 'cuz my aunt said I wasn't. She always claimed that my parents were both still alive. I lived with Aunt Moira who insisted that she was indeed my real aunt. Since her last name is the same as mine — O'Quinn — everyone thought she was my mom. But she wasn't! She said she was Michael's sister. Michael and Moira O'Quinn, brother and sister, born to Grandma and Grandpa O'Quinn, whoever they are — or were.

But Aunt Moira had been good to me, and I think she loved me, if kindness is love. I called her my phantom aunt 'cuz she always travelled, was seldom home for more than a couple of weeks together. The house where we lived was beautiful though — sitting in the pretty little village of Alta at the edge of nowhere Canada — an interesting but ancient house that Aunt Moira had refitted "with all the mod cons", as they say. She even added an indoor pool just for me. In addition to the pool, and more to Aunt Moira's taste, were the two large living spaces with modern elegant lines, three full bathrooms equipped with sauna tubs and showers, four luxuriant bedrooms, one modern study and a brushed nickel and black kitchen/dining area that was simply stocked, since neither Aunt Moira nor I could cook — all professionally designed and tastefully furnished by some posh interior decorator whose creations featured regularly in our community magazine. But nothing in this house said 'home' — no family photos, no heirlooms — just modernistic bric-à-brac scattered about to add gashes of colour and interest to the slightly weird designs. All posh and artistic, cold and impersonal.

My own room was decked out just the way I liked it though, with pearl grey walls, a cozy armchair upholstered in deep red velvet big enough for two of me, a squishy round area rug to match said chair, and a soft Queen size bed draped in a white coverlet and heaped with bright cushions of every primary colour! Oh, and all sorts of tech toys. I lacked for nothing.

Sort of.

Aunt Moira always swerved my many questions about my parents. As a kid, she usually got away with it by distracting me with some silly toy or favourite food. But by the time I reached the age of ten and had developed a stronger sense of self, I began asking the more serious questions and insisting on answers with threats of tears. I remember the day when I stopped asking those questions. Her answers had become so dissatisfying and I had become so demanding that after dodging the first few, she suddenly grabbed my arm in a vice like grip and whispered right up close to my ear …. quietly … urgently … exhaustedly, "I'm cautioned not to tell you more — yet."

What? What was that? Cautioned? By whom? Now I was even more confused, and hopelessly frustrated. But the urgency in her tone stopped me from asking those questions again. So from that day I was silenced, although it confirmed what I long suspected — that my truth was not only mysterious, but for some reason, ominous as well.

Nethermost Regained

Because Aunt Moira was on the road all the time, I had nannies, hoards of them when I was little, right up to age eighteen. I never got too attached to any one nanny. They didn't stay long enough for any of us to care. Not because I was a bad kid. I was an angel. But after all, we did live at the back of beyond and these nannies were young women, living alone for the most part with someone else's kid in a village so small that it had no public transit, no pubs or restaurants, no theatres and just one general store. So each of them, in turn, got bored and left, even though my aunt paid a top nanny wage. By the time I turned eighteen, both my aunt and I were thoroughly weary of nannies, or 'companions' as we started to call them after my fifteenth birthday. In fact, Aunt Moira practically kissed me on the mouth when I suggested that, at the ripe old age of eighteen, I was now too old for either nannies or companions — and then they were gone from my life for good.

I've said it before, and will do so again, Aunt Moira was kind to me. But she never figured out how to be anyone's idea of a parent. From moment one, she wanted to be my friend, my protector, which was nice but I often needed more guidance than friendship, something for which she was completely ill equipped, and too often the very thing that I craved. I was stricter with myself than she ever was. If I got low marks on a test or assignment in school, I grounded myself until I 'picked up those grades'. If I broke a plate from loading the dishwasher too carelessly, I gave myself extra chores until I felt I had 'repaid its cost'. Gosh I was disciplined! So, by the time I was eighteen, living for the most part on my own in a big old house on the border of the forest primeval, I truly felt that I had reared myself, with my aunt providing all of life's necessities, a large dollop of life's luxuries … but never that quality in life that I deeply desired.

What I desired was a witness to my life, someone to notice what I did each day, someone to praise me when I did well, to care enough to send me to my room when I was petulant, to hug me when I was sad — as I often was. But with no one like that around me most of the time, my life was unwitnessed. Even when Aunt Moira was around, she didn't see me. When she wasn't busy, she was distracted — but never by me, that permanent visitor in her home.

And I was ignored by others. There weren't many people my age in the village for one thing. I was bused to the nearest high school eight kilometres away where the kids also ignored me for the most part. I'm sure I would have been hard to spot in a crowd in any case. I didn't exactly stand out. I viewed myself as plain and average in every sense of those two words — neither beautiful nor ugly, neither tall nor short, neither fat nor thin — and far too shy. And because I needed to get on that bus at the end of each school day to get my only possible ride home, I couldn't join any after school clubs or sports teams. But even if I hadn't needed to board that bus after class, to be honest, I wouldn't really have joined in.

And that's the long way of explaining why I paid more attention than most people did when Mánús was hanging around outside The General Store.

Chapter 2: Ol'Ben in The General Store

After graduating high school, my world felt even more aimless. In my final year, I had wanted to do what so many of my classmates were doing, which was to apply to universities and colleges, some in province, some further abroad. Aunt Moira was dead against this. As she put it, "Stay here? … just for a year more, dearie. How about taking a gap year?" When I started to look for gap year jobs, she begged me to choose one which would allow me to continue living in the house. "Just for a year longer, dearie. Just one more year with me, huh?" Aunt Moira had always been so … kind. Surely I owed her this much.

So Aunt Moira arranged for driving lessons, bought me a car, and I stuck around the house for another year before launching myself in a new direction. After successfully snagging a driver's license by mid July, I tootled about the countryside exploring beyond where I'd been able to venture as a pedestrian. I found this new liberation exhilarating. I was still not allowed to remain away from the house overnight, just as I had never been allowed to travel with my aunt on either business or vacation at any point in my life, but there were lots of places to be explored that could be reached, there and back, in one day — albeit an exhaustive day, ending in aching shoulders and cramped knees from driving such long distances.

The first thing I did was to list all the public beaches in southern Ontario, the 'land of a thousand lakes', and set out to discover them all. I spent a lot of hours swimming and lying on their warm beaches or rocky shores. I included waterfalls in this list as well — of which there were many, especially the mother of them all, Niagara Falls. In my explorations, I would choose the snaky back roads even for my city shopping jaunts, not because I feared highways, but because I found it fun twisting and turning up the hillocks, around farmers' fields and through woods, to challenge my new driving skills.

I will certainly not bore my reader with tedious descriptions of my numerous driving excursions — they have little to do with this story after all, except insofar as they explain a newfound confidence and the satisfaction I felt as I took honours in my self constructed proving ground. I was gaining a strength of personality, a self assurance that had been so lacking for someone my age, likely from being held thus far in virtual captivity. As I gained in perspective, and as I understood my world better, I trusted my own opinions more. I trusted my observations of Aunt Moira, for instance, in whom I sensed a distinct change since my graduation, and not necessarily for the better. She got noticeably nervous whenever I mentioned my solo shopping trips to the city. Although she could no longer forbid her now adult niece from doing so, Aunt Moira seemed to be attempting to shape my choices by showing an unnatural enthusiasm for my countryside excursions. Such uncharacteristic responses in my aunt caused me to question, and not for the first time, a certain nervousness of voice in her, an unusual clinginess — as evidenced in her not wanting me to go to away to university, in resisting my taking a job away from home, in being uncomfortable with me exploring the cities. It led me to wonder if she was hiding me away from someone, or something, for some reason. But as she continued to be as kind and sincere as ever in her good wishes, I let the matter drop … again.

As summer sunburns were replaced by winter chilblains, I began to look closer to home for adventure, and oddly enough found it at The General Store. I had history with that store; it was like a friend to me. Or rather, I really liked the old fella who'd stood behind its counter since Queen Victoria was a baby — Ben McCauley was his name, known to all as Ol'Ben for as long as I ever knew him. Ol'Ben was a character as they say. His entire body was shaped more or less like a lowercase *b.* He had a small egg shaped bald head with four or five white hairs right on top that stood on end and breezed about each time the shop door opened. His well worn clothes never varied, taking on the look of some sort of weird uniform. The polyester wrinkle free shirts in faded pastels to cover his sunken chest were usually buttoned too high to hide his flaccid chin. In old age his weight had settled into his midriff which he then bifurcated mid belly with a worn leather belt that he used to hold his threadbare trousers in place. Their bagginess camouflaged his lower bits, where his belly joined up with his stubby white legs and thin ankles. Twelve hours a day Ol'Ben stood at that cash register, anchored to the floor by puffy feet entombed in frayed bedroom slippers.

As I read this description back to myself, I realize that although it is technically accurate, I may have given the misimpression of Ol'Ben as being a wizened old grump. But Ol'Ben wasn't like that — not even a little. The bubbles and bumps on Ol'Ben were adorable, especially when considered as part of the whole package. Because here was a wise man who could make anyone feel good. By pausing his day to joke, giggle and listen, Ol'Ben told us all that he cared, that however grumbly or petty we were being when we came into his shop, he had time to listen to all our conflated nonsense with a soothing, unprejudiced ear.

Ol' Ben noticed me. He did a good deal more than notice. He thought I was interesting, and to prove it, he would ask for details about my day, and actually listen to my answers. Furthermore, he would set aside treats that came into the shop which he thought I would enjoy — candy, magazines and the like. And even if I didn't like or need what he saved for me I would never say so because I loved that Ol'Ben did it just for me, as one would do for a granddaughter — or, given his age, a great-granddaughter.

I tried to stop by the store to visit Ol'Ben daily because if I didn't, and especially if he knew Aunt Moira was out of town, he'd be on my doorstep making sure I was okay. Actually I enjoyed his visits to the house even more than my visits to his store, because there would be more time for conversation, or in all honesty, more time for Ol'Ben to listen to yet another of my blithering tales. I fancied my travels were making me more interesting, and as I continued relating them to the old fellow, I'd chance to make bold enough to throw in the occasional opinion, and that felt very good indeed.

*****

About two years before my real story begins, Ol'Ben had taken on an assistant to help out in the store, to take the strain off him in his advancing years, even though he was still there most of the time. Just lately, he'd taken to using a stool behind that counter. This assistant's name was Loo Blakely, a nice sort of guy, born and bred in the village, who I'd known more or less all my life — handsome and keen, if a bit too full of himself. He had strong and balanced facial features framed by dark blond hair that was forever falling onto his forehead, and that he kept swooshing back unconsciously with his fingers a couple of hundred times a day. His well developed muscles strained the fabric of all his shirts in interesting places and left no room for the imagination in his tight fitting jeans. Although he wasn't exactly a fussy dresser, his clothes were always clean, crisp, fresh smelling, and presentable to customers. I knew that he had graduated high school three years before I did, so that working at the general store seemed to be more than just a gap year job for him.

Loo liked the work and he performed like a son of a gun to please Ol'Ben. He kept the shelves well-stocked, the floors well-swept, the stock room well ordered. He worked long hours too, I suspect so that Ol'Ben would feel easier about heading upstairs to his apartment earlier of an evening.

One day, on a frosty November morning, when I had popped into the store to have a moan about how the snow was putting a serious crimp in my travels, Ol'Ben blurted out of the blue: "So, come work for me! That'll keep ya' off the streets, what?"

"But you've got Loo. You don't need me, and you can't afford to pay two people."

"It's true I can't pay much, but you don't really need the money do ya? I want you around Cait. I'm starting to slow down a wee bit. Loo's a good fellow, but he's no rocket scientist. … plus … plus …" he sighed, "I think *you* need to be here too Cait. Just think on it," he implored, adding a whispered "… what-what?"

I did 'think on it' — plenty. Furthermore, when I ran the idea past Aunt Moira, she enthused so much that my answer was made up for me. I started working at The General Store on a cold Saturday morning in November. Two weeks later, on the first of December, Ol'Ben slipped on some ice in front of the store and broke his collarbone in two places.

What was especially worrisome was that, even though Ol'Ben seemed amazingly tough, he also was amazingly old. Although the breaks were fairly easily set and immobilized in a sling without surgery, Ol'Ben's doctor was worried that, with only one workable arm, Ol'Ben would unbalance himself, making him vulnerable to more falls or worse. So before the hospital would discharge him, the doctor informed the old fella that they would need to find a vacancy in a home for him to transfer to until he could show that he was able to care for himself again.

I was there when his doctor gave him the news, and I saw the terror in Ol'Ben's eyes, which changed to a sad brave smile the instant he noticed me watching him. He seemed to shrivel in size right before my eyes though, slumping more deeply into the folds of his hospital bed after the doctor left the room.

"A *home*! A nursing home?" I panicked aloud.

"Now don't go fretting, Cait." Ol'Ben did his best to pour calm waters on my emotional flareup, "this was always gonna to happen … bound to, ya know, sooner or later. Better a collarbone than a leg … what-what," he added with a nervous smile. "I mean, you have no idea how … really ancient I am! No," he laughed, holding up a hand to my obvious next question, "Don't even ask. I don't want to have to lie to you now, do I?" His sad, dull eyes were making a valiant effort to conjure up a tiny twinkle.

Resignation and stoicism — I couldn't have that! Nor could I imagine Ol'Ben in a nursing home. Just as I was learning to love him, for goodness sake. I couldn't lose him now! It was all too soon. I shouted back, "No Ol'Ben! No. I'll look after you myself. I won't let this happen! I'll ... I'll ask Aunt Moira to let you move in with us. Sure! She'll say yes ... I think."

 Ol'Ben smiled and shook his head. "Not Moira ... she wouldn't ... and she shouldn't. Nope ... no," he muttered. "She's a good girl, but no ... nope!" His decision seemed final.

And this is where Loo stepped up to the plate, good man. He was just arriving for a visit after closing the shop early. He had brought along some truly unhealthy goodies from the store's shelves, presumably as a gift for Ol'Ben, but was doing a pretty good job of scarfing them down himself as he entered the room.

"Z'up?"

I instantly teared up, blurting out my anxiety charged version of the doctor's 'plans' for Ol'Ben, escalating my tone into a fevered soprano. "I mean, it's a *home* Loo, a *home* for old people — for Ol'Ben! I can't stand it ... Not him ... No ... I won't!"

Loo looked from Ol'Ben to me and back again, munched some more chocolate coated raisins and drawled in his ever laidback way. "Um, why don't I just move in with ya Ol'Ben. I don't like that crumb-box where I'm living anyway. So ..." he added, wiping away the last of the chocolate from around his mouth with the back of his hand and tossing the box at, but entirely missing, the bin by the bed, "unless you've got any great objections ..."

Ol'Ben had no great objections.

Chapter 3: Mánús in The Snow Squall

I'd been watching the lone dog parked outside the shop for hours on the day of that late February snow squall. Heavy snow had filled the sidewalks and high winds were whisking more of it up against the storefront. It pounded away at the dog, covering it in a thick layer of icy whiteness as the beast paced back and forth to keep from freezing. I saw no sign of an owner though I watched for hours; no one stopping to pet it either. Like me, it seemed invisible to all passers by.

By early evening I had determined two things: one, that the storm was showing no signs of stopping anytime soon; and two, that the poor hound, looking more miserable by the hour, must be either lost or abandoned. By early evening, I'd decided to stage a rescue. Holding the heavy door steady against the brute force of those howling winds, I beckoned the dog to come inside using treats that I'd liberated from the store's pet section. In its desperate condition the dog took no persuading, quickly pushing the door open wider as it brushed past me, not stopping for a treat. Now inside under the harsh fluorescent lighting, I could get a better look. *It* was a *he*, and *he* was shaking with cold, matted with ice. It was hard to determine just what breed of dog he was even up close, certainly none I'd seen, but even in his bedraggled state I could see that he was both tall and muscular, with close cropped grey fur darkened by the dirty snow and ice that were now melting in rivulets of mud all over our doormats. His huge paws were cracked and bleeding between the claws.

"Poor guy! Just look at those feet!" I whimpered, as I locked the front door and retrieved an old towel from the store room. I wiped him down as best I could, cleaning away the worst of the gritty water while he stood patiently in place. He cooperated beautifully, seeming to sense that I was trying to help him. But even after I had him more or less dried off, I could see him shivering still and panting, no doubt from the excruciating pain of his paws unfreezing. I decided to take him upstairs to Ol'Ben so he could warm up by the wood stove. As we climbed the stairs to the second floor, I shouted out, "Visitors, Ol'Ben. I've brought someone to see you. He needs your fire to thaw out."

Ol'Ben held out a beckoning hand to the dog as he lumbered uncomfortably across the floor and nuzzled his nose into that ancient palm, as old friends reunited would do. Then he lay at Ol'Ben's feet while I found a water bowl and opened a can of dog food from the downstairs shelves.

While the dog drank volumes and devoured his supper, I raged with clenched fists: "I swear he's got frostbite! Honestly, I don't know what his owners were thinking — sending him out in vile weather like this! That's cruelty, that is!"

As always, Ol'Ben's soothing voice cooled my wrath. "Don't go presuming Cait. You don't know that. Maybe he snuck out without saying he was going."

"Huh! Or maybe he was tossed out. Ever think of that?"

"Sure … yeah. I'd just prefer to consider the innocent explanation first I guess. After all, look at his collar. Someone cared enough to put a tag on it, see. Read what it says, will ya?"

I grabbed the thick leather collar on the dog's neck, turned it until a tag came into view, and read … "'*Manus'*. Interesting name for a dog."

"What was that name again Cait?" asked Ol'Ben, pushing forward now and looking alert. "Spell it, could ya?"

"M-A-N-U-S. Oh, wait, there's a couple of accent marks over the A and the U."

Now Ol'Ben was looking even more intently at the dog, who was licking the last bits of food from around his chops. He held the dog's muzzle still with both hands and stared keenly into Mánús' eyes. Then he inspected the tag on the collar himself. " Maw-noos. It's pronounced Maw-noos, Cait," adding, "I wonder … could it be? … do you suppose?"

"What are we talking about Ol'Ben? Do I suppose what?"

But Ol'Ben was leaning back in his chair, turning his head upwards to stare at the ceiling. For a full minute he sat frozen there while I waited all fidgety, before he finally turned back to me, almost dreamily, "It's most likely not important. Let's make this fellow more comfortable, what-what?"

*****

My first view of Ol'Ben's apartment was on the day we brought him home from the hospital. It was full of … let's call it *character*. Just like Ol'Ben, it was old and dusty. Except for a separate bathroom, the entire floor was open, a loft space with twelve foot support beams placed strategically here and there to support the roof. Heating and water pipes were exposed in raw rafters, as were some of the electrics and insulation. The pine floor was worn and grooved, once amber in tone, now darkened with age and grime. A kitchen of sorts had been plastered against the back wall with an ancient range style stove and a grubby bar fridge which sat slightly askew on a stained formica countertop. Tatty cupboards were anchored against a dingy sheetrock wall at a worrying angle.

The condition of the loft's front wall was no less problematic. Although its forty foot expanse had been divided up by two three-paned windows, the wall was otherwise encased floor to ceiling in unvarnished wooden shelves, filled to overflowing with books and weird relics all disarranged and cattywampus. Those books that were too large for the narrow planking had been exiled to the floor and were stacked high against the contents of the lower shelves, making it virtually impossible to get close enough to view their titles.

Along one of the loft's bricked side walls, a tiny area had been arranged as a bedroom — with its narrow bed shoved up against the dark brick, an antique oak trunk, presumably serving as Ol'Ben's clothes cupboard, at its head. Although tidy and clean, the bedclothes were somewhat threadbare, including the friendship quilt that added an ounce or two of interest and colour to the area. On the brick wall opposite, stood a high stack of firewood and a potbellied stove, the only obvious source of heat for the entire space. A wooden rocker and a shabby easy chair were cozied up to either side of the stove. Besides a few dim overhead Edison bulbs, the space was lit by a garage sale floor lamp next to the easy chair and a goose necked table lamp which craned over the bed's headboard from its perch atop the trunk. There was no dining area to speak of, or in any case no table or chairs at which to eat or prepare a meal.

After Loo struggled Ol'Ben up the stairs and set him carefully in the easy chair, he strolled about to absorb the atmosphere of his new home. "Awesome!" he declared, as he spun around in glee. "I'm living in a warehouse. Woo hoo! Lemme just grab my gear from the car."

With such a scarcity of furniture, there was plenty of space for Loo's possessions, such as he had. His 'gear' consisted of a couple of suitcases, some weird gewgaws in green garbage bags, a collection of old car magazines, and a massive television set with a games console that looked humorously incongruous in the vintage space. He was just in the process of selecting a suitable spot to set it up, when Aunt Moira burst into the room like a human tsunami.

I hadn't realized that she'd returned from her latest trip. I did wonder how she could have found out about Ol'Ben's accident, as she'd been away since it happened. She answered all my queries at once. She had just 'popped in' to tell me of her return, she explained, when she heard the commotion upstairs. She looked so travel weary — short sculpted auburn hair now tousled, beautiful violet blue eyes now puffy, tastefully applied makeup now smudged, stylish clothes slightly untucked. Her fatigue translated into impatience: "What *have* you done to yourself old man?" she admonished in a booming voice. "And what kind of a space is this to live in?"

"Now look Moira, you can't just come charging into a fella's place unannounced and start roaring!" Ol'Ben retorted, becoming hotter than I'd ever seen him. "You just leave us here to settle Loo in … what-what."

"Loo? And just who is Loo?"

"My em-ploy-ee," he drawled, "for the past two years, as if you didn't know. Now my roomie as well, 'cuz apparently I'm suddenly an old man too feeble to be trusted on my own!" he grumbled uncharacteristically.

"Well you are old, you fool! You've been old for thirty years! And look how you live! This apartment's not fit for you, let alone for this young man," she added, pacing about and clicking her tongue. She turned on Ol'Ben, hovering menacingly over his armchair. "Right then, here's what we're going to do …"

"Hold on there missy! This is my place. I decide."

"And my niece works in this squalor..."

"She does not! She works downstairs, and you know I keep that store in immaculate condition. Squalor, bah!"

"And can you tell me she won't be coming upstairs all the day long to help you out, now that you have that … broken wing?" So began an exchange of clipped remarks which finally distilled into a set of negotiated repairs and enhancements …

- o A professional cleaning crew to scrape years of dust and grime from the entire loft

- o   A new stove and refrigerator for Loo's use to prepare proper meals
- o   Refitted kitchen cupboards for proper storage, painted in a colour of Ol'Ben's choosing
- o   An additional armchair for the living area
- o   A small dining set, and
- o   A plan for organizing the books and gargoyles by the front window, including either better or more shelving.

"Ahhh … just one thing Ol'Ben," said Loo, as he read over the proposed list, " … where do I sleep?" So the list was revised to include …

- o   A new bed for Loo, with a decently large chest of drawers and a coat rack for his hangable items.

One thing about Aunt Moira which cannot be denied … that woman could sure make things happen. By the following weekend, the purchase of the additional furniture and fittings, *and* the repair, cleaning and paint jobs had been accomplished. Aunt Moira went a bit off list in the end to sneak in a modest sofa in earth tones to which Ol'Ben silently acquiesced with a shake of his head and a barely perceptible smirk. The results were transformative!

I had never been able to figure out the relationship between Aunt Moira and Ol'Ben. They weren't friends exactly, yet there seemed a familiarity, like they'd known each other for some time. They neither liked nor disliked, but did respect one another. And whenever I tried to prize more detail from either of them, each became tight lipped.

With Loo happily tucked into his new living quarters, we set out to establish a daily routine. I came in at 6:00 a.m. most days to tidy up below from the previous evening, and to set up the coffee maker and tea urn before opening up. Loo got Ol'Ben sorted with showering and dressing, making him breakfast and clearing everything away, before joining me downstairs at 7:30 a.m. when we opened the doors for the village's commuters to grab their first coffees or teas before heading off for work. About mid morning I took a proper break to visit Ol'Ben with a fresh cup of coffee and his favourite morning newspaper. For the most part, Ol'Ben amused himself by thoroughly reading all the dailies before turning on Loo's TV which had been hooked up to cable by then. It took him a while to learn the ins and outs of the controller, but once he did, he surfed the hundreds of channels expertly, dwelling most often on nature channels, news programs and classic old movies.

Loo and I tag teamed back and forth throughout the day; one of us would pop upstairs to see to Ol'Ben, while the other remained below in the store. About 6:30 p.m. each day, Loo knocked off and headed upstairs to prepare our evening meal, which we ate after I had closed the store at 8:00 p.m. Mondays through Thursdays, and 9:00 p.m. Fridays and Saturdays. We didn't even consider taking a day off, nor did either of us seem to mind.

Loo's self professed culinary prowess was well deserved. With the minimal supplies in Ol'Ben's kitchen, to which he added some key extras, and after a few practice runs with the new stove and oven, Loo's dinners were becoming more and more interesting, so that I gave up any idea of eating at home, even when Aunt Moira was in town. What Loo could do with tomato sauce, fresh herbs, a few veg, and a whole chicken was inspired, and his pasta dishes were positively mouthwatering. Even Aunt Moira had to agree, on the few occasions when she invited herself over to share in our meal, that Loo's skills verged on the gourmet.

As peaceful and happy as we had all become, after six weeks of rest and mending Ol'Ben became bored and restless. We were certain that he was improving when he began to agitate about returning to the shop. Although the doctor would not agree to a full day, he nonetheless approved of Ol'Ben going downstairs for short stints on the cash register and yakking to the customers, provided he did so from a seated position. Aunt Moira inserted herself into the equation once again by arranging delivery of an ergonomic chair with a footrest that could fit in very nicely behind the cash till.

It might well have been expected that the arrival of Mánús' in late February would disrupt such domestic harmony, but somehow his presence only enhanced our lives, adding both magic and mystery — magic because of his obvious super doggy intelligence and intuition — mystery because we had no idea where or to whom to return him.

On his first day with us, Mánús did little more than lay by the fire and sleep, giving his paws time to heal. But from the second day onwards he made himself useful, fetching and carrying for Ol'Ben — slippers, newspapers, even reading glasses. When he himself needed water or food, he found the correct bowl and kicked it in front of either Loo or me, waiting patiently until we got the message. If Ol'Ben needed our help and we were downstairs, Mánús would come to fetch us, pulling us by the sleeve towards the stairs. In the evenings after dinner, he loved to play ball, or twirl on his back legs either as a solo act or as a dance partner for Loo or me — with or without musical accompaniment.

For the first three days after Mánús' arrival, the snow accumulation more or less confined us all to barracks, with me bunking in on a fold up cot instead of trying to dig my car out right away. We kept the store open for those few brave soldiers who struggled through the drifts to pick up a few staples for their families, while Loo spent hours tunnelling out, opening up the long stretches of sidewalks that led to the store and the driveway alongside where we parked our cars. Mánús and I took an airing every few hours so he could 'answer the call', but other than that we hunkered down, focused on each other, and quite frankly had the best of times.

It was almost disappointing when the village dug itself out enough to continue the daily commutes and the school days. With the roads now clear, Aunt Moira insisted I return home in the evenings to sleep in my own bed again. I continued to spend very long hours at the store, however.

My affection for Ol'Ben was strengthening by the day, my attachment to the dog was already undeniable, and my regard for Loo was widening and texturing as he continued to surprise me with previously unsung skills and loyalties. Even Aunt Moira was relaxing again, that is until one night while taking her evening meal with us, she suddenly turned her gaze on the dog, started and stared deeply into his eyes.

"You see it too," Ol'Ben commented. "'Bout time you noticed. I'm surprised it took ya so long."

"Well, for the simple reason that I wasn't expecting it so soon Ol'Ben. And Mánús doesn't look much like he did back then — different species for one thing. Can it be ….?"

"Dunno," Ol'Ben sighed. "Guess we'll find out sooner rather than later though."

"Find out what?" I asked — again with their cryptic non answers! Why wouldn't anyone answer my questions? And so I waited for 'sooner rather than later' to happen.

Mánús seemed content to be with us for the time being at least, while we looked for news of a missing dog at the usual rescue agencies and websites. Then one afternoon in mid March Loo came up to me as I was ringing in a customer's order and muttered lowly, "That guy over there thinks he knows where Mánús belongs."

Nethermost Regained

Chapter 4: Sinead in The Cottage

In the end we decided not to tell Ol'Ben, not yet anyway. The man in the store had identified a lone cottage five kilometres east on High Point Sideroad as where he had first noticed Mánús. He said he didn't know who lived there, didn't know if it was even occupied, but he 'reckoned it was worth a look see'.

The difficulty was in finding a time when Loo and I could drive out there together, neither of us feeling confident enough to go alone. We weren't yet comfortable leaving Ol'Ben for any length of time either, and we weren't sure how long it would take us to find the house and check out its occupants.

The opportunity presented itself that Sunday, our one day off each week, when a dear friend of Ol'Ben's dropped by for dinner at noon and agreed to stay with him while Loo and I took Mánús for what we outright lied was a long walk. Loo had prepared us a midday dinner, after which I quickly cleared up. Then we settled our visitor and Ol'Ben by the wood stove with post dinner coffees, piled Mánús into the car and headed off. It took us just ten minutes to reach the end of the driveway in question, where we parked and debated our best approach. In the end our plan was determined for us, because at the sight of the stone cottage, Mánús yipped excitedly to be released from the car. Before Loo could open the door completely, Mánús was launching himself up the snowy walkway and scratching at the front door. It was opened by an elegant woman leaning on a carved shillelagh, the door's dark threshold emphasizing her tiny body. At the sight of Mánús, she threw her arms about his neck hugging him to her. Perhaps I was imagining it, but I could have sworn that Mánús winked in her direction, then stood still while the wee thing pulled herself onto his back and hung on to his collar as he carried her easily along the snow packed driveway and back up to the car.

"Hello-ooo," she called cheerfully through the driver's side window, "do I have you to thank for my companion's return?" When we nodded, she shouted out again, "Come in then, I've got the tea steeping in the pot." She signalled Mánús with a twist of his collar to return to the house, not waiting for a reply.

We had no option but to follow. When we entered her home through the door that she'd left ajar, we gasped at our first view of the room before us. Although not perhaps by modern standards the most stylish, nonetheless the great room that we had just entered was easily the most fascinating living space that I'd ever seen, and I'm sure Loo was impressed as well. Although not exactly cluttered or messy, the room was, to say the least, full. To begin with, the furniture was pristine yet not prissy. The chairs and sofa were velvety soft in lush tones of blues and purples. End tables, fashioned of exotic woods, hugged the corners of the upholstery. Ornamental area carpets of elegant blues defined two conversation areas. But most exciting of all were the glass paned china cabinets she had filled with remarkable ornaments and apparatuses, museum pieces really, of undeniable antiquity and mysterious functions, each perhaps telling a story about generations long forgotten.

As we hesitated by the door in our outdoor gear, the little lady beckoned, "Oh do come in and tell me how you take your tea," adding, "Boots off on the mat; parkas, hats and scarves on that rather intriguing coat tree. Quick, quick … tea's getting chilly."

Tea would not have been my first choice, nor I suspect Loo's, but at that moment it didn't seem to matter much. Having said that, it was the most delicious blend I'd ever tasted, and soon Loo and I were nestled together on the sofa across from this elf like creature sitting in an armchair four times too big for her. In stature, she was the size of a five year old, but she bore the demeanour of a queen. Her clothes had simple lines, skirts draped to mid calf length covering fitted leggings, fashioned of shimmering taffetas rich with colour. Beneath this sumptuous fabric, her thin legs looked mismatched, perhaps the explanation for her walking stick. It was impossible for me to decide how old, or how young, she actually was. She seemed ageless — with the wispy white hair of the aged, the smooth skin of the young, the textured eyes of the experienced.

"Tell me," she said, proffering a plate of scones stuffed with strawberry jam and clotted cream, "How is Ben McCauley? And for that matter Moira O'Quinn? Just how is Moira, dear girl? And you — little Cait?" she queried, peering at me intently. Then returning her teacup to its saucer, she turned her attention on Loo, "Welcome to you young man. I don't know you, do I?"

"Don't think so. I'm Loo Buckley," said Loo awkwardly.

"And what is your story Loo?"

"I … I don't have one," said Loo, pinking from all the attention. "Not an interesting one anyway."

"Oh I disagree!" I pitched in with more thrust than I usually play. "Loo's a man of hidden depths. He stays in the shadows, so you sometimes forget he's there. But when things get tough, before the situation gets desperate — there's Loo, level headed, totally unflappable, stepping forward in a really cool way. And that makes … has made … all the difference."

"Congratulations Loo," said the little lady, "hidden depths is it?"

"Dunno."

"That's just what I'd expect him to say," I added boldly. Why was I telling a stranger so much? But I wanted to acknowledge this man of few words. "Ben, Ol'Ben as everyone knows him in the village, has been unwell you see … and without Loo things could have gone really … well … wrong … for all of us. He takes care of Ol'Ben … takes care of us all … makes our lives so much easier … happy really."

Loo turned to me, with a hint of the misty about the eyes, and answered me alone. "I just wanted to make Ol'Ben well again … just wanted you to be happy, Cait."

I stared back in astonishment, for the first time appreciating the man before me, for the first time not regarding the stalwart employee who did a decent job in the store, but taking in the essential Loo, a man of undeniable strength of character, whose approval was becoming something to which I now paid more heed.

"So," our hostess observed, "somewhat more than a friend ..."

Loo turned his gaze quickly back to her again. "How do you know Ol'Ben and Moira then?"

"Oh … I guess you could call us old friends, although with Ben, it's been a while."

"H-how do you know *my* name?" I asked. "Have we ever met?" At this moment I was nervous about what her reply might be.

"Well yes … although you were just a baby," she explained. Changing directions abruptly, she chirruped, "Thank you so much for escorting Mánús home. I was missing him."

Missing him? I asked myself. But not desperate, I thought, not out searching for him? "We found him outside The General Store during that big snowstorm — bits of him got frozen. He was in pretty bad shape," I retorted with a bit of heat, and more than a hint of disapproval.

"Oh dear, you didn't tell me that, Mánús … you poor fellow," she addressed the dog.

Well that was a shock to the system! Just how would Mánús have communicated that? I was intrigued and appalled at the same time. "Well, he's just a dog …" I began.

"Oh, dear no!" she giggled delightedly, "Mánús, a dog? Oh my dear, you couldn't be more wrong. Mind you," she added, "looking at him in this light, he does look a bit more doglike at the moment. But no, not a dog."

"That there's a dog," Loo affirmed, pointing an accusing finger at Mánús.

The room was palled in awkward silence. A full minute went by — Loo and me sitting in confusion on the couch worrying about what we were beginning to suspect was a madwoman who had just declared, albeit good-naturedly, that her dog, her pet, was not … a dog!

Of course she sensed our confusion and discomfort, and made an effort to turn the conversation. "I … I…. Hmm … Hello … my name is Sinead. I should have opened with that I am sure. Rude not to really."

"What?" I mumbled, still reeling in confusion from the dog issue.

"Sinead … yes, there you are … my name. Pronounced Shin-Aid but spelled quite differently. Shin Healy, I call myself."

She calls herself? What do others call her, I wondered. Curious and curiouser.

"You can call me Shin, if you wish," she added, as if reading my thoughts.

"Umm," I stuttered, my head feeling woozy now, yet still determined to return to the question about the neglect of one's pet. "Why weren't you frantic with worry when Mánús was lost?"

"Oh dear! Mánús were you lost, dear boy?" she asked, laying a tiny hand atop his head. "He says not. He was relieved to have found you he says, since that was his mission in the first place. He's sorry he caused you to worry."

"Well, I was worried of course! He was hurt and … lost, I thought." The forcefulness behind my voice trailed away in befuddlement.

"That must have been so upsetting for you! Dear me! So regretful. Of course that snowstorm added a wrinkle to the works, didn't it Mánús?" She stroked his fur lovingly. "He was just trying to do me a favour you see."

"A … a favour?"

"Yes, I was keen to be in touch."

"W-Why?"

She disregarded the question and ploughed forward. "Mánús was a leader of great strength in the old realm. Indeed I believe he is the most revered of his race. Don't be modest dear fellow, you know it's true. It's a well known fact that my race wouldn't even exist anymore, were it not for the loyalty and protection of Canomorphs. Indeed we would not!"

How was I to unpack that statement? What was a Canomorph? And if Mánús was a Canomorph, what was she? What made Mánús a great leader of his race? And why was *I* — insignificant little me — Mánús' mission? Now nausea was beginning to set up in competition with wooziness. Swallowing back my panic, I plunged forward: "Wh-what do you mean when you say 'the old realm'?"

"Oh … no, of course you wouldn't remember … silly me. Nethermost. The old realm, that is … Nethermost … although it takes a great deal of imagination to discover it, let alone to live there."

"Well, that's me out," Loo jumped up like he'd been tasered, "no imagination — just how I like it." Pulling me to my feet, he steered me to the door. "You're welcome for the dog!"

Chapter 5: Beyond Belief

"Well, that was an experience and a half!" Loo spat, as he steered our car down the road putting some distance between us and the stone cottage. "That female … thing … is mad, she is. She, her dog, and her weird cottage!" he added, finally slowing the car down as we reached the first crossroad.

"It was shocking," I agreed, selecting my words carefully. "But … I … I … I … ahh…"

"But what?" Loo exploded, pulling over and slamming on the brakes. "Look Cait, I know *Looney Tunes* when I see it right? And that there was *Looney Tunes*! I'm just sorry for the dog!" He revved the engine and jumped the car back onto the gravelly road.

He drove in silence for the rest of our return journey, while I made a futile attempt at fortifying my own emotions. Was it only a few minutes ago that I had been praising this guy's steadfast nature? Now I was beginning to see a slight downside to Loo's bread and butter view of the world — a narrow mindedness, a resistance to possibilities. Now I considered that there may be occasions when being steadfast and grounded were not always strengths.

*****

For two days afterwards, I was shocked — outraged at Shin's declarations and off the cuff references to things mysterious, even magical, to realms that stretched beyond my earthly knowledge and experiences.

For two days after that, I was upset — queasy at the very suggestion that I was in any way connected to such weirdness; that my aunt and Ol'Ben had somehow known of it too and had been culturing secrets. So while Loo was freaked by the suggestion of a fairy tale world, I was more freaked by the possibility that a fairy tale world held the bizarre explanation of my own beginnings.

After all this shock and upset … curiosity kicked in.

Loo and I did not discuss the goings on in that stone cottage any further, especially the weird ideas voiced by that strange elfin creature, nor were either of us keen to discuss our adventure with Ol'Ben or Aunt Moira. Of course Ol'Ben was curious about Mánús' disappearance, asking us both separately about it. Fortunately our stories more or less jived — Loo stating curtly that we'd dropped the dog off with his owner, 'no problem'; I adding details to my tale, such as that the reunion was a happy one, that the dog had been sorely missed, and that his owner seemed grateful to us. Neither version was technically a lie, but then neither was it the entire truth.

Amazingly enough my brain didn't reject outright the idea of imaginative realms with unusual creatures, and I couldn't explain why. It's not like I had any innate recollection of such things from infancy. Yet night after night for the first week after that visit, and in the privacy of my own room, I mentally replayed Shin's words through my brain until every neuron ached. I even searched the internet for whispers of a world known as *Nethermost*, for hints of *Canomorphs*, for descriptions of elfish creatures in history that looked like Shin. But except for the traditional fairy and folk plots of escapist genres like science fiction and fantasy, I could find nothing resembling an explanation.

I kept grappling with reality and kept losing. I confess there were moments when I wanted all that Shin had asserted, in her squeaky blasé voice, to be the truth. But there were more times when the practical me felt certain that if such a world or such characters existed, then surely someone, somewhere on the internet — the ether world of a nearly infinite collection of minds and experiences — would post a clue, or the tiniest of hints. But … zilch.

Taking another approach to my research, I delved into the possible origins of the words Shin used, starting with *Nethermost*. 'Nether' refers to somewhere likely beneath the Earth, 'most' was a superlative descriptor referring to the highest degree or extent. Could I presume then that Nethermost was a subterranean realm located the greatest distance off, but still of the Earth, so to speak?

Next I tried to analyze the term *Canomorph*. Could 'Cano' be a prefix referring to something doglike? And 'morph' brought to mind the idea of change or transformation. Could a race of Canomorphs be doglike somehow and capable of transforming? Frustrations built up, doubts overwhelmed me until finally I threw my tablet computer under the bed, appalled by my own wild assumptions.

Still I couldn't get Sinead, or Mánús for that matter, out of my head. Shin's words preyed heavily on my dreams, becoming my constant companions in sleep. So when a week later Mánús appeared in the store again with a note attached to his collar addressed to me, I was as much grateful as Loo was annoyed.

"*Cait*," it read, "*Please come to tea next Sunday*," with the post script, "*And bring Mánús back with you then.*"

"So, you're on loan to me are you?" I said ruffling the ears of the gentle giant standing before me. "She knows how much I love you. She's bribing me to come see her again by lending you to me for a few days. You're a piece of candy to tempt me to follow you down the rabbit hole, Mánús, that's what you are!" Mánús bowed.

I knew I would go, but before I did I had a lot of questions for Ol'Ben.

*****

I chose my mid morning coffee break the following day to speak with Ol'Ben alone, when I knew Loo would be occupied downstairs. "Ol'Ben?" I began, sitting close to him and lowering my voice.

"Yes, Cait?" he answered, twigging instantly to my conspiratorial tone. "What is it dear girl?"

"Ol'Ben," I began anew, "we weren't exactly honest with you the other day, Loo and I, about dropping Mánús off at his home."

"Of course you weren't dear," he said, quite matter of factly.

"What! Why do you say that? How could you know?"

"Because you both failed to mention *her*. And she is at the centre of it all, is she not?"

"Do you mean Shin?"

"Oh is that what she's calling herself these days?" Ol'Ben replied.

"Yes, Shin Healy. That's how she introduced herself to us."

"I must say she's chosen an interesting twist on her name this time," Ol'Ben chuckled. "That last name, Healy, is a particularly nice touch."

"Why's that?"

"Oh … because she *is* … healy. That's her race … healy — wise ones, or elders if you like. That's what healy means." He smiled and shook his head.

"She said some pretty strange things Ol'Ben, to Loo and me. Is she dangerous?"

"No, no" he assured me. "The healy are not dangerous beings, although this one's arrival in the village is a clear sign of imminent danger. Very worrying. Very … worrying … what-what."

"What can you tell me about her and this 'old realm' of hers, Ol'Ben?" I asked, having slid forward to the edge of my seat now.

"Almost nothing dear, almost nothing, for I've never been there. But I've heard it called … Nethermost … if I remember rightly."

"Yes, that's what she called it," I affirmed. "Then what do you know? She called you an 'old friend'. She said Aunt Moira was one too."

"Ah, did she? That was kind, if a bit exaggerated." He turned in his chair and reached out a hand for me to take. "First off, I hope you will forgive me for keeping your origins, such as I understand them, a secret from you all these years Cait."

"But why did you? Could you not see how restless I was? Was there nothing you could have said to make me more hopeful, less lonely?"

"I gave my solemn promise that I wouldn't, dear girl, an oath demanded by wiser minds than mine. Moira and I were directly charged with your safety — thus indirectly charged with the safety of an entire continent, as I understand it. How was I to do otherwise? Can you forgive me?"

"What you say next will matter a good deal. Take great care that it's the truth. Lucky for you that I love you old man. Now … spill!"

"Yes. Yes, of course. The truth. In truth, I ... I'm just an ordinary fella, boring really, born in this village several generations ago to a young country couple who ran this same shop as a grocery store back then, in the days before travel was easy. Then at some point the main roads were paved, everyone could afford cars, and folks found it easier, and cheaper, to drive to the next town for most of their groceries. So when I inherited the store, I turned it into a general store, for quick stock everyday items.

"Yes, well …. my parents raised a simple child who was happy with his country life — except for some brutal years I spent as a soldier in an appalling global war. Or maybe it was *because* of those wretched war years, that I was content to live the rest of my life here. Yes, maybe that was it.

"In any case, I married a local girl, a few years after returning from the war. And after a few years more, my wife and I were blessed with a wonderful son — Riley, we called him. Only one child, mind you, but it was enough for us. Yes, Riley was quite enough to make us feel blessed. Unlike his father, however, Riley was not content to remain in the village. Rather, he had ambitions and expectations that exceeded our small lives. We were distressed, but not surprised, when almost from the moment that he blew out those candles on his eighteenth birthday cake, Riley packed and left on what he laughingly referred to as his 'world tour', keeping in touch with us only with a rare postcard. For his mother's sake, I wish it had been more. We had faith in his goodness, although we constantly worried for his safety, and desired only that he be happy.

"Years later, although not soon enough for my wife who died awaiting his return, Riley showed up out of the blue, looking travel worn and weary. But he did not come alone. Can you even imagine my delight at his return, my gratitude and, dare I say, elation when he asked to work alongside me in the store? It was all I could have hoped for — at least that's what I thought initially. But despite Riley's willingness to stay, I sensed a profound sadness. It took little imagination to understand that he was now a broken man and aged beyond his years.

As I said, he did not return alone. Riley brought with him an adorable little girl, his natural daughter, clearly the sole source of happiness in his broken life. He had named her after my wife, dear boy … He named her … Nora."

"Nora!" I gasped. "But my moth…"

"Yes, Cait, your mother. Nora is your mother."

"And Riley is …"

"Your grandfather …"

"And you are my gr…"

"Great-grandfather … I am your great-grandfather, for my sins, as they say."

"Stop! Instantly! I need to think," I squeaked, jumping up and moving about to outpace my agitation. Ol'Ben stayed frozen in place, not speaking, not looking in my direction.

I hadn't expected that! Ol'Ben my great-grandfather! "How could you, you selfish old man?" I reeled on him and cried, "How could you not tell me? How could you listen to my aching heart almost daily and have said nothing? How could you have ignored my solitude, you heartless … heartless …?" I grabbed a glass from the kitchen cupboard, filled it with water and took a long drink, trying to slow down my panicked breathing. Loo, who had heard my shouting from below, raced up the stairs in alarm, with Mánús close on his heels. He stood now at the top of the steps looking from Ol'Ben to me.

"Leave it alone, Loo," I whispered.

"No … Something's wrong!"

"I said … leave it!" I spit my words at him, in my distress and outrage. "Please," I softened. He grabbed the dog's collar and pulled him downstairs with him, while I exhaled deeply, slumped onto the sofa, leaned back and closed my eyes.

"I know..." Ol'Ben rasped.

"What do you know Ol'Ben?" I jumped in. "What?"

"I know … *I* was lonely … I could only suppose that in some ways you were too," he mumbled. "But you didn't know who you were lonely for. I did. I knew you were my great-granddaughter, knew I had to stand by silently and watch you grow up, while only being allowed glimpses of your life — not allowed to enjoy you, not allowed to spoil you — beyond being that friendly old shopkeeper at the corner store. You were my only family, Cait! I knew what I was missing. You didn't. At least you … didn't."

When I opened my eyes again, I saw a tiny old geezer slunk low in a broken down armchair dabbing away at his eyes with a frayed and faded handkerchief. I saw … oh goodness, my great-grandfather!

Nethermost Regained

Kneeling at his feet, I took him in my arms, blending my own tears with his. I'm unclear just how long it was until I pulled back to wipe the rest of Ol'Ben's tears from his grizzled chin, but whenever that was, it was also to say. "Okay … okay... Enough."

We sat silent, in recovery mode.

"Nora, your mother, was special in ways that are hard to describe Cait. And you are so much like her."

"Pht! Poor girl!" I interjected.

"Why do you say it like that? Do you not know how exceptional you are Cait? And that is not just through a grandfather's — a great-grandfather's — old eyes. Ask Loo! Loo knows! Or look in the mirror; although a mirror can only reflect your physical beauty, not your generous heart."

"So," I prompted, after another beat, "Nora was exceptional … ?"

"Exceptional, certainly. Physically she bore a rare elegance. But there was something even more rare within. A magic I might say, although I have no knowledge of such things, but yes even as a small child, she was magic! Oh I am utterly failing to describe her! She was kind, never petulant, more wise than intelligent but never a showoff; observant and discerning, diplomatic and encouraging. I fancy I ended up imitating some of those last qualities in her, if I may make so bold.

"But I am most grateful to her for the strength she showed with her father. I have said that she was the high point of his life, that he focused on her alone, and this is true. But it was she who cared for him really, even from a very young age.

"One day, not long after they arrived in the village, a five year old Nora told me why she had become his carer, something she said in all innocence that first alerted me to the existence of Nethermost. She was playing on the shop floor one morning while I manned the till and her father stocked shelves, playing with the cans of peas, stacking them like blocks — to build a palace, she explained, when she stopped suddenly, saying to herself: 'I miss my Mommy, but I mayn't talk about her …'

"Naturally this shocked me as you may suppose. Riley had said nothing about his wife, her mother. Not so much as her name, or her whereabouts. Nothing. So I sat down beside her on the floor and whispered: 'Where is your mother, Nora?'

'She's in Nethermost. She was swiped away from me and Daddy ...'

'She was swiped?' I prompted aghast. 'Who swiped her'?

'The Appa ...' she began but halted mid word as her father came nearer on his path to fetch some more boxes. He stopped, scowled and shook his head slightly before walking through to the back.

When he was gone, I repeated softly, 'Who swiped your Mommy, Nora?'

'The Apparatchik. (*appa-rat-chick*) He's wicked! He swiped Mommy and hurt Daddy. But I mayn't speak about him.' She stopped talking then and went back to building her tin can castle."

Ol'Ben shut down at this last detail and leaned back in his chair, plastered against its cushions like a soggy noodle. I took in a breath, held it, and released it slowly: "A wicked Apparatchik?"

"Yes," he sighed, staring straight ahead now.

"He swiped her Mommy?"

"So she said."

"And hurt her Daddy?"

"Just so."

"Where is her father — your son — now?"

"He died when Nora was sixteen."

"Where is she now?" I asked. Ol'Ben's shoulders were positively drooping with sadness.

"I cannot say. Perhaps in Nethermost. We're not sure."

"Who's we?" I asked, anxiety creeping into my tone again.

"Moira, Ambassador Sinead, me … many others I would guess."

"Is she alive?" I breathed nervously.

"We hope so. That's the hell in which I've been living Cait. Now it's your hell as well.

Chapter 6: Nethermost is The Beginning

The following Sunday I sat down to the second of many cups of tea I would share with Sinead at a bistro table in the kitchen nook of her cottage, a small round table overflowing with cakes, buttered toast, interesting jams, two pots of tea, warm milk, lemon slices and sugar lumps. There was barely room left on the table top for the tiny bone china cups and saucers, side plates, miniature teaspoons and butter spreaders made of what looked suspiciously like pure gold. I felt like a six year old playing house with her little friend and a fancy doll's tea set. Sinead … my little friend.

Mánús made himself useful while we sampled the goodies. He added a cushion to Shin's chair to raise her up closer to the table. Then he removed her shillelagh and placed it against the wall, out of harm's way. Just before we began our meal, he rolled in a tea trolley from around the corner of the L shaped kitchen, stacked high with more goodies, placing it alongside the table to add to the fare spread before us. Watching him work, I made a mental note to find out more about Canomorphs when the opportunity arose.

"Did you bake all this yourself," I asked, licking some jam surreptitiously from my fingers.

"I bake at home," Shin said, "but I'm a bit small to be useful in this full sized kitchen. No, most of what's in the cottage now arrives in my daily diplomatic pouch."

"Your diplomatic pouch?"

"Yes, from our embassy."

"You have an embassy here in Canada?"

"We call it so, although in truth, it is a citizen support service, unknown as such to the Canadian government," she laughed lightly. "We have trade agreements with private citizens of this country of course. But ours is unlike any other embassy on Earth because its primary purpose is not to establish a diplomatic relationship with this country, but to track and inventory all our Nethermost citizenry living anywhere outside of our continent. I humbly claim ambassador status," Shin added with a slight bow of her head. Pushing her chair back from the table, she signalled to Mánús for her shillelagh. "Shall we continue our conversation in more comfy chairs?" Once relocated in her parlour by the front window, Shin wriggled into the cushions of her oversized armchair, playfully clicking her heels that dangled over the edge of the cushions. "Now that our tummies are happy," she began, "what would you like to know?"

"I hardly know where to begin …"

"Nethermost *is* the beginning, Cait."

"Where is Nethermost, Shin?"

"Ah, now that is the question isn't it Cait? Where? And it is also the key to opening the doors to 'why' and 'how' as well. It is a difficult question, so I will answer as clearly as I can. Shut your eyes, if you will Cait and imagine going on a journey … a very, very long journey along a rigid, unforgiving, northbound path … for days and days — and days — until you feel that you cannot imagine taking a step further… There!" she exclaimed, "There is Nethermost … Most on-Earthers don't have the patience to push themselves so far. But that is where we are nonetheless — have been for centuries — undiscovered and unseen. That step further! Do you understand?"

"Not really."

"You will dear — all too soon, I fear."

There she was again, saying weird and ominous stuff, and then leaving them hanging like that — unexplained. For the moment, I wasn't biting. Instead I commented: "Ol'Ben says that my mother was born there."

"And your father … and you."

"Me? I was born in Nethermost?"

"Yes, my dear. Or rather, at Nethermost Gate. You are one of our most valued assets."

"I am? How can that be when I don't know a thing about Nethermost?"

"Then let me begin your instruction. How many continents are there on Earth, Cait?"

"Seven: North America, South America, Europe, Asia, Africa, Australia and Antarctica."

"Very good. And *under*-Earth? How many?"

"I beg your pardon? Did you say *under* Earth?"

"Just so."

"None."

"Correction, respectfully, one continent lies under-Earth, in a vast expanse located deep beneath North America, floating on a pool of liquid gold. It is, in fact, a large fragment of the Earth's mantle that eons ago broke away from the larger whole, to rest beneath the massive root system of Canada's unexplored and largely virgin forests. The under-Earth continent of Nethermost."

"Nethermost … a floating continent … under Canada?"

Shin giggled and clapped her hands. "Magical, isn't it?"

"Impossible!"

"Improbable, I'll grant you, but not impossible, because it does exist! And it is easily the most beautiful continent of them all —the richest — although not the biggest. It's not much larger than New Zealand, in truth."

"But Northern Canada is cold — so very cold! Doesn't everything freeze solid that far north?"

"We are not *in* Northern Canada, Cait, we are *under* it. And we are not at all cold. Being beneath the Earth's surface, we are closer to its warm core, and floating on liquid gold as we do, our climate is constant. It's a delicate balance, to be sure."

"But, isn't it too dark beneath the surface?"

"The rock and earthen surrounds of Nethermost are well seeded with quartz crystals known as 'vitreous of life'. Its phosphorescence glows in the presence of the liquid gold to provide us with a consistent light source that we control with our own special brand of magic. We also use skylight technology on an enormous scale, as a source of daylight brightness and to enhance our breathable atmosphere. These UV rays are essential to our wellbeing, essential in the photosynthesis of our plants. Combined with the skylight technology, plants and trees provide us with most of our oxygen. Water of course is free and pure in Nethermost, tapped from our underground lakes. There you have the practical stuff — everything else is the twiddly bits and magic — the icing on the cake. Whatever we need, we borrow, buy, or steal from on-Earth. Since on-Earthers steal our minerals and forest products, we feel justified in harvesting some their more interesting natural resources in return. There's so much to wonder at and admire in Nethermost. How can one describe a realm in a few words? Indeed, mere words cannot begin to do it justice."

"You mentioned magic Shin, and I suspect that you and Mánús are somewhat more than run of the mill folks. Is everyone in Nethermost magical?"

"If not in the under-Earth, then where? Magic cannot be trusted in the hands of on-Earthers."

"And you said that I was born in Nethermost … or rather at Nethermost Gate?"

"Most assuredly — from the greatest of bloodlines."

"Am I magic too then?"

"You just could be the most magical of all Cait — you and your sister. In fact, we are counting on it."

"My sister?"

Chapter 7: The Father Daughter Bond

Standing in front of my bathroom mirror, I studied my face critically. "So, where's the magic then," I asked my evolving self.

It had been some time since I last took real notice of my reflection, beyond a quick peek as I swiped at my hair and applied a splotch of makeup each morning. Today I paused longer. I was sensing that there was a new person in that mirror of late, and I wanted to get a good look at her. I had to admit that the face before me had changed in the few short months since I left school. Now that I had let my hair grow longer, more due to busyness than anything else, I found its wildness appealing. It was curling in a more flattering manner, softer than those rigid comb backs I had kept it in as a student. The fluffiness brought out red highlights, not unlike my aunt's auburn hair. My previously pale complexion now had added tones of tawny pinks. And my eyes looked — how? — bluer somehow, sharper, with a steadier gaze. Was that a spark I could see behind them?

My self-indulgent mirror gazing was suddenly interrupted by Aunt Moira standing in the doorway, photobombing my reflection. "You do look more beautiful these days Cait. What's your secret?"

I turned on her with uncharacteristic hostility: "My secret? What's yours? A sister, Aunt Moira? I have a sister?"

"Ah," she replied, exhaling deeply and slumping a little at the knees. "Should I presume then that the Ambassador has come?"

*****

Despite my shocking tea party conversation with the remarkable Shin, I opened the store on time the next morning. Having tried, and failed, to sleep for more than ten minutes at a time on Sunday night, I adjusted my expectations altogether. Sleep would be a long time coming yet.

At this point I was running on adrenaline. I felt like an ill prepared athlete standing knock kneed at the gate of an imposing cross country race course, dreading the crack of the pistol. I was that out of shape hurdler wondering how she found herself at the starting line in the first place, certain that she would prove incapable of achieving enough pace and trajectory to negotiate the first basic hurdle, let alone the more treacherous ones to follow.

Not only was I unprepared, but this particular course was obscured by a thick fog of ignorance and confusion. The only thing of which I was certain was that it was sign posted Nethermost, my supposed homeland, about which I knew very little beyond the whisper of its name. Heck, I still needed to be completely convinced of its existence. At this point all that was certain was that I had more to learn, although I suspected that the more I was told, the more I would want to discover.

Of course my anticipation was obfuscated by fear. Bravery was a new idea for me after all. Although I desperately wanted to feel such strength, I knew that nothing I had ever done in life so far could earn me a hero's medal. Yet Shin led me to understand that I had potential, that within me was the magic essential for the wellbeing of Nethermost. And while her words inspired enthusiasm, I was paralytic with fear at the very idea of failing its myriads of citizens in need who, to use Shin's exact words, were 'counting on' me.

On top of all this, I had family. Not just an emotionally distant and often absent aunt, but parents to discover, and astoundingly, a sister. And while in theory the idea of saving an entire continent was a powerful image and more than a little intriguing, my need to reunite with family was as essential to me as breath itself.

No wonder then that on Monday morning, although I was physically on the job, I was in mental disarray. My brain felt overstuffed. I needed to digest each huge meal of information served up by Shin — the beginning of my 'instruction', as she called it.

As a first step in easing the pressure I was feeling, I decided to nobble Ol'Ben once again at my morning coffee break: "I have a sister?"

"What? I never heard of a sister. Who said?"

"Shin. Does she lie?"

"Not in my experience. All I know really is that you were left in Moira's care, with me as back up, when you were a tiny baby. There was never any mention of a sister. But, in truth, I always felt with the Ambassador that much had been left unsaid. A sister, eh? That's a shock, what-what?"

"Yes, it is. But you do know about Nora, about my mother, and I want to hear it all. Make me know her as well as you know me. And be warned old man, now that I know you're my loving great-grandpa, I am not above applying a little emotional blackmail to extract the truth. Just keep that in mind, eh?"

"No need, my dear. I do love you, always have — more than life itself." The truth in his voice made me shiver. "Consider this ancient relative an open book. In any case, to speak about my Nora is a pleasure, not a burden."

Over the course of the next few days, in snippets of time stolen from work, Ol'Ben orally uploaded a mountain of detail about my mother into my head and heart. In fact I think it gave him strength to be able to relive her story, to remember her as she was — his biggest adventure. It strengthened me.

Nora McCauley, as Ol'Ben had known her for much of the time she lived with him, was an open, loving child who filled his cloistered life with joy. Almost from the moment she arrived, Nora's big personality attracted playmates by the score. Although her best friend was indisputably her father, Nora's heart had a great capacity for love. From the beginning she would bring her collection of friends into the store, certainly getting underfoot, but always in innocent, playful ways. Seeing Nora interact with her friends taught Ol'Ben a great deal about his fellow man — how to listen sympathetically to each life story, how to accept everyone for who they were, how to soften their woes with the simplicity of a kind word.

Although she kept her friendships, although she found time for her grandpa, Nora primarily focused on her father, placing his needs before anything, before herself. Riley made every effort to hide the fact that he was in severe pain from Nora and Ol'Ben.

Even so, they were reminded daily of the hurt inflicted upon him by 'the wicked Apparatchik' as that five year old Nora once had innocently blurted out — a wound that placed his life in mortal peril. It was a deep ugly slash to the forearm that refused to scab over and was haloed in a sick yellowy glow that crept up his arm and beyond, claiming more and more territory along its insidious and relentless path; a wound beyond the expertise of traditional medicine.

Nora sensed that this injury was slowly sapping her father's life-force. Even with this understanding, or perhaps because of it, she remained calm in his presence. She seemed to be savouring him for as long as she could. Ol'Ben felt certain that it was the strength of this father daughter bond that enabled his son to continue for as long as he did.

The hours spent together before bedtime seemed the most important to them both — Riley whispering urgently to his small daughter; Nora, the ever attentive student taking notes in her cloth bound journal that she kept in a locked wooden box stuffed beneath her mattress.

When Nora was just sixteen, Riley succumbed to his wound, and for some time afterwards she would continue to study her journal daily before restoring it to its cubby. The untimely loss of her father triggered a new maturity in Nora. While she still kept in touch with friends, she kept to herself more often and was less inclined to party. Even though Ol'Ben did not expect her to work in his store, she insisted on spending time there, working alongside her grandfather. "She took such good care of me," Ol'Ben remembered with a twist of a grin, "that I kept checking my pulse, just in case I was on the way out too. When I joked with her about it, she answered in all seriousness, 'I'm not sure how much longer I can stay with you Grandpa Ben. We must make these days count the more for it.'"

At the time Ol'Ben had no idea what she could mean. The answer came a few months before Nora's nineteenth birthday in the form of the creature Ol'Ben now knows as a healy, who appeared in the company of a huge black dog one morning. She was so short that it took Ol'Ben a few minutes even to notice her peeking over the shop's countertop — an elfin being unlike anything Ol'Ben had ever encountered. Dressed in colourfully flowing robes that draped well past her knees, she commanded more space than she occupied. "Good day sir," she chirruped in a squeaky but formal voice, "The Nethermost Ambassador to speak with Nora McCauley … if you please." When told that Nora was off picking up stock for the shop, the strange little lady exited the store and sat outside by its front entrance, leaning heavily against the massive black dog — a stalwart beast with the profile of a St. Bernard. He would not have looked out of place with a small cask of brandy about the neck.

Ol'Ben kept a careful eye on the duo for the next two hours until Nora's return and witnessed their strange ritualistic greeting of his granddaughter as she approached. Woman and dog each bowed deeply in front of the girl, remaining in place until Nora laid a hand on both their heads, took each of them in turn by the shoulders, and pulled them to their feet. She invited them up to the apartment, while Ol'Ben remained below astonished.

What followed were days of back and forth visits — Nora at times disappearing for entire days, she and the Ambassador at other times closeting themselves upstairs. The dog stood faithfully by, waiting to fetch and carry for his mistress. On the few times when the Ambassador's visits extended into the evening, Ol'Ben had the occasional opportunity to converse with her, although he confessed to me that Shin's lofty demeanour and inscrutability made him feel shy and jittery. He did recall their first conversation in detail, however, as it was the moment when he was involuntarily inducted into an elite club of on-Earthers entrusted with information about the existence of the hidden continent.

Their first talk opened with a rather bold question from Ol'Ben. "Why do you and the dog bow before my granddaughter?"

Shin, who had been quietly napping in Ol'Ben's comfy chair by the wood stove while Nora and the dog prepared an evening meal, suddenly snapped to attention fully engaged, her squeaky voice at full pitch: "My dear Ben, I have been so rude! How could I have neglected to introduce my escort and assistant, Mánús, a Canomorph of great distinction and no mere dog!" The hound stepped forward and cocked his head very slightly in Ol'Ben's direction. "And, to answer your excellent question, we bow to your granddaughter because this is her due. She is of the first bloodline, and a future sovereign of Nethermost."

"A queen? Nora — a queen?" Ol'Ben asked.

"In your terms yes, only this regal office is known to us as Swayer, historically so named because it is gender neutral. When Nora comes of age on her nineteenth birthday and receives her talent, she will become regent to the throne in her mother's absence — although while Nethermost largely remains in a state of gilt, this title is honorary only. But … we live in hope."

Shin then went on to define the 'we' she referred to as the people of Nethermost. Ol'Ben had been given little more than the briefest of sketches of that subterranean world, leaving him more than somewhat confused and largely dissatisfied, with more questions than the Ambassador was prepared to answer. But from that point onwards, he had become aware of the world's eighth continent, and aware that his granddaughter's destiny would somehow be determined by it.

By the end of my entire week of chats with Ol'Ben on his favourite subject, he seemed noticeably brighter, stronger to be sure. As the recipient of these well guarded secrets, I too felt lighter, with just a smattering of hope. Family, eh?

I did have at least two follow up questions for Ol'Ben though...
1. What was a *talent,* and why would Nora receive one on her nineteenth birthday? and
2. What on earth did Shin mean when she said that Nethermost was in a state of *gilt*?

Ol'Ben had no idea.

Chapter 8: The Good Ol' Days

Aunt Moira and I sat across from each other in the tastefully designed dining area of our well restored house — me looking her straight in the eye, she trying to avoid mine.

"Look Aunt Moira," I began kindly, "I understand that there may have been secrets to be kept and for very good reasons, but I have a sister? How could you keep this particular detail from me?"

"It was important to keep it secret, dearie," she replied with a look pleading for understanding, "especially from you."

"How so? Why? Whatever … answer one of those questions! Please!"

"Because you would have wanted to meet her, to know her, to be raised with her; and that could not be allowed." She correctly interpreted my drooping posture, "Please allow me to explain … in my own way, and at my own pace.

"First, let me tell you of my happy childhood with Michael … with your father. Yes Cait, I really am your aunt. Michael and I were born in Nethermost, in the time before the gilding, when our continent was glorious and all its citizens prosperous. My father and mother both held the same political office, that of Chief Counsels to the Swayers of Nethermost, Her Grace Fianna (*fee-na*), and His Grace Canice (*can-iss*), regals of the first bloodline, sovereigns of Nethermost.

"Michael and I, as members of the regal household, were given more licence than most citizens, although having said that, there was really no poverty or want in Nethermost at that time. Everyone was assured of a prosperous life, with a generous allotment of liquid gold, our greatest natural resource. But Michael and I nonetheless were even more fortunate, because we were allowed direct access to their Graces. Our education was more complete, our experiences more exciting, such as attending royal events at the palace, far more opulent that anything I have witnessed here on-Earth.

"We were provided with excellent tutoring, not only in the culture, values and workings of our own continent, but in the ways of on-Earth, as diverse and textured as it is. Both of us were expected to learn a few on-Earth languages; both of us were allowed an on-Earth tour. In addition, our education shaped us for continuing in our family tradition of service to our sovereigns.

"At the time of my birth, their Graces Fianna and Canice were already parents, their two children fully grown. Nicola, their daughter, was a young woman of great character, elegance and compassion; Peadar (*pad-dar*), their son, and the younger of the two, was a man of great ambition and an insatiable inventor.

"Since my part of this story involves my association with the lovely Nicola, I shall leave the account of Peadar to Ambassador Sinead, his tale being the more complex and troublesome.

"As I said at the outset, the royal children were closer in age to my parents than to Michael and me, and my first memories of Nicola are of her as a very young woman. When she came of age and received her talent, the expectation was for Nicola to marry well. Although she had many suitors vying for her affection, none seemed to catch her eye. Indeed the populous in general wondered if she would ever marry; yet marriage and offspring was essential for the continuance of the bloodline.

"In Nicola's twenty-first year, a stranger pierced the borders of our continent from above. He called himself Riley McCauley — a traveler of great strength and unusual charisma — especially for an on-Earther."

"Ha!" I erupted as Aunt Moira came to this point in her tale, "My grandfather!"

"As you say, dearie, your grandfather. Although that was an idea far from ripening in anyone's thoughts, or desires, at that time. Whether he was searching for Nethermost in particular, or came upon us by accident, I never knew. But when he did arrive in The Capitol, his presence was the subject of widespread gossip, eventually reaching the ears of the Swayers.

"He was brought before them to be questioned, and although he did not realize it then, his fate depended upon the quality of his answers."

"Gosh!" I squeaked, fully engrossed in the drama.

"Gosh, indeed," smiled Aunt Moira, "now hush up, dearie, while I continue."

"Consider my mouth zipped, Aunt," I responded, "I want to catch your every word!"

Aunt Moira laughed and reached her hand across to squeeze one my own. "You were always such a dear girl, you know. So like your mother … so like your father. Hmmm … But to continue …

"Riley presented as a keen explorer, as a man of honour and a great curiosity. His enthusiasm was infectious and he brought fresh eyes to our society, the eyes of a man inspired by all that he witnessed, utterly challenged to contribute, to be useful. He begged to be allowed to serve at court in any capacity and, as such, was given the lowliest of tasks, jobs demeaning to the most unfortunate citizen. His positive attitude in his duties impressed our Swayers and eventually came to the attention of their daughter Nicola, who watched Riley from afar for some time before she permitted him an introduction.

"But once that introduction took place, so did a friendship launch. Soon Nicola was showing Riley her most favourite sites on the continent, soon she was listening to his own tales of adventure, soon they were falling in love, soon they were begging her parents to marry.

"Such an idea, of course, went beyond all historical precedent, well past the traditions and expectations for the royal lineage. There was strong opposition to the proposal. There were those who were convinced that it would pollute the bloodline, those who feared that to allow an on-Earther into the regal family would be to invite the general co-mingling of the two disparate levels of Earth. And of course, there were the whacky superstitions — that a marriage between two individuals from the two surfaces of Earth would bring about catastrophic events — massive earthquakes, tsunamis, appalling climate change.

"Not all, but a great deal of public opinion was against it. Although once the clamour died back, saner heads seemed to be able to assuage the foolishness. Besides, it saddened the hearts of Their Graces to see their daughter so broken hearted and at the mercy of a continent of opinion. So in the end they allowed the marriage. Riley continued in his service to the court, as Chief Functionary now in service to His Grace Canice, and of course he stood as consort in waiting to his wife, Nicola, who was destined to become Swayer, she being the elder of the two regal siblings.

"Within two years, Nicola and Riley, along with nearly all of Nethermost, celebrated the birth of a baby daughter. Michael and I were only small children ourselves at the time. Nevertheless the birth was so memorable, that even as a young child I paid attention to the many celebrations of her birth across the continent. They named their daughter Nora, after her paternal grandmother ..."

"My mm ...?"

"Shh," Aunt Moira giggled, "you're spoiling the drama. But yes — Nora — your mother."

"Oh I have to ask Aunt Moira, I can't keep zipped up any longer. How did the happy birth of that baby girl go so badly wrong? How did her mother go missing, how was her father mortally wounded? And how did Nora end up working at The General Store in our village and living over the store with Ol'Ben?"

"Yes, something went very wrong, dearie, very wrong indeed. But for a few years at least, baby Nora was honoured and nurtured by the most loving of parents, and spoiled by the most indulgent of grandparents. But when Nora was just four years old, our beloved Swayers died in rapid succession of each other, which altered the fate of Nethermost in ways that no one could possibly have imagined."

"What happened? Wha ..." I didn't know what to ask next.

But Aunt Moira had stopped speaking now and was rising from the table to signal the end of our conversation. "You know Cait," she added, "although there is so much yet to relate, I feel that the next part of this tale should be entrusted to the Ambassador — to Sinead. It is her duty after all. And so I suggest that you and I go to see her very soon, and have one of her famous afternoon spreads. It's been a while since I've seen her in any case, or tasted her amazing teas."

"Oh, just give me a hint Aunt. A hint is all I ask."

"A hint? Hmmm. What happened was ... Peadar ... Peadar happened!"

"And my sister?"

"She — and you — come much later in this story. Be patient!"

Chapter 9: The Gilding of Nethermost

Be patient, indeed! Could you be patient, I ask you? Finding patience had always been hard for me; now it was making me crazy.

My aunt's story filled in the blanks of Ol'Ben's account, which fitted in perfectly with Shin's tutoring. Each day the information I was absorbing made it more and more convincing that a floating subterranean continent was not just an alluring idea or a dream, it was all too real.

But there was one guy who was having none of it and that was Loo. One morning when I was yawning back my fatigue, the by-product of many a night spent in fitful sleep, as I tried to synthesize all the details and the emotional blowback of recent events, Loo challenged me mid mop stroke.

"You're not pulling your weight anymore Cait. What's with matter with ya?" Rain was pissing down outside and our early morning customers were dragging in muck off the streets by the gallon, making a fine mess of his once clean floor.

"How dare you say that?" I retorted, failing to suppress another yawn. "I do plenty, and if I don't pull my weight I expect to be taken to task by Ol'Ben not by you. You are not the boss of me!"

"Listening to fairy tales," he grumbled, disregarding my reaction entirely, "making a fool of yourself."

"What *are* you talking about?" I demanded hotly, "Where is this coming from? … from Ol'Ben?"

"Na, I just hear things."

"Things?"

"Stuff … like dogs that aren't dogs, continents that aren't there, weird twisted little ladies with highfalutin' manners and impossible names. Nethermost — what's that? And you and Ol'Ben shouting at each other, then whispering together — clamming up whenever I'm near. When's the old Cait coming back? I miss her."

I tried to see things from Loo's perspective. We did keep shutting him out. And if I weren't standing in the eye of this supernatural hurricane, I would be more ruffled too. I was now receiving my instruction in manageable bites, even though I still struggled to digest each new meal. So I couldn't imagine what it must be like for good old dependable, unimaginative Loo to swallow what could not be seen or proven from afar.

And I hated to tell him, but I wasn't at all sure that the old Cait was ever coming back.

*****

True to her word, my aunt booked us a tea date for the end of the week.

"Moira's caught me up with what you know so far," Sinead began, "She's taken all the good bits, of course, leaving the nasty stuff for me."

"The nasty stuff? About the Apparatchik, or about the gilding of Nethermost?" I asked.

"Both actually, it's one and the same. But let's not refer to him as Apparatchik, he deserves no such title. He usurped the throne from his sister after all, naughty boy. I shall refer to him simply as Peadar."

"My great-uncle," I volunteered proudly, having worked out the kinship beforehand.

"I suppose so," sighed Shin, "but you would do well to shun that connection. It will be easier to bear the rest of this tale, if you disassociate yourself from that villain.

"Let me start first with the 'good ol' days', which is where I understand Moira began. Picture a land of prosperity, overseen by benevolent sovereigns, where resources were plentiful; where nature was both predictable and consistent. That describes Nethermost in its glory — for hundreds, even thousands of years — that is until four decades ago.

"Nethermost is home to a number of sentient beings. Of course by far the largest race on the continent, and the one most familiar to you, is human. But there are six other species of magical creatures living there too, beings who dare not live on-Earth. The healy, in my totally biased opinion, are the most noble of all living creatures. Although small in stature, we healy are large in wisdom. In fact, the birth given talent of the healy is that we are natural seers. Because of our ability to recount the past, interpret the present and foresee the future, the healy have taken on careers in Nethermost that draw heavily on this talent: teachers, judges, librarians, farmers, ambassadors — to name but a few.

"My own position, as you know, is that of Ambassador. As such, I am required to be diplomatic, understanding, and fair. I must represent my continent beyond its borders, broker fair trade deals between on-Earthers and under-Earthers, inventory emigration — and do all this without drawing too much attention to Earth's eighth continent, Nethermost.

"Because of my mammoth assignment, I was off continent a great deal, unable to keep abreast of home front news except through diplomatic reports. For this reason, the subtle tensions that were building within the royal community eluded my notice — until they had gone too far. Other healy should have known, should have stopped it long before it happened. Sad to say, we let the whole continent down, in this most important of instances. But he had always been such a charming boy," Shin murmured, "which is no excuse ..."

"Excuse for what, for who?" I asked.

Ignoring my question, Shin pushed on with her tale. "Peadar and Nicola were the hope and the future of the crown. It was always understood that the elder child, Nicola, would become the next Swayer, upon the deaths of their parents. Peadar would rule by her side as Apparatchik, her loyal lieutenant. Even if either or both siblings married, these roles would not change. Their spouses would be consorts with diplomatic, but no official, powers.

"The children's education was customized from the outset to shape them for their futures. Nicola, being both wise and compassionate, developed the softer skills essential to leadership. She was also encouraged to pursue an interest in geography, especially climate control and land development, subjects that her parents felt would guarantee prosperity and safety for the homeland. They knew that Nethermost's position beneath the forests' roots was a delicate balance at best.

"Peadar, always a bright boy in school, was especially good at maths and sciences. Because his future duties would be less arduous than his sister's, he was given more latitude to expand his studies, and to travel as much as he wished. At university, his interests included engineering and the art of invention. Although he did not share his sister's interest in geography, he was passionate about history, the history of warfare on-Earth especially, and he collected a library of books on the subject.

"The siblings came of age five years apart from one another. At her coming of age ceremony, Nicola asked for, and was granted, the talent of balance — not frivolously so that she could climb trees, and sit atop buildings, but more for the supernatural ability to address the imbalance of nature and climate — a huge responsibility shared with dwarves. She had noticed small changes in our continent's stability — a slight tilt, a few earth tremors, a squirt of gold erupting in odd places. With the magical talent of balance Nicola was able to stabilize such imperfections, to shore up the effects of time and erosion. Her ability was so powerful it was legendary, although only a few appreciated how much she was forced to use it to maintain the health of the continent.

"On his nineteenth birthday, Peadar asked for the talent of alchemy. Traditionally alchemy is the power to transmute base metals into gold. Since Nethermost is literally floating on an ocean of gold, this was viewed as frivolous, but it was granted nonetheless. Little did anyone realize how Peadar would pervert his talent, would weaponize it, and in doing so would destroy generations of peace and prosperity.

"Shortly after Nicola ascended the throne, Nethermost experienced its first major earthquake. It shook buildings, toppled spires, left gaping cracks in roadways — a shock of ruination which took lives. The population was in turmoil. As balancer, Nicola was flummoxed.

"Was anyone even paying attention to Peadar, I wonder, during this catastrophic event? Did anyone even notice? Peadar was calm, Peadar was cool … Peadar was smug! In fact, he used the aftermath of this crisis to sow the seeds of doubt about Nicola — about his sister's ability to lead. In hindsight we know that it was Peadar himself who began those early rumours, delivered in whispered tones which guaranteed that they would spread all the more quickly.

"The rumours were about as subtle as cancer and just as harmful … What kind of weak Swayer could allow her subjects to die? Was Her Grace Nicola neglectful or was she sadistic? Given her magical talent of balance, shouldn't Nicola have been able to avert this disaster?

"And the most popular, harmful and loopy rumour — Was this disaster caused by the marriage between Her Grace Nicola and the on-Earther Riley McCauley?

"Such rumours inflamed our more vulnerable citizens initially, then spread exponentially as these same citizens became the messengers of even more insidious speculation, again fuelled by Peadar.

"In public Peadar's behaviour was impeccable. He openly flattered his sister and fawned over her young family like a doting brother and uncle. Then one day he applied to her highness for permission to build a separate residence for himself, in anticipation of the day when he too might marry. He petitioned for a tract of land within the grounds of the palace itself — an area of prime real estate near the main gate, on green space reserved for parkland. He had been so clever, so doting, that Nicola had no reason to suspect his intentions were anything more than as declared — 'to start a family as lovely as yours, dear sister.' She assumed that he had always dedicated his life, as she had done, to the service of its citizens, and she was delighted over his ambitions to dip his toes into the pool of family life. His request was granted.

"Over the next year, Nicola gradually became more and more alarmed — and suspicious. She was alarmed that Nethermost was experiencing even more earth tremors, with inexplicable fluxes in temperature, for the first time in the continent's history. Indeed, it took all her strength as balancer to stabilize the realm.

"She was also suspicious of the goings on in the parkland. Peadar's new home was enlarging so much that it now overshadowed the size of the palace itself. With the assistance of an army of tradespeople working night and day, Peadar's new home was finished in ten months. It was built almost entirely of gold inside and out, at a price which must have been a thousand times the value of our historic castle. Nicola berated herself for not overseeing the work, and expressed to her brother her desire to view its progress, even though the building was near completion. So Peadar graciously guided her through his home's two hundred rooms, dressed in his father's coronation robes, strutting and swaying through a cluster of handpicked onlookers, who followed them on their tour, applauding from one room to the next. It was a pomp clearly designed to eclipse Nicola's office as Swayer, while puffing up his own as Apparatchik.

"After this outrageous display of supremacy, Peadar's followers increased in number. They became more rowdy, not only disrespecting, but also shouting daily at palace officials. This groundswell of change had gone too far by the time Nicola took action against it — against a brother that she had loved unconditionally all their lives. First she asked her husband Riley to conduct a quiet inquiry into her brother's financing of his opulent lifestyle. She also tasked him to determine the harm Peadar's followers were inflicting on the palace's operations. Although Riley lacked a magical talent at assist him, Nicola was so beleaguered with suspicion of everyone that she felt she could trust no one but him.

"What Riley discovered was beyond Nicola's wildest imagination. In brief, he found a regency on the brink of toppling. He witnessed a dangerous over mining of the continent's gold foundation by magically enhanced techno gear invented by Peadar. He found munitions factories built by his brother-in-law that were reassembling ancient weapons and converting them into lethal super weapons, through the application of a poisonous transmutation of liquid gold. Most abhorrently, Riley uncovered warehouses of gilded creatures who had been either killed outright or placed in suspended animation — he wasn't sure which. In short, Riley witnessed the inception of Peadar's insidious plans to overthrow the Regency of Nethermost by a brother-in-law consumed by a malignant envy.

"Before he could report on his findings, Riley's activities were uncovered. He was overpowered by Peadar's ruffians and brought before the Apparatchik himself, who trussed him up like a turkey and strapped him to wrought gold fretwork. He tortured his captive with his weapon of choice — the family's most revered artifact, the Swayer's sword, a ceremonial symbol, now perverted through alchemy. During this lengthy torture session, Peadar himself swung the sword wildly, slashing the air centimetres from Riley's vital parts, threatening death with each swoop. In a brutal finish to his fiendish ritual, he angled the sword next to Riley's head, poised as if to decapitate him with the next stroke. He was so consumed with hatred that drool oozed from his lips. The tension was beyond bearable — he sliced the air with the blade and aimed it at Riley's exposed neck. A millisecond before it reached its mark, Peadar veered off, arched upwards again, then quickly downwards to slice Riley's forearm, screaming maniacally, 'Why kill you outright when with one simple stroke I can guarantee you a life of torturous pain, and a slow miserable death, you vile on-Earther!'"

Shin stopped to ingest a couple of gulps of air, in an effort to control of her quavering voice as she continued this appalling tale. "The lethal edge of the sword had the desired effect on its victim. The poisonous substance coursed through his veins, numbing the wound site, sending Riley into a coma. One of Peadar's evil cohorts unbound him, threw him over his shoulder and carried him to the palace gates. Dropping the incoherent Riley to the ground, he encouraged his co-conspirators to stomp on the consort's unconscious form, as they fell in step behind their leader. They marched into the palace, their newly invented gilding guns blazing, covering everyone in sight in a thin layer of gold. When he reached the throne room, Peadar zapped the palace guards before they could reach for their weapons, grabbed his sister roughly by the hair, and violently dragged her from the room, while dozens of courtiers, including myself, watched aghast!"

Shin's vocal reach soared to a sickly crescendo, then shattered in a gulping sob, as she slid to the floor, grabbing clumps of her grey/white hair on her thin scalp and howling, "Stupid, stupid, stupid!"

Aunt Moira raced to her side and lifted her into her arms with a strength I didn't know she possessed. She placed Shin on the couch, calling for Mánús to bring cold towels, and applied one to Shin's forehead and one to back of her neck. Lying limply on the cushions, fully outstretched, a defeated Shin barely whispered, "I was there! I should have stopped it!"

"How?" I piped in helplessly. "How."

"Precisely!" Aunt Moira agreed, "How indeed." Then she turned to the Ambassador and asked her softly, "May I finish up, Ambassador? She cannot go home today without knowing this last bit."

She nodded, closed her eyes and Aunt Moira continued …

"Shin acted quickly, as only a healy has the presence of mind to do. She called for Nora's nanny, barked for her to prepare the child for departure, and was gone from the palace within minutes, the child and her nanny in tow. Having discovered a nearly dead Riley at the gates, she ordered three guards, Mánús amongst them, to pick him up and follow. How they managed to leave the city without being discovered is due in part to magic, in part to Shin's prowess. But, suffice it to say, Shin did escape with her troupe of refugees, leading them to the farm of a healy friend in the hinterland, who took a great risk in sheltering them from the searching eyes of the usurpers.

"They dared not move from their camouflaged hideaway for some weeks, only staying long enough for Riley to be able to continue the journey. Shin knew that Peadar would eventually spot a major flaw in his wicked plans. He would not care that he had allowed Riley to live; that made no difference one way or another to him as long as Riley suffered. But what he would care about, once he thought it through, was that it was a mistake not to snatch the child as well, who upon her mother's demise, was the legitimate heir to the throne."

Chapter 10: A Conversation Long Overdue

I called in sick the next day.

It was not a matter of whether I believed that the under-Earth continent of Nethermost existed, or about whether it was my homeland. That was no longer in question. Its truth had been reinforced by various witnesses from various points in time and from various perspectives. It was now a matter of my emotional resilience.

The morning after my latest audience with Shin, I awoke with a fearsome headache, complicated by second hand heartache at the loss of family I'd never known in the first place. And it wasn't so much an awakening from restful sleep, but more from a series of lapses into unconsciousness from which I was jerked to the surface regularly by nightmarish visions of scary men holding swords over my head, or grabbing me by the hair and dragging me off.

I was in shock, no doubt. After all, I had just begun to enjoy dreaming of a hidden world, stocked with wondrous magical creatures, and dogs that weren't dogs. I loved the idea of pools of liquid gold, of illusionary stars that were actually luminescent quartz, of a society where poverty was a non issue, of a weather report that always called for shirt sleeves temperatures.

Now I was struggling with nightmares of the worst sort. Now I saw a homeland I could only imagine in peril, its citizens living in exile, its geography and climate in ruins — an entire society not just dealing with poverty and disease, but a realm that had virtually been destroyed by greed and unimaginable violence.

As I repositioned my sick head on my softest pillow in the hopes of waiting out the pain, I mused not for the first time about my grandparents, Nicola and Riley. Riley I knew had passed on after years of appalling pain, salvaged in part by the daughter he cherished. But what of Nicola? Was my grandmother stacked in the corner of some warehouse, gold plated? Was she slowly rotting away in some draughty dungeon in an obscure corner of the realm? Or had she been extinguished too?

Nethermost Regained

And what about Michael and Nora? What about my elusive sister? Where did they come into the narrative? Where did I come in?

I perseverated on these unanswered questions for so long, that my eyes began to water again, my head to throb even more. Though I was drenched with misery, I could still hear the door to my room open, and correctly assumed that it was my aunt.

"I can't face work today, Aunt Moira, and I can't face people. Just leave me on my own, will you?"

"Of course," she whispered, "Just brought you aspirin and some cocoa. Get this down your neck."

I sat up gratefully and polished off the aspirin and warm drink in a few gulps. "Are you psychic? Is that *your* talent?"

"No. Not psychic dearie. That's my mother. My talent is teleportation. Sleep now, talk later."

"I wish! I can't sleep!"

"You will now," she whispered, "I put a 'wee dram' of magic in that cocoa. Sweet dreams."

I don't even remember falling back onto my pillow. I slept though, deep and long. I remember getting up for a quick pee mid afternoon, before crawling back into bed for round two. When I awoke for the second time, it was early evening and Ol'Ben was sitting on my bed, absolutely still and waiting. That felt cosy.

"Hey, Ol'Ben What are you doing here? Am I fired for skipping work?"

"Dear me no," he protested, "Am I fired for being a crap great-grandpa?"

"Dear me no," I echoed, reaching for one of his hands.

"She awake yet?" Loo popped his head around the doorway. "'Bout time you stirred. Brought some leftover dinner for you and your aunt. I'm heating it up now. Five minutes okay?"

"More than okay, I'm ravenous."

"Oh, and sorry I for being a dick the other day. Didn't know you were ill."

"I wasn't ill, just unbearably tired. And you weren't a dick, you were concerned. I get it."

After Loo left, Ol'Ben looked worriedly at me and asked: "Why was Loo being a dick?"

"He wasn't a dick, more dick adjacent. But we need to decide what to do about him. Either we keep him in the dark and make sure we never speak about the witchy stuff when he's in the same building, or we include him altogether and trust that he can cope."

"It's more up to you than me, Cait. What are you thinking?"

"I'm thinking … I'm thinking … we should ask Sinead."

*****

After Ol'Ben and Loo had left, and Aunt Moira and I were lying back contentedly on our comfiest furniture digesting our latest Loo Special, I trial ballooned another subject. "So, you teleport. What's that like?"

"Well it saves on time and air fare," she laughed. "But seriously, I believe I chose my talent well."

"Okay, let's take one step back. We've been skating around this feature for a while now. What is a *talent*, in Nethermostian terms?"

"Nethermostian? That's a mouthful. A talent is the one special magical gift that each human citizen of Nethermost can access through supernatural rings held in trust by the Magic Council. They may petition for a talent ring when they reach the age of their ascension into adulthood — that is the age of nineteen. It is considered an honour, not a privilege. Of course most species, like the healy, are multi magical from birth. We humans are not. We can manage the use of only one ring — *only one* dimension of magic in our limited lives, but we are given a strong voice in the selection process, so it pays to choose well."

Aunt Moira went off to the kitchen to fetch us more coffee and some of Loo's oatmeal cookies. When she returned, she repositioned herself on the sofa next to me, sipping quietly away at her drink in nervous contemplation. "Did I do right by you Cait? Was I a good provider?"

"Were you a good provider? Yes, of course, you gave me everything money could buy."

"There's a *but* coming, I'm thinking …"

"*But* … I was often bored, and more than a little lonely."

"I wanted to do such a good job with you Cait, and I blew it! When my brother charged me with the care of his little girl, I knew it was an onerous responsibility, and neither of us wanted to entrust you into anyone else's protection — not even to old Ben McCauley, who was non magical and even then as old as dirt. But clearly I got it wrong."

"No, Aunt Moira, not wrong exactly. But I did feel like some exotic animal raised in captivity, left alone in its cage for too long. I have been given very little freedom, and feel largely unprepared for the upper layers of Earth, let alone for its challenging under realm. I've been too meek, too lacking in confidence, too nervous to stick my head out through the bars of my habitat."

"I thought I was teaching you independence — testing you on how to cope on your own. Instead you thought I was being neglectful and uncaring. I never wanted that!" She paused and stared at the fire. "For the record, I love you very much. There's nothing I wouldn't do for you."

For a while we sat side by side in stillness. This had been a conversation long overdue. I felt half embarrassed, half elated. Aunt Moira looked totally miserable. I knew it was up to me to close this chapter, so I changed subjects entirely, and rather effectively I thought. "So, when you go travelling, are you actually teleporting?"

"Yes, although I can only teleport in real time," she explained, the worry lines beginning to smooth away already. "That is, I can't jump into the past or leap into the future. For most of my adult life, I've been senior staff at Shin's embassy, working directly for, but seldom seeing, the Ambassador. You might argue that I perform some of Shin's more active duties. I'm her arms and legs so to speak in immigration rather than trade. My primary mission is to identify and pip tag all Nethermost citizens currently living on-Earth. As you might expect, at the time of the insurrection, those loyal to Her Grace Nicola were left in fear of their lives. Those openly hostile and resistive to Peadar were arrested and gilded immediately. Some fled to the hinterland to keep a low profile and stay off of his radar, while still more left Nethermost altogether.

"We need to know where everyone ended up, and so I was set the assignment of finding and tagging those outside Nethermost's boundaries. It has been a daunting task. But we need to know where everyone is in preparation for the day of our return."

"Did you say you 'pip tag' your citizens?"

"I use the term loosely but the results are the same. As long as I can get three seconds contact time with the skin of a person, I can leave a magical powder that gets absorbed and remains in their bodies forever. My tracking software shows me where anyone can be found at any given time.

"In actual fact, almost everyone I tag submits to it voluntarily. They want to be kept informed, and they want a panic button to push in the event of their abduction."

"Abduction?"

"Oh yes! Peadar's scouts have been sent out to roam on-Earth to discover and nobble those citizens who are actively working to find a means to stop the usurper. The trickier, more hazardous part of my job has been to find and pip tag the agents of Peadar. It requires stealth and finesse. So if a citizen is caught by these madmen, I can track their whereabouts and send in rescue teams."

Now Aunt Moira paused and grabbed me by the shoulders "Now listen Cait, this next bit is tough, but I urge you not to panic. Okay?"

"Oh no … why do I feel that this is about me?"

"Because you're smart, and you see where this is going. There are also agents whose sole job it is to find you."

"What have I done to deserve this distinction?"

"You are of the first bloodline and are positioned to inherit. And who knows, you may have the power to defeat your mad uncle. That is why I needed you to stay close to home under my continued protection in this village whose boundaries have been camouflaged for years with all the magic we could spare. That is, until you are needed. We must avoid your enemies Cait… now more than ever!"

"Oh help! I want my Mom!"

Aunt Moira smiled conspiratorially. Her gorgeous violet eyes positively twinkled as she presented me with the best bit of news so far. "Will Dad do? Cuz he'll be here tomorrow."

Chapter 11: Previsions in Paint

I had thought that there would be little to astonish me about another session with Ambassador Shin. I had expected to be challenged by her stories about an elusive realm populated by magical folks, to be instructed in the responsibilities of the first bloodline, to be appalled with a description of all the rotten doings of my nefarious uncle — all delivered by a remarkable and flamboyant character straight out of Disney Studios. And, I would expect all this to be served up alongside a lovely cup of tea.

But she did it to me again. She went and blew my mind. When Mánús opened the door to Aunt Moira and me on this occasion, our nostrils were greeted not by the aroma of freshly baked teacakes, but with the stench of chemicals — turpentine, oil paint, and linseed. And instead of a formal greeting at the door by Shin dressed in flowing robes of state, there was the mute Mánús bowing low, and behind him, on the far side of the room, the paint spattered backside of a healy casually slouched on a stool in loose fitting denims, studying a half completed canvas clamped to an easel.

"Do come in ladies," she called over her shoulder from her distant paint station, "I'm just finishing up an idea here. Mánús will see to your needs."

I was utterly flummoxed. Then my eyes took in yet more surprising detail. The pristine furniture from the front parlour had been shoved to one side, and in its place, dozens of oil paintings were set out in orderly rows along the outer edges of the area carpets, with dozens more leaning along the baseboards all around the great room.

With Mánús' assistance, Shin slid off her stool, retrieved her shillelagh, and hobbled across the room to where my aunt and I stood — my mouth, at least, agape. As if nothing was out of the ordinary, she enthusiastically extended a paint stained hand to both of us in turn. The act of returning her handshake left our own hands smudged with oils. "Ahh, that's interesting," said Shin, examining my palm like a fortune teller, "let's look at those colours. Ooo, lovely! That's called "celestial blue", that one "vivid violet" and that "orchid mauve" — a combination that perfectly captures the spectrum of lavender grown by the field full in the western hinterlands, under a late August afternoon's skylight. Or it used to, anyway," she sighed, wiping her hands back and forth on her jeans.

As if on cue, Mánús arrived with hand wipes to clean away the mess. He then pulled some dining room chairs forward to form a rough sitting area. "Why don't you serve our guests the sherry, Mánús," Shin suggested, "while I make myself more presentable."

"Good Lord!" I hissed when Shin had left the room. "What's all this?"

"Actually it's rather interesting," Aunt Moira explained, "and very useful."

"What's interesting? How useful?"

"The paintings are interesting … and you'll see how."

Shin entered again with an apology and an explanation of sorts. "I had intended to clean up before your arrival, but I had a vision that needed capturing. Now, where were we?"

"The room full of paintings?" I suggested. "Or the large glass of sherry I'm drinking instead of tea?"

"Oh yes, of course. The paintings are here to tell their stories. The sherry is for the shock."

"What shock?"

"Well … more of that later. First, the paintings. Let's start with these ones," she said, leading me over to four paintings leaning against the wall in the dining room. "Take a look at this set."

I was guessing that this first group of paintings was conveying a visual narrative of Nethermost in its prime. The scenes seemed to represent different angles of the same event. Besides the obvious humans, I recognized a healy in an inner circle directly in front of an ancient castle. To one side, bearing an orb on a pillow was a guardsman, standing tall and stiff in his earth tone uniform. In one of the paintings I thought I recognized doglike features in the face — slightly oversized floppy ears, small dreamy eyes, and a prominent nose.

"Is this guard a Canomorph?" I inquired.

"Yes, indeed. Most Canomorphs serve in the military because of their great strength and bravery."

Behind the palace guard, hoards of creatures pushed forward, straining to view the characters in the middle. Although features were blurred and simplified to symbolically suggest a larger crowd, I thought I could discern differently constructed beings scattered amongst the obvious run of the mill humans — some short legged, others long necked, tiny creatures with veined wings — a full range of skin tones, all dressed in their fineries. Central to each painting, a young couple of obvious distinction — bejewelled, be-robed and glittery. From their poses, props and costuming, I was sure that it must be a ceremony of sorts.

"Ah," I said, "How interesting! Is this the coronation of my grandparents — of Nicola and Riley?"

"A coronation indeed, but that is not Nicola and Riley. That impressive young couple are your great-grandparents, Their Graces, Fianna and Canice at their self coronations, eighty years ago."

"Wow! These paintings represent a significant memory in Nethermost history. They're stunning!"

"Perhaps they are a memory now, but when I painted them eighty years ago, they were a forecast."

"You painted this — eighty years ago? Not as a memory … but as a forecast? Just how old are you?"

"You know I don't really keep track anymore … somewhat north of one hundred and fifty years."

"And what do you mean by a forecast, not a memory?"

"Yes, this of course is the key point. Have another sherry while I tell you about my paintings, and why I had a large sample of my collection conveyed here from the Embassy for your inspection. I am not simply being vain, although I fancy I have some skill as an artist. Rather, let me convey to you why I paint, and how I came upon this skill.

"I understand that Moira has described to you the coming of age ceremony in which talents are granted to humans born in Nethermost. She will also have mentioned that one talent only is granted to each human. For most humans, one magical talent is all they can manage. Some humans even have trouble coping with the one. But it's different for beings born into magic, magicians in generic terms, for whom the supernatural is simply a way of life. When magicians of all species come of age, instead of acquiring a new talent, they are granted an *assistive device*, a tool to help them enhance one particular magical attribute and to turn it into a truly exceptional asset.

"When I came of age I asked for the ability to paint as my assistive device, not just to paint for painting's sake, but to make me a better seer. In that first set of paintings, for example, I had a prevision of the induction ceremony of our beloved regals even down to their specific guests. I do not see it in my mind, I see in through my fingers. It flows onto the canvas through a wondrous brain to hand symmetry that even I cannot fully understand, and over which I have no conscious control."

"Are your forecasts ever wrong?"

"No, but my interpretations of them sometimes are — at times with horrendous results. Come over here, if you please. You may find it interesting to see images of your homeland, along with some of your family in these next paintings."

I trailed her about the room, viewing the remaining canvases lined up against the walls. By the end of the tour I had a much clearer impression of the magic and beauty of Nethermost. I had also viewed several artistic impressions of members of my own family. Just viewing the canvases caused me to fall in love with their likenesses, and I wanted to dive into the paintings to set up house immediately.

But another collection of paintings, those bordering the area carpets, were not so lovely or inspiring. They illustrated the bad times times — images of the insurrection during which my grandmother had been abducted, my grandfather ruined, my mother exiled. They showed the devastation of those same landscapes that Shin had painted as glorious and luminous in the previous cluster of paintings. Now her paints were smudged, smokey, and muted, except, that is, for some images of Peadar's new home — all garish and overly ornamented — and the backdrop for Shin's horrifying reenactments of suffering, violence and degradation. These were the hardest to bear — especially her portrayal of citizens being caught at the point of gilding and, for all anyone knew, frozen for all time.

"Please! Stop!" I whimpered, shocked and horrified by the fear and loathing on their frozen gold faces. "How could you bear to paint such images?" It was one thing to hear carefully worded summaries of hardship and battle, quite another to witness them.

"It was not my choice or my doing. I was compelled to do so," Shin repeated.

"Then I am truly sorry for you, living in this exile, painting such hopeless visions." I felt drained and defeated by the evil encapsulated within the paint. I was beginning to be fearful of the canvases Shin had yet to show me, unequal to whatever she expected of me. "Aunt Moira, may we please go home?" I pleaded, "My headache is returning."

"No!" Shin shouted, "you must allow the canvases to continue their tale! You must see the rest of the paintings. This next sequence of paintings tell another story entirely. They are a warning, yes, but they also suggest a reason for hope. They contain hints, opportunities on how to return to our sad continent, warnings about rescuing Nethermost now before it crumbles and melts into its basin of liquid gold. Cait, I must make you understand *why*!. Why we still can hope … why we have come for you. Time is running out! We must act soon!"

"You hope! I can't. It's too hard. I'm just a stupid girl of little significance, leading a very dull life on a very small bump in the road. What do you want from me?"

Aunt Moira raced to my side and put her arms around me, holding me tightly while I sobbed uncontrollably. "For goodness sake Michael, I know you're here!" she shouted out loudly, angrily.

"Yes … yes of course," a disembodied voice came from the direction of the stacked furniture. "I have remained in the shadows far too long." From an armchair shoved into the corner, a man emerged before my eyes. He was a tall, imposing man, dressed in jeans, a brown leather jacket, deep green jersey and black boots. His face was rugged and weathered — with black hair greying at the temples, piercing blue eyes, and a well trimmed beard — a face that I could well imagine looking fierce when need be, but at this moment softened by a loving smile. It wasn't that this dark man was so quiet that I hadn't yet noticed him, it was that moments before he hadn't been visible.

I was certain that we'd had never met … but I knew him nonetheless. "Hello, Cait. I'm Michael O'Quinn."

Chapter 12: Love in a Cold Climate

I awoke in my own bed again, feeling drugged and hung over. This time it wasn't Ol'Ben sitting on the edge of the bed, but Michael O'Quinn lightly dozing in my chair. From the moment I stirred, he was alert and kneeling at my head, stroking my hair.

"Hello again … daughter."

"Cripes! Please don't tell me I fainted. That would be too damsel in distress."

"More like daughter in shock. I shouldn't have dropped in that way."

"Why did you? How did you?"

"It's my talent — invisibility. It's been very useful for sneaking behind our enemy's back. It's also been invaluable for keeping an eye on my daughter."

"What? You've been watching me? Why didn't you show yourself?"

"Because it would have exposed you to danger. My face is too well known to Peadar's agents. I am a key player in The Nethermost Gate Resistance Movement, a small but determined fighting force dedicated to breaching our continent's impenetrable borders in an effort to regain Nethermost."

"Then why show up now?"

"We have good reason to suspect that Peadar is actively searching for weaknesses amongst members of this movement. In his pursuit of me, his agents have already unearthed a few clues, and even though they are all louts and dunderheads to a man, they will eventually find you. We need to make plans to remove you from here."

"Sinead did mentioned that time was running out, and Aunt Moira spoke of scouts. But I thought I was being cloaked by magic somehow, that the village was camouflaged."

"True and it is still working … for now. But as much as they are truly undeserving, these madmen have talents too. And one of them seems to have a talent for detecting magical fencing. From there, it would be a short leap to discover what, or rather who, I'm hiding in this village."

"Where's Mom?" I blurted suddenly. She was always on my mind. "Is she here too?"

"No, Cait, she was captured just after you were born and hasn't been seen since. But Shin feels confident that she still lives."

*****

"My dear, I fear I have been doing such a bad job as your counsellor," said Shin, again with an apology. "I can see that I should have been much gentler in my approach. I thought the sherry would have cushioned the shock, especially as I slipped in a soothing powder. Can you forgive me?"

Aunt Moira and I had invited the Nethermost refugees to come to our home this time. We didn't have anything like the hosting skills or the frippery that Shin could conjure. Our collective best effort was coffee and bakery cookies.

In attendance were Shin, Mánús, and Michael, a.k.a. Father. "You must think me such a wimp," I said, red faced.

"No, it's my fault," Aunt Moira piped in. "I failed to prepare her adequately."

"And I just plain failed," added Father, sorrowfully.

Something inside of me suddenly juddered into the *on* position. Was there a suspicion of bravery igniting within me? I certainly felt quite tetchy at this moment, irritated at all the apologies flying about the room, and with the realization that twice within this week I had been drugged against my will. And because of that, I felt the strong need to stick up for myself. "Enough," I pitched loudly. "There's plenty of blame to go around. But it isn't useful and frankly it's annoying. So, let's stop tiptoeing about. Let's all try plain talk. The truth would be good. *No* speaking in parables Shin, no softening the blow ..."

"Ooo! Hark at her," Aunt Moira smirked. "Maybe I didn't do such a bad job after all!"

"No, you were crap as a parent, Aunt Moira, but your heart was in the right place." When Father cast Aunt Moira a sour look, I added, "And lay off your sister. At least she was here!"

I surprised myself just then. Here I was spewing forth feelings I'd held onto for years, pushing back against the heaviness of inadequacy and isolation, tossing them aside in one single, forceful thrust. I was on a roll ... it was liberating! Thus emboldened, I turned to Shin.

"Ambassador Sinead, I know by now, after all these interviews and cream teas, that your advice is sound. You are a seer after all and I trust your wisdom. But no more cups of tea! I hate tea! And one more thing ... no more roofies!"

"How could anyone hate tea?" Shin pouted, "and what's a roofie?"

*****

"Your mother and I had an arranged marriage," Father began. "I understood my destiny from an early age. Even though we would never have resisted the wishes of our parents, it was wonderful, nonetheless, that we did actually fall in love before we wed."

This was precisely what I wanted to hear. I was getting my first glimpse of my parents as a couple and I was giddy with excitement. This was going to be a love story …

"I was ten years old when Peadar seized power. I remember that wretched day all too well. My parents racing to our classroom, grabbing Moira and me, and shoving us into an overstuffed hover limo, bursting at the seams with hastily grabbed items. As we peeled away from the palace, I was heartsick with dread, understanding even at my young age that we were fleeing for our lives, and that I might never see my home again.

"While most of the courtiers headed for the hinterlands, my parents knew that, as high ranking members of the regal household, we would either be regarded as high value assets for Peadar to use to leverage his sister's cooperation … or we would be gilded and stuck in storage somewhere.

"Many didn't trust their safety to the hinterlands. These folks raced over the borders and scattered to more remote locations on-Earth. My family did neither. We crossed the border but stayed on the upper side of Nethermost Gate, along with a couple of thousand exiled patriots, and we constructed an outpost of resistance and rescue. We held back Peadar's troops from crossing at that main exit point at least, while offering the Nethermost refugees medical care for their injuries, and emotional support for their trauma.

"This is where Moira and I spent our teenage years, as outlaws enduring a rough, no frills lifestyle — living, loving, rescuing and fighting shoulder to shoulder — humans and magicians alike.

"Due to his dire injuries, Riley was of little use to our ragtag band. While our magic staved off the immediate impact of his injuries, he required advanced medical attention, regular meals and the warmth of a good hearth in a proper home. Besides, it was his primary duty as royal consort to nurture and protect his daughter, the legitimate heir to the Swayer-ship. So it was decided that he should return to the village of his birth and remain there with Nora, living with his father Ben, protected at a discreet distance by the ambassador and her agents. Riley would prepare Nora for her future duties as best he could, and then just before her nineteenth birthday she would return to Nethermost Gate for her ascension ceremony, talent assignment, and to join the resistance movement.

"Life in our Nethermost Gate community was uncomfortable and cold. Although we found caves and air pockets within the northern forests to shelter away from the worst of its arctic blasts, we were cruelly exposed to long winter months of unreasonable amounts of snow and ice, until our very bones ached and our fingers and toes were waxy with frostbite. Over time, we acclimated, as you do. Our masons expanded the caves into complex caverns, our builders found ways to winterize our homes, but I for one never learned to enjoy life in a cold climate.

"Our money and supplies dwindled all too quickly, and we found ourselves in need of an income to keep ourselves in food and clothing. But just because we were outlaws didn't mean that we were thieves. So in the summer months, we formed ourselves into a troupe of acrobats, actors and musicians, using our magical abilities to create an impressive traveling road show. We initially toured the northern towns and villages nearby, but as we became more popular, our performances became more elaborate and our tours countrywide. Although we didn't exactly become rich, we were nonetheless financially comfortable and quite popular. We were able to earn enough money, not only to survive, but to acquire some interesting on-Earth tools, which when combined with the magic at our disposal, provided us with powerful devices to assist in our plans to breach our borders and regain Nethermost.

"When Nora returned at the age of eighteen years and ten months, Nethermost Gate was a much evolved and somewhat prosperous community. She was such an outgoing and loving young woman that it was not only I, but an entire settlement, that fell hopelessly in love with her. At her coming of age birthday party she chose her talent wisely. Perhaps because she regretted not being able to ease her own father's suffering, she chose the talent of healer. She developed this ability so quickly and so well that she was soon teaching more experienced healers a skill or two, especially in the area of diagnosis.

"Our courtship was brief but intense and captured the romantic spirit of the entire Gate community. Even though the doting community promised us privacy and space to advance our courtship, we often sensed prying, eager eyes. We rejected activities of traditional dating — taking meals together, long walks, mindless entertainment — relying more on more practical activities to better prepare ourselves for an uncertain future. I taught Nora survival and combat skills. She in turn, filled in the gaps of my interrupted education with subjects such as maths, reading, and sciences. She even taught the entire community the newest on-Earth dance steps — modern, slick moves which then became a community pleasure, and the primary entertainment at our wedding.

"There were times when we almost forgot our life in exile, sustained as we were by love. As respite from the cruel climate and an essential pleasure for my wife, we visited the village of Alta at least twice a year to stay with Nora's grandfather, Ben McCauley. I especially liked to pop by in the winter months to enjoy the warmth of his potbellied stove.

"After we had been married for two years, Nora delighted me with the news that she was expecting a child. I was overjoyed, and overwrought at the same time. The arrival of a regal child represented a source of hope for the future. But it also placed us all at risk, should word should ever reach Peadar's ears. And then to discover that we were in fact expecting twins …"

"Twins!" I yelped.

"Twins, yes … identical."

Chapter 13: Romance and Betrayal

"What's her name then — my twin sister?"

"Rhue."

"And where is she now?"

"She lives with my parents … at Nethermost Gate."

"Ah-ha … How come you kept her and gave me away?"

"I didn't give you away. I separated the two of you. You were raised by family too. We knew that Peadar would be unhappy at the thought of even one royal child. But two would enrage him beyond imagination. If he knew about you girls, he would not have stopped until he had destroyed you both."

"Why are we a bigger threat? We're only third in line to the throne, if Nicola and Nora are still alive."

"This goes beyond a competition for the leadership of Nethermost, Cait. Regal twins could just be the very weapon needed to challenge Peadar's power — and the key to his ultimate destruction."

"How so?"

"As two separate people, you and Rhue will very soon be granted one talent apiece. Because you are twins, one twin can lend her talent to the other twin for brief periods. That fact is well established. But there have been cases in which *identical* twins, such as you and your sister, have *cloned* their talents, and this would be powerful indeed."

"Cloned?"

"Cloned in the sense of making a precise copy. So, you could have your primary talent and also a cloned copy of your sister's talent. She could have her primary talent and a cloned copy of yours. One human with two magical talents has depth and strength. Two doubly talented humans, working together — well that would be a force to be reckoned with.

Nethermost Regained

"Wow!"

"Wow, indeed."

*****

I was sitting across from my father at the dining room table in the still of night, finishing off my last coffee for the day. All the lights in the house had been turned off except for the stove light on the kitchen range, leaving us largely in darkness. The other guests had left, and Aunt Moira had gone to bed.

"Tell me how you lost her," I put the question to him. "How did Peadar get his hands on Mother?"

My father grabbed his head and slapped his hands over his tortured face. I thought that he was going to refuse to answer. Instead he raised his head again, drew in a bushel of air, and began …

"You asked for truth, plain and simple. While I agree that this is the best approach, the truth can be complex and textured. My fear is that I cannot do it justice. Which doesn't mean I won't try. You deserve that …

"From the beginning, we had been following Shin's paintings for intelligence on the enemy's movements. For the most part, the canvases kept repeating themselves. They showed villains in high numbers patrolling all the internal borders, including Nethermost Gate itself. While we had always been able to defend The Gate from our side, Shin's forecasts were warning that any effort on our part to break though this barrier and return to Nethermost would be easily thwarted. And so years elapsed without a major confrontation from either side of The Gate. We were at a stalemate.

"When Nora arrived at the settlement, she quite understandably wished for any intelligence on her mother. She begged Shin to paint a forecast of Nicola's fate. But as Shin explained, she could not control her visions. So even though Shin herself greatly desired a image of Nicola to flow onto one of her canvases, this prevision never came.

"We formed our own hypothesis of Nicola's condition, not from what we saw, but what from we didn't see in Shin's paintings. Of course, many of the canvases depicted upsetting images of exploited resources, and of Peadar's ruffians plaguing unhappy citizens. But while we were witnessing human suffering, what we weren't seeing in any of the canvases were images of a continent falling apart — no earthquakes, no tsunamis, no volcanos. And we asked ourselves why.

"It couldn't be because Peadar was no longer fracking or strip mining unconscionably. His exploits had been the cause of climate crises even before he usurped the throne. So it stood to reason that this unchecked exploitation of our natural resources would create geological emergencies regularly. So why was the continent not cracking or erupting? Why wasn't it melting into the magma upon which it floated?

"The answer we felt sure was Nicola. Almost all our small numbers of balancers had escaped over the border or were hiding in nooks and crannies throughout the continent, not daring to expose themselves. Furthermore, it would take a number of balancers as a unit to do the job that Nicola was able to do, so we reckoned she must be employing her advanced balancing talent to hold the continent together. This made us hopeful that she was still alive, and we gave thanks to her for preserving our homeland from an apocalypse."

Father stood and paced uneasily before adding this next bombshell of a detail. "It also made any strategy for her rescue more difficult."

"Why would Nicola's good deeds make your mission more difficult?"

"Her heroism and talent alone seemed to be keeping Nethermost intact. But … if we staged her rescue, well …"

Of course I saw where this was leading and it wasn't towards a happy ending. While he was struggling to find the words to deliver this grim truth, I assisted by stating the obvious: "She couldn't leave, cuz even though escaping Nethermost would perhaps save *her* life, rescuing her could mean the destruction of Nethermost. Is that what you mean? She needed to remain inside the boundaries for the greater good? One woman's freedom versus one continent's salvation. Right?"

"Right, only I would take that argument even further. Not only was Nicola saving Nethermost, she was also keeping both levels of Earth alive. What would happen if a portion of the Earth's mantle erupted and crumbled beneath the surface? Even if we knew where Nicola was being held, even if we could breach this well defended border, we couldn't rescue her."

"But something did change at the border ... because my mother was lost."

"Something changed alright … and I'll never forgive *her* for it."

"Forgive who? My mother?"

"No. I can never forgive Ambassador Sinead!"

"What! Why?" My brain was fogging again. I could see my father losing his battle against his suppressed feelings of rage. He was barely keeping himself in check to complete his story. So I pulled my chair next to his and placed my hand on his forearm arm to quell the surge. "Michael … Father. It's okay. Leave it for now …"

"No," he whispered, smiling at me and gathering strength again, "No … best pull the bandaid off quickly … that way it hurts less.

"Nora and I could never imagine ourselves being happy with life confined to The Gate. But once we found out about Nora's pregnancy, the anticipation of the double birth lightened everyone's lives. The settlement felt doubly blessed. To be on the safe side, we planned to return to Ben in the village for the delivery, where the closest hospital was a mere eight kilometres away. We also thought it wise to remain with Ben for the babies' first year. But Nora gave birth early, and at The Gate instead of in the village. Although we still planned to go to Alta, we stayed put for a few more weeks until it was safe to travel with the infants.

"One day, about a month after you were born, while I was taking my turn at guard duty, Shin dropped by with a gift for the new mom — a painting still wet from her easel. The painting portrayed her mother Nicola languishing on a gilded bed in a gilded cell. With all the gold fittings, her whereabouts was obvious. It was Peadar's residence.

She looked emaciated and wretched. Her hair was so thin you could see her scalp, a clear sign of malnutrition. She was dirty and lacklustre. You can imagine my wife's reaction. Having just become a new mother herself, she was more vulnerable, inconsolable and pining for her mother all the more."

I was having trouble grasping his objection and told him so. "I can understand that you might not want Mother to know that her mother was ill. But the painting was proof that her mother was alive at least. Surely that would console her. After all, she had been begging Shin to forecast Grandma Nicola's whereabouts since the moment she arrived at The Gate."

"But that's not why Shin brought the painting to Nora. That's not what she wanted Nora to see. That's not what she wanted Nora to do. And that's why she waited until I was away from the house to show the painting to her."

"Then why? If not to comfort, then why?"

"Nora was a healer remember, and Nicola was clearly dying. And if she did die …"

I picked up the thread, "… earthquakes and volcanoes would erupt and soon it would be too much for the continent to endure!"

"Just so. Shin wanted Nora to go her mother … to heal her … to keep her alive … to keep her on task."

"And she knew you would never agree."

"Yes. She also knew that there was zero chance that Nora would be able to rescue her mother. In fact she counted on it. The best she could hope for was to be captured … to be imprisoned alongside Nicola … to become her personal physician."

"So Shin manipulated Nora, my mother … and you into the bargain."

"She didn't even give me a chance to find an alternative solution. When I returned from guard duty that evening, I found Shin minding the babies and Nora gone. And when I saw the painting lying on the coffee table, I knew where my wife was heading. I raced to the border just after Nora had slipped through the upper gate. Making myself invisible, I rushed through in pursuit with every intention of pulling her back before she could be detected by the enemy. But I was too late. Three ruffians had already tackled her and were pinning her to the ground. Without thinking and in a rage, I piled on top, hoping that my surprise attack would cause them to let go of Nora and give her a chance to escape. But even in my invisible state I still had a solid body and as I attacked them wildly, one thug seized me and held on with a vice like grip, while his two deplorable comrades ripped Nora from my grasp and dragged her away."

"Oh Lord! How did you escape?"

"I didn't. I knew as I struggled with this giant of a man that I was no match and was quite literally fighting for my life. They would not be interested in taking me prisoner, as they were with Nora. I would have been collateral damage, insignificant. I swear to this day that I would have lost that man to man combat were it not for the swift response of Mánús who, unbeknownst to me, had followed me. Transforming himself into his full werewolf incarnation, Mánús lunged at my captor, sinking his teeth into the man's throat and holding on until he released his grip on me. Then while I scrambled out of harm's way, Mánús shook his opponent savagely, until the man went limp and lifeless. Then the blood soaked canine warrior rushed to my side and, despite my insistence on pursuing my wife, dragged me gently but nonetheless firmly back through the lower gate.

"The following day Peadar sealed the lower gate with his alchemized binding agent, and reinforced it with perimeter magic. From that day nearly nineteen years ago to this, there has been no activity at the border."

My father sat beside me now, completely spent. I hesitated to even touch him. I worried that a sympathetic response from me would cause him to lose it altogether. I knew I was aching. I could only guess at his turmoil. My grief was second hand. I suffered, had always suffered, vaguely. But that was from the *lack* of a mother. His suffering was more intimate. His grief came from the *loss* of a love he had cherished all too briefly; a life as dear to him as his own. I gave him the time he needed to compose himself, while I reached out for his hand, leaving mine there until he returned the pressure.

"So … what would you have done differently," I asked quietly, "if Shin had not been so underhanded?"

"For the life of me … I don't know."

"One woman's freedom versus the salvation of a continent, and I would argue, a planet," I repeated.

Nethermost Regained

Chapter 14: This is NOT A Drill!

We were totally unprepared for the breach when it came.

****

I was in the store at six a.m. the next morning despite my late bedtime. It had been two days since my last shift and I was craving the comfort of a daily routine and the companionship of my workmates. Ol'Ben could always be relied upon to recharge my emotional batteries. But I especially needed Loo, to be honest, and his grounded perspectives. With Loo I could be sure I wouldn't be pulled off furtively into some corner for updates on skullduggery. He would want the shelves stocked, coffee and tea prepared, and Ol'Ben made comfortable. In Loo's world, the end of a good day would be the satisfaction of a job well done.

Our partnership thus restored, we began ticking away adequately for the morning coffee and tea trade, reaching maximum velocity by noon. Although we had agreed not to discuss the witchy subjects in the open, I allowed myself one whispered comment to Ol'Ben about having to catch him up later on compelling developments.

In welcome contrast to the constant upheaval of the past couple of weeks, this day seemed destined to be routine. Nothing out of the ordinary, thank goodness. Then about mid afternoon we were surprised by a visit from Shin, Michael and Mánús, who announced a desire to visit Ol'Ben. Although he was slightly taken aback, Ol'Ben seemed pleased enough to see them, and led them upstairs to his newly refurbished apartment. I settled them in with mid afternoon coffees, while I remained below with a distinctly grumpy Loo and the ever stalwart Mánús.

"What's she here for?" Loo muttered, "and who's the guy with her?"

"That *guy* is my father."

"Your Dad, huh?" Loo softened the edges of his tone, "I thought you were an orphan."

"I never said that, although I met the man for the first time only two days ago."

"And he's friends with the old dear?"

"Sort of. They have mutual interests, let's say."

Mánús had been staring out the front window at a figure in dark trousers and jacket, slowly making his way up the street in the direction of the store. His interest became more apparent as the man drew closer and when another fellow in similar dress suddenly fell into step behind him, my puppy pal went ballistic. He switched from being a watchdog frozen in place, to a canine projectile, suddenly launching himself at me, grabbing my forearm and pulling me to the floor behind the counter. A startled Loo rushed to my aid and tried the pull the dog off me, but Mánús held him at bay with a fierce growl, a baring of teeth and a quiver of jaw.

"Dad!" I shouted, "Quick, something's wrong with Mánús!"

Within seconds Father was in the doorway assessing the scene, "What happened?"

"I think it may have something to do with that man down the block there; maybe even the other guy behind him."

He dropped and slid along the floor to a low corner of the front window, allowing himself a quick peek, which apparently was enough to activate a well rehearsed drill. "Good job Mánús! Cait, you remember those guys we talked about? The ones Shin wouldn't even think of inviting for tea?"

I decoded that immediately, my insides turning to jelly. "Yes, Father, I remember. How does this go from here?"

"You — upstairs with Mánús. Let Shin know what's happening, and get Ol'Ben into something warm. Take nothing but your cold weather stuff, understand?" Turning to Loo, he said, "Hi, I'm Michael, you don't know me, but I'm your best friend at the moment."

"What? W-what the hell …" Loo sputtered, turning about slowly in the middle of the floor, looking confused.

"Hell is exactly what this is. If you want to live, do what I say. Walk to the front door very casually and turn the lock without seeming to be doing anything out of the ordinary. Those guys are after *us*, but they'll kill you too in a heartbeat."

Loo did just as directed with more calm and deliberation that I could have mustered. Meanwhile I crept along the floor until I reached the stairs, Mánús pushing hastily from the rear. I took the steps two at a time, not chancing the loss of a single instant. Even before I reached the second floor, I was calling out, "They've breached the village's perimeter barrier Shin. Let's get Ol'Ben ready to go."

I shoved Ol'Ben's arms into his winter jacket while he protested, "I'm no use to ya." As I continued with his hat, scarf and gloves, he added, "Look, no one's going to hurt an old man. Leave me here. I'll only slow you down."

"You're coming," Shin and I shouted together.

Michael and Loo reached the top of the stairs seconds later, pausing only to take a quick breath. "We toppled a few shelves in the front room to slow their progress," my father informed us, "but it won't give us much more than a few minutes at most."

"How do they know I'm here," I asked, surprised I was even keeping my sanity.

"I don't think they do," Father explained, "it's the magic auras of Shin, Mánús and me that they're sensing. You're not magic yet, so they can't pick you up on their radar. But they're going to figure it out — and soon. Loo, you've got a car I'm guessing? You're going to take Cait and Ol'Ben to Shin's cottage on the fly, and wait for us there. Shin, Mánús and I will deal with this lowlife and join you there as soon as ... If anyone follows your car, do your best to lose them. Once you reach the cottage, get down to the basement, find the panic room, lock yourselves in, and wait for one of us to open it. Once you're inside, switch on the barrier lock. You can't miss it, it's the only pulsing red button in the room. They won't be able to penetrate it."

Loo protested, "I'm not running away from a fight, while you wrestle these dudes with an old lady and a dog!"

"Look kid, there's no time to argue. The old lady and the dog perform tricks you and I will never be able to do. Beside, I'm entrusting you with my family for goodness sake — my most treasured possession — don't blow it! I refuse to lose another family member to that bastard Peadar!"

We could hear the front door rattling, first softly, then more loudly, then violently.

"Right!" he barked. "You guys leave by the fire escape, but don't put a nose out the door until we have distracted the enemy. I'm guessing the first thunder blast from Shin should grab their attention. Wait for the boom, then scarper."

We stood at the back door awaiting the signal — me first with Loo's car keys in my hand, then Loo with Ol'Ben hoisted on piggyback style. At the sound of the deafening roar, I pushed the door open, checked that we weren't being observed, then whizzed down the fire escape at warp speed by holding onto the rails, lifting my legs and letting my mittens slide me along. I raced to the car, opened the nearest back door for Ol'Ben, scooted around to the driver's seat and turned on the ignition. Loo was far quicker than I would have thought possible with Ol'Ben on his back. By the time the engine had turned over, he had already strapped and locked Ol'Ben into the back, and was making a beeline for the driver's side, barking, "Scootch over, Cait. I'm faster."

Loo raced that car along those country roads like he was going for a win at the Indy 500. He barely braked at the corners and treated all stop signs like mere suggestions, as we made that dash for our lives. Once at the cottage, we parked in the rear and tried to enter through the back door. When we found it locked, Loo took a single beat and coolly suggested. "Okay, Plan A — I pick the lock; Plan B — I find a rock."

"Just quickly," I growled.

"Plan B it is." He grabbed a fist sized stone from a sleeping rockery and threw it at the single glass door pane, then reached around to twist the knob from within.

"Well, that was surprisingly easy, especially for a witch's house," he declared.

"Shin's not a witch."

"Then what is she?"

"Never mind that now. I'll save that for your bedtime story. Let's find that panic room and get Ol'Ben settled."

It took a few minutes to find the room in the basement, partly because it was really dim down there, and partly because the door was camouflaged. Except for a few storage crates stacked in one corner, the basement was entirely bare. But I ran my hands along the unpainted concrete walls searching for anything unusual in their smooth surfaces, until I found a small round recess two centimetres wide and two deep in the middle of the back wall. When I placed my baby finger in the tiny hole and pushed hard, the entire wall slid to one side, revealing another short set of steps taking us half a floor down. At the bottom was a chamber of sorts — compact, low ceilinged, but comfortable. We bustled Ol'Ben in, sat him down in the only chair, and I gave him the once over to make sure he was still doing all the expected — like breathing in and out. Then in rapid succession, we found the switch for the overhead light — turned it on; spied a button inside similar to the one outside — pushed it, thus moving the wall back into place. An air circulation system began to hum as the door closed, which reassured me that the room was well ventilated and siege ready. I had almost forgotten the double lock feature, but was reminded of it, by its throbbing glow next to the door button. I knew I got it right after I read the label: 'perimeter fence'. I pushed that one as well. Only then did I feel assured that we would be reasonably safe, although the irony did not escape me that as we were eluding our foe, we were also imprisoning ourselves.

I looked around the eight by eight foot space and found it well stocked with supplies. Against one wall, floor to ceiling, were shelves charged with groceries and sundry other items to sustain us for many days. In the way of foodstuff, there were bottles of water, boxes of crackers, jams and peanut butter, cans of meats, fruits and vegetables, and a fair variety of candy bars. But there were also blankets and pillows, sleeping bags, down filled parkas, boots in a few different sizes, a shovel and a pickaxe as well. No bathroom, so that was disturbing, but empty buckets for the purpose I guess. I grabbed a couple of bottles of water, opened one for Ol'Ben and drank one off myself in several gulps. Turns out running for your life is thirsty work. Loo lunged at the chocolate bars and scarfed a few down, while declaring "I could sure go for a coffee about now."

"We got water," I said, "that's it."

Ol'Ben wiggled around uncomfortably in the chair: "I'm feeling pretty useless, kind of like a heavy piece of luggage. I really think you young people should have left me there. I would have been okay on my own at the store."

"I'm pretty certain there's not much of a store left, Ol'Ben. That's what you get for having me as a great-granddaughter, I guess."

"Great-granddaughter? Since when?" Loo asked.

"Since always. I've only known about it for a couple of weeks."

"What about you, Ol'Ben? How long have you known?"

"Since she was five weeks old."

"Well," Loo drawled, "Still waters, eh?"

I looked through the selection of boots, found some in Ol'Ben's size and persuaded him to put them on. Next I found a pair for myself and added a down filled parka over my own inadequate jacket. Finally I pulled a blanket off the shelf and tucked it around Ol'Ben's legs for extra warmth over his arthritic knees. I wasn't taking any risks with this old heartthrob of mine. I knew we were all in for a bumpy ride whatever happened next, and I needed to make sure he was in good form. Then I tossed a pillow on the floor beside his chair, plunked myself down on it and rested my head in his lap. While he stroked my head, Loo paced.

I guess it was only half an hour that we were in that room, although it seemed so much longer. When we heard noises overhead, Loo cheered, "They're here, praise be!" and began checking the shelves for cold weather gear for himself.

But the commotion seemed too violent for it to be our friends — sounds of furniture being tossed about, dishes smashed, doors opened and slammed, then deep guttural noises growing louder as they advanced towards our hiding spot. All too soon we could hear them enter the basement and start pounding the walls. I motioned a finger of silence to my lips.

The room started to ring from all the pounding outside and I knew our villains must be using something like hammers to open up the walls. While their vulgar threats grew louder, the locked door remained inviolate. After several minutes of this bombardment, Ol'Ben was beginning to look distressed, and Loo winced a few times. As for me, I don't mind admitting I was terrified. I kept swallowing back screams in my throat, and held onto Ol'Ben tighter than ever.

Suddenly the remote and abusive tones turned to yelps of surprise and screams of pain as a thunderous clap rocked the basement, followed by a long, blood chilling howl from some kind of beast. There were sounds of bodies being chucked about and cries of protests suddenly strangled mid sentence. From what I was hearing, coupled with my recollection of Micheal's recent account of a similar skirmish years before, I knew it was a transmuted Mánús at the throat of one more villain, an assault that thug could never survive.

Then silence.

The next sound we heard was the automatic click of the two buttons next to the door as it released and opened wide. Before us stood our rescuers, looking blood smeared and disheveled. The wall parted in time for us to witness Mánús in the final stages of transforming back from his fighting werewolf shape into the familiar dog that we knew. Shin looked a bit singed and smudgy about the fingers and hair, but otherwise robust. Father was bruised, his clothes stained with blood, apparently not his own. Mánús was calmly licking his chops to clear the pinkness from around his lips and nose. I raced forward to hug all three in turn.

"It's not over," My father announced breathlessly, "more are coming. Everyone back in the room."

"You get on with it, I'll be with you directly," called Shin as she made her way back up the steps. "There's a painting I must save."

"Impossible," Father shouted.

"Imperative," she retorted, as she disappeared through the door.

"Foolish old woman," he muttered as he stood by the door, jiggling up and down in frustration. She was back within a minute but it was thirty seconds too long, for just as she handed me the rolled canvas and prepared to step in, Father shouted "Watch out!" Shin turned to face yet another dark man bearing down upon her from the top of the lower steps, directly before our chamber. She shoved him inside the room ahead of her, shot a bolt of lightning from her fingertips, struck the madman dead centre, stepped into the room, and pushed both wall buttons at once. The last thing I saw as the wall slid into place, was that man on his knees, shuddering in his last moments of life, falling forward to land a hair's breadth from the entrance.

Now that we were all crowded safely into the space behind the double locked doors, we took several deep breaths to calm down. Loo was the first to break the silence. "Okay … now what? What happens next?"

"Next we open the second door," Shin explained calmly, pushing aside jars of peanut butter to expose yet another sneaky button. This time the door opened just like a standard one, only what was beyond was anything but mundane. We were no longer inside Shin's cottage, but had entered an underground tunnel, like the entrance to a mine. More of the same food supplies were shelved against the uneven rock walls, to which were added more boxes of outdoor clothing, blankets, tents, camping gear, and piles of animal pelts in wooden crates, all stacked high beside the tins and bottles. Everything needed, in fact, either for a woodsman's hunting trip or for a fortress under siege.

Most fascinating of all, parked at the end of a rail track, were two vehicles that looked like a combination of roller coaster cars and miner's carts, only with a lot more flair. They were a sleek polished teal, with magenta style lines. The front car had a streamlined nose and a squared rear; the second car was blunted at both ends. They both were completely open with seating for six, coupled together with a hitch, outfitted with head and tail lights on each cart, a complex control panel on the dashboard of the first cart, and a black box welded to the rear of the second.

"What's that?" Loo whistled, walking around the strange vehicles as he would a new model car in a dealer's showroom. "This is some sweet ride. Where's the engine?"

"Those are what's known as tunnel pods — these two models are called Launcher I and Launcher II … and the engine is contained in that tiny black box. Microtechnology," Shin explained, "There are magic assisted power boosters on each wheel for when we need a bit more juice." I thought she was going to try to sell it to him, she had become so businesslike.

"Cool. What's the mileage like?" Loo asked, and I swear he was looking for tires to kick.

"One ounce of liquid gold should fuel it for a couple of thousand kilometres, although I have never paid much attention … never had to."

"Right … well …" Loo mused thoughtfully, "You know, if you'd have said that to me yesterday I'd have called you a nut job. But today, after that performance out there, I wouldn't even think of messing with ya."

"You have proved yourself to be someone not to "mess with" either Mr. Buckley," said Shin, with a bow.

I swear I saw a bit of swagger in Loo's step, as he sauntered back and forth scrutinizing the tunnel pods even closer. "So, now I'm guessing this Nethermost place is real too. And I think we've all just seen the inner Mánús right enough." He gave a flourishing bow in Mánús' direction, "… and this dog is not really a dog."

Overhead, we could again feel the vibrations of a renewed home invasion, and even though we were secure behind the double barrier,

Father urged us to load the supplies into the tunnel pods sharpish, buckle up, and prepare for takeoff.

Shin lifted up the seats to show us deep storage bins. We filled Launcher I with food, water, and extra bits of clothing, and Launcher II with sleeping bags, tents, lanterns, and cookware. Then we lined the seats with the animal skins, setting some aside to put over us. I belted Ol'Ben into the front seat of Launcher II, cocooning him all around with the skins and strapped myself into the seat directly behind him.

Now layered with extra clothing, Father, Shin and Loo selected their seats in Launcher I. Father took the first seat position in front of the control panel. Loo called shotgun and plunked himself behind my father to rubber neck over his shoulder while he operated that strange train. Instead of taking a seat of her own, Shin shoved in beside my father, buckling herself into the same seat belt. Then she unscrewed a small cap on the dashboard, and poured in the contents of a tiny gold bottle. The engine hummed as it revved, while I belted Mánús into the caboose.

Father listened for the motor to reach full throttle, then announced like a pilot pre flight: "Hang on tight … the first ten seconds are a real pip!" And he wasn't kidding. As he released the handbrake, the Launchers propelled as a unit into the darkness at two hundred klicks at least, and our stomachs stayed behind at the starting gate.

Chapter 15: From Zero to Warp Speed

When you're traveling through an inky black miners' tunnel in tandem carts going faster than the speed of light, you don't see much I can tell you. After that zero to warp speed takeoff, Shin switched on the head and tail lights so we could at least see rock walls whizzing by, albeit in a blur. When I checked over Ol'Ben's shoulders, I saw his eyes tightly shut against the gale force wind, his poor little cheeks and chin flapping mightily. I wished I had thought to truss him up better, with goggles at the very least. I myself dared open my eyes only when facing sideways or behind.

Father thrust us through the darkness at this velocity for a full thirty minutes, before allowing our speed to slacken. Then for another fifteen, he geared down gradually until we were moving at a crawl, finally stopping entirely by a luminescent stop sign. Once we were locked in place, Shin switched on some side spots to brighten our surroundings, causing us to blink from the shock.

Father unbelted and jumped from the pod, hopping in place to release the stiffness in his legs. "Stretch break," he announced. "There's an earth pit outhouse over there in that little lay-by for the prudish, or a wall of your choice for the bold."

I got Ol'Ben unfurled and tried to get him out of the cart on my own, but his knees started buckling so Loo stepped forward like the vigilant caregiver he had become. He rubbed the old man's legs, paying attention to the knees especially, then massaged his shoulders and upper arms. After this, he lifted Ol'Ben like a baby from his seat and set him down gingerly on the ground, holding on until he was certain that his charge had his balance. My eyes misted up at the sight of this simple, intimate ritual between two of my most cherished companions on the planet.

Although the tunnel seemed wider now, there seemed little of interest about our current parking space, apart from the strange outhouse signposted by a single stop sign, that is. But I wasn't griping because, while this tunnel lacked scenery, it also lacked murderous villainy. For the first time since Mánús had tackled me to the floor a mere two hours before, I considered the possibility of standing down on the tension a smidge.

"These tunnels are so claustrophobic," said Shin, creeping up behind me unannounced and making the hairs on my arms stand on end. "Although there is something quite remarkable and naturally spectacular just around the next bend. May I show you? I promise you it's quite special." The mystery in her voice was intended to pique my interest, I was sure.

I checked to see that Ol'Ben was okay, finding him slouched on a pillow, taking a catnap. "I guess I'm not needed … so yes."

"Can I come with?" Loo asked.

Micheal produced a strong flashlight to illuminate the track beyond the scope of the pod lights, and all four of us followed the track for a couple of hundred metres, until we could see a blue glow emanating from beyond a curve in the tunnel and could hear the swoosh of running water. "I almost feel that I should have you both close your eyes so I can lead you to the best vantage point and surprise you," said Shin with a twinkle, "but you've both had a lot of heart stopping moments today already, so I'll let this unfold … as it unfolds."

As we rounded a slight turn in the track, the swooshing noise intensified, the air moistened with mist, and the tunnel widened into a cavern. We seemed to have triggered a motion sensor light which sprang to life suddenly and bounced a beam off the ceiling and walls studded with sparkles.

"Those are vitreous of life crystals, the phenomenon I tried to describe to you Cait. You see how they actually intensify that beam of light? Somehow it defies description, wouldn't you agree?" Shin observed, enjoying the depth of my amazement.

"Check this out Loo," Father added enthusiastically. Loo stepped forward fearlessly, while I contented myself with a more cautious viewpoint twenty feet back. Even from this perspective I could appreciate the drama of the scene. Here the track left its rock solid path to hover in air over a fast flowing water spout that shot its impressive volume over the canyon wall into the abyss beneath.

"I can't even see the bottom from here," Loo announced with a laugh, "and would you look at the angle of that track. How the heck …"

"Magic!" Shin shouted over the din, "awe inspiring, is it not, Mr. Buckley?"

"If I'd known I was going to get pulled into an adventure like this," Loo declared, "I would've paid more attention in school. Cuz I'll need more adjectives to describe all this!"

Despite the allure of the setting, I took a beat to study my no nonsense friend once more. I'd been worrying about Loo's lack of imagination and need for routine — worried that he would think me and my family mad. Yet here he was caught up in the moment, wide eyed with wonder.

"So, Ms. Healy," he said, sidling up to her, "All done with magic … a trick of the eye, huh? But you'd need to get the speed and angle just right too to land this puppy on the lower deck. Am I right?"

"You're catching on, wonder kid," she replied with a laugh. "Plus a little rain gear might not go amiss."

Before we continued our journey, I rummaged around in the Launchers' storage bins for something to protect Ol'Ben's face and eyes, finding the exact right thing — a balaclava with goggles sewn into the fabric. "I bet I'll look like a bug in this," Ol'Ben observed, but he pulled it over his head nonetheless. "What do you think Loo? Will I do?"

Loo guffawed when he saw Ol'Ben in that headgear, laughed until he choked. "Nah man, you look great!" he said, his shoulders still shaking with mirth, while at the same time giving Ol'Ben two gloved thumbs up.

Father stood before our ragtag team and barked out further instructions. "Okay, we will be dropping about one hundred metres in this descent of the falls. Things will get a bit warmer further down, so maybe remove one layer of clothing before putting on one of these rain slickers.

"This next instruction is critical, so listen well. The track arcs over the waterfalls and descends at a steep angle. It's twice as scary as the worst roller coaster you've ever ridden. So belt yourselves in — not just the lap belt, but also the one attached to your seat back. I'll take us first to the very edge of the falls and stop just at the tipping point. Before we start our descent, lean back as far as you can in your seat, and push back with your feet."

He nudged Launcher I forward slowly into the mist, until I could feel the back of Launcher II begin to rise, at which point he applied the brakes. The pods creaked, weaved and nodded a bit as they balanced between equilibrium and disaster.

My father looked forward, his face full of tension, and called out over the roar of the spray. "No sudden moves. Shin, have you got some magic to apply to this enterprise?"

"Absolutely," she confirmed rubbing her hands.

"Everyone lean back as far as you can … now." But Ol'Ben panicked and his movements got a bit wild, causing the carts to pitch erratically.

"Sorry, sorry, Michael," he cried out, then muttered, "useless, useless."

"No problem. Second take. First lean back slowly … on the count of three ... One, two … three ..." We leaned back in unison, slow and sweet. "Now brace your feet on the floor pushing back as you do until you feel well wedged in." Fourteen legs (taking into account Mánús' four) all braced.

The Launchers quivered but stayed in balance. "Okay, no screaming on the way down, it makes me jumpy. If you're scared of heights, close your eyes and think happy thoughts." Father held onto the emergency brake, easing it off slowly as he prodded the two carts over the falls, down the angled tracks — brakes groaning, straining — towards the darkness below. I could see Shin keeping her arms fully extended like a high wire dancer's balancing pole. It must have taken all of Father's concentration, plus all of Shin's magical whatevers to pull it off, but the tunnel pods did stay on the track and we did land safely on the canyon floor, no bones broken or lives lost. Though it must have taken less than five minutes, it was the longest five minutes of my life, and by the end of it I wasn't sure if I was more wet from the water or from my own nervous sweat.

Father moved the Launchers forward slower now as we followed the river's course for several kilometres. The cavern treated us to spectacular views of its myriads of stalagmites and stalactites, designed, it seemed, to play with our imaginations. It was so humid in the cavern that the walls were sweating and the stalactites drippy, bouncing the occasional calcium rich splotch onto both vehicles and our rain suited heads. After a few kilometres of weaving back and forth around these rock icicles, the river veered off and descended to lower depths, while our tracks continued straight on. Although we had now lost our impressive views, the simpler tunnel allowed us to pick up speed, as we did until Father halted once more an hour later.

"Okay," he said, "that was perfect teamwork. Let's store the rainwear before we begin the next leg of our journey."

"How many legs to this journey?" Loo asked.

"Depends what you mean by a leg. The entire run takes a day and a bit at top speed. However, we're nowhere near top speed and we had a late start today. Most of the route is subterranean, although the last leg is overland and very cold indeed, even though it's the first day of spring in the south."

As we rearranged ourselves, an appalling thought suddenly hit me square between the eyes. Of course I could blame the circumstances of our panicked departure. Even so, I was ashamed that I had not thought of it before. "Oh hell, what about Aunt Moira? Do you think she might have been captured, or worse?"

"Don't fret, Cait!" Shin piped in. "She teleported to Nethermost Gate early this morning on Embassy business. And she's got you tagged, so that an alarm bell rings whenever you step beyond the village perimeter. She would have caught on almost at once. I bet she's glued to her holo screen right now, trying to figure out what actually happened. She'll also have picked up the pip tags of those villains in the village. So, while she'll likely be wringing her hands in frustration and anxiety, nevertheless she is safe."

"She tagged me?" I asked.

"From infancy dear. Did you doubt it? I'm tagged, so are Michael, Mánús, Ol'Ben. Loo too."

"I'm tagged?" Loo looked startled. "What does that mean?"

"It means you're now globally traceable," I explained, "It's weird, but it's not terminal."

"Is that legal? Should I feel violated?"

"I'm sure there's some sort of official complaint form you can fill out when we reach our destination — in triplicate," Shin offered, with a smirk.

"No, I'm good," Loo replied, smirking back.

The next leg of our journey was just plain tedious. With the threat of being followed well behind us now, Father no longer pushed on at super speeds. Nevertheless, being pummelled persistently in the face and body in open air vehicles, even at a reasonable pace, would ravage any unprotected body, and I felt exhausted. I could only imagine what it was doing to Ol'Ben. I tried several times to signal to Father to stop for Ol'Ben's sake, but with the winds deafening our ears and wiping the words from our mouths, communication was all but impossible.

Ol'Ben kept sliding down in his seat until finally his head lolled to one side and I knew he was either asleep, unconscious or expired — all of which caused me alarm. I began to wave my arms frantically trying to catch the eye of anyone in Launcher I, but no one was turning around. Just as I was about to lose the plot entirely, I heard a sustained bestial howl coming from behind me. Mánús was baying loudly and was not letting up. I turned around startled to determine why, and realized from the sad look in his deep brown eyes that he was worried about Ol'Ben too. A howl like that could almost wake the dead, and it certainly did the trick in alerting the folks in Launcher I, that Launcher II needed a time out. Father, Loo and Shin all turned at once, as I pointed a deliberate finger in Ol'Ben's direction. The Launchers moved at a snail's pace until the tunnel widened again, and Father pulled us gently to a stop.

I couldn't extricate myself from my seat fast enough in my effort to reach Ol'Ben, but as usual Loo was ahead of me, rubbing his extremities and calling his name. I slipped into Ol'Ben's seat from the other side and pulled off his balaclava, trying in my amateurish way to assess the situation. His colour was good, but he was clearly spent. He opened his eyes and smiled, but I knew we were in trouble.

I expressed my concerns to Father and Shin. "We can't go on like this for Ol'Ben's sake. He can't take the wind and the jerking. He needs real rest at the very least and we'll need to make adjustments to our flight plans."

"Of course … without question," agreed Shin. "Let's unload, set up the tents, and fashion a cosy bed for Ol'Ben from some skins and blankets — get him lying down. Then we can see to other comforts."

The little settlement we constructed was impressive, if compact. We set up two, no pegs required tents, lining their floors with animal skins, and stacking one corner 10 cm. deep with pelts as a bed for Ol'Ben. Then we helped him out of his restrictive outdoor paraphernalia, and stretched him out with more pillows and skins to soften everything surrounding his frail body. Lou brought him some pieces of thinly sliced tinned ham on crackers, garnished with diced tinned peaches. To wash it down, a bottle of water doctored by Shin with some sort of mysterious magical powder. As the rest of us left him to his slumbers, Mánús crawled in beside him to serve as a living hot water bottle.

Loo and Shin set up the butane burner away from the tents and started preparations for a rustic hot meal. They worked in silence opening and combining tins, heating their concoction in a cast iron pot. As dessert, they laid out a selection of chocolate bars, and heated water for coffee and tea. Meanwhile Father and I arranged the sleeping bags, pillows, etc. over the pelt floor of the other tent, then positioned a few lanterns around the perimeter to brighten our twenty by twenty metre sanctuary.

Our post prandial conversation was devoted almost entirely to the best means of supporting Ol'Ben for the remainder of the journey to Nethermost Gate.

"What's really killing him is the wind bombarding his ancient body." I argued, "I don't even know how old he is but …"

"Ninety-three. Mr. McCauley is ninety-three years old," Shin affirmed, matter of factly.

"What! Then what are we doing shooting him on a fast moving projectile through a freezing rock tunnel under unexplored forests towards the coldest place on earth?" I cried, tears of panic escaping from the corners of my eyes.

"Saving his life," Shin replied with a sigh. "But you are absolutely right, Cait. We had no plans in place for transporting a medically fragile person through such an inhospitable climate. I find it hard myself these days and I'm used to it. How foolish of us not to protect him better."

"Okay, I'm sure there are enough brains hereabouts to figure this out so that the old guy arrives in one piece." Loo interjected, "He can't have the wind blowing him over any more, he can't keep upright all day on a jiggling track, and he definitely needs more breaks. So … taking this one issue at a time …"

I was never more proud of Loo than I was at that moment, and he'd already had a few great moments recently. Before we turned in, we had a care plan in place. The adjustments were fairly straightforward and definitely sensible …

- o Father and Loo would build a low roof over the storage space furthest back on Launcher II as a windbreak, using the canvas from an extra tent. They would remove the back seat, clear the storage bin, and install a thick lining of skins and pillows for Ol'Ben to stretch out on. To fortify the structure, Shin would add a modicum of barrier magic.
- o We would travel no more than an hour at a go at speeds of less than one hundred klicks. Rest stops would be a full fifteen minutes.

Shin bunked in with Ol'Ben and Mánús that evening, insisting that she needed to dose him magically throughout the night. I was too tired to argue. I crawled into the middle sleeping bag in the second tent, between the very warm bodies of my father and Loo, and within seconds was out for the count.

Chapter 16: A Desperate Plight

It made no sense, under the circumstances, that I would sleep so well on that foundation of rock, but apparently I did because I had to be awakened by Loo rubbing my arm and whispering, "Sorry Cait. It's getting late … coffee's going out there."

Every bone and muscle I owned complained as I tried to navigate out of my sleeping bag. I did my best to make myself presentable — tucking in my clothes, straightening my hair, finger polishing my teeth and slipping on my ski jacket, before pulling the tent flap back. The guys were busy packing up already, while Ol'Ben was limbering up his extremities by hobbling around in wide circles, flanked on two sides by Shin and Mánús. Under the glow of a single lantern I could see my breakfast waiting — a cup of steaming coffee, some crackers slathered with peanut butter and jam. Perfect!

"Good morning sweetheart," Ol'Ben said in a croaky voice. "I'm afraid the outhouse is a bucket and a dark corner. Enjoy!"

By the time I'd finished breakfast, Loo and Father had packed up the second tent as well, and were busy constructing Ol'Ben's cocoon. I set to work relocating some of the exiled items from Launcher II, by making better use of every ounce of space in the other storage bins and saving some of the softer items to ride up top with me.

Ol'Ben fit into his car bed just fine, although there was little space for him to wiggle about, making me glad of our decision with respect to rest stops. The journey began well enough and the pace seemed fine for the most part, although I did notice Ol'Ben's voice growing more crackly over the course of the morning. When we extricated him from his covered bed at lunchtime, he was looking distinctly flushed, although he still ate a decent lunch.

Shin took me aside: "He's still not weathering the ride all that well is he?"

"I agree. What would you suggest?"

"I have two options for your consideration. One, we stop here for the night … "

"But won't that mean it will take even longer to get to The Gate … and maybe two or three more nights on the road?"

"Yes, but he's working up to a bit of a fever at the moment and the ride is taxing him. Our second option is to press on longer than planned. Then we could stay the night with some friends of mine near the overland entrance. If we do this, our accommodation tonight will be soft and warm, and the final leg much shorter. This way we could conceivably reach Nethermost Gate tomorrow by midday. The downside to this option is that the longer journey today will be very tough on the poor fellow … It's your call."

"It's not my call, it's Ol'Ben's." I went over and knelt next to him. He was perched on a boulder next to his bin bed, sipping some of Shin's magic water. I presented the options to him, then waited while he considered.

"Cait, do you know how happy I have been these past four months with you and Loo? I couldn't believe my luck when a broken collarbone brought the three of us together so beautifully." He reach down and patted my head, tears pooling at the edges of his bloodshot eyes. "I don't guess life could be much sweeter, and if I were to go today, I'm ready.

"You're asking me to choose what to do next? I don't fear dying, but I choose to fight for an even happier ending, and if I make it, hurrah! If by some remote piece of luck I get one more wish in an already blessed life, it would be to witness you meeting that sister of yours for the very first time. That's my brass ring. So, let's push through today, hard as it will be. Let's drop in at Shin's friends' place this evening and get to Nethermost Gate all the sooner tomorrow."

And push through we did, for hours, stopping regularly still, but for no more than fifteen minutes each time. By early evening Ol'Ben wasn't even trying to stir from his travelling bed any more, sleeping through the rest stops entirely. The fever Shin had noted in its early stages was now undeniable, and his chest was rattling audibly. The only reaction I got out of him now was when I placed my cool palms on his forehead and cheeks. This made him smile his gratitude.

Although Loo left the task of comforting to me, he stood close by and brooded in the background, shadowing everything I did. It was like he was thinking that to ensure Ol'Ben was okay, he had to make sure I was as well. So he brought water and snacks to me before I even knew I wanted them. And he tucked me into my seat before seating himself at the start of each new lap.

About two hours before we reached our destination, I could feel a gradient change in the slope of the tunnel and realized that we were slowly rising towards the surface. The temperatures were cooling so much that at our next rest stop, we pulled out the cold weather gear again and decked ourselves out. I didn't try to struggle Ol'Ben into any more clothes in his current condition, but I did add to the layers of skins and blankets that surrounded his poor body.

We didn't reach our destination until nearly midnight. I knew we had arrived when the glow of our headlamps illuminated a red railway car parked on a side track, away from the main. By my estimation this unique dwelling was ten metres long and three metres wide, with a three step walk up. In its heyday it must have been a first class carriage. The cladding and paint on the car was in good repair and, although the temperatures were well below zero at this time of year, there was an outdoor sitting area which suggested that for some of the year at least, temperatures got warm enough to allow the owners some outdoor pleasures.

The clatter of the rails and the glare of our tunnel pod lights must have startled Shin's sleeping friends awake. But their glee in seeing her was apparent, nonetheless, and they welcomed us all into their home without hesitation.

For some reason I thought they'd be human, perhaps healy, but they were neither. Our welcoming hosts, although similar in height to Shin, were more earthy than she was, meaning that their features and clothing were earth toned and coarse and they looked altogether more weathered than Shin with her white hair, milky smooth complexion and colourful garb. Shin introduced them to us as Aspen and Larch, and identified them as root elves, an ancient race. The elfin woman, Aspen, fussed over Ol'Ben and insisted on placing him in their own bed. We couldn't even rouse him now, and he was dead weight in Loo and Father's arms. Loo stripped off most of Ol'Ben's clothing, while I checked his temperature and pulse. His forehead was raging hot, his skin alarmingly pink and dry, his pulse rapid and weak. Aspen got some cloths and tepid water for us to wash him down to reduce his fever. Since he wasn't taking liquids by mouth, Shin smoothed her magic dust on his forehead and chest in powder form to absorb through the skin, before we swaddled him in layers of bedclothes. After we'd done all that we could for the moment, Loo huddled up against the wall at the end of the bed and kept watch, while Mánús slept on the coverlet next to Ol'Ben.

*****

Were it not for our dire circumstances, I'm sure I would have enjoyed our evening with the elves. The temperature outdoors was colder than I'd ever known, yet these folks had insulated and heated their tiny house so well that it felt positively cosy. With few exceptions, the compact rooms were constructed entirely of wood with carved trim in botanical and forest creature themes. The overall effect was that of a homey, personalized space which was, I suspected, a fair reflection of the character of its owners.

Someone had seated me on a soft chair in front of one of the wood stoves with a plate of reheated stew in my hand that I picked at automatically rather than out of hunger. I was cloistered within my own thoughts, vacillating between hope and despair. I resurfaced somewhat when I overheard a conversation between Shin, Father, Aspen and Larch. They were discussing the use of overland snow vehicles, they referred to as SnowSquallers, for the last lap of our flight and detailing a plan for attaching a storage sled to one of them for our patient. Father was discussing the use of this sled to house Ol'Ben and outlined the required modifications. Aspen was promising to warm the sled with hot water bottles next to Ol'Ben's skin. Shin offered to supply the gas powered engines with liquid gold to increase their speed and reliability. It all sounded efficient and impressive, but I knew that with even such excellent adaptations, it would be touch and go the next day.

When I had consumed as much as I could manage, Shin came over and sat by me. She stayed close and silent for some time, respecting my mood. Finally she whispered, "It's at times like this that I wish I was a healer."

"What do you mean? You've been slipping Ol'Ben medicine for the last day and a half."

"First aid, my dear. It's only first aid. Healy are seers, not healers. We have a modest range of magical skills in a broad range of areas, but we are not doctors — a deficit I have never regretted more than at this very moment."

"You're making him comfortable; that counts for something."

"You make him happy. That counts for a great deal more."

At last Shin convinced me to rest, so I grabbed a pillow and a couple of blankets and curled up next to the stove, while the others found softer areas to land. But I couldn't get Ol'Ben out of my thoughts, so I got up, grabbed a couple of chocolate bars for Loo, and tiptoed into the bedroom where he was still on watch. I handed him the chocolate and cuddled into his arms. He pulled some of the lower bedclothes around us both and stroked my hair in reflection.

"Did Ol'Ben ever tell you how he came to hiring me, Cait?"

"No, he's not said a thing. I just know he likes you … thinks you're a good worker."

"What do you remember about me in school?"

"Not much. You were a lot cooler than me. I was younger and stupidly shy. I figured you didn't even noticed me."

"I don't guess I did at that time. But it wasn't anything to do with you; it was because of me. In twelfth grade, my Mom died of cancer. It happens, right — happens to kids all the time? One parent leaves their lives suddenly and the other parent steps up to the plate. That's the usual scenario. That's what saves the day.

But my waste of space Dad didn't see it that way. I think he cared about Mom right enough, although he didn't do much by way of helping out after she got so sick. And when she died, he did even less.

"I was hurting, didn't know how to grieve. Maybe Dad was hurting too, I wouldn't know; he never let me close enough to find out. If he was hurting, he should have said. He should have fixed himself and then fixed me. He was the parent so he should have noticed … noticed that his kid wasn't doing so hot. Why didn't he see how I was getting into trouble, doing stupid stuff that could easily have landed me in jail? Petty stuff, destructive. Why didn't he see that as evidence of my grief? So in those final days of high school I wasn't the cool guy at all. I was a screwed up kid whose Mom was no longer *there*, and whose Dad was no longer *present*.

"Ol'Ben noticed. For me, life started getting better the day he let me know he noticed me … swiping chocolate bars in his store. He was so cool about it … didn't let on he'd seen anything … didn't blow his wig. He just came up to me as I was leaving the shop with a rucksack full of candy and said, 'Come work with me after school in the store young man. And after you finish paying back the value of those candy bars you stole, I'll even consider giving you a wage.' Just like that. So simple it was, but just like that he changed me … listened … made me feel worth listening to."

"Ol'Ben noticed me too." I whispered. "What if he doesn't get better Loo? What then? How will we …" the tears were slipping freely down my cheeks and chin, and I squeezed my eyes tight to stop their flow.

Loo cupped his hands about my face and held it a breath away from his own. He slowly placed his soft experienced lips on my own innocent ones, and kissed me long and sweetly, until my tears were stilled. He stretched my body out and placed my head on his knees, surrounding me with even more covers, then leaned back and closed his eyes.

Chapter 17: Not A Step Further

Shin had already cajoled a semi-conscious Ol'Ben into downing a few spoonfuls of porridge and was going for more. "How's the patient?" I asked cheerfully. "Are you feeling better Ol'Ben?" The lack of a reply from either of them provided the answer I dreaded.

"I think Michael wants to get started at first light, Cait," Shin said matter of factly.

As I sipped my warm drink and munched a square of toast, I watched through the frost painted windows of the railway carriage, while Father, Larch and Loo loaded the disassembled materials from Ol'Ben's covered bunk into the back of an old Dodge pick up and headed down a trackless tunnel. From the lack of items in the back of the truck, I assumed that most of our stores were remaining with Aspen and Larch. It made sense to streamline our load to increase our race pace across one of the world's most bitterly frozen landscapes. We were engaged in a desperate effort to save the life of our critically ill friend after all.

"Good morning Miss Cait," said Aspen, placing a bowl of porridge on the table before me, "You will need more than that scrap of toast to fortify you today. Larch and the men are organizing your trip forward and there's much to do. Since you won't be stopping along the way, I will prepare pocket food to nibble in flight. You will need to dress yourself more warmly and prepare your ancient friend as well. I've laid out some woollen undergarments for you both. They will be far too short of course, but you are tiny in the waist so a pair of mine will fit you in the critical places. I've found something that my late father-in-law used to wear for Mr. Ben. This open country is inhospitable, even in March. It is the kind of cold that freezes exposed skin in minutes, snaps your nose hairs off without a balaclava and hardens your eyeballs without goggles."

*****

We looked like aliens, geared up as we were. The men were so disguised that I could barely tell Father from Loo. Larch used his pickup to take us to the tunnel opening where two open aired ski vehicles, called SnowSquallers, awaited. We loaded in a matter of minutes, despite the assault of the harsh elements. Ol'Ben was tucked inside the covered sled with Shin and Mánús. The rest of us rode uncovered, in the open air.

I hadn't realized that Larch would be coming along, but of course we would need a navigator to make sense of the endless and unvarying landscape of snow and trees. The convoy was lined up in this order: Larch with Loo behind him on SnowSqualler I, hauling the sled with Shin, Mánús and Ol'Ben. SnowSqualler II piloted by my father came second with me in the bunker seat, belted to his waist.

The winds were still, the sky a crisp blue, and an early morning sun pinked the snow. It was a stunning view few would ever witness. I was glad for the warmth of my father's body and the protection it provided from the full force of arctic air pushing against us in motion. We wove back and forth across a path fraught with tree obstructions. At the same time we bobbed up and down, as the undulating snow drifts gave us the experience of a fall fair ride. Was Shin as busy today as yesterday with her arms outstretched under that canvas magically orchestrating a smoother journey? I wondered. It killed me that I wouldn't know the fate of my old great-granddad until we reached journey's end. But Mánús' body warmth and Shin's hocus-pocus was what he needed more than me. So I hardened my resolve, clung on and tuned out, allowing my thoughts to roam, while entrusting my life to the man I barely knew yet as father.

In the five hours it took to reach Nethermost Gate, I rethought my entire life. I didn't ignore the years of emotional isolation, but now I focused more on what was good about those years. It was good that I had felt safe in an enriched learning environment, that I had been challenged to become an independent thinker, organizing my life and my surroundings without feeling any lack in comforts. I had been given the opportunity recently of reappraising my relationship with my aunt, my primary caregiver, who loved me after all. Although this was a renovation job just begun, it was full of promise and texture.

I thought of Ol'Ben and how he had known about me all along, but was forbidden to declare himself as kin, of how he had subtly instilled himself in my life despite these restrictions, and found ways to watch over me. His calming personality counterbalanced my emotional insecurities. I marvelled at how he took on my pain, while nursing much deeper wounds himself.

My parents' absence was the substance of childhood nightmares. While I still bore some anger towards Father for staying away, I could appreciate his impossible decision to forgo the pleasure of watching me grow, in order to keep me safe. Michael, a grieving husband and alienated father, setting aside personal happiness for the greater good. He made his decision, not based on family, but on the slight chance that his offspring might become the saviours of an entire realm. So as much as I wanted to fault my father, to rage against my enormous loss, I was gradually replacing resentment with understanding.

And my mother … did I dare to hope to meet her … to envision her still alive her, enduring half a lifetime in captivity with her own mother as her sole companion, praying to be rescued from the erstwhile Apparatchik whose perverted leadership caused a continent of people to go mad? A jealous brother and unconscionable coward who groomed an army of weak minded citizens to do his dirty work, sending them out in numbers to betray their own parents, spouses, siblings, friends, and neighbours. Could there be a time when his reign would end? Was that end in any way connected to me and my sister?

Rhue. As much as she was always in my peripheral vision, I almost feared the introduction. What would it be like to run into your own doppelgänger? Having been raised apart, how would we compare? Would we share more than genetics? The possibilities were exciting and unnerving. Yet before the end of the day, I could be meeting her and begin to answer a multitude of questions.

There was Mánús, the full canine spectrum, who served as my introduction to this remarkable world. A mute agent and forceful protector who carried out his mission no matter the cost to himself. A faithful servant who led me to Shin, my mentor and advisor, whose job it was be to prepare me for my inevitable future.

Shin, a seer — an irritant at times — but ultimately more right than wrong. My regard for her was textured. She instructed, protected, entertained, showed compassion. But I knew her loyalty was to the realm first and, like my father, I felt resentment mixed with regard.

Nethermost Regained

Loo was the wild card. The simple working man. The sanity in a world out of control. What was his role in my life? What role did he want in my life? He had shown himself to be a faithful friend both to me and to Ol'Ben. He was undoubtedly the glue that fused our lives together. But was he more than that? Was his inclusion in this mad ride accident or destiny? Was his kiss last night comfort or passion?

When I finally roused myself, the sun was directly overhead, bouncing its blinding glare off the untouched snow. Returning to consciousness inevitably meant returning to reality — to a head aching, a stomach lurching, fingers and toes numbed with frostbite — a reality from which I longed desperately to be finished.

It was then that I recalled Shin's words about the whereabouts of Nethermost. She had been so annoyingly enigmatic, describing a long, unforgiving, northbound path that must be traveled "until you cannot imagine taking a step further." That, she underlined, was where Nethermost lay.

Now I understood the metaphor. Weakened in body and sick at heart, I wanted to let go of my father, to drop off the back of the SnowSqualler and float away into oblivion. You're right Shin, I thought, I've reached that desperate point. I can't go on … not one more …

In that very instant Father turned his head and called over the wind, "There's Nethermost! Hang on Cait, just one … step … more!"

Larch & Aspen

Chapter 18: Doppelgänger

"Why did you come Loo?"

"Dunno."

"Not a good enough answer. You can't just give me one of your verbal shrugs … not this time. You've let yourself be dragged into a war, a civil war in a subterranean realm that until three days ago you refused to believe even existed. So, why *are* you here? I had to come, but you chose to."

"Did I? I'm not so sure. Anyway, someone wanted to hurt you and Ol'Ben, and I wasn't going to let that happen, was I?"

I reached out to touch one of his hands with one of my own heavily bandaged ones. "Well, you're a marked man now. You aided and abetted."

"Sounds good — *noble* — how's that for a word? Just wait til you see this place Cait. It … is … awesome! I want to be the one to show you around. Remember that kid's book <u>Peter Pan</u> and the words they shout at the top of their voices to save Tinker Bell? 'I do believe in fairies! I do! I do!' Well, that's me," he laughed throatily, bending over the bed to give me a hug and a squeeze, reinforcing it in a whisper: "I do believe in fairies, Cait … I do … I do."

*****

It was Nethermost Gate II, the outside barricade, that shares its border with the Canadian wilderness, not Nethermost itself. In fact, it was just a sheer rock face peppered with a thin dusting of snow. The two vehicles pulled in close, noses almost touching the barrier and extinguished their engines. Loo slid off his seat, jumping in place, then ran over to unbelt me from my father. Father's dismount was slower but no less graceful. I stayed where I was, fused to my seat. I was not at all sure I could shift my legs; I was fairly certain that my feet wouldn't support me, they felt that frozen. If I'd had anything at all in my stomach, I would be losing it now. I let myself lean forward, resting my head on my father's vacated seat, hugging the residual warmth of his recent departure.

I was vaguely aware of movement about me, but I just didn't care. I shut my eyes and prayed for unconsciousness. Then I felt a jerk, a click, and the sensation of the vehicle being dragged, heard the sound of rock creaking and scraping, and felt a gust of warm air surge over me. When I opened my eyes a slit, I witnessed both SnowSquallers, coupled to winches, being hauled inside a great gap in the rock face. The last thing I remember was this wave of people rushing me, lifting me gently from my frozen position — and me, not caring a jot what they did, letting go of everything.

*****

I got an entirely different perspective on what happened from Aunt Moira …

"I returned to Nethermost Gate that morning, Cait, after our evening with the other Nethermost émigrés, feeling you were perfectly safe with your father at the house, and with the Canomorph and the Ambassador close by. Besides, I was planning on returning in the evening as I often did, since teleporting makes the jaunt between the village and The Gate a bit of a dawdle. I was keen to catch up on my data entry though; I was behind with the new pip tags for what I call my GTS — Global Tagging System. I remember feeling especially elated that morning because you and I had had a meeting of the minds the night before. It was a relief to learn that I hadn't messed up your life entirely, and that you were inclined to forgive my little messes. Indeed you also seemed ready to flex your muscles and face your destiny. The idea of returning home in time to invite myself over for one of Loo's gourmet meals positively delighted me.

"So I was puzzled, taken unawares, when your pip tag started alarming on my wrist band mid afternoon. I thought it odd that you would be driving outside of the perimeter fence, although I could think of a few reasons why it might be natural to do so. But, being extra cautious, as I am to a fault, I checked on your pip position with respect to any nearby villains, and was horrified to discover that a particularly bad cast of actors had breached our village barrier.

"Shoving panic aside, I began to piece together a possible explanation from the GTS holo screen alone: villains in the village — Cait outside the barrier. Next I checked the whereabouts of Michael, Shin, Mánús, Ol'Ben and Loo — all pips showing up with yours on my holo screen, creeping northward as a unit towards Nethermost. I could only surmise that what we feared all these years had finally happened. But it was more than a little intriguing that for some miraculous reason you all had been able to escape the village and the agents who were stalking you. I had no idea if there were injuries amongst you, but I had to assume that there were. I just knew that you were on the tunnel pods shooting rapidly along the subterranean rail trail, effecting your escape.

"I know our RNC, Rescue and Cleanup Strategy, backwards and forwards. While cleanup crews were dispatched to the village, I stayed where I was at The Intersect, at our Central Dispatch Kiosk, and prepared for every eventuality. Healers were readied, hover transports positioned, Security Support alerted — all poised to move on Gate II. I expected some of your party would require treatment for frostbite and snow blindness. I feared that you could have been double tagged by an agent of Peadar during your escape, and that you may unwittingly be leading them to our front door, the precise location of which, up to now, has eluded him.

"The guards at both boundary gates were trebled because Peadar was also quite capable of using the village assault as a distraction, while he tried to pierce our inner boundaries. So, in addition to our active militia, warrior reserves were assembled and run through their paces to hone their fighting skills and magical trickery.

"The delicate bit was keeping my parents (your grandparents) and your sister Rhue from panicking. There was much handwringing all around, mine included.

"After this prep, I seldom took my eyes off the pips on the holo screen. Two hours before your expected arrival, Michael activated his panic button indicating a medical crisis. Now I knew to send both primary and secondary healers along with advanced life support equipment in the ambulancia. I was aware almost to the nearest minute when you would arrive and was there out in front to greet you, to witness the dramatic moment when you first glimpsed your homeland.

"But all that changed the instant I saw them carry you unconscious from SnowSqualler II, looking so small and broken that I thought my heart would shatter. I know I was never your mother, Cait, yet I felt a mother's love, even as I kept reminding myself that you were only on loan to me. But as I watched them load you into that hover ambulancia, I couldn't bear it, seeing you so damaged, and you became that helpless infant again. I had every intention of coming with you to Hub Medical, but Loo shoved me aside, jumped in and slammed the door, before I could begin to voice my objections.

"I was doubly shocked to see Ol'Ben lifted from the sled a minute later, with Mánús plastered to his side, ridden by Shin looking quite elderly and beaten for the first time since I've known her. Ol'Ben was so far gone that the healers didn't dare move him without first oxygenating him and running a line of IV fluids. Mánús shadowed their every move, growling if he thought they were jostling Ol'Ben too much. At that moment Mánús was a Canomorph conflicted — showing loyalty to two masters. Who to choose?

"In the end, Shin chose for him. As the healers loaded Ol'Ben into the second hover vehicle, she nodded for Mánús to attend Ol'Ben rather than her. How touching to watch the Canomorph, ignoring all protests, shove his way into the vehicle, slip under the stretcher, and hold his ground with a snarl.

"I brought Shin, Michael and Larch back with me, heading straight for Hub Medical where family and friends awaited."

I interrupted my aunt at this point, my stomach flip-flopping in dread. "How is Ol'Ben doing?"

"The short answer is that he's still unconscious, but let's not count him out yet. He was barely breathing when he reached Gate II, dehydrated and running a high fever. Since then, using sound medicine, with heavy doses of jiggery pokery, his fever has come down, his breathing improved, although he is still oxygen dependent and on IV fluids. But he won't wake up. On the one hand, he's improving, his vitals stronger — but he just won't open his eyes. There is no rational explanation, except that he's ancient."

"Can I see him?"

"I will ask first, of course, but I don't see why not. I do have better news for you though Cait. Your sister is here and asks to meet you. What do you say?"

What I longed for and what I decided were diametrically opposed. Of course the answer should have been yes. Instead I answered, "No … I mean of course, yes, nothing would make me happier, but … no … I can't … not yet. When Ol'Ben was facing the possibility of dying en route to Nethermost, he spoke of a happier ending. He described a brass ring moment that made him want to survive the battle waged upon his frail old body — he wanted a front row seat to 'The Big Reveal', when long lost sisters met for the first time. He held onto this one dream while riding through hell, Aunt Moira, bouncing about in an ice box for two days, culturing a raging fever. All for his happy ending. He's come too far to miss it now! Heck, I didn't even get a chance to tell him that Rhue and I were twins, let alone identical ones.

"So if he does wake up — how can I deny him his exciting brass ring moment? I must wait for him. I owe him that … and more. Can you try to explain to Rhue?"

*****

I spent my first three days as a returned citizen of Nethermost Gate getting to know Hub Medical pretty well. Apparently, by the time we arrived at Gate II, I was in pretty grim shape. Even though my hands had had the benefit of gripping my father's warm body, my fingers were whitened with frost nip. But this was nothing compared with my feet. I recall screaming with pain as my poor toes began to thaw too quickly in the shocking warm air, once my boots had been cut away. Not only were they white with cold, but the tips of my toes were a dark pinky/grey from advanced frostbite. I was never so grateful to anyone as I was to that healer in white, with the elegant long neck, who took me quite literally in hand and quelled my pain with a simple touch of her magical fingers, after which I could watch more calmly as the damaged areas were cleansed, and a mysterious salve applied and covered in gauzy bandages. I was then offered water, that no doubt had been spiked with magic, because I dropped off to sleep within minutes, and was out for the next twenty four hours.

As I had been forbidden from walking until the salve had finished its job, Loo took me in a hover chair down the hall from my room on my first visit to Ol'Ben. The old dude looked comfortable enough but small as he lay so still on the softest bed I'd ever seen, like floating on marshmallow. All care was clearly being taken, of that I was certain. I addressed his unresponsive form. "Hey, Ol'Ben … looking cozy there … surrounded in luxury. No wonder you're sleeping in. We're all safe at Nethermost Gate by the way … no more bad guys trying to singe our butts. I'd have brought cut flowers, but apparently they don't grow that well at minus fifty degrees Celsius."

I kept up the endless chatter for half an hour, trying to waken him with the sound of my voice without success, at which point I gave up and asked Loo to return me to my room. As we floated down the corridor looking with interest from side to side at Nethermost's fascinating versions of medical equipment, I heard a familiar grumble coming from a semi-private room, and peeked in to overhear a very distinctive voice barking out orders: "I've lived with this damned leg for forty years now you young whelp, and I plan to live a good forty more. Now hand me my shillelagh!"

We hovered in the doorway, jaws agape at the sight of Shin, bare legs dangling over the edge of the bed, in a red satin nightgown and matching bed jacket. I remembered Aunt Moira saying she was looking elderly, and she did look a bit older it's true, although I could see that her spunk had returned. But that was not the shocking bit. The shocking bit was that one of her legs was gold, from the top of her ankle to mid calf. I knew from all the stories what this was. Loo did not.

When he saw her golden leg, Loo exploded, "What the hell, Shin! What's that?"

I murmured, "Is that Peadar's handiwork? Did you get that when he stormed the palace and took my grandmother Nicola? You didn't mention anything about being gilded at that event."

"Yes, well, it's a part of the story I'd like to forget," Shin confessed, with a sigh. "I did tell you that Peadar and his villains gilded the Palace guardsmen and others along the way, as they entered the throne room. But I failed to mentioned how he also took aim at half the court and gilded them mid pose also, before he savagely brutalized his sister and pulled her away. I was not hit directly, only splashed a tiny bit, which is why I have yet to succumb. I was stunned, I'll admit, and offered no return to his fire. To this day, it is my very great shame."

"That's what killed my grandfather … killed Riley?"

"Sort of. But I was gilded by alchemy and he was poisoned by the bastardized liquid gold. His wound was far more serious than mine and went deep. The inevitable outcome of my gilding is taking years, with years more it is to be hoped."

"I repeat, what the hell! Somebody please … catch me up!" Loo pleaded.

Nethermost Regained

While Shin gave him the *Reader's Digest* condensed version, I tuned out and reflected on the challenges before us. Hearing the story was one thing, seeing an actual outcome was quite another. It made me realize just how unprepared I still was.

Aunt Moira surprised me the next day by bringing some of my belongings from the house, including the nicest of my clothes, to which she had added some new stuff more suited to the cold weather. "Got some great bargains at the end of winter sales," she announced triumphantly. For Loo she brought his clothes, T.V. and games console, although she complained mightily about how heavy the technology had been to hold while she teleported.

Loo kicked up with glee at the sight of his T.V. especially. "So, what kind of reception are we talking here? How many channels?"

"None I'm afraid, but I thought you might like your video games."

After Aunt Moira departed, I poured a bubble bath, slipped in, and covered myself in a blanket of foam. There were nooks and crannies on my person that could benefit by an invasion of good honest soap and soothing warm water. I believe I may even have nodded off for a few minutes, coming to when the water turned tepid. In the time it took for my long soak, dry off and to be clothed like a normal person, Loo had set up his T.V. and console and was madly engrossed in one of his more violent video games. "Just getting in some target practice," he smirked, "you know, for when we trounce the bad guys."

*****

It was day three and I was allowed to walk about the Hub to test out my foot repairs. If the rest of the Gate was anything like its medical facility, I knew I was in for a treat. Loo took me to what we would call a hospital cafeteria, but here was known as Dr. Coffee Klatch. It was like an upmarket bistro, with an array of warm drinks on hand and table upon table of delights to tempt the most fussy of eaters. I selected a foamy coffee along with something resembling a croissant, sprinkled with a rather pleasant but mysterious spice, and sat with Loo at a mushroom shaped table with puffball chairs facing a sparkling rock wall that kept changing colours and intensity every minute or so.

After this, Loo took me to an area he'd found earlier — a solarium under ultra violet lights, filled with exotic florals and ferns, soft seating for patients and staff, interesting twisty walkways and trickles of water. It triggered a memory I had of a book I'd read in school — James Hilton's <u>Lost Horizon</u>, a work of fiction about a haven nestled amongst the frozen mountaintops of Tibet, a refuge known as Shangri-La. How many more of these utopian clones had been reproduced here in the caverns of Nethermost Gate, I wondered.

On our return to my sickroom, we stopped by again to visit Ol'Ben, as we'd been doing every few hours since I woke up. There was little reason to expect any change, yet I still needed to see his face. I berated myself for the danger he was in now, reasoning that were it not for me and my family, he would still be behind that counter in The General Store. Then I recalled that he was family too, and that his blood ran as much through my veins as did my kin from Nethermost. Thus primed, I drew in close to his bed.

"Ol'Ben, don't make me come in there and pull you out. You need to wake up … now, dammit! You've been such a brave soldier, you *were* such a brave soldier … in the war, remember? A war you fought in and won. You fought again on the home front to make a good life for Riley. You fought for Nora, helped prepare her for greatness. And now for me … you've been fighting all along … for me!

"You were holding out, you said, for that happier ending. But you've made it to that happier ending *now*! You just have to open your eyes to find that brass ring moment. Please, Ol'Ben, please … reach out for that damn brass ring!"

He opened his eyes and smiled at me long and sweet, then looked over my shoulders and beyond me, his eyes expanding to saucer size, his jaw dropping in amazement, mouth widening with joy. I turned around and saw in the doorway … me!

I saw me!

Chapter 19: Secrets and Clues

… or a better version of me. With my exact same face, but more confident, more muscular, with long reddish hair plaited into a braid, clothed in a khaki jumpsuit, belted at the waist, with a holstered dagger looped in. Her boots were no nonsense too — weathered but well polished, clunky and sensible. She was a warrior from top to toe, and she was, by anyone's measure, fiercer than me.

"Cait?" she began tentatively, in a similar a tone to mine, though without my Canadian accent. "Sister … Cait?"

"Oh Lord!" Loo interjected, jumping to his feet, disrupting an otherwise exquisite moment, "Another plot twist! This should be good!"

"Rhue." I whispered, creeping forward to meet her, as she advanced to me. We stopped short of each other … to just stare ... each hypnotized by the image before us. My hand reached out to touch hers … then to grip hers … then to pull her to me in an embrace aspiring to make up for all the embraces that we'd been denied for half a lifetime.

We were pulled apart by the sound of Ol'Ben blubbing from the bed, and turned to see him dabbing away at his tears with the bedsheets, his stare transfixed. "Would you look at that Loo!" he cried, "My two great-granddaughters. And identical twins — or am I seeing double? You didn't share that tiny detail, Cait. Now that's worth waking up for … what-what?"

I brought Rhue to his bedside for introductions. "Rhue, this is Ben McCauley; also known as Ol'Ben. And he is perhaps your oldest living relative. Ol'Ben, this is Rhue, clearly a better version of me."

Sap that he's always been, Ol'Ben pulled himself up on the bed, arms outstretched, weeping still. "Are you shocked that this old geezer is your Great-Grandpa?"

"Indeed not, for I have always known about you … and about Cait. I even have a scrapbook of pictures of both of you. But I have waited far too long to meet you face to face."

"You've always known?" I gasped, "Yet I was only told a few weeks ago. Heck I didn't even know Ol'Ben was kin."

"Greater minds, I'm told, have been planning our past, present and future. I know from Aunt Moira that you wanted to include Grandpa Ben as witness to this moment, but I am an impatient person. It is truly my greatest fault. I had to come as soon as he woke."

"But he's only this second opened his eyes! Are you psychic … or am I bugged as well as tagged?"

"Neither. I am a little sneak, I'm afraid. I have been shadowing you for two days, watching and waiting."

Loo guffawed. "Who needs television? This is prime time stuff!"

"Well, now that you've barged in Loo," I turned on him and chided just a little, "I guess I will leak the plot spoiler. Without going into it too much, this is my twin sister, Rhue. We've never met." Then to my sister I said, "This is Loo. He's the sane one in the bunch — if you can believe it."

As he presented his 'pleased to meet you' smile, Loo was muttering to me under his breath, "You *are* going to give me the longer version of this later Cait, right?"

*****

When I finally met my grandparents, I thought I was being escorted into the presence of royalty. Even the invitation I was sent was formal, especially in light of the fact that this was a meeting of long lost family, not of heads of state. The invitation was for me alone, although I understood that Rhue would also be present. I consulted with Aunt Moira about what to wear and she offered, "Oh anything clean dearie, they're not that fussy." But then she confused me by fussing herself — pulling out the cornflower blue sweater she'd just bought for me, which she matched with navy woollen slacks and a stylish ankle boot, laying them all out on my bed and adding a red print scarf for 'a gash of colour' about the neck.

Rhue came by on her hover scooter to fetch me and bring me to their in cavern dwelling along one of the more remote corridors off the central maze area, known as The Intersect. We'd only been acquainted ourselves for a couple of days, although I thought we'd used our time together productively.

*****

Now that I had actually met Rhue, my bitterness resurfaced. I felt that being denied our growing up years together was the worst kind of theft. It would take years to share even the most basic information about our lives, let alone an understanding of how our experiences had subtly shaped our values and personalities. More than once I pulled back on my urge to kick Shin right in her damn gilded leg. In other words emotionally I was still struggling with the audacity of it all. But intellectually I guess I could credit the argument that we were treasures of the realm, its most valuable playing pieces in a war game whose rules depended as much on strategy as it did on thrust and parry. What I dared not do at this point was examine just how this was going to play out exactly. Greater minds and all that.

During our first shared meal at Dr. Coffee Klatch, Rhue had opened the occasion with an introduction that had me absolutely floored. "You are so much more beautiful and sophisticated than me, Cait. You have lived in that enormous, stimulating upper world with access to the most brilliant of minds, the most powerful technology and invention. In its sheer potential, it must seem infinite and mind boggling. You drew the long straw. I know nothing of the upper world. I know only about this small air pocket of life, cloistered beneath a frozen landscape on the threshold of a realm in crisis."

Well, I didn't see that coming! Here I was envying her, and in practically the first breath out of her mouth she voices this? This was reshaping my expectations entirely. "I am not beautiful …"

"Your friend Loo thinks you are."

"What? No!" I objected, "I'm astonished! From my perspective, you've had the richer life. For one thing, you've been raised with family about you — including our father — and have lived and worked shoulder to shoulder with the most unique citizens of Earth. These extraordinary human and magical beings have gifts beyond anything I've ever seen upstairs. Besides, I may have lived on the layer of the planet with the greater amount of real estate, but I was still raised in a protective bubble of sorts. You are much fiercer than me. I've spent most of my life being afraid. You frame any doorway you walk through with confidence and courage."

Rhue contemplated my words, before observing, "Perhaps this is precisely what these 'greater minds' had in view. Perhaps it will require the sum total of our two utterly different lives to fortify our daunting mission."

It was a good, honest beginning to our twin partnership. From that moment, we created a running inventory of what abilities we wished either to acquire or to share. First on my list was Rhue's combat skills.

We had only just begun our unique home schooling when the invitation to my grandparents' residence arrived — a visit that would change us both, in exciting and unanticipated ways.

*****

As I entered the O'Quinn's bio pod, I felt nervous and weak at the knees. It was not a palatial home, space within The Gate community was at a premium after all. No one was granted more than was due them. Nor was it extravagant. No one person could possess more than another, just as their exiled existence was equally shared. But their home was tasteful and staged to impress. For example, there was one table only in the front foyer, chipped from stone, smoothed and polished to perfection, upon which was displayed one exquisite gold sphere, filigreed and set with red gems. "That is the Orb of Power," Rhue explained as we passed through on our way to a central living space, where a couple awaited, in simple but tasteful dress, poised to receive us. Rhue introduced them as Aileen and Fergus O'Quinn, my paternal grandparents. In their features I saw many parts of both my father and my aunt. Aileen, for instance, was the likely suspect for my aunt's auburn hair and violet eyes, although her auburn was now streaked with grey, her violet eyes framed with character lines. My father's dark colouring came from his father to be sure, whose black hair and sooty eyes were similarly salted with age. At a guess, they were in their sixties, lean, alert, and full of joy at the sight of Rhue and me entering the room.

"Could anyone be more welcome than you dear Cait? How we have longed for your return!" Aileen effused, while Fergus swooped me up and crushed me in a firm embrace. Rhue reached for both of them in turn with an easy greeting, and I was reminded that they had essentially been her parents, even though my father popped in and out of the picture between war preparations. It brought both joy and envy to my heart.

"It seems that our daughter Moira has raised you pretty well," Fergus observed, in a booming voice. "You look very polished, different from your genetic counterpart, but yes, well turned out." Suddenly Aunt Moira's care in selecting my outfit for the day made more sense. She had wanted her parents to see that she had done a decent job with me. I felt a bit under the microscope, and wondered if I would have to perform.

Grandma Aileen took charge, seating us in soft chairs and offering warm drinks, and fresh breads served with butter, jams and thick cream, to relax and settle us in.

"The night you two were born," she began, "was the happiest in the short history of Nethermost Gate. If we could have had fireworks inside the caverns we would have, but the celebrations were spectacular nonetheless, from spontaneous neighbourhood parties to formal balls. Everyone wanted to wet the heads of the newborns. To a group of weary exiles, you two represented our greatest hope. But in truth, it was completely unfair of us. We should not have added to the already heavy burden of brand new parents trying to raise two newborns under such harsh circumstances, with our lofty ideals and suggestions of a higher purpose."

Grandpa Fergus continued the account. "No one was more conflicted or upset than us on the night of Nora's departure and subsequent capture. She was our daughter-in-law, the mother of our grandchildren, the love of our son's life. We were appalled when we heard of Shin's manipulation of a situation that fractured our family, and all but destroyed our only son.

"But Shin was not acting alone. After this prevision appeared on her canvas, she took it immediately to the Elders' Council, of which we are members of course. But in light of our obvious bias, the council excluded us from its *ad hoc* session, knowing too well what our objections would be. It was the council, not Shin alone, who conceived of the plan to ignite Nora's maternal feelings and to virtually send her off to save her own mother."

"How despicable!" I shouted, "Is this the same council that would have my sister and me lead some sort of rebellion against Peadar? After shredding our childhood and sacrificing our mother?"

"The same," Aileen sighed. "And yet … we cannot deny the ultimate wisdom of their decision."

I knew that. I just needed to vent my spleen once more. "So, now I'm here and it's likely that Peadar is aware of me, right? Rhue and I will be turning nineteen on our birthdays in May. What do 'greater minds' expect?"

"First of all," Fergus added to his wife opinion, "Let me say that it's very likely that Peadar knows *one* of you exists, because it would have been obvious that Nora had given birth not long before her capture. But he still may not know of his double jeopardy. We may still have that card to play."

"An advantage described with a lot of fuzzy speculation and wishful thinking wouldn't you say?" I observed.

"Yes," Aileen agreed. "But we have asked you both here today for a very specific reason — a reason about which even Rhue does not yet know."

At these words, Shin entered the room, limping badly and carrying a rolled up painting. Well, blow .. me .. down, I whistled inwardly. She planted herself centre stage. "I may not be the most popular person in the room at the moment," she acknowledged, "but I believe I possess the greatest piece of intelligence that we've ever had in our lengthy fight to regain Nethermost. This is the painting I was so desperate to show you last week, Cait. This is why I risked our lives back in the village to retrieve it, even with our enemy at the door.

"What Rhue appreciates, from years of hanging around my studio, is the *oddity* of my previsions. Here, let me show you ..." she said, unrolling a travel battered canvas onto the coffee table. All four of us moved forward to peer. "What's the first thing you notice about this painting, Cait?"

The scene was dark and obscured, an indoor setting, a couple of characters in odd dress — occasionally streaky because ... "It's moving," I said, "the paint and the figures ... moving," The action was incomplete and undefined, seconds only in length, repeating on a loop.

"What does this oddity mean?" Shin was addressing my sister this time.

"It means that this scene is still in a prevision state, and not a memory," she replied. "This has not yet occurred."

"Yes," Shin affirmed excitedly. "You know too well from years of watching me paint. Rhue loved to scrutinized a moving canvas, waiting for it to freeze, to become a memory. Once the painting stops moving, the vision is fulfilled, you see.

"So, this prevision has not yet come to pass! Now look again closer … all of you," she commanded in her no nonsense voice. "Where is this and who are these people?"

The room represented in Shin's oils was cluttered with books, test tubes, dirty clothes, and a few pieces of animal artwork. "I recognize that room," Fergus exclaimed, "from years past! This is Peadar's old room in the palace. Just as it looked when he was a boy. He was always messy, that one. But wait, that is not Peadar."

"That's Cait … that's me!" cried Rhue, eyes bulging. "What are we doing?"

"I've studied this canvas for hours and am no closer to figuring that out," Shin acknowledged. "But it must be important, don't you think? Two things we may surmise — one, that in the future, Rhue and Cait will be inside Nethermost itself; and two, that somehow Peadar's bedroom is important. Otherwise you would not be there. But why?" She rolled up the canvas again, and handed to me.

"You girls will be nineteen in less than two months and will be formally granted your magical talents. I know Michael has described the potential of that ceremony — the possibilities of identical twins receiving individual talents. What you each choose for your talent will be critical. But I implore you to study this painting, as well, night and day if need be, for I am certain that it is meant to guide you."

"Choose well." Shin drank off a quick cup of tea, grabbed her shillelagh, and left the bio pod.

We sat in silence, dumbfounded — until I broke the spell, "Wow! Now that's a great exit line."

I caught Fergus and Aileen exchanging looks, nodding in some sort of agreement. Aileen left the room, returning a few minutes later with a carved wooden chest, and placed it on the table before us.

"I saw you notice as you entered, Cait, the unique ornament on our front hall table, and I overheard Rhue telling you that is the Orb of Power. We display it publicly to inspire our citizens. We mean it to attest to our certainty that the Swayer-ship of Nethermost has always been, and remains, supreme in all our hearts.

"While Shin wisely scooped up Nora and Riley before fleeing the palace on that fateful day forty years ago, we ran for our own young children of course. But we also had the presence of mind to grab up the symbols of power — the orb, the sceptre, the crowns … and the two rings worn by Their Graces Fianna and Canice."

She stopped in her narrative and retrieved a key from around her neck, using it to open the box. From it she retrieved two small leather pouches and gave one to each of us. "These are the rings worn exclusively by Fianna and Canice. That last detail, especially, is important. While the other symbols of power are traditional and inherited, these rings are the love tokens that Their Graces gave to one another on their coronation day."

She waited while Rhue and I opened our pouches. The rings were fashioned of the purest gold and heavily jewelled with rubies, sapphires, emeralds and diamonds, encrusting a masculine crown in one ring and a feminine crown in the other. Not something you would wear everyday — far too heavy. "Not only should these rings inspire you and remind you of your ancestry, they should also focus you on your duty to throne and realm. That would be enough reason to give them to you. But they contain two attributes of inestimable value, about which not even Peadar is aware.

"First of all, the rings combined are a key to a hidden entrance to the old palace. This secret door was commissioned by Fianna and Canice sixty years ago, its precise location known only to them. Used together, the rings form the only key to their secret door. There may come a time during this conflict when access to our ancestral palace becomes critical, when stealth is essential. Secondly, each ring, given and worn in love, holds the residual talent of the wearer. Look at yours, Cait, and marvel that this is the ring which for four decades graced your ancestor Fianna's royal finger. When she died, Fianna transferred a trace amount of her lifelong talent into this ring — a minuscule amount, mind you, but sufficient to allow her talent to be used once more … only. It was gifted to her in love back then, given in love to you now Cait. It is your legacy."

"What was Fianna's talent?"

"Teleportation."

"Like Aunt Moira's?"

"Exactly. Moira will be a useful resource in providing you with instruction, although you must not tell her, or anyone else, of this ring's existence."

"Not even your own daughter?"

"No one. You must promise!"

"As for your ring, Rhue, it belonged to Canice, a man well known for his great courage and stamina. In fact, you remind me of him very much. That ring contains the final issuance of his talent, to be used one time only."

"I am so honoured," breathed Rhue. "What talent does Canice's ring hold in reserve?"

"As chief warrior, Canice's strength lay in combat, and with his talent, he was able to shoot thunder fire, such as the healy magicians do. In fact, Shin was his mentor in developing his talent. Again, while she should be studied, Rhue, Shin must never be told about this ring."

Fergus added one final warning. "Carry these rings in secret; never leave them unattended, never let them be seen. We have reason to believe that citizens loyal to Peadar may be living amongst us. As you prepare for your ascension ceremony, consider the vital resources stored in these rings, before choosing what further talents you require."

"Use them … wisely!"

Chapter 20: Why The Dirty Clothes?

I caught Loo hunched over a large sheet of parchment, madly sketching with a stick of graphite and nursing what was called a 'coffee noir', an extra strong black coffee, in a quiet corner of Dr. Coffee Klatch. I'd been camping out in the Relatives Support Apartments at the Hub in order to be near Ol'Ben, who was still at the medical facility. At this hour, Ol'Ben was getting the once over by his doctor and being prettied up by his caregiver, so I'd popped by the bistro to wait. It was going to be Ol'Ben's first full day out of bed, and he was excited to be getting a brief view of Nethermost Gate, even though it was only a tour of The Hub. I was excited at the prospect of showing it to him, the highlight of which would be the solarium that

151

had become my favourite hangout. In fact, I'd now taken to calling it Shanghri-La — a name that was beginning to catch on with the staff.

"Whatcha doing?" I asked, plunking myself down at Loo's table, and jostling his paper as I did, "Are these your plans for taking over the planet?"

"Ha, ha. I've been staying at Michael's, which incidentally is little more than a closet with a toilet and shower … but hey ho. It's been good though, cuz Michael's been filling me in on a lotta stuff. I'll have followup questions for you later."

"Of course."

"Anyway, something he said got me thinking. He told me that he and Moira have been organizing a volunteer militia made up of those Nethermost folks who are living on the upside. I guess they're hoping to pull this army together over the next few months, which isn't a long time, considering all the organization and training involved. It's going be massive — lots to plan, supplies to bring in, billets to arrange … and hundreds of folks shooting through those underground tunnels, which apparently run all over North and South America, did you know that?

"So, I got this idea … about those tunnel pod thingies that brought us here; that are really little more than miners' carts with some seats screwed into the ore bins. I outlined some ideas to improve them with Michael and asked him if he thought it could help the cause. He seemed pretty keen … said he thought it was worth a look see. Long story short, I've got a meeting later this morning with the head honcho at the motor pool, or whatever the witchy equivalent of that is.

"How I see it, Cait," he shifted his position leaning in closer, his eyes brightened with enthusiasm, "How I see it … they've got the technology of those Launchers down pretty well right? *A+* for engine development, speed and agility … especially the awesome magic gizmos — not Formula One standards but hey, they haven't got Formula One money. But *D-* for aerodynamics and comfort. Biggest mistake? Those things should never have been open topped! They need roofs and windbreaks dammit! It nearly killed Ol'Ben. Also, the insides need a boost … not comfy on the bum. But there's no money for modifications since any spare cash goes to building this militia. So I'm coming up with some cheap solutions."

It might have been the most I'd ever heard Loo say at one go, and he was positively gushing. "This is so impressive Loo. Well done you! You haven't let grass grow … So … would you say you were happy … I mean here at Nethermost Gate?"

He stopped his sketching, looked up and gave me that delicious smile of his. "Yeah, I guess. I hadn't really thought about it much. No time really. But … I like the people, like the setup, like the challenge, like the respect. Love you … and Ol'Ben of course."

"You l-love me?"

He looked down for a few beats longer, smiled to himself, then looked back up at me, catching me square in the eye. "Yup, I do … and Ol'Ben of course."

(Of course).

*****

A few days before Ol'Ben was due to be discharged, I moved in with Grandma and Grandpa, (that still sounded odd) and was sharing a bedroom with Rhue. What I lacked in privacy, I made up for in sister time. We needed to fast forward our schooling for one thing. Our skills set had to be pretty much evenly matched. We also had some massive problem solving to do before our birthdays — like what talents to ask for (and how), like what the painting was telling us (and why), like how to use the rings (and when). For much of this we were on our own, or at least we had many secrets to keep to ourselves. Except for our choice of talents, we could be completely open with Grandma and Grandpa, and could still ask a few judicious questions of others as well. But ultimately the final decisions were ours alone, and neither of us felt even remotely up to the job.

I still wasn't certain that an insignificant and inexperienced young pup like myself was capable of even a tenth of this … heir to some sort of throne … leader in some sort of war. I didn't feel like a queen or a warrior. Was I even considering doing all this? But every time I got myself worked into a tizzy, I remembered our mother Nora and her commitment to the greater good over personal happiness, and I was humbled.

It was mid April already and time was wasting away.

The move to my grandparents was extra sweet because I knew they were planning on asking Ol'Ben to move into Grandpa Fergus' study, converted for the purpose. Not only was I over the moon to have Ol'Ben so near, I was tickled that my grandparents were leaving it to me to invite him. I felt positively giddy when I entered his hospital room that day. But when I told him, he looked uncomfortable and unsure. I had to ask why.

"Come on Cait. I'm an over the hill shopkeeper who's only known life from behind a store counter in a remote village all my life. How does that compare to all this? How would I fit in? From what I've been told, these people were high ranking members of the palace household, for goodness sake — counsellors to the royal family, no less. I'm deeply honoured, of course I am, but I think I must say no. Just find me a room in a home somewhere, and maybe later I'll go back to the store … someday, what-what."

In a home? I screamed inwardly. No! It hadn't been acceptable back in Alta, it was even less acceptable up here in the Ice Box of the World. I doubted they even had 'homes' for the elderly. So I went back to my grandparents feeling blue and told them about Ol'Ben's reaction and decision. The following morning Aileen showed up at Hub Medical and floated into Ol'Ben's room unannounced, with the poise of an aristocrat, but the humility of a commoner. She approached his bedside, and bowed lowly. "Mr. Ben McCauley I believe. I am Aileen O'Quinn, sir. I must express my great regret that we have not been introduced. It is unforgivable that my husband and I should not have introduced ourselves before now."

I could see shock register in Ol'Ben's face. That this society woman should bow before him, should apologize, was quite beyond his grasp. I wasn't sure where Grandma Aileen was going with this, but I could see that Ol'Ben was looking even more intimidated than before. Fortunately, she could see it too. So she tried quite a different and very clever tac which made me love her all the more. She pulled a chair up next to the bed, sat close to him and lowered her voice, "In truth, I've been longing for your advice … about the girls."

What a brilliant woman she was, and I have to say, absolutely genuine. She asked about Ol'Ben's experiences with his great-granddaughter, me, and shared her own tales about her granddaughter, Rhue. Ol'Ben listened with rapt attention (his best attribute), and with good humour (his best response). In the end, Aileen didn't even bother asking him to stay. What she did was far more subtle. She asked if he could be of help with Rhue and me as we were getting to know each other, and to help smooth the coming of age process for us. By the end of an hour together, they were best friends, laughing themselves to tears. When Aileen rose to leave, her offhand parting comment was, "Shall we say Thursday for your move in?"

To which he replied, "I'll check with the Doc. But I think that should be fine."

Brilliant woman!

*****

The final flutter about his resettlement came when I told Ol'Ben that none of his clothes had survived the attack at The General Store. That was an outright lie, a plot I'd contrived with Aunt Moira, about which I was a little ashamed, but I could live with it. All that polyester and pastel, all that fraying and tattiness. Also, we argued, he would need clothes befitting his new position at Nethermost Gate, as great-grandfather to members of the first bloodline. That was a load of codswallop too, although I knew that with Ol'Ben's people skills, it wouldn't be long before he'd be treated as the wiseman that he truly was.

Aunt Moira and I went to a community tailor to discuss clothing style options for the older man and ordered three different looks for Ol'Ben. The tailor met and measured him a couple of days before his discharge, and on move-in day morning showed up at Hub Medical with all three outfits, carefully wrapped in tissue paper.

Ol'Ben disappeared with him for fifteen minutes, while Aunt Moira and I waited in his room all expectant. While we knew anything had to be better than his old look, we had no idea how good it would be. When he entered that room again, Ol'Ben had a hint of a strut — he was a new man and proud of it. Having lost a few pounds due to illness, his midriff was less pronounced, and the dark corduroy trousers hugged his waist comfortably, rather than bifurcating his belly. He wore a crisp cotton blend shirt in a subtle blue check under a heather grey double breasted sweater jacket framed at the neck by a shawl collar. His shoes were soft and sensible, but still stylish, with a good tread for stability. Up top he wore a flat cap, pulled low over the forehead. He also sported a cane, ornate like Shin's, and leaned on it as he stood as tall as possible before us.

"What d'ya think? It's good huh? And look at this — best of all!" He pulled off his cap and lowered his head to reveal a bit of stubble on his noggin. "They've been splashing some fairy goop on my bald pate for weeks now and it's causing my hair to grow back! Heck, I've been combing my hair with a wash cloth for forty years or more. At this rate, I'm going to need a haircut before Christmas!"

*****

"Grandpa Fergus, what are these jars and beakers on the desk?"

Rhue and I were examining Shin's painting for the umpteenth time in the privacy of our room and had called in Grandpa Fergus for his opinion. For a couple of weeks now we had been deconstructing the canvas bit by bit under a magnifying glass, trying to determine the significance of every brush stroke, like in a 'Where's Waldo' picture, only worse because we didn't know what Waldo looked like in the first place, and not finding our 'Waldo' had direr consequences.

We felt strongly that the images of us in this painting must be for the purpose of retrieving something vital from that room. But what? We would have to search the room after we got in. But where? We noted every brushstroke and postulated places where this item may have been secreted. We figured it wouldn't be left out in the open for just anyone to find so we made a checklist of drawers to open, books to flip through, shelves to scour, secret buttons to discover; stuff to look under, over and through.

Once we finished that list, we began analyzing the purpose of every item in the room and had come to the question of the chemistry clutter.

"Why were these items in Peadar's bedroom, Grandpa Fergus?" Rhue asked. "He would have had a big laboratory to work in after he received his talent, would he not?"

"Yes, of course. And he slept in this room up until he moved into his own hideous monstrosity. But I remember that as a child, he would set up his chemistry experiments in his bedroom suite. He would stink the whole place out, and his mother would scold him something fierce. The servants assigned to clean his room were very unhappy. Perhaps later in life he kept these items still as mementos."

We scrutinized the canvas along this vein until late evening, assigning a purpose and context to each item. We finally called 'lights out' about midnight, our eyes bloodshot and our brains fried. I had just nodded off when I woke up explosively, turning on my bedside lamp. At the exact same second, Rhue did the same.

"It's not the *what*, *where* or *why* that we should be trying to figure at first, is it?" I cried.

"No, it is not. It is *when*!" Rhue answered excitedly.

"Yes, yes! And why are there dirty clothes on the floor?"

"Precisely!"

Chapter 21: Back to Basics

"I don't like that guy," Loo hissed, while rubbing peppermint oil into my grumbling muscles after a particularly rough training session. He's too hard on you. It's like he doesn't want you to succeed … wants you to give up. Think I'll join his training class ... keep an eye on him …"

"He's building me up quickly," I protested. "You know … tough love. He wants me fighting fit."

"We'll see."

*****

My fitness instructor Donal Fadden was a task master. I thought it would be Rhue who would teach me fighting skills. Instead she made a case for Donal. She trusted him, believed he was the guy to get me into shape the fastest. She'd been using him as her trainer for years. Heck, she'd been dating him for the past six months.

My combat training wasn't going that well, if I'm honest. I didn't have the advantage of years of body building that Rhue had, or Loo had for that matter. My gym experiences at school were basic — track and field, volleyball, basketball. I'd been a decent runner, or least I didn't disgrace myself. But since I didn't do any intramural sports, the sum total of my fitness regime came from PE classes that everyone attended as part of the overall curriculum.

I wasn't a complete weakling, and I was giving it a good go. My muscles screamed at me on a daily basis, but I wasn't wimping out, although Donal did seem a bit harder on me than he was on Rhue. When he made me do pushups, he'd load weights on my back and keep adding on until I collapsed under the pressure. He didn't do that with Rhue.

And I was getting fit, but that may have been due more to the supplementary sessions I was doing with Loo, who used gentler exercise, but more of it, with plenty of massage in between.

I was better at the hand to hand stuff, again because of Loo. He would put me through defensive karate moves until they came to me like dance steps, rhythmical and choreographed. I was also a decent fencer, using the same dance principles, more for parry than for thrust. Since I was best at the defensive skills, coupled with the knowledge that we were running short on time, I abandoned Donal's intensive training program which really annoyed him, working with Loo instead on the skills that showed more promise.

Loo offered an opinion one day that made perfect sense. "You're not going to win this war by assaulting the enemy with your limited combat skills, Cait. Big galoots like me can do that messy stuff. You're going to win by using your wits. No one can get battle ready in a couple of weeks. Best you can hope for is a few effective defensive moves that will keep you out of trouble when a villain comes at you. Count on having the militia, magic — and me — at your back."

*****

Rhue and I identified academic subjects that needed strengthening before our mission. What we lacked, believe it or not, turned out to be basic knowledge like history and geography. For instance, I knew nothing of the layout of Nethermost. Rhue knew nothing of on-Earth geography, including that Nethermost was under the northern edges of Canada's great forests. I needed to understand more about the customs of my homeland and how to behave. She needed to study the history of warfare, and read the same reference books that Peadar used when developing his wicked blueprint for seizing the throne. If we were going to be pulled into this, we wanted to be more than pawns in this war game between the Elders' Council and the Apparatchik. We wanted to be major players on the board.

At the community lending library, we chose books for one another. Besides all this reading homework, Rhue would sit for hours listening to accounts of upper Earth from Ol'Ben, paying particular attention to his war stories. I, on the other hand, would grill Grandpa Fergus about Nethermost, especially the general layout of the continent, with a special interest in best routes from Nethermost Gate to the palace. He gave me a slew of historical photos taken of landmarks, especially of the palace. Even though it would be forty years out of date, I got him to sketch a layout of the Palace as well, identifying rooms, corridors, hiding places, including the general outside area where its secret entrance might be.

*****

Now that Rhue and I were certain that the prevision in Shin's painting involved time travel, we put that at the very top of our list of talents to be considered. Our birthdays were only three weeks away now, and we needed to make our minds up soon.

At our next mentoring session, we opened with a question about time travel. "Is time travel a talent Shin?" I began.

"Yes, of course. A *talent* by definition is a skill or attribute that exceeds the normal capabilities of creature kind, or that defies the laws of physics. While humans often wish to travel in time in their wildest dreams, the laws of physics prevent it. Magic is the ingredient that allows us to defy these laws and to exceed our pathetic limitations. So, time travel is definitely possible with a talent."

"How does it work? Is it limited in any way? Can we go back to the beginning of the world, for instance?"

"Technically yes, practically no. While your movement through time is completely fluid, it does not include movement in space. Unless you knew exactly where that first amoeba was culturing in the primordial ooze, it would be impractical to expect to be able to travel back to that time and location both."

Hmmm. So this meant that we had to physically be inside Peadar's bedroom, or the space it used to occupy, *before* travelling back in time to the 'when' of our picture. Despite this extra challenge, time travel was still the number one candidate on our list.

Keeping our grandparents warning in mind, we were sneaky about our next set of questions. "Shin," Rhue asked, "I've been told that our Great-Grandmother Fianna's talent was teleportation. Is this true?"

"Oh yes. In fact, it influenced your Aunt Moira's decision to request this talent herself, and I've heard her say on many occasions that she felt she had chosen wisely. But Fianna was the role model here. I remember how impressed I was about how Her Grace used her talent. She had her fun with it, yes, but she used it more often for good. When she became stressed by her duties, Fianna would teleport to a place that gave her peace — a swimming hole, a waterfalls, a natural garden — places off the beaten track where no-one would know who she was, where she would not be disturbed. The solarium at Hub Medical is dedicated to her for this very reason. It is designed to represent the sort of haven that Fianna would have loved."

It made me feel shivery to connect in this tiny way to my royal great-grandmother, to know that we both found solace in such surroundings. Shin continued, "Fianna more often used her talent to reach out to her subjects on a personal level. When she would hear of a citizen in distress, she would be there within minutes to offer consolation or practical support. She was selfless, never bragging about her good works openly. Her subjects loved her, not only for her support, but for her discretion."

"Would that I had known her," Rhue remarked wistfully. "His Grace Canice had one of *your* great talents did he not?"

"Yes, one of the primary talents of the healy is the throwing of thunder fire. But I must warn you that this talent comes at great cost. First of all, using it is exhausting and accelerates the aging process. And one thing more ..." Shin sat back in her chair, closed her eyes, and sighed. "You no doubt remember, Cait, what Michael calls my 'thunder blast' in our combat against the enemy at The General Store and again at my little cottage."

"I remember it all too well."

"It was a fight both of honour and necessity, and it saved our lives. If I hadn't used my powers then, we would all have surely died. Nevertheless, I took three lives that day. Taking life, no matter how noble the cause, or villainous the victim, exacts a toll. That day not only aged me noticeably, but took a piece of my soul — as indeed it should have."

I could hear Aunt Moira's words again about now much older and knocked back Shin had looked upon her arrival at the outer gate the day of our arrival. Now I knew why.

"No matter what talent you choose, think about the consequences girls. These talents are not parlour tricks and must not be treated as such. Although it is often remembered as a one liner from Stan Lee's comic book series <u>The Amazing Spider-Man</u>, it was actually the brilliant writer and philosopher Voltaire who penned this ageless truth, 'With great power comes great responsibility.'"

We spent hours over the next two weeks, interviewing Shin and discussing talents in detail. With each talent discussed, she sketched its benefits and side effects. Every evening before bed, we reviewed each one, either dropping it off or placing it on the possibility list.

By the day before our birthdays, we had selected time travel as one talent to request, and two single use talents of thunder fire and teleportation stored in our rings. We needed to choose one more from our short listed candidates …

Invisibility — Father has this talent and finds it useful for espionage. Although it makes him invisible, he remains solid while undetectable and often forgets this fact.

Transmutation — This is primary magical gift of Canomorphs like Mánús, although it is possible for a human to possess it as a talent. Again used as disguise, it is an excellent espionage tool. But it can also be weaponized. Canomorphs move through the full canine spectrum for instance — from the benign to the ferocious —from humanoid, to dog, to wolf and everything in between. At the extreme end is the werewolf, a weapon of destruction. Like thunder fire, this talent holds dire consequences for the user, as well as for the victim.

Telepathy — Grandma Aileen reads minds and she was almost irreplaceable in the aftermath of the coup for treating people suffering from stress. It explains how she was able to understand Ol'Ben's issues so quickly. The warning here is not to delve too deeply. Deep diving into someone else's psyche should not be attempted without permission. Otherwise it is theft or invasion of privacy.

Flight — Grandpa Fergus can fly like the fairies, leap over structures and hover in mid air. He finds it useful as rapid transit, but it also gives him a panoramic view of a landscape, so he is the right person to assess the overall battlefield and to advise on strategic positioning.

The downside of this is that it isn't practical for use outside Nethermost because you are visible to outsiders on radar.

Balancing — This talent, as we have already discussed at length, is what was saving Nethermost, but killing Grandma Nicola. She has a rare balancing strength that exceeds even the dwarves and she can do the work of ten dwarves. Most humans would not have her strength.

Healing — This noble talent, chosen by our mother Nora, is one of the most selfless. It saves lives where traditional medicine may falter. But as with other talents, there is a price to be paid, of overextending oneself and aging prematurely.

Transference — The ability to put oneself in someone else's shoes is the positive end of this talent. It allows the bearer of the talent to become empathetic. But taken to the negative extreme, this talent is something akin to personal assault, when the take over of another person's mind or body occurs against their will.

While our mentoring sessions with Shin could be intense, they also provided us with an encyclopedia of choice. It was going to be a daunting task to select that final talent.

'With great power comes great responsibility.'

At the close of each session, Shin would conclude with exactly the same caveat, "Remember ladies, although *what* you chose as your talent is very important, *how* you receive it is critical too."

That annoying healy and her little riddles.

Chapter 22: I Can Explain

"Why don't you like Donal?" I asked Loo a few days before my nineteenth birthday, during a rare moment of relaxation. Rhue was on a date with Donal — which made me happy because I had the use of our shared bedroom for the next few hours undisturbed, to spend with Loo and finally answer some of his more burning questions. But he was spoiling it now by being grumpy.

"Small stuff. His expressions are all wrong ..."

"Expressions! Wrong … how?"

"I'm trying to put my finger on it." Loo frowned, reaching for the correct explanation. "Okay … example. I'm no Freud, but a guy who frowns when his trainee does well and smirks when she screws up is at best a bad instructor right? At worse … he's either half a bubble off of plumb … or a bad dude! Don't you think?"

I *did* think, and now I was grumpy too. "How sure are you?"

"Believe me, Cait, I was watching."

*****

Grandma Aileen and Ol'Ben were planning a splash-up celebration for our nineteenth. Although there were surprise components from which we were excluded, Rhue and I joyfully watched their frenzy from the sidelines. We were elated, of course, but a bit nervous because we still hadn't chosen that last talent and we were only hours away from D-day.

My biggest excitement, however, was how Ol'Ben was thriving these days. Aileen took great delight in cooking for him and, with all the nutrition she was shoving into him, he was getting rosier in the cheeks every day. The evenings when Loo came by and tagged teamed with Grandma Aileen in the cooking department were quickly becoming legendary, and usually evolved into an impromptu party with old friends and new.

There was one old friend we were always happy to see. He appeared on our stoop the day after Ol'Ben moved in, dressed in a supersized version of the khaki jumpsuit that Rhue always wore. He was large featured to be sure, with a strong, bold nose, trim beard over a long jaw, dark fuzzy hair and deep brown eyes that darted about the room constantly. Under the tight fitting uniform you could appreciate his well toned muscles, and where the uniform ended, a shocking amount of body hair began. Ol'Ben stared up at his six and a half foot frame for a good two minutes, before sputtering, "Mánús, my dear fellow! How very good of you to come!"

Mute though he was, Mánús seemed to communicate with Ol'Ben just fine, and they easily renewed their friendship with almost daily visits. It was Mánús who took Ol'Ben for walks these days, thus adding gentle exercise to his fitness regime. Ol'Ben didn't look a day over seventy-five now, with even more stubble on his erstwhile bald head.

The two day celebration began with a trip to the travelling roadshow which was running in preview prior to its cross country tour — this to be followed by a pre birthday soirée hosted by Ol'Ben and my grandparents. Although it was all kicking off in the late afternoon, I was starting early as it would be my first opportunity for a leisurely walkabout of Nethermost Gate. I'd had been staying here for seven weeks already and had never really had the chance to enjoy the caverns themselves, let alone the area directly surrounding the inner border gate. So while some of the others in our party were travelling by hover car to the five o'clock show, we young folks were walking and meeting up with the rest at the event itself. We set off just after midday, Rhue and Donal, Loo and me.

I think Rhue would have been happy to enjoy my touristy reactions, but Donal was showing obvious signs of boredom barely an hour into it, so she suggested we split up to meet later. That suited me fine. Loo and I felt like kids in a candy shop, absorbing the sights of this organic architecture made more beguiling by a smattering of magic.

It was always daytime in the caverns. The maze of connecting tunnels were lit by white/blue beams, powered by a combination of solar and wind energy. Although I understood that the continent ceiling beneath was more quartz rich, still there were sparkling areas within these caverns too, where the vitreous crystals had been found and exposed. As an aid to navigation through the maze, each tunnel was lettered and each bio pod numbered. For instance, my grandparents lived at P49, about a kilometre northeast of the central business district known as The Intersect, along Tunnel P. The Intersect was located midpoint in the caverns, a hundred metres from the main tunnel entrance. Major landmarks such as Hub Medical and Intersect Security were signposted, not only over their entrances, but also on directional maps posted in each tunnel.

The maze of caverns spanned about 3 kilometres in length, but only 200 metres at its widest point. Everything was compact due to the fact that these hollowed out rock pockets needed to house more than two thousand people.The remainder of the refugees lived outside in homes constructed of rock and wood, which was nice for them in the summer months, but a real struggle the rest of the year.

We took our time making our way to the tunnel entrance, even though we had walked these paths so many times before. But in my constant daily rush, I had never stopped to appreciate the wonder of it all, or to enter the intriguing shops, as Loo and I now did. Loo led me into the goldsmith shop that I had been to before called Jeremy's, with off the shelf and custom made jewelry, small ornaments and dining accessories. While most of the items had been fashioned of gold, there was the occasional silver piece as well. The gemstone insets were mostly amethyst, from a mine that had been unearthed nearby. As we entered the shop, Loo nodded to Jeremy, who went off to the back room, and returned with a tiny leather box, which he handed mutely to Loo.

"Tomorrow is going to be a huge day for you Cait." Loo began, "You'll be getting so many gifts to mark the occasion that you won't remember who to thank. Then there's that small matter of your new *magical appendage.* I wanted to get in first … so maybe then you'll remember." He handed me the box. "It's a pinkie ring," he blurted out, before I could open it. I guess he didn't want me getting any notions.

It *was* a pinkie ring — so suited to my particular pinkie and my taste. A thin gold band with three tiny dark green emeralds set in a row. "That's you, me and Ol'Ben," Loo explained, reddening a bit in the face. "Moira popped by Brazil to pick out the dark green emeralds herself, like she was off to the corner store, and Jeremy put them in this setting for me, with pure Nethermost gold."

I tried it on and it fit beautifully. "How did you know …?"

"Rhue, of course, I measured her finger. But I chose it all by myself, the design I mean." Well, that did it. That made me mist up — and in public too. "Is it okay?" Loo looked worried. "Are those tears of joy?"

I stood on my tippy toes to get up close. "It's … just … perfect!" I breathed, brushing his lips lightly with mine. He responded by pulling me closer, recapturing my lips with his own and holding them hostage in a tender, lingering embrace.

No mistaking that one. That was passion.

*****

While the bio pods inside the cavern had obviously been created with the assistance of magic, the homes in the outer community could have been erected by tradesmen from Alta, they looked that normal. In fact, this settlement was not unlike Alta, except for a shocking lack of vegetation. Though not extravagant, these outdoor homes were well constructed and properly maintained, solidly built of thick rock and wood in order to withstand the subzero conditions. The buildings had been placed along a five kilometre central lane with some short cul-de-sacs branching off at intervals.

It was likely a lack of imagination on my part, but I had expected the actual entrance gate into Nethermost would be a sheer rock face in a mountain, to match to the look of the outer border gate. But of course it wasn't. It looked more like the entrance to a subway. There were no mountains in sight on this side, and the entrance to the downward portal was camouflaged by a massive wall of boulders all along the entire five kilometres of the northern perimeter. This wall was guarded 24/7 by militia in kiosks, every hundred metres or so, armed with swords, longbows, and nunchucks.

There was nothing of particular interest outside the cavern besides the residential homes and one massive inflatable tennis dome, the headquarters for the travelling road show, known as *Magic is Real*. Apparently they resurrected this structure each spring, as both a rehearsal and a performance space, packing it up again in early October when the first snows begin. Inside the dome was a skating rink sized performance space, ovular in shape and surrounded by bleachers on all sides. But on this day it was tarted up like a Barnum and Bailey extravaganza, complete with vendors walking the aisles with popcorn, chips, and cold drinks. The audience was full of fun seekers; the two fancy staging areas on the polished stone floor were poised for takeoff.

At five p.m. exactly, the lights lowered in the audience, and a single spot shone down on a tiny fairy in a top hat hovering three metres above centre stage, an oversized microphone grasped in both hands. "Ladies and gentlemen," he squeaked, "boys and girls, magicians and non magicals … welcome to the greatest luminary experience of your life! Welcome to *Horoscopy: Your Future Foretold*!"

And with that, a rush of fairies dropped from the rafters weaving a pattern of fireworks midair, which rose like Aladdin's flying carpet, flew around the outer rim of the bleachers, then fell like snowflakes to the floor. This was followed by a ring of Magicians entering the stage from all sides, flicking colourful sparks off whips and sending them in the direction of a gasping audience.

"This is already better than last year," Rhue whispered to me, "and that one was marvellous." She leaned forward for a better view.

The performances were flawless — one act overlapping another seamlessly, as the audience's attention bounced from one stage to the other. Jugglers tossed and caught flaming batons in ever increasing numbers, then those batons became white doves which vanished into the rafters on their final throw. Tightrope walkers not only danced *on* their high wires, but *under* them as well, tipping themselves over completely, hanging down like bats, holding on by their toes alone. Aerialists floating ten metres above the floor on ribbons of fabric, dropped to within a hair's width of the ground, then reversed like an old motion picture reel and rolled back up using their core strength alone.

As the acrobats faded into darkness, fog rolled in and with it singers appeared back lit from the coloured mist, dancing in silhouette, while filling the air with song. At the end of the first chorus, front lights lit their beaming faces and sparkling costumes as musicians joined the singers on stage. Their instruments bounced in vivid colours, shooting light beams to the musical beat throughout the dome. Leaving their instruments to play on their own, the musicians lent voices to the singers, expanding the volume and texture of their powerful refrain.

The finale fused it all into one melodic surge — performers blended their talents to raise the rafters quite literally in song. The birds scattered into nothingness; the self playing instruments rose above both stages; aerialists somersaulted and froze in air; contortionists tied themselves into bows — and all raised their collective voices in harmony: "All Hail Nethermost! All Hail Swayer Nicola, All Hail Rhue and Cait!"

The final chorus of voices gave way to instrumental music alone while a trap door in the floor slid aside to release hundreds of brightly coloured balls into the air. As the music softened and faded, the balls alone remained, silently hovering over an audience holding its breath. All eyes focused on the balls, watching as they evaporated slowly into fairy dust, wafting tiny white leaves of paper about, each one bearing a secret — a 'future foretold'. The leaves floated through the crowd until each one identified its own personal target — the individual palm of a predestined audience member.

A mesmerized crowd was silently compelled to open their fortunes at once. Mine said: *You are destined for greatness*. Peeking to my left, I saw Loo read his, chuckle and whisper, "I knew that." To my right, Rhue read her fortune, screwed it up and looked sour.

The hush was truly eerie, as everyone reflected upon their 'fortunes foretold', the spell finally breaking by the sound of a single person clapping. A stunned audience revived from their stupor *en masse* roaring their approval, sustaining this applause until each performer had taken their bow. I felt elated, light hearted and drenched in sweat, having given myself over to the experience quite utterly.

*****

It was an evening of elegance, the anniversary eve of our births, and trays of the finest foods and drinks were circulating. Everyone brought their company manners. Ol'Ben was the most impressive, in a bespoke black evening suit and silk bow tie, shaking hands, laughing easily, and accepting honours quite immodestly for his part in our births. Loo looked so handsome all dressed in a well fitted black tux, no tie but an impressive rhinestone stud at the top of his crisp black shirt. Shin's robes had extra colour and flow, Aunt Moira's choice of gown was predictably impeccable, and Aileen's red diaphanous number was positively daring.

While Rhue and I had decided to cooperate with Aileen's dressmaker and stylist, we felt that our presentation should reflect our differences as much as our similarities. Rhue therefore wore a simple long gown of sparkling teal, with a single green gem about the throat and emerald stud earrings, her hair woven into a work of art. In contrast, I wore peach chiffon, closely hugging my contours above the waist, but gathered into yards of flowing fabric to the floor. My hair fell loosely about my shoulders in soft tresses. My only jewelry pieces were tiny emerald stud earrings given to me by my aunt, and my emerald pinkie ring — now my most treasured possession. As Rhue and I made our entrance into my grandparents' receiving area, there were such gasps and ooo's from everyone that I had to hold my breath to keep the unsophisticated giggles from surfacing.

Grandpa Fergus went about the room once more charging glasses with wine, then stood on a stool and cleared his throat. "Gentlefolk, please be upstanding." The room hushed. "Tonight we are poised once again on the threshold of a great moment. Nineteen years ago on this very night, we were a community of one mind, as we nervously awaited the safe arrival of the regal offspring."

Voices muttered in the background, "Here, here!"

"Tonight we again stand as a community of one mind. Our babies have grown into strong beautiful women, powerful members of this community, and future leaders full of promise!"

More voices, "To strong leadership!" … other voices admonishing, "Hush, give him his moment!"

"Gentlefolk all, I give you Rhue and Cait O'Quinn, heirs both to the throne of Nethermost!"

Louder voices calling out, "Cait …Rhue … Nethermost … Long life to you … to us all!"

I made the rounds with Shin for a good portion of the evening, as she introduced me to people I 'should know'. Then I shifted my allegiance to Ol'Ben and tried to persuade him to sit and let others come to him. But he was having none of it, until Mánús crept up on him that is and growled in his ear, which made him 'sit and stay'.

All evening I kept trying to catch my sister's eye. All evening she avoided mine. It was so uncharacteristic, so worrying. When she thought she wasn't being watched, she dropped her pleasant façade and became sulky, sad.

I finally caught up with Loo, just as he was leaving, insisting there was something that 'needed doing' before the next day's celebration. "You were just going to leave then, without saying goodbye?" I admonished.

"No, I was just going to do this … then scarper." He kissed my cheek briefly and was gone.

By midnight people were beginning to disperse and, by one a.m., we saw off the last of our guests. Aunt Moira and I had decided earlier that, having not contributed to the preparation in any way, we would manage the cleanup. And so the elders were sent to their beds, along with Rhue, who looked pale and was complaining of headache.

It felt good to work alongside my aunt, just the two of us again. I used the opportunity to share my ever niggling concern. "We haven't settled on our talents yet, Aunt Moira."

"You will dearie, you will. You will be standing on that platform tomorrow in the presence of all who love you, and that moment of clarity will come at last. Trust me … it will come."

The doorbell sounded, followed by a rapping on the wood. When we failed to respond immediately, knuckle rapping turned into fist pounding. Within a minute Grandpa Fergus was by our side, nunchuck in hand.

"Stand back. I will get it." He looked through the peephole, then slid the bolt aside and opened the door .

A sergeant and a corporal of the boundary guards stood on our stoop, presenting themselves with an air of authority. The corporal was lowering an unconscious man to the ground; the sergeant held tightly onto another bound at the wrists. "We regret the disturbance Elder O'Quinn," said the sergeant, "but we caught these two men at the border gate effecting an escape. This one insisted we bring him here." The senior officer nodded his head toward the manacled man, who only now raised his head.

Loo!

"I can explain everything," he said.

Chapter 23: Double Deception

By now the entire household was awake, huddled in the front foyer and peering through the doorway. Fergus waived us back and asked the grim cast to come in. Then he closed the front door quickly to avoid the attentions of gossip mongers and alarmists.

Loo was plopped on the floor and landed with an awkward oof, while the unconscious man was laid on the settee. The latter was showing signs of arousal, struggling into an upright position and in doing so revealed his identity — Donal Fadden.

"Don't let him wake up," warned Loo, "whatever you do. That man can walk through walls. I saw him. Please Aileen, zap him or something!"

Aileen went up to the stupefied Donal and put her hand on his forehead. He was out like a light again. She sighed, checked his pulse, and remarked, "That may not have been the best use of my talent."

"No, Grandma Aileen, it wasn't!" Rhue screamed, running to Donal and pushing her aside roughly. "Zap *him*, Grandma … Zap *Loo!*"

"Oh no you don't!" Ol'Ben stepped forward and placed himself between Loo and Aileen. "I've known this young man since he was a little gaffer. He's been like a second son."

"That doesn't mean he's innocent!" Rhue shouted in response.

"No," Ol'Ben agreed. He took a beat, looked at Rhue with pitying eyes, and slowed his reaction to diffuse some of the tension in the room. "What I was trying to say … is that he should at least be allowed to explain."

The sergeant from the Border Patrol agreed. "Someone's got to start talking. Or we can wait for Intersect Security, and do it all at the station."

I went over to Loo and crouched by his side. He was battered and bleeding, in need of medical care. But I took Ol'Ben's lead and voiced my concerns quietly. "Did these soldiers do this to you?"

"No, these guys were great!" Loo attested, "I'm glad they were around. They kind of saved my butt — and maybe more."

"What do you mean 'maybe more'?

"Show them what you found on the ground," he said to the sergeant, "when you got to us … show them … please?"

The sergeant reached into his tunic, pulled out a battered piece of canvas and handed it to Grandpa Fergus who smoothed it and stared in astonishment. Even before I had moved in closer I knew what it was. "Where did you get this young man?"

"I pulled it directly from the hands of that thief, just as he was dissolving into that boulder by the gate. I hauled his forearm — and this painting — back just in time."

"Hold on Loo," I said, "Take this back a step or two. You're giving us the end, without the beginning and the middle."

"Right … good call Cait." Loo took a snootful of air and released it slowly. "Remember Cait I'd been telling you how something wasn't right about this guy, and how I'd been watching him?"

"Yes, we spoke about it a couple of times."

"You did?" asked Rhue, "if you were so worried, why didn't you say something? You could have said."

"No, Rhue, I couldn't. I didn't have anything solid on the guy, just a feeling. I didn't want to stir the pot if there was nothing there to stir. So I watched him — a lot. Then tonight at your party I saw him doing something really weird. I saw him walk straight into Rhue's and Cait's bedroom when he thought no one was looking."

Rhue retorted, "That's evidence of nothing! Donal has been in our room plenty of times."

"On his own?" I asked, plenty creeped out at this thought.

"No, never!" She shot back angrily.

"You're both missing the point!" Loo insisted. "I said he walked straight *into* the bedroom, I didn't say he opened the door first — cuz he didn't. He walked through the door itself — through the wood! And he didn't come out again!"

"How could that be?" Rhue asked.

"Exactly. So I excused myself and darted outside for a quick look see, and there he was halfway through the outside wall on the east side of the pod, where your bedroom is Rhue, carrying that rolled up canvas. I know that canvas. I saw it in Shin's hands that day in Alta. That's what she went back for when those bad dudes were on our heels. I could hardly forget it; it nearly got us all killed."

"That's true," I affirmed quietly.

"Right," Loo continued. "So I ducked down until he went by, and I followed him at a discreet distance since I've got no magic *what's it* myself. It was plenty hard to keep up with him, cuz he kept taking short cuts through walls and the like. I nearly lost him a couple of times. That's why he succeeded in starting through that barrier before I could grab him. I pounced onto what was still visible and held on like fury! Guess his arm was still solid because he was holding the painting.

"He's a strong S.O.B., but then so am I. It was a toss up which one of us would succeed. But I shook his wrist 'til he dropped that canvas and had to come back to retrieve it, which is when I jumped on top and wrestled him to the ground. Now that we were both completely on this side of the border, we went at it hammer and tong. But his blows were hitting home more than mine, so I guess he was getting the better of me. That and the fact that some of my punches went straight through him. Then these two guards came up with big flashlights and one of them shone his in Donal's eyes which caused him to stop to blink. Luckily I had just one more punch left in me, so I hauled off and socked him a good one — right in the jaw. That's when his lights went out. And that's when these gentlemen stepped in and arrested us both. I don't blame them. It looked pretty bad."

"I can only confirm those final statements, Elder O'Quinn," said the sergeant. "I thought it odd that this young man wanted to be brought straight to you, sir, but it wasn't completely inappropriate, as part of your council duties is to serve as judge and arbitrator. I hope I did right."

"You did well sir," Grandpa Fergus agreed. "But hold off for now on the arrests. If this Donal fellow can truly walk through objects, no jail, manacles, or hover van will be able to hold him."

"Doesn't Donal get a chance to defend himself too?" asked Rhue.

"Perhaps," Grandpa Fergus replied, pulling his granddaughter into him his arms in a comforting embrace. "But consider, my dear, if Donal truly has the talent of intangibility, a rare talent I am bound to say that I've never seen in humans before now, then he just may choose to run rather than to offer a defence. We must consider this carefully.

"Aileen, my dear, we need to convene the Elders' Council right here in our home within the hour. And would you please call for the Healer and the Mesmerizer? This situation needs the full power of the council to debate it — and a bit of medical care."

*****

My father was stating his case to the Council and members of his own family. "Just give me two hours with the both of them. I'll get some answers."

"Not unless this man can be restrained," Shin warned, "I have a grave suspicion that Loo may be right about our peril."

"Who is Loo to us?" Rhue asked, still very much on the defensive. "He's a newcomer. Why believe him over Donal? Doesn't Donal get extra credit for being a Nethermost citizen?"

"We none of us get extra credit when it comes to espionage." Shin explained. "And *both* sides of this conflict are Nethermost citizens. What possible motive could a non citizen have — what stake in the outcome of this struggle?"

"I-I have a suggestion … if I may," I piped in, plucking up the courage to step to the fore. I'd been idling at the curb of this debate for a while now, watching and listening, and an idea suddenly popped into my brain. "If … now don't get mad Rhue … I said *if*, Donal Fadden is a spy and *if* he walks through solids, then it stands to reason that this is not his first border crossing. There could have been dozens. And if" (I looked at Rhue again, hold up my hands in a gesture of peace), "*if* he's been across the border before now, leaking information — as and when — what are the chances that Peadar has been briefed about some pretty vital pieces of intelligence already — like that Rhue and I are the royal twins, like that we're coming of age soon, like that the Council is raising a militia cuz they think the time to resist is fast approaching?"

The councillors muttered amongst themselves, and the atmosphere in the room became exponentially bluer.

"That being the case," I continued, slowly building my argument, "we may have lost the element of surprise on several fronts — strategic advantages that we'd been counting on. Peadar may have researched the power of twins, for instance, and may be fortifying his defences. So," I paused here because I had finally reached the strength of my argument and wanted their complete attention. "So Councillors, we need to find another strategic advantage — another surprise."

"Exactly!" Shin chirruped excitedly, "And if I'm reading you correctly Cait, you have thought of a good one? Am I right?"

"You are … I think … but it all hinges on you Shin, and how fast you can paint. What if you were to paint a fake scene that *looks* like a prevision but isn't. One that would take our evil relative on a wild goose chase. Dirty it up in your own special way to look like the other one from the outside … you know like it's been through a battle … then put a little magic wiggle into it so that it moves like a prevision and then …"

" … and then wipe Mr. Fadden's memory," Shin added, now completely on my wave length, "place him, with the painting, near the border with a dusting of waking powder on his eyelids. If he returns the painting, it has all been a nonsense and everyone is happy. If he escapes, as Mr. Buckley suggests he will do, then this is an admission of guilt. The Apparatchik will have disinformation to throw him off the scent. Mr. Fadden will be out of our hair which is just as well, because he would have been an nightmare to incarcerate. If Mr. Fadden comes back, he will be dealt with. If he stays with Peadar, we will meet again on the battlefield some day. Brilliant! As far as I can see, there is no downside to this."

"Providing you can paint fast enough Ambassador Sinead," Grandpa Fergus added.

"Give me plenty of cups of tea, and I'm your girl," Shin boasted.

"Meanwhile, Loo's got to be jailed!" Rhue added. "If you're going to *chemically* restrain my boyfriend, you can *physically* restrain hers!"

I paused, stunned at the shock and grief in her poor little face. My heart was breaking for her. "Good idea!" I said.

"What? Why?" Loo asked.

"Because… it will give you the best of alibis and reduce the possibility of error. Don't look so worried Loo, I hear the beds are quite comfy in the hoosegow," I smirked.

Aunt Moira and I accompanied Shin to her studio, set her up at her easel, her paints and turps all around her, and produced cups of tea on demand. It was going to be a real nail biter to get this critical prop prepared, to set that stage and to have the actors in place while it was still dark outside. We needed to work fast.

In the end, we allowed ourselves to have a bit of fun with the painting. We set our fake scene at a gold refinery, where liquid gold was being over fracked. This would take the focus away from the palace entirely. Next, Shin painted an image of Peadar as the central figure. That would get his interest — the narcissist. Finally, at my suggestion, Shin added an ambiguous figure with a tattooed arm entering from the foreground, holding the regal sword gold tipped with poison. Aunt Moira prepared the drying element to cook the paint; Shin concocted a dirty wash to make the canvas more convincing; the magic squiggle Shin added moved the sword up and down over Peadar's painted image — just like he did to our grandfather Riley — the bastard! By four a.m. we stood back to view the finished piece. It was superb!

But … time was running out!

We rushed to the border gate to meet up with Father and Grandpa Fergus, who were standing by impatiently with the border guards and a mesmerized Donal. They returned Donal as closely as possible to his escape position. After Shin applied a hint of revival dust to his eyelids, we took cover and waited. As rehearsed, as soon as Donal showed signs of recovery, the two guards made some noise in the distance like they were responding to a disturbance further north. The rest of us stayed behind our cover, and watched the drama unfold.

*****

By six o'clock in the morning, I was waiting outside Intersect Security with a cup of foamy coffee in my hand, and handed it to Loo as he exited the building, "Morning."

"You're wrong," he grumbled. "Those beds aren't the least bit comfortable." I laughed as he jiggled his joints about and tried to tuck his bloodied shirt into his ripped trousers. "What about Donal?" he asked.

"Scarpered" I reported, "dived straight through the rock."

"And the fake?"

"Went along for the ride. An inspired performance by Shin, I thought, although I take full credit for the best bits of that fiction."

Loo let loose a howl, grabbed me up and swung me about. Then he threw one arm about my neck and led me towards Tunnel P, weaving like a drunkard on his way home from a bender. "Come on Cait, let's get you magicked! Happy Birthday!"

Chapter 24: Giving and Receiving

It took the efforts of most of the O'Quinn household to pull Rhue together that morning before our ascension ceremony. Grandpa Fergus made her coffee — she let it chill. Grandma Aileen made her waffles — she pulled them apart untasted. She just sat on a stool in the midst of the breakfast rush, moping, lacklustre.

It was ten o'clock and our ceremony was at noon. I looked across the kitchen to my aunt and nodded. We choreographed a singly intended move towards Rhue. Each taking a hand, we pulled her off her perch and waltzed her down the hall to the bathroom.

Aunt Moira turned on the rain spout and we stepped into the shower stall as a unit, nighties still on, Rhue still between us. We lathered her up and soaped her hair, throwing globs of foam at one another — like children and their bath bubbles — until Rhue joined in and returned fire twofold, laughing hysterically. Then suddenly she was no longer laughing, no longer part of the game, but had sunk to her knees, in gurgles of anguish, trying to catch her breath. We dropped down to her level to encircle her, letting the warm rain pummel away our fatigue, and cleanse tears and regrets, until Rhue was silent once more. Then we left her to compose and dry herself, while we waited for her in the bedroom.

"The world is full of mankind using love to betray womankind, dearie," Aunt Moira murmured, "Women do the same to their men. It has ever been thus." She gave Rhue a kiss on the forehead, then picked up her wet things and left the room, calling out as she departed, "We leave at eleven thirty sharp!"

I sat on my bed across from Rhue. "I guess you really loved him, huh?"

"Yes … no … I don't know … maybe."

"Well, that's clear then," I mocked gently.

She went over to her dresser and opened her jewelled music box to extract a tiny ball of white paper which she handed to me. I recognized it as her fortune from the Horoscopy performance we'd seen hours before. "Read it," she said.

I smoothed the slip out and read aloud, "*You will be betrayed.*"

I refolded it neatly, handed it back, and searched for the correct words to console. "Rhue, I can't begin to imagine what it's like to lose a love ..."

"No, you cannot Cait," she pouted, flopping down on her mattress again. "But I cannot let you think that I am mourning the loss of a love. It is a matter far worse. I despise myself!"

"But you weren't to know!" I protested, rising to my feet now and pacing, "How *could* you know?"

"Loo knew! How could he know from his brief exposure to Donal — and me not?"

"Loo has hidden depths and ... and ... 'love is blind'?" I tried pathetically.

"I did not love him Cait! We went out — occasionally — that is all. There can be no love right now, no affairs of the heart. There will be a better time in Nethermost's future for feelings of love. I am not that foolish. I have been ridiculous in other ways." She flopped down on the floor now, folded herself up and held her head in her hands. "When I received that fortune from the travellers, do you know what I felt?"

"Well, you looked angry ... upset."

"I was to be sure. And torn between belief and disregard. I dismissed it, yet all the while I felt that this was no mere frivolity, but the truth. But Cait, not for one moment did I feel that it was Donal who would betray me!"

"No? Then who ..."

"You! I thought the note was referring to you! How could I have possibly thought that? But I did. And it festered within me like an abscess all last evening until I could not think straight. Thank goodness I was able to hide it from you."

"You're not that good an actress, Rhue. I knew something was very wrong."

"Oh," Rhue dropped her gaze and picked at her fingers, chipping away at her nail polish.

I reached over and stilled her hands. "Stop that! We don't have time for another manicure! Now, listen here, missy. You're a member of an elite set of warriors — *unusual* but nonetheless powerful. Collectively you are a fierce opponent of the forces of evil. Direct that self loathing towards a more deserving target. Weaponize it against Great Uncle Peadar. Ugh, the very name!"

"But what about the Ascension Ceremony? We are not prepared. What will we ask for?"

"You know," I replied, feeling just as strong and focussed as my aunt said I'd be. "I think I've got this covered. Just follow my lead. And Rhue…"

"Yes, dearest."

"Happy Birthday!"

*****

It was nearly noon at The Intersect and it was standing room only. When I had waited for Loo on this very spot six hours before, it had been deserted, devoid of creature kind. Now, hours later, a dais stood under The Intersect Clock that hung suspended in midair. The platform was constructed of polished hardwood, hexagonal in shape, symbolically representing all six magical species of Nethermost. At each angled corner of the hexagon, a member of the Magic Council stood waiting. A stone pedestal had been placed centre stage, upon which sat a plain wooden chest the size of a bread bin. Each Council representative was dressed in scarlet robes, Rhue and I in white robes. As applicants, we stood to either side of the central pedestal.

That was the extent of the frippery allowed by the Magic Council for this ritual. Although families could plan celebrations before or after such an event to be as extravagant as they wished, the ascension ceremony itself was intentionally unadorned.

I was still mostly ignorant about the Magic Council and its hierarchy, but I had been schooled enough to match each species of magician to their primary role in essence …
Fairy — horticulturalist   Healy — seer
Canomorph — warrior   Dwarf — stone mason
Elf — forester   Ziraph — healer

The clock struck twelve — the ceremony began. A long necked ziraph named Afric stepped towards us. "Cait and Rhue O'Quinn, are you prepared with your petitions?"

"We are," we answered in unison.

"Cait, as the elder twin, you may select first. What talent do you ask of the Magic Council?"

"I ask for the talent of intangibility," I announced, with no hint of emotion. It was obviously not what the Council, or anyone, expected. Council members looked to one another, with more than one raised eyebrow amongst them, while they considered my request. At last they each nodded to their ziraph leader who then opened the box, searched for and finally found the exact thin gold band. She placed this ring in the palm of my right hand.

"Cait, please place this band on the middle finger of your right hand which will give you the privilege of possessing the talent of intangibility."

I took the ring, but instead of adorning the middle finger of my own hand, as everyone present expected, I walked over to my sister and placed it on her middle finger instead, making the following pledge, "Rhue, I freely give you my talent for your forever use." Then, I pushed the ring into place on her hand and stepped to one side, leaving Rhue with Afric centre stage. The audience gasped and rumbled lowly.

Without even raising an eyebrow, Afric continued. "Rhue, your selection is no less important than that of your sister. What talent do you ask of the Magic Council?"

Rhue looked at me with a hint of a smile and said: "I ask for the talent of time travel."

This petition, a more common request, received instant Council approval, and the ziraph elder opened the box again to retrieve the more common band imbued with the talent for time travel. She placed it on the palm of Rhue's right hand.

"Rhue, please place this band on the middle finger of your right hand which will give you the privilege of possessing the talent of time travel."

Rhue took her ring, walked up to me and placed it on the middle finger of my right hand, saying: "Cait, I freely give you my talent for your forever use," and she pushed this band into place on my middle finger. The audience could barely hold still.

Now Afric declared, "As much as these sisters have freely given their talents to each other, it is the rare decision of this Council to grant them the use not only of their own talent, but that of their genetic identical — in perpetuity. Congratulations both on your strength and wisdom. To seal the bargain you must merge the two rings.

I'm not sure how I knew to do this, but I took up my sister's right hand once more and touched my ring to hers. In doing so, the rings merged, turning from solid into liquid gold, absorbing into our skin — no longer mere tokens of power but the nucleus of a grand metamorphosis. As we bowed in thanks to the Council, our white robes turned to scarlet, and our audience exploded with an almighty cheer.

Afric

Chapter 25: Community Hearts

"Do not even attempt to use those powers, until you have received my instructions first," warned Shin, at our gift exchange that afternoon. "Open all doors before you walk through, and stay in your own time lane!"

*****

This was the second of three celebrations of the day and for me, of all the birthday events, this would be the most significant. In the direct aftermath of the ceremony, we were gathered at our home for the clan event, although Shin, Mánús and Loo had been included as honorary members as well. I was raised with a regretful lack of relatives. When I was a little kid, Aunt Moira was generous to a fault, but our celebrations always consisted of just her and me. She thought she could fill those holes in my family tree with lavish elegance and garish gargoyles, which never filled the void. But this occasion truly had the sense of a relaxed get together — no pomp, no company manners. It was thrilling! I could think of nothing better.

Aileen and Loo had flexed their cookery muscles, this time with our favourite finger foods. And no round the table nonsense — we balanced plates on our knees, in easy chairs or seated on the floor. For 'afters', the central coffee table had been stacked with wrapped gifts and one double birthday cake. It was not just exciting for the birthday girls. Everyone was atwitter with anticipation. "Will they like my gift best"?

Rhue and I had foreseen this scenario, and had prepared a benevolent *coup*, a 'turning of the tables', so to speak. We had discussed this beforehand and had agreed that what we wanted most as a birthday gift was to become the givers. With Shin as our go between, we had commissioned the goldsmith to mint special issue coins with a limited edition of ten. On the face side of the gold piece, was the effigy of our current Swayer Nicola engraved underneath with the single word NETHERMOST. On the reverse was the old palace, the traditional seat of power, with FOREVER engraved beneath. As Grandpa Fergus made to call the company to order, Rhue and I stepped forward and gazumped him. "No, no, Grandpa, not this time!" said Rhue. "Let us begin as we mean to carry on — in our pledge of honour to our kith and kin." Then we circulated the room stopping at each loved one, dropping our rare coin into the outstretched palm of each, and sealing our gift with a double cheeked kiss. The room misted up with tears of love and nostalgia. We had united and conquered!

"Well," Ol'Ben cleared his throat and wiped his nose with his cotton hankie. "What can I say to beat that? I did kind of agonize about what I could do for my great-granddaughters that might hold meaning for them. I'm just plain country folk, after all, an old geezer who sells non magic stuff in a boring old store, completely out of step with the world." We all protested but he continued just the same, "And this world I'm living in now, my life with all of you, is so full of wonder … and excitement. So I asked myself, what could I give my girls that would make a difference?" Rhue and I went over to hug him again, to reassure him that having him with us was blessing enough. Still he ploughed on.

" … but I did think of something rather special … had to ask Moira to rummage about in the ruins ... but ladies — great-granddaughters both — nothing would make me happier than if you accepted these." He handed two identical boxes to us, "These are my most treasured possessions … my dear wife's engagement and wedding bands. She was your great-grandmother after all, and your own mother is named after her. So, if you don't mind a keepsake from the more *vanilla* side of the family." The company tittered.

In my box, was Grandma Nora's wedding band — ten little diamond chips set into a thin rose gold band. In Rhue's box, the matching engagement ring — a one third carat diamond solitaire, set in rose gold offset with two diamond chips to either side. They were emblems of love and a humble reflection of Ol'Ben's youth, and of the leaner times after the big war when he and Grandma Nora struggled for money. Even as their coffers increased, I knew from the stories Ol'Ben would tell, Grandma Nora never wanted to replace her rings with a gaudier set. This was her reminder, he said, that love was really enough.

If every gift was going to be so emotional, I thought, I was going to need a couple of fresh aspirin.

Grandma Aileen and Grandpa Fergus were next to the plate. "Rhue and Cait, you are of the first bloodline it is true," Grandpa Fergus declared hastily before anyone else could step forward before him. "But you are also members of the clan O'Quinn, a family that has always taken pride in its honourable history of service to the crown."

"To represent our clan connection," Grandma Aileen continued, "we offer these bespoke pendants bearing the O'Quinn family crest — a reminder of our commitment to all duly crowned Swayers of Nethermost. May that be you someday!" The crested medallion, dangling on a simple gold chain, bore the symbol of a figure kneeling before a crown and a throne. This time the entire family applauded.

Our father stepped forward. "Rhue and Cait, I find shopping and gift selection quite beyond me. Furthermore, I must represent your absent mother. I am your father and a warrior both. As a parent, I love you dearly and would give my life to protect you. As a warrior, I want to arm you, to keep you safe. With this gift I hope to do both. Although the conflict you face is unlikely to be on bloody fields of battle, there may still be occasion for a subtle but effective defence. Please accept these dirks, which may be secreted upon your person for that extra bit of *confidence*, shall we say." He handed us long thin boxes concealing polished steel blades with plain silver handles engraved with our initials, sheathed in tooled leather guards. A murmur of approval from the family.

"I too must concern myself, at all times, with your safety." Shin now declared. "Although it may not have always seemed to be the case, I have ever had the welfare of this family at heart. Of this I am clear. There will be times going forward when you find yourselves in the dark — actually and figuratively. I therefore offer you these wands with the magic to light your darkened paths and to ease your fears." From one of the boxes, she pulled out an eight centimetre rod made of *vitreous of life* crystal fused onto a carved ebony handle. "*Fiat lux,*" she commanded, and the rod glowed with a blue/green light. "*Finis lux,*" she called again, and the light extinguished itself. "Be careful who knows you have these," she warned.

"Well I feel silly," said Aunt Moira, "I thought only of this as being your birthdays. And in upper Earth society, these things are often commemorated with birthstones. May is the month of the emerald, quite the most beautiful gemstone in my opinion. I gave you both your gifts last night — the emerald stud earrings that you wore with those gorgeous gowns. But I didn't forget today's events altogether, so I popped over to Paris to bring you a selection of the latest in perfume. Select what you like and I'll return the rest. You are girls still after all, no matter what expectations have been lain at your feet."

Rhue and I threw our arms about her and twirled her around with girlish laughter. Thank goodness for that dose of normality, I thought, in an otherwise surreal world.

"Mánús wants me to interpret his gift to you both," Shin announced. Mánús stepped forward and stood before this small audience in humanoid form. Then he began to transmogrify right before us — first into the doglike shape I had first loved, then into the werewolf configuration I had feared, and back again into the soldier version I had now come to expect. "This is Mánús' gift to you both." Shin explained. "He means to pledge his life, in all its forms, for your protection. It may well be the most valuable gift you will receive today — or ever for that matter."

All this while, Loo stood off to one side. One gift remained on the table, addressed to Rhue. Aunt Moira handed it to her now. "I know this one is for you Rhue, although the giver seems to be very modest," she commented, looking in Loo's direction. Rhue opened it to find a living orchid with three deep purple blooms and two more in bud, resting in a deep green glass bowl — a rarity in these parts. "How absolutely beautiful!" she effused.

"Well, I just noticed that there weren't a lot of flowers up here. And I know how much your sister enjoys the elegance of orchids. She visits them all the time at the solarium in Hub Medical. Just thought, you know, if Cait likes them so much, they must be something special."

Rhue went up to him and kissed his cheek, "Special indeed, Loo, thank you. But what about your gift for Cait?"

"Ah … she got hers yesterday," he explained modestly. I lifted my left hand into the air to show off my pinkie ring. All the women gathered around to inspect. "You know dearie, he made quite a fuss about this ring's design. It had to be just right," Aunt Moira told me softly.

"It's a friendship ring, Aunt Moira. The stones represent Ol'Ben, Loo and me."

Aunt Moira corrected me, "It's a love token … and it's a promise."

*****

When Rhue and I were born nineteen years before, as my grandfather had told us, the entire community celebrated, with elegant balls and street parties. So, for this final anniversary celebration of our birth, it seemed appropriate to hold a community wide event. The Council of Elders sponsored a series of street and tunnel parties for any or all of its twenty-five hundred citizens.

The main venue for the parties was held under the *Magic is Real* dome. All the food contributions were pot luck — bring a dish, fill a plate — or two. Ol'Ben sat at the entranceway with Rhue and me framing him, greeting and shaking hands with everyone as they entered. There were no rules of conduct beyond the dictates of mutual respect. People could be sedate in their dignity or crazy in their repressed craving for a roaring good time. I witnessed both.

The great room was tarted up with streamers and balloons, and had been edged with a single row of makeshift tables crowded with hundreds of potluck dishes, each trying to outdo the other in deliciousness. At the end of every second table, enormous bowls of punch were set out, filled with weird brews of mysterious origins. People loaded their plates and mugs and sat on the bleachers in groups scattered throughout the audience sections, some returning several times for refills. As they ate and chattered, the *Magic is Real* irregulars weaved their way through the crowds eating fire, walking on stilts, juggling balls, somersaulting — something for the amusement of all.

At around nine o'clock, the overhead lights were dimmed, and spotlights were raised to flash coloured beams back and forth across the darkened room. Music was cranked to full pitch, and the dancing began. People were bopping and rocking to the oldies, moving with the dance steps taught them years ago by our mother Nora in her glory days, along with a few new steps that Loo was trying to insert into their repertoire, with limited success. The canvas of the dome reverberated so much that Ol'Ben was becoming uneasy, shifting restlessly in his folding canvas chair and holding his hands over his ears. I gave Loo a heads up to leave.

We returned Ol'Ben in a hover cab to P49 and settled him in with a book and some tea, leaving the others to party into the wee hours. Then Loo and I set out again, on foot this time, to visit some of the smaller tunnel parties in the main cavern. These more intimate groupings provided their own unique entertainment with home grown rhythm instruments, guitars and fiddles, bongos and kazoos. Folks raised their voices in song — traditional tunes, for the most part, about happier times. The purity of their voices wafting throughout the tunnels quite captured my heart.

There was one exquisite yet haunting moment I am unlikely to forget — ever — at a party not far from The Intersect where a young girl stood before a group of a hundred or more, as they listened in reverent silence to her sweet *a cappella* voice …

Just to hold a child in life weary arms — a seed of humanity
And view the world through her tiny eyes — I treasure all they see.

Why rant against the shadows, why grieve success unborn
*Why not embrace **the children** — so dear to the soul.*

I stumble into these open hands — a moment of charity,
And pressing onwards with my strength resolved — I sense the community.

Why rant against the shadows, why grieve success unborn
*Why not embrace **the friendship** — so dear to the soul.*

I melt into love's tenderness — a jewel of security,
And trust my secrets to belovèd heart — I feel our eternity.

Why rant against the shadows, why grieve success unborn
*Why not embrace **the lovers** — so dear to the soul.*

Restore inside life soothing havens — pools of tranquility
Build the fresh dreamscapes — creative ideals
Witness astonishing moments — see the possibilities.

Why rant against the shadows, why grieve success unborn

*Why not embrace **each other** — so dear to the soul.*

*So dear to the soul — so dear to **my** ... soul.*

As these final strains echoed throughout the tunnels, I was momentarily imbued with an sense of what it must have been like to have lived through the ruination of a paradise, to have endured a decades long exile in an inhospitable land. What strength it must have taken to turn struggle and loss into survival and promise. And how it could only be achieved by clinging to each other utterly. That was the true story of the folks at Nethermost Gate.

I turned to Loo, who was wiping away a tear of his own. "If I *ever* complain or lose my way Loo," I said, my voice overflowing with feeling, "just remind me of this moment will you?"

He folded me into his arms and held me close.

*****

I can't say that I was sorry to see the back end of that day. I was overstimulated from being on such display, and emotionally drained from all the sentiment expressed. Now, late in the evening, I was grateful for the simplicity of being alone with Loo and Ol'Ben — just like the quiet of those precious nights in our own tiny paradise over The General Store.

"I have a confession to make Ol'Ben," I said, as we lingered over our bedtime cocoa. "Do you remember what we told you, Aunt Moira and I, about your wardrobe being singed in the attack on the store?"

"Yes," he said, "what a load of codswallop that was! As if a villain focused on knocking us to kingdom come would stop to destroy some old clothes. Besides … Moira's already confessed."

"Oh? And what do you think? Are we forgiven?"

"I told her to burn 'em. What do I need them for now? Look at me, I'm gorgeous." He chortled, polishing off his warm drink.

"Are you worried about the store?" I asked. It had certainly been on my mind more than once of late.

"Moira has taken care of that as well," he said. The rivalry between Ol'Ben and Aunt Moira seemed to have taken quite the turn for the better of late, I thought. Our common enemy makes friends of us all. "She's had it fixed up, she says, like new. She let it be known in the village that we'd had an explosion — blaming my potbellied stove. As if! That thing always worked beautifully! I bet she's made some changes of her own as well — *improvements* I'm sure she'd say," he laughed.

"She's circulated the rumour that we've gone off on holiday — some long holiday, what-what? Anyway, the place is being run by some folks from Nethermost Gate for the time being — John and Mary Smith. That's their names, I kid you not! I've met them actually; they're very nice, and quite sensible. They're running the old place now at a greater profit than I ever did. Don't think they need me at all!"

"Do you think you will ever go back?

"I'm not saying yes or no, not just yet. What I am saying is … well … I heard from some of the folks that my granddaughter, Nora — your mother — may still be alive. Is that right?"

"Perhaps. It seems possible that Nicola, her own mother, is still maintaining continent stability over Nethermost, with her balancing talent, and that Nora, as her personal physician, may be fortifying her efforts. So it's now my life's goal to work with those dedicated to their rescue — with all our powers united, if need be. If she is out there, we will find her."

"Good girl! I won't even consider leaving Nethermost Gate until I know her fate."

After the old man had gone to bed, I cuddled up with Loo on the sofa. "Rhue said something to me this morning, Loo, that made me think. She said that there can be no love right now, and that there will be a better time in Nethermost's future for feelings of love. Do you agree with her?"

"I think that Rhue has a cynical view of love, and maybe that Donal guy is to blame. We cannot choose when to love or, to some extent, who to love," Loo replied. He drew me to him and passionately kissed me once again, letting the flats of his palms trail down my body … deliciously… from my neck to my knees. "But if she meant that this is no time for *distraction*, or to be caught up in the passion of *new* love," he sighed, "then I would have to say that she was right."

He kissed me again beginning with my lips, moving slowly down to kiss my breasts, until I ached with desire. Then he stopped himself with a shudder of regret. "Consider that a bookmark of sorts, Cait. You have a job to do … and I'm determined to be your backup, not your distraction. That's got to be our focus from now on, don't you think? Plus there's that small matter of you being a queen of sorts …"

"You're right," I agreed reluctantly, "about our need to focus … not about the queen thing."

*****

Chapter 26: Licensed for Magic

"Let's explore the talent of intangibility first," Shin instructed. She went over to her wall of books with its rolling library ladder and tried to climb onto the first rung, wincing as she did.

"You are in pain, Ambassador," said Rhue. "Please let me assist."

"It's a bit awkward is all," Shin protested. "I can't get this leg to behave at times. But of course, you will be able to retrieve the book I'm looking for more easily. Do you see that red leather volume high up near the ceiling?" Shin pointed five shelves up, "Pull that off the shelf cautiously. It's bound to be dusty."

The book in question was half a metre tall, and thick — very thick. Though Rhue did grab it 'carefully', she nonetheless managed to disturb decades of dust, which now puffed her full in the face, and showered us below. But she struggled down the steps with the monster tome, entitled: <u>Intangibility: Grasping the Ungraspable</u>.

*****

I loved visiting Shin's studio. It was full of character and promise, stuffed with interesting, artistic clutter — blank canvases in one corner, completed canvases in another. One wall was dedicated to books on the subjects of magic and art, for the most part, leather bound and tooled, works of art themselves. There were deep shelves against another wall, heavy with bins of paint tubes, varnish, brushes, palettes, and such supportive mediums as gesso, turpentine and linseed oil. A whiff of chemicals assaulted the nose upon entry, despite the flow through of air.

"I suppose this would be the right time to confess to you both that I do not possess the power of intangibility." Shin continued, "In fact, there's only one species in the realm that does. But we should be able to figure it out. So, let's begin at the beginning, shall we? Page one."

Intangibility

Definition: In non magic terms, intangibility refers to the state of becoming something so undefined or improbable that it is unable to be touched or grasped. Examples would be ideas in the abstract or impossible wishes.

An infusion of magic can take this illusive characteristic to its next level of illogicality. Thus the ungraspable now includes living beings whose transparency allows them, not only to elude capture, but to move through solid matter.

"Well …" she paused looking quite flummoxed, "that seems simple enough. So … I would assume … that you will need to imagine yourself … invisible … or without a body …"

"No, no! That won't do!" A little voice chirruped from the direction of the bookcase. A tiny winged creature appeared from amongst the books on the shelves, flicking library dust from her gossamer wings and diaphanous clothing. She sneezed, flitted over to a nearby workbench and sat down crosslegged. "If you do that, you'll give your noggin a good crack!"

"You're late," said Shin. "Rhue, Cait … meet Zinnia, a Flower Fairy."

"I am never *late*," Zinnia retorted. "No, just eavesdropping before announcing myself is all. You started off well enough Shin, but then you started to go all cattywampus."

At this point, she looked in our direction as if she hadn't noticed us before this very moment. "How do you do," she said, holding out a tiny hand, "Zinnia Flower, at your service. Call me Zee."

"How do you do Zee," I replied. Trying to show the greatest of respect, I went to take her hand only to find myself grabbing at thin air, causing Zee to giggle with glee.

"Now you see why fairies are quite impossible to catch young lady," she declared. "You can see us at times I'll grant you, but try as you might we cannot be caught because we are simply ungraspable."

Rhue and I exchanged an implied raised eyebrow.

"Let's go over the rules of intangibility," Zee stood on the bench before us now for lecture time.

Number One: Don't walk through people. It's an unpleasant sensation for both parties.

She stopped there and sat down again.

"Is that all?" asked Rhue, "It seems like there should be more."

"There are lots of sensible things to consider, of course, like watching where you're going, and only carrying inanimate objects on your person, but you will best find out these thing through practice and experience."

She then handed us two tiny stud pins with the letters 'TL' engraved on them.

"'TL'? What's this for Zee?" I asked.

"It stands for **T**alent **L**earner. Put them on your shirt collars. While you're practicing, it lets people know you are a newly licensed magical, and should therefore be given a wide berth."

"Fair warning," said Shin, "Fairies can be quite the bossy boots."

"Hush, you!" squeaked Zee. "Here's your first exercise … Contrary to what Shin has told you, translucency is very difficult to imagine. Certainly don't imagine yourselves invisible, as she has suggested — that way madness lies. You will not be invisible, you will be *translucent*." She stared at Shin triumphantly. "Imagine instead that the solid you are walking through is curtain fabric, and as you approach it, sweep it back with one arm. Eventually you'll become so good at it, you won't even need the arm motion.

"Try these paintbrushes first. Picture them like feathers." We focussed on the brushes. Then Rhue passed one hand through the stack and back again. "It tickles," she commented.

"It doesn't always tickle," Zee remarked, with an ominous look. "Walls and other thick solids make the body feel quite heavy. It's like walking through treacle."

Zee had us try various small items first, moving up slowly to larger ones. As we walked through objects in Shin's studio, the clutter remained undisturbed. Then she had us walk through our first wall — the thick outer rock wall to Shin's bio pod. Zee wasn't wrong. My body did feel heavier and my footsteps held down by a sucking feeling. But something also she hadn't mentioned. I gulped and swallowed … hard.

"Oh, yes," Zee added. "That's what I was forgetting. The nausea. It can be rough on the tummy."

Our homework that night was a half hour of wall walking in our own bio pod. Before I could sleep that night, I needed a witchy brew for the queasiness.

*****

"Time travel is quite within my own bailiwick," Shin boasted on day two of our accelerated talent orientation.

Zee had turned up for our class again, clearly invested in our tutelage, but sat silently giving Shin the stage.

"We have covered the topic of time travel before now at an introductory level. So you understand already one of the important limitations of this talent. That is, when you travel in time you do not travel in space. So you must start your time leap in the exact place you mean to land. And when you return, you must also launch from that exact same place, or things could go very wrong. They sometimes go wrong in any case. You could be standing in a open field amongst the cows, for example, and leap forward a century only to find yourselves inside the wall of a building!

"There is one more hard and fast rule to obey absolutely with time travel. You must not affect the timeline! If you affect any event or even the mindset of anyone in the past, this may drastically alter the future!"

"Dear me yes! Disastrous!" interjected Zee. "Why I remember…" She stopped mid breath after a withering glance from Shin.

"But what if we need to find something in the past that will help us defeat the Apparatchik?" Rhue asked.

"Is that what you're thinking girls? That there is a clue to be found in the past?"

"We have reason to interpret your painting as being set in the past," I explained.

"Oh … brilliant girls! Of course! The dirty clothes on the floor shows that Peadar was sleeping in these rooms at the time! And this explains your choice of talents too! How exciting! How inspiring! We must take you to the Elders at once."

"The time travel!" shouted Zee, flying before Shin's face and grabbing an ear in her tiny hands to focus Shin's attention. "Finish the time travel tuition first, Shin. One … thing … at … a … time."

"Yes," Shin nodded, "Yes of course. It is really all quite delicious. But … ahem. Your conduct in the past must not affect the future. You can't go back and prevent the coup from happening for instance. It happened. If it had not, for example, would the two of you even have been born?"

"So we can't change the past. Why would we travel there then?" asked Rhue.

"To find a clue, a weakness, a strategy that will inform the future," Shin explained.

"But we may not bring anything back with us?" I asked for clarification.

"Only what you had on your body when you entered the past can be brought back."

"Can we take photographs or sketch things? Can we ask anyone from the past for information?"

"Yes to the first two questions, but be very careful with that last one. You need to ask yourself, 'will my question alert this individual in any way or change the course of their future'? If the answer could be yes, then you must not ask it."

The exercises we worked on to understand this talent involved moving in time back and forth within the current studio session only, which was very confusing as we nearly bumped into ourselves in flight to the recent past or future.

Our homework that evening was to synchronize our time travel with each other, which was a bit trickier and required more focus. But we found an empty section of tunnel and played tag — one twin projecting a few hours into the future or the past, challenging the other twin to track her through time and arrive at the same moment. We got pretty good at it almost immediately.

As I fell into uneasy sleep that night, I recalled Shin's warning from a few weeks before: "These talents are not parlour tricks, and must not be treated as such. 'With great power comes great responsibility.'"

Zee

Chapter 27: Council & Catastrophe

True to her word Ambassador Sinead convened a Council meeting to which we were invited. She felt the information was so significant to The Nethermost Gate Resistance Movement that attendance at this meeting was expanded to include the Council of Magicians and the League of Warriors as well.

It was to these conjoined councils then that my fearless sister presented our theory …

"Honourable members … my sister Cait and I have now reached the age of ascension and are eager to take our place amongst those who fight to restore our realm to its citizens of good conscience. The talents we requested were selected for the sole purpose of making this happen. Besides our new talents and the support of your good selves, we have been given additional useful gifts.

"One of the most valuable of these gifts we believe, and perhaps even the pivotal clue to change all our fates, is the prevision shown in this painting." Rhue rolled out the canvas onto the round table to allow it to be circulated amongst the attendees.

 "You are all aware of the wondrous talent of Ambassador Sinead of the healy. Her seer ability reaches prophesy status at times, as her magically directed paint skills produce critical visions of the future. We must surely all agree that over the years her truths have ever guided us — in many cases pulling us in the nick of time from the brink of disaster.

"Not many weeks since, the Ambassador painted what we feel is a critical scenario … a prevision … this very image you are now examining.

"With much consultation and hours of study of this painting, my sister Cait and I firmly believe that …

- o the room in this painting is Peadar's childhood apartment in the old palace
- o the figures in this painting are Cait and me

- o we will be entering this room in the near future in search of a critical clue, and
- o this room, as it is furnished, does not exist in the present, but rather it *did* exist in the past."

The joint council members murmured amongst themselves, and Afric, head of the Magic Council, stood up to address the body. "How certain are you that these rooms are Peadar's?"

"Absolutely certain," Grandpa Fergus interjected, "I have been to this chamber many times as Councillor to Their Graces Fianna and Canice. I remember that clutter all too well."

"And why should we expect that this event took place in the past?" Afric asked again.

"I would not phrase your question quite in that manner," explained Shin, now standing beside Rhue. "To be clear, this action has *not yet occurred* as you can see from the fact that this painted image is moving still, on a six second loop. But the room setup, as painted, could only be as it looked *in the past*. It would not look like this today."

"What made you come to this conclusion?"

"First of all," Rhue explained, "it is unlikely that Peadar would still sleep in this room today. He will undoubtedly be living in his gilded residence. After all, he did nearly destroy an entire nation to build his opulent home. If this messy room is used today, it will not be by him.

"Second, there is the matter of the clothing dropped on the floor. A lab coat, a pair of old blue jeans, stained boots, old knickers, a tatty satchel — gear that would never be worn by the richest man in the world, as the Apparatchik certainly is now. No, these would undoubtedly be worn by a slovenly, spoiled young man, in the habit of dropping his grubby clothes to the floor before going to bed. This is a person quite used to be picked up after — these discarded clothes are likely left for the housekeeper to tidy up the next morning. It is a nighttime scene, of course. See the twilight coming through the skylight, barely lighting the chamber, and showing only a few shadowed details.

"Councillors, although this evidence may seem sketchy, it is nonetheless the prevision of a seer of great repute. It *will* happen, and Cait and I must see that it does. We must therefore pierce the border into Nethermost, travel to that palace, enter that room, choose the correct timeline, and find the essential clue."

Afric continued her line of questioning. "How will you determine the exact timeline?"

At this point Zee piped in. "Perhaps this is where I can help. I am friends with a woman who worked in the palace forty years ago. I well remember her complaining about having the unpleasant task of picking up after young Peadar. If we were to show her this, she could perhaps provide some wisdom."

"Does she live at Nethermost Gate?"

"No, she remained in Nethermost after the fall. But I plan to go with the young ladies as they make their way through Nethermost to get to the old palace. If anyone can find her, it will be me."

Zee's statement brought Father to his feet. "How can you even think of sending my two young daughters alone into this unknown territory — a land under the control of wickedness itself, patrolled by ruffians wielding goodness knows what weapons? We ourselves cannot know what to expect from a realm we haven't seen in forty years. Can we really be this desperate?"

"First of all, Michael," Zee retorted angrily, wagging her finger his way, "They will not be alone, because I will be with them."

"And second of all, Zee? What is second? What else can you offer? What protection could *you* possibly provide?" He dropped to her eye level and stared her down. She met his glare for a full minute, before turning and fluttering off.

Father stood up and turned his gaze to the rest of the council, "I think you take my meaning." As he took his seat again, I heard him mutter, "Isn't it enough that you sacrificed my wife?"

The awkward silence that followed was interrupted by a trembling of the room around us. Several councillors were shaken from their seats, bits of wall fell to the floor, and the conference table collapsed. The shaking continued for several minutes, after which warriors and councillors alike ran from the chamber to their action stations, Rhue amongst them. Left on my own, I tried to make my way back to P49 to make sure my family was safe.

The evacuation alarm had sounded, and many were already streaming toward the exit tunnels helping the elderly and the walking wounded. Hub Medical personnel were out amongst them, evacuating their inpatients on stretchers and hover chairs; more were racing with medical bags towards the partially collapsed tunnels where the injured were being stacked along the entranceways.

I made my way east towards The Intersect. There I found Aunt Moira, passing out hard hats and red vests to emergency captains — stone masons, warriors, fire quellers, fairies — all reporting in to the Central Dispatch Kiosk for instructions. As I caught her eye, Aunt Moira nodded and shouted, "Here, grab a hard hat, Cait, then check out Tunnel P for Ol'Ben and Aileen. I left them home stirring sauce on the stove not half an hour ago."

Compared to what I had just witnessed, Tunnel P was not too badly damaged, although there was one crush point where a ziraph was holding up a collapsing rock face by pure white magic while a dwarf mason was hewing a support boulder into a column, and fusing it to the damaged wall. At the junction of tunnels P and Q, fire quellers were pouring water onto a small blaze caused by an erupting solar transformer. And at P23, a fairy had flown behind its collapsed doorway to report back to rescue teams on the number of folks trapped inside.

As chaotic as it sounds, the coordinated response was well structured; everyone seemed certain of their assignments. My biggest problem was just keeping out of the way, as I gradually picked my path through the broken rock and timber to reach P49 — to Ol'Ben and Grandma Aileen. Just as I reached our front door, I ran into Mánús and we entered the pod together.

We split up to conduct a quick scan of the rooms. The place was still intact, although rubbished — objects were broken, furniture disarrayed, including the orb of power which had fallen from the foyer table, and had rolled along the floor into the sitting room and under the coffee table. But I wasn't seeing my grand folk anywhere. Then I heard the now familiar Mánús howl coming from the kitchen. Seconds later, my eyes were assaulted by a heart wrenching sight — Ol'Ben bent over my grandmother who was lying unconscious next to the stove, the pot on top still on the boil. The old man was holding a cloth to her head, calling out in his croaky voice, "Aileen! Aileen! wake up dearie, what-what" — and she completely non responsive. I lacked even basic first aid skills and was out of my depth, but I did try my best to assess the scene. As far as I could see, my grandmother had a head wound and was losing a lot of blood. Ol'Ben's instinct to apply pressure to stem the blood flow seemed effective, and even I knew that this pressure must be maintained until we could get her to more effective help. The evacuation alarm was still sounding; we needed to leave the caverns immediately. The problem was one of coordination — how to get instant help for Aileen, and how to ensure that my ninety-three year old great-grandpa could escape at a pace that would not overwhelm him while we travelled those lengthy, hazardous tunnels to reach the safety of the out of doors.

Mánús grabbed Aileen up in his arms and was already making his way to the exit with Ol'Ben struggling to keep up, still hanging onto the pressure bandage. I was certain that this would never work. "Stop, stop!" I screamed, pushing back my own panic instincts to find a reasonable solution.

I raced to my grandmother's lingerie drawer and pulled out several scarves — balled up two to place over the wound and tied one more around her head to hold my makeshift dressing in place with sufficient pressure to keep the blood from flowing again. "Okay, Mánús, take her now, gently but quickly towards The Intersect, and don't stop until you find someone with a medical bag. Ol'Ben and I will follow at a more reasonable pace."

I grabbed Ol'Ben's hover scooter from his room and pulled it into the front doorway. "Come on Ol'Ben let's go!"

"Hold on!" he said, a look of panic registering on his face.

"Now don't go telling me that you're too old, that I must leave you to save myself, because I won't!"

"No, Cait. I was going to say … brace yourself. I think this is an aftershock!"

Sure enough, the floor began to sway, if anything, more violently than before. I pulled Ol'Ben against the nearest wall and held him up as the worst of it passed. While the bedrock continued to hold, now the pod walls were flaked and crumbled. The worst of the damage this time was to the outer doorway, where just moments before, I had intended to seat Ol'Ben on his hover transport. The threshold had collapsed, crushing the scooter, and barricading our exit under a pile of rocks stacked two thirds up the opening. Had Ol'Ben not stopped me when he did, our fate would have been the same as the scooter's.

Although I felt our good luck, the problem remained — we were penned into a stone bio pod, our only exit blocked. I might be able to struggle through the narrow gap at the top of the doorway myself or simply walk through the rock pile, but there was no chance that an old man could. I crawled up the pile to the small opening, stuck my head through to the tunnel, and shouted loudly. I knew it was a long shot, that the evacuation would be well along, but I continued my cries nonetheless. Several minutes later, feeling hoarse and defeated, I climbed back down and checked on Ol'Ben. He was sitting still and mute, so paralyzed by shock that I wondered if he was still alive. Seeing him like that brought forth the tears, which up until now I had held in check. I allowed panic to disrupt my thoughts and defeat my hopes.

I reached for Ol'Ben and held him close, wondering if this truly was where it all had been leading. Had I prepared myself only for this end? Had I searched for family for so long, finally finding them long enough to fall in love with them, only to have it all taken away moments later? Such thoughts dried my tears and replaced them with feelings of rage. How dare this happen! It would not happen!

I climbed back up the crush of boulders again, calling out while picking up rocks one by one and tossing them in the direction of the broken foyer table. I was lifting pieces far heavier than I should have been able. Perhaps the months of fitness training was kicking in, and combined with an ounce or two of adrenaline — who knows? Toss a rock, call out … call out, toss a rock.

After a while I realized that the cadence of my shouting and rock tossing had changed. A new beat had been added. Now it was … call out, toss a rock — *Cait!* … call out, toss a rock — *Cait!* …

I stopped … listened. "Cait!" — and the sound of rocks being pulled away from the other side. A voice that I knew — the voice that had promised to always have my back.

"Loo?"

"I'm coming, Cait! Let's get this done." It was the way he said it, I guess — like we were stacking shelves and making coffee for the morning commuters at The General Store. Same teamwork — different product. In half an hour, with both of us tossing the rocks aside, we had made a pass through that Ol'Ben could use.

Loo rushed in, gave me a quick squeeze, and then went over to Ol'Ben who still hadn't moved. "Hey old feller … 'zup?"

Ol'Ben's eyes shifted for the first time in an hour, as he was slowly being released from his fugue state "Loo? Did you see that, Loo?" he called out in confusion, "The walls just came down!"

"Yup, they did," Loo agreed, maintaining the calm. "And this is no place to be Ol'Ben. Hey, remember that day at The General Store when those bad dudes zapped their way in? And we escaped out the back door just in time, you piggybacking on me? That worked out just fine right? And you're even skinnier now. So hop on. Let's blow this joint!"

*****

I awoke the next morning huddled under the same blanket with Rhue on the floor of the canvas domed arena, Ol'Ben on a mattress to one side, and Grandma Aileen on a stretcher to the other. Both were resting comfortably, although the gravity of my grandmother's head wound still placed her in serious condition.

Then I realized what had awakened me. Father was shaking my shoulder a second time. "Girls … we need to talk." I roused my sister and we followed him outside, out of earshot of the masses collected in and around the dome.

"Rhue … Cait … I'm not sure I can bring myself to say this …"

"But you want us to go to Nethermost." Rhue assisted him.

"Yes …" he sighed.

"When?" I asked.

"Today."

Chapter 28: Subtext

I had never seen Loo cry before — I never want to again. But just as Rhue and I were about to place a first step through the huge boulder that blocked the border gate, I turned to catch his eye once more — brave face smiling, arms waving me forward — tell tale tears on his cheeks that betrayed the subtext in his heart. There would have been 'a better time', as Rhue suggested, but I confirmed from those tears that he loved me … and that he was scared.

Loo loved me … and I … him.

Up to that point, he'd been so upbeat and calm — the Loo I'd come to expect — filling me with confidence about setting out on a mission that all reason would suggest had little chance of succeeding. My sister was the trained soldier, I was not. But together we had skills. We didn't quite know how that would give us the advantage, but we had to trust that it would.

Loo built onto that mood of optimism and confidence by reasoning with me that Shin's painting itself was the evidence that we *would* travel in safety to the palace and actually enter the room at the correct moment in time. It was a prevision after all. How could we fail? 'Done deal', as Loo put it.

Of course the getting back was not covered by Shin's prophesy. That fate was yet to be written, or painted as it were.

But Loo remained my rock throughout. He was even more protective of us than my father had been when it came to the preparations for the journey. He flatly denied the War Council a meeting with us until Rhue and I had been allowed enough rest. He tracked down Aunt Moira and insisted she find us a quiet room with proper beds to give us no less than six hours of uninterrupted sleep after our wakeful night post disaster. When we awoke, he'd organized a spa mistress to come by with her oils and magic fingers to smooth away our muscle cramps and bruises from the day before. Then he made us a huge meal of waffles and bacon, with a fruit compote, washed down with plenty of coffee.

While we slept, he helped pack our bags, which included essentials such as a digital camera with extra batteries, a sketchbook and several sharp pencils, a long length of rope, bottled water, trail mix and protein bars, along with items he got from my father — maps, blueprints, compass, old reference photos, gold discs for currency, towel, blanket, and one change of clothes, as we were traveling grubby — the poorer and dirtier we looked, the less interesting we would be.

He had my back alright.

*****

"At first we thought a bomb had gone off and we were looking for the ignition point," Father explained. "We felt certain that Donal must have crept back in and planted it under orders from Peadar. The aftershock told us a different story. Now we know that this was not a bomb but an earthquake, and that almost certainly its epicentre is within Nethermost proper."

He paced the floor obviously conflicted between daughters and duties, but he waved off any other council member's interference and continued the briefing himself.

"If this is the case, we have danger to overcome, and opportunity to turn to our advantage. The danger is that Nicola is unable to balance the continent effectively any longer — either because she is too ill, or because the geological damage has become too extreme for just one balancer. We must adjust for both. We could not only lose our own realm, which would be a disaster of monumental proportions, but we could also seriously damage the entire globe, which would be Armageddon, the end of days.

"The opportunity we have here is the earthquake itself, and the damage to Nethermost that will become a distraction for Peadar and his minions in their continental cleanup. The last thing they will expect now is a breach of their borders. It will give you girls the chance to make your way to the palace relatively unobserved. That is why we are sending you in immediately. It is perhaps premature, given your youth and inexperience, but I wonder if one can really be readied for such an assignment."

He directed his next instructions to Rhue. "Rhue, you and Zee are to meet with our cartographers who will show you the best routes to take, along with some locations of our allies with safe rest stops along the hundred kilometre journey to The Capitol."

"And Cait …"

"Yes, Father?"

"Yours is the weightier assignment, I'm afraid. The events of yesterday have now doubled your burden. Now, you must not only retrieve this mysterious clue, but you must also find your mother and grandmother in their cells, under the watchful eye of Peadar himself. Not to effect a rescue, as compelling as that would be, but to bring them aid to fortify their efforts in keeping our realm in balance, while we race to find a permanent solution."

He pulled me to him in a hug, and whispered in my ear, "Yes, my dear, it is heartbreaking I know, but trust that there will be a day of reckoning." Then for all to hear, he added, "You need to meet with Moran the ziraph healer, and Darragh the dwarf mason."

*****

While Rhue and Zee met with the map experts, my father and I went to see Dr. Moran, head of Hub Medical, and Darragh, Nethermost Gate's master builder in a meeting chamber at The Hub.

Dr. Moran had the characteristic long neck of the ziraph, with clear fair skin and long blond hair. I guessed his age to be similar to my mother's and I wondered if they had worked together nineteen years before.

"I am concerned that there now may be a lack of medicine to sustain Her Grace Nicola," said Dr. Moran, "but it is impossible to know what may be wrong. It is my plan, therefore, to send along some powders and oils to strengthen Nicola's constitution and provide extra nutrients. I dread to think …" Dr. Moran was silenced by a withering look from my father.

"I'm not a child … " I began.

"No, but it will do no one any good to 'dread to think,'" Father asserted. "That only adds anxiety to an already tense situation."

"You are right Michael, as always," Dr. Moran agreed. "Suffice it to say, that the magical ingredients I am sending will cure an array of sicknesses and fortify a number of weaknesses. They are highly concentrated, so they will not overburden your backpack either. I have labelled them with instructions, and leave their use to Dr. Nora."

That was the first time I had heard my mother referred to as Dr. Nora and it felt pretty good. I liked imagining her as one of the medical team at The Hub. Indeed, had she not been held captive all these years, she may have been running the show by now.

"I am here to address the balancing issue," said Darragh, the master builder. Although I knew dwarves lived long lives, nevertheless Darragh looked very well seasoned. His long black hair and full beard were streaked with white, skin wrinkled and callused in unusual places, leather clothing weathered and repaired many times over. He stood proudly before us now, his tone deep and noble.

"This situation is perhaps even trickier than concerns for Nicola's health," Darragh asserted. "Again we cannot determine what has caused this earthquake, so we must send along a solution that will address the unknowns.

"Dwarves are famous for their ability to balance geography and climate. No other magical species possesses it and only a handful of humans — none currently living at Nethermost Gate. As architects and builders, we dwarves are routinely required to balance our builds. We work with the toughest materials after all, in the most inhospitable climates.

"Whether the issue here is a weakened balancer or resource exhaustion due to over mining, I can think of no other solution than to give the talent of balance to your mother Nora, so that she can assist Nicola in her arduous daily duties."

"Is it just a matter of sending a talent ring for her to put on?" I asked.

"I will certainly send along the *balance band*," he corrected, "although it is not a simple matter. To provide Nora with this second talent will require a sacrifice from someone who is willing to give away their own balance abilities — just as you gave your talent to your sister, Cait. The strength of this additional talent lies with the giver and the strength of the sacrifice."

"But Nora has no twin or even a sibling," I observed, my head spinning from his roundabout presentation.

"But she can acquire this additional talent by a non-family member, if it is offered freely and without condition. I therefore offer my own talent to the good lady."

"You are lending her your talent? That is generous indeed."

"I am *giving* my talent away. When *given* it cannot be taken back." Now I understood the care he was taking with his explanation. He was, in effect, cutting away a vital piece of himself, and offering it on a platter to another.

"How will this sacrifice affect you?"

"It is a disability I am willing to endure … for the greater good." Darragh stood noticeably taller as he proclaimed this. I was touched, and once again impressed, by the indomitable spirit of these people. "Be so good as to take this band to your mother, Mistress Cait," he said as he pulled away at his middle finger until a band appeared and dislodged, "… with my words of explanation."

"I will do, Darragh. I only hope that I can transfer the nobility in your voice along with it," I replied, to which he bowed silently, looking quite spent.

The final preparations included a wardrobe of vile looking clothing selected by Aunt Moira to make us look unapproachable — along with a temporary dye job to our hair — Rhue's hair becoming grey to make her look like my mother, mine turning a limp, mousey brown, again to take the focus away from us, as we travelled incognito.

"Could you make us look a bit more homely?" I asked my aunt, facetiously.

"Well, I could add a scar to your face Cait, or a nasty boil or two," she returned wryly.

*****

"I hope I have prepared you both sufficiently for this mission," Shin looked sadly at me, all trussed up with my gear. "I gave Rhue a closeup photograph of that one section of the painting — the bit with the crumpled clothing — to show to Zee's friend. It is too risky to take the entire painting."

"Thank you Shin. That image is indelibly imprinted on my brain in any case, so I know all the nooks and crannies in the room I'm going to search already. As to my readiness, I cannot swear to it, but I hope I do you proud."

"Just stepping through that gate does me proud Cait. You could not possibly disappoint."

The grand-folk were especially difficult to leave. Grandma Aileen was still woozy but expected to recover. Grandpa Fergus was looking fussy, conflicted about leaving her to perform his community duties. But Ol'Ben was by her side, refusing to leave for a moment, caring for Aileen this time as she had cared for him.

When he saw me all ready to go, Ol'Ben smiled in an effort to keep it light. "Well if I'd known you needed to wear such awful clothes, I'd have saved my old wardrobe for ya, what-what! … But Cait …"

"Be careful?" I suggested.

"Yes, of course. It's just so hard ... what I want to say … Cait … Believe in yourself … trust your own strength."

"Well, I was going to say that!" said Father, as he and Aunt Moira came up to say their goodbyes. They hugged us both silently, their pride needing no words.

"Aunt Moira, a moment …" I said, pulling her aside. I had forgotten one important piece of information I still needed to know. "If someone were learning to teleport for the first time, what should they do?" I was thinking of Fianna's ring secreted inside my satchel.

"What? Why?" she began to question. Then she took a beat, changed directions, and reproached herself, "Never mind, I don't need to know. You have your reasons — and your secrets I dare say. There *is* one essential thing. You must imagine the look of the place to which you are teleporting in great detail. Close your eyes, envision yourself there. The actual experience will make you want to vomit, so hold your breath and keep still until you come to a complete stop."

"Can one teleport while holding another living being?"

"No, that being would not survive."

"Thank you aunt, and thanks as well for everything you have done to get me here today."

"It has been my absolute honour, dearie — daughter of my heart."

As I walked over to join my sister, Aunt Moira called me back, whispering, "One other thing Cait … very important. I have tried, and failed, to teleport across that border into Nethermost. All of us teleporters have tried. It can't be done dearest. The magic barrier in front of that gate is crazy strong. Don't even attempt it."

Rhue and I waited until the pitch of night before setting off with Zee. Father, Grandpa Fergus and Loo escorted us in our final steps.

Before we reached the gate, Loo grabbed my hand and hauled me to one side."You're my most favourite person in the world, Cait, do you know that?"

"Well … me … and Ol'Ben, right?" I said, like he always did.

"No … just you Cait." he said, emphasizing his point with one of his delicious kisses. "And you know what? You're gonna be great! No worries. Just get back quick, okay?" I held him in an long embrace, then kissed him a second time — one more for the road.

We lined up before the boulder — Rhue holding Zee in one arm, all set to melt as intangibility met with igneous rock — me behind, ready to move on her signal. As we stepped forward, I looked back once more, saw Loo's tear soaked cheeks, and in that final instant —

I bestowed my love.

Chapter 29: A Blind Path

That first step was a doozy. The boulder was so dense, my legs so heavy, that I felt fatigued after just ten metres. But then we were through, standing at the top of a downward staircase, the wrought iron upper gate with its boulder barricade in our rear view mirror. A weak light emanated from a wall sconce at the top step, but beneath that, profound darkness. I knew from our briefing that these stone steps dropped for a kilometre beneath the surface, and that only a handful of creatures had even tried to access them in the past forty years. Such a derelict space was bound to host all manner of creepy crawlies. Zee had her baton out already. "Wands on, ladies." Rhue and I pulled out our crystal rods and chanted: "*Fiat lux*". The wands' beams were so dim, we couldn't even see our feet, let alone light the next step.

"You've got them set too low sillies," Zee chided. *Maxima* … say '*maxima*,' … hurry, hurry."

Now the beams if anything were too bright, their blue/green glare filling the passageway. The stairs were thick with dusk, cobwebs dangled from the ceiling and dozens of millipedes made a beeline for cracks in the stone. It was my worst nightmare. I gave up on 'trick or treating' as a kid to avoid less terrifying scenes than this.

Zee wafted leisurely in front of us, watching the steps for more bugs and routing the occasional rodent. At first I stepped tentatively onto each step, praying that I would avoid stepping in anything nasty. I held my wand up high in one hand and balanced myself against the slimy walls with the other. I tried to distract myself by keeping track of our progress. Father had calculated that these crumbling stairs were at least five thousand steps long. In order to prepare me for what to expect, he said that they were almost three times the height of the world record breaking staircase in Toronto's CN Tower. At first I marked our progress by counting each step as I walked, but I got tired of that after the four hundredth step, and hummed tunes in my head from then on, while watching where I placed my feet. Within half an hour I was feeling significant pain in my knees and calves, despite my rigorous training, and I was willing our descent to be over — not that I was looking forward to the other end.

Nethermost Regained

I recalled Father's description of the Gate he knew forty years before — a glorious arched throughway, adorned with effigies of the old Swayers to either side. The lead up to the gate had been formally landscaped with sculpted hedges, bordered with glowing moon flowers. The entire green space, in fact, had been so friendly back then that it served double duty as a public park.

The few fairies who had crossed the border since told a different story about today's Gate Park. Their scouting reports described the boundary on the other side as a fenced in area with ugly barbed wire, lawns had been replaced with tarmac, with spotlights running day and night. It looked like a demilitarized zone, five hundred metres square — no people allowed, nor flowers nor greenery. The gate itself had been altered by changing the effigies of Fianna and Canice into unflattering images of Peadar. The gate's latches and edges were fused with an alchemized compound, formulated and forged in Peadar's nefarious factory. The heavily welded edges made the inner gate impenetrable. Nevertheless, there was also increased security at the guard kiosks, stationed at four locations along the fencing, two armed guards at each one.

My watch read ten o'clock as we reached the bottom. You could see by the light of our wands that this inner sanctum had once been ornate, almost Art Deco in design, with flourishes of stylized vinery chiselled in the rock, framing its threshold. The iron gate itself was fused shut with an alchemical weld, but the gold was tarnished with age. At this end as well, a giant boulder completely blocked any view of the other side.

It was here that Zee dropped to her feet and implored us to sit. "Confession time, ladies," she announced, with less enthusiasm than she generally exuded.

"What are we confessing Zee?" Rhue asked.

"You aren't — *I* am," she sighed, leaning up against Rhue with whom she had become quite pally. "I may not have been as forthcoming as I should perhaps have been. I may have neglected to mention that we cannot cross here."

"What!" I exclaimed, my voice bouncing off the walls and echoing up the stairwell. I dropped the volume. "Then what are we doing here?"

"Oh, we will cross — just not here. It's reinforced both with alchemy and a barrier of magic — intangibility doesn't work at this particular spot. And besides, just beyond that gate there are too many guards. So, not the best idea." She snuggled into Rhue even further, trying to build alliances and to avoid an angry stare from me.

"But you must have had a plan in mind," my sister cajoled, coaxing the fairy to explain. I held my temper for Rhue's sake, although I wouldn't have been as kind if she weren't protecting the little sprite.

"We will have to walk along the inside edge of this rock face," Zee explained, "until we get further away from the main access point."

"Great," I said, "How far along?"

"Half a kilometre should do it," she quipped, like saying it lightly made it simpler.

"We can do that … can we not, Cait?" offered my optimistic sister, looking to me for confirmation.

"Well … there are a few challenges," Zee's voice was getting more and more tentative.

"Okay! Zee," I said, trying to keep a lid on. "Just tell us everything, because clearly there's a problem right?"

"If only it were just the *one*. The truth is … fairies can't fly through rock. Their wings are not strong enough. They have to walk. So the only fairies who have ever completed the annual scouting mission have been the very strongest of us who trained for years to endure such a challenge, and even then, it weakens them cruelly. It's the pullback of the rock you see. You must have felt it coming through the boulder at the top step and you are ten times bigger than me. What I told you is that it's like walking through treacle for you humans; what I didn't say is that it's like walking though quick dry cement for we fairies."

"Then why did you come?" I asked.

"Because … you needed me! … needed my guidance and my knowledge of magician kind on the other side," her eyes teared in frustration. I saw now how I had misjudged her. She wasn't being pompous or deceitful, she was being noble — the 'greater good' thing again. I reined in my attitude.

"I will carry you on my shoulders then dearest," said Rhue.

"Oh! yes please," Zee clapped, her enthusiasm returning. "That should work! … yet there is one more thing …"

Oh help, I thought inwardly, what now? "Our wands will not work inside rock." Zee explained. "No light can penetrate the darkness of solidified magma. So, in effect, we will be walking blind. But I have a solution … I think. You two will hold onto each other and walk as a unit, keeping as straight a path forward as you can. I will sit on Rhue's shoulders and count off our steps as we go. Four hundred human long paces should do it."

Her bossy boots attitude had returned, and Zee was in her comfort zone again. "So," she summarized for clarity, "right turn into the rock … pace out four hundred steps … stop … turn left and creep forward one pace and at a time, until we feel a breeze. I will poke my head through first to check that the coast is clear. Once it's safe, we extrude ourselves and become tangible once more."

Our progress was beyond slow, the sensory deprivation unnerving. Were it not for my sister's brave leadership, I wondered, would I have turned back? Zee's little squeak counting off the paces somewhat anchored me and I tried to envision cool clear air to counterbalance the nearly suffocating feeling of this thick morass. My legs were screaming with fatigue, my feet heavier with each lift, begging me to stop. After the two hundredth step I was fully committed, because with each step now, the easier way out was to go forward not back. It couldn't have been more than fifteen minutes altogether, but it was a lifetime nonetheless, and my heart went out to those fairy scouts who had endured this blind path every year in order to provide Nethermost Gate with intelligence. No wonder it aged them.

After I heard Zee call out the final pace and felt Rhue coming to a halt, I stilled my feet. Now Zee directed, "Turn left in place … one step, two step …" it took us ten paces before I could feel that my left foot had broken through to the other side. "Stop!" Zee commanded. I could sense her dismounting from Rhue's shoulders and imagined her poking her head through the rock face. "Coast clear, ladies. But be warned — we will not come out at level ground. We will be on a narrow jut in the rock about three metres from the floor."

I stepped cautiously, leaning my face forward to catch the air first and regain my bearings. I could see what Zee meant. The rock we stood on, in our tangible bodies, could not even be called a ledge. It was indeed a 'narrow jut', hardly wide enough for our feet. I watched Rhue manage her descent first. She turned around in place like a slow moving toy top, bent her legs, grabbing some edge pieces, dangling one leg over first until her foot gripped another bulge in the rock. Her second leg followed the first, seeking another foothold. When she felt stable, she pushed off and let herself drop to the ground, landing in a crouched position, completely intact. She coached me through my descent and was there to catch me in my wonky flop. Almost instantly, Zee was pushing us back towards the shelter of some dead wood, to survey our surroundings undetected.

"The land of course is in twilight," Zee explained. "The crystal ceiling dims for twelve hours a day to simulate nighttime. What time is it *on-Earth* time Rhue?" she asked.

Rhue consulted her watch. "Ten-thirty exactly."

"Good, so the skies will lighten at six o'clock *on-Earth* time. Dawn here is not a gradual process, like the sunrises at Nethermost Gate. When it dawns in Nethermost proper, it is instant — like someone switched on the lights. We wouldn't want to be caught in the open when that happens."

I could see why she called it twilight. Every detail of the landscape was dimmed but not completely obscured, and distance viewing was very hazy. It was not like the nightfalls I was used to. I could appreciate that it was going to be tough travelling in the open — day or night. We were going to have to choose a route where the ground cover was high and the potential to encounter fellow travellers low.

Before we proceeded, Zee insisted that we memorize our entry point, so we could rendezvous here if we got separated. I memorized the look of the rock face and the idiosyncrasies to either side. We had entered a safe distance away from the actual gate and all the guard kiosks. Even so, we needn't have worried. The kiosks were empty, the guards nowhere in sight. Instead, right in front of the barrier, there was a steaming crevice from which oozed pale gold magma, slowly cooling. It created a gash in the earth as it travelled jaggedly along the rock wall to beyond the fenced in zone, like an ill stitched and oozing wound.

Clearly, the earthquake in Nethermost proper had been far worse than our surface experience. I could sense Zee shudder and take a deep breath before she lifted into the air. "Time to go," was all she would say.

The going was relatively easy, with the continent otherwise engaged, not defending their perimeters. We made our way unobserved for several kilometres before Zee would allow us to rest. While I downed a few sips of water, Zee and Rhue consulted their map, plotting our path. I was so tired from our boulder walking that I must have nodded off, because the next thing I knew, Rhue was nudging me awake. This time we followed in the same direction as an unsurfaced road we'd found, bordered by woods to either side. We travelled, not on the road itself, but well back in the trees.

Our watches read five-forty-five at our next rest stop. "Time to find cover for the day," Zee announced. We moved at least a kilometre into the thick of the woods where there were no signs of human life. Rhue and I found tall trees next to each other to climb. Once again, I was grateful for my endurance training, although my legs were still complaining from our rock dive. We tied ourselves onto thick limbs and leaned against the trunks, trying to rest as best we could. Zee seemed determined to stand guard, which was fine by me. I was spent and had nothing more to offer. I snacked on half a protein bar and drank a few more sips of water. Then I leaned back, closed my eyes, and ran images of the best bits of my life past my eyelids while I searched for sleep, finally nodding off to an enjoyable dream sequence of Loo's full lips pressing its warmth onto mine.

Darragh

Chapter 30: Welcome to Carrickbeg

I awoke the next morning to the sound of Zee rooting through my bag of trail mix picking out the raisins. I was full of cramp, unable to shift myself without jabs of pain, yet watching one of the funniest sights I'd ever witnessed in my life — a greedy, raisin addicted fairy 'jonesing' for a fix. I would have gladly given them to her, but I was too entertained watching this act of petty larceny. She was demonstrating the very spunk we needed to continue.

"Okay, Missy Thief," I said, with a chuckle, "Just for that, you have to rub my legs to get my muscles working again." Along with my laughter, came a rush of endorphins that helped ease my discomfort.

Rhue was up already consulting her maps. "It looks like we've covered twenty-five kilometres already. I am amazed. I've just been studying our map, considering the options. We want to get to the palace as quickly as possible of course, but if we go slightly off track, we can contact Zee's kinfolk here on the Pinnacles of Pons." She pointed to a region northeast of our location. We would more or less follow our current road east for ten kilometres, a route marked in detail, then head north into a section on the map marked only by the cartographer's symbol for high ground, with 'PINNACLES — OF — PONS' slashed across the carrot shaped markings. While most the other areas were well labelled, this region was not, meaning that it was unexplored by the mapmaker. Furthermore, I noted that the palace, our ultimate goal, was directly east, rather than northeast. Then again, that more direct route involved travel through several settlements, where our presence could easily be observed. It was a head scratcher, and it made me favourably consider the wisdom of Rhue's suggestion.

As if reading my thoughts, she elaborated further. "It is a little off our path, I know, but still in the general direction. We might be wise to go there first. They may be able to tell us more about current events on the continent, and our intelligence is hopelessly out of date. Also, although I'm sure we are capable of travelling a hundred kilometres on foot, perhaps we can borrow transportation which would save us a great deal of time.

"I am intrigued about this Pinnacles of Pons region," she concluded. "Its mountain folk are 'special' shall we say, and it seems they have stayed off the radar for centuries. We need to make as many allies as we can, especially amongst the magically gifted.

"Also, Zee may be able to get word about the whereabouts of her friend who cleaned Peadar's rooms. You know as well as I do that we need more clues before invading that space. And it has to be said that we need better sleep than our tree napping affords."

All in all, it seemed a good decision.

We set off a couple of hours before twilight, keeping to the woods and staying far away from signs of settlements. In the brighter light, I could better witness the earthquake's damage — the uprooted trees, shattered rocks, and pools of golden lava oozing from tiny fissures in the ground. Never mind that the lava was pure gold, the most precious of earth's metals. Here within Nethermost, Earth's precious gold had become a threat, taking life and scorching everything in its path.

Zee flew ahead as scout to ensure our safety. We had gone at least ten kilometres by six p.m. when the twilight setting switched on. Rhue chose a rest stop at the base of a tall hill that clearly made Zee giddy with excitement. "That is Grace Pinnacle," she explained, pointing a tiny finger upwards. "The first of thirteen hills that make up my homeland. Whenever I see 'The Grace', as it is known, it starts my blood bubbling and my wings twitching."

"When was the last time you were home?" asked Rhue.

"Well, of course we've been in exile for 40 years, and I was in service to the family of the first bloodline for twenty years before that."

"But, you're just a child!" I exclaimed.

"My parents would certainly agree that I am little more than a girl. But I am also 90 Earth years old." Would I ever get used to those kind of answers, I wondered.

From this point we travelled upward, our progress slower, our path safer. I remembered Father telling me that Peadar had always given magicians a wide berth. He was more interested in bullying those less able to fend for themselves. As we climbed, I saw evidence of the cavelike dwellings carved into the hillside itself. Zee commented on one halfway up the slope, "That's where Blossom and Clover live. If I were at my leisure, I'd pop in for a bite of peach pie."

"My homestead is on the third pinnacle," she continued. "At least that's where my parents live. It's called Carrickbeg, and it's by far the most beautiful — or it used to be."

She had scarcely finished her explanation when we were surrounded by mountain folk of all shapes and sizes, bearing wands, flares and torches that effectively blinded us, making us blink uncomfortably. I took my cue from Rhue, who took hers from Zee. "Lay down your wands, girls," Zee instructed in a whisper.

"Why?" I whispered back.

"Because it is an act of submission. It lets them know that we mean no harm."

We laid down our wands and stood silently in place. Two fairies, looking so much like Zee they could be her sisters, pulled her away leaving Rhue and me standing alone … waiting. It was an unnerving half hour before Zee returned. When she did, she barked instructions to our captors in an unfamiliar language. Two dwarves stepped forward to remove our back packs and hoist them onto their own shoulders. They rushed us into rickety hover pods parked near an opening in the hill. Rhue and I were separated — she in one pod with an Elf driver, me in the one behind her, driven by another. We entered a gloomy tunnel and travelled along a subterranean roadway that twisted and climbed for fifteen minutes before slowing and coming to a stop under the arch of another hole in the hill. What lay ahead was a most extraordinary sight — an ancient looking settlement full of bustling creature kind, poised and expectant for our arrival it would seem. Zee flew in from high overhead, shouting joyfully, "Welcome to Carrickbeg!"

Though the crystal filled sky was still in twilight mode, I could still observe some intriguing detail. Built into, on top of, and around the pinnacle itself, were wood and stone dwellings, not unlike the photos I'd seen of Swiss alpine homes. At a guess, I would say there were fifty such structures surrounding a central business space with outdoor stalls and tiny shops, their *closed* signs up for end of day. But everyone seemed out in full force, or least two hundred plus were … watching three or four deep by the tunnel entrance, or perching on overhanging cliffs.

Zee pushed her way through the small crowd to the front row with her parents Ren and Saffron in tow. After brief introductions, she whisked us away to the largest public building off the square, a meeting hall I suppose built to accommodate big people. Here we were escorted to the great room and seated on one of the long couches near a central fire pit. A flurry of anonymous workers placed small cups of nectar tea and biscuits before us, along with our returned knapsacks and wands. Our onlookers tittered nervously.

"Zee tells us you are here on a secret mission, and that she will box our ears if we ask anything more." Ren began. "Even though we mayn't know, let me just say that if it has anything to do with ridding the continent of that wicked Apparatchik, then count us in!"

It was a bit too much sharing for the first five minutes of an acquaintanceship and Rhue's answer reflected as much. "You are most kind," she replied carefully. "All we can think of at this moment is that our legs are sore and our throats parched. Perhaps more of your nectar tea … and a few minutes on this sofa?"

"Oh we can do better than that," Zee proclaimed. We were bustled into a spa where two tubs had been filled with steaming hot bubbly water. Our sad looking clothes were removed with no heed to our objections, and an army of fairies scrubbed our stained skin and dyed hair until they returned to their natural colours. We were dried, coiffed, our muscles limbered and toned with fancy smelling lotions. Then they left us wrapped in warm blankets, with fresh clothing folded on a bench for us to redress ourselves. Had I been at home preparing for a date, I would have been pleased with the look. But here on this hilltop, on a secret mission into enemy territory, when we were supposed to be traveling incognito, the look was more alarming than pleasing.

Zee knocked on the door and entered. "That's better," she enthused, "much more party ready!"

"It's not better Zee," I argued. "That ugly look was our disguise. These clothes may look pretty, but they put us in danger."

"If it were anywhere else, I would agree," she replied, "but in Carrickbeg you are safe. Party tonight, business tomorrow. We can make you look as filthy and grim as you like then."

When we returned to the great room, everyone gasped, giggled and talked behind their hands. "Well, that's a bit rude," I whispered to Rhue.

"They are stunned dearest. Aunt Moira's camouflage was very convincing, so they hadn't realized before now that we were identical twins. In fairy lore, this is great good fortune! To them, identical twins represent the promise of better times. You and I have neither acted nor dressed identically before now. Actually, seeing us in the same clothes and the same hair style is a shock to me as well."

In our absence, flourishes had been added to the great room — leafy boughs, alpine blooms, pillar candles — and long tables charged with food and drink. The community folk were a pleasing blend of both magic and non magic folk, whose common ground seemed to be a love of mountain life and simple things. As I found out later, all the creative food dishes were thanks to a host of chefs of all species, and the produce they'd harvested from their slope farms and alpine herds. Our plates were filled for us, our cups recharged, and we were ensconced once again on the comfy furniture. Musicians brought out stringed instruments and played gentle refrains throughout the delicious meal.

During dinner, Saffron engaged us with her stories of happier times. She related treasured memories of the old Swayers, describing their traditional annual climbs through the Pinnacles to visit the more remote areas of their realm. Back in those days, she said, travel back and forth to The Capitol was commonplace for mountain folk — for supply shopping, feast days, weddings, and parades. These days they seldom stepped foot from the hills, sending a few brave representatives only to stock up on essentials twice a year.

After the meal was over and we were replete, the dishes were cleared and the tempo was revved up on the music. Now singers and dancers stepped up with an enhanced band to entertain us with folk tunes and country reels. For a few hours at least, I put aside the mission and focussed exclusively on the company. It was well past midnight when the children were ordered to bed, which made them complain loudly, not wishing to miss a thing.

"What if I were to tell you a bedtime tale?" Rhue suggested. She sat on the floor, and they collected about her. "Once there was a magical kingdom built on a huge island beneath an enormous forest, resting on a pool of gold. The people of this kingdom were very happy, and lacked for nothing ..."

"Oh I know that kingdom Miss!" said one wakeful child.

We all knew that kingdom. But in Rhue's story, rather than an evil Apparatchik, there was a fire breathing dragon who burned their houses and singed their bottoms. And the heroes she described who rode in on horseback brandishing swords and shields to slay that dragon and restore peace to the kingdom, were knights in red armour all handsome and brave. I couldn't help sniggering at the description of her red knights — and thinking how far removed they were from the two redheaded girls, fresh out of school, with a couple of magic tricks in their repertoire, and a pair of fancy rings.

Later in the evening, Rhue and I found a quiet corner to meet with some of the Elders, and receive their updates on Nethermost. While the countryside was of little importance to the Apparatchik, they reported, beyond supplying The Capitol with an overabundance of food and other raw materials, the settlements were quite a different matter. Guards patrolled the streets during the day, taking whatever they wanted from the businesses and the homes of hard working citizens. There was a curfew imposed after twilight, and all violators were instantly gilded. They were fearless bullies so long as they carried these vile weapons, and they used them far too often, without considering the consequences. The numbers of gilded 'statues' were said to be stacked high in several huge warehouses. Peadar's guardsmen were fat and uncouth, while the rest of the masses were thin, weak and sickly from doing without. It was a hardship story about the whipped masses being dominated by the wicked technology of the boorish few.

Without being too obvious, we questioned the elders about the royal parkland on which both the palace and the Apparatchik's house sat.

A young huntsman named Keane Sweeney was sent for, an apparent expert on the subject.

He arrived at once, as if he'd been standing by waiting. As he made his way across the floor, I saw my sister's eyes sparkle in his direction. He was the perfect specimen of a warrior, with a dark mane of hair that he unconsciously pulled across his forehead with long tawny fingers — a gesture that I'd seen Loo do hundreds of times. His azure blue eyes looked even more pronounced against the complexion of an outdoorsman. He was 'well fit', as they say, muscles bulging from the appropriate regions of his leather tunic and leggings. Indeed, he could have passed for any of the Hemsworth brothers in an action packed Hollywood film.

When asked about the palace grounds, Keane responded confidently. "I don't know how recent your facts are …"

"Assume we know nothing since the day the usurper took power," I replied.

"In that case, I must first describe the facts, as related to me by my grandparents when I was a child. They worked as servants to the royals, Their Graces Fianna and Canice. And for a time under the Swayer-ship of Nicola, bless her soul."

"Why do you say that — 'bless her soul', I mean?" Rhue asked.

"Because she has been locked away by her brother these forty years. I despair for his immortal soul. There can be no excuse for such cruelty!"

"Do you know for sure that she is still alive?"

"Sadly no, but there have been innuendo and rumours. They say she is locked away in The Golden Palace, forced under some penalty or other to do His Grace Peadar's bidding. Beyond that I cannot say."

The Golden Palace, eh? That was no palace. Nethermost already had a palace and that wasn't it! What had become of that old seat of power, I wondered. And *His Grace Peadar?* Two generations had passed now, with people now used to calling Peadar 'His Grace'. It was shocking. Now I understood that there was a mindset to shift as well as a legion of enforcers to rout. But would an entire realm so physically abused and mentally enslaved for decades have the strength to fight back?

Keane returned to his briefing at the point he'd left off. "Grandfather was one of the horse guard, because of his talent with animals. He was a 'whisperer' you see."

"A horse whisperer?"

"He communicated with all creatures, understood their languages, and could train any animal in the land. Grandmother was a companion for the royal children and supervised the household staff who tended to their needs."

I filed that juicy detail about his grandmother for a future chat.

"On that dark day, after Peadar had stormed the throne room and had taken Nicola away, Grandfather drove the transport that whisked Ambassador Sinead, Consort Riley and little Nora away from the palace in the nick of time. When he had deposited them at their safe haven, he returned on horseback to the palace. He freed all the royal horses and instructed them to meet him along the eastern border to The Capitol. Next he went in search of my Grandmother, finding her at the mercy of one of Peadar's henchmen, who was forcing her to fill a suitcase with Nicola's clothing and carry it to what would all too soon be known as The Golden Palace. Perhaps this is another reason to suppose that it was never Peadar's intent to kill her — and to hope that she is still alive.

"Grandfather followed his wife at a discreet distance and waited until she was released from her grim tasks before snatching her from under the noses of the ruffians, who had by then drunk themselves into a stupor.

"He coaxed as many of the palace staff, willing to brave it, to escape with them, leading them to rendezvous with the horses. Some chose at this point to go their own way, while others followed my grandparents. They rode the horses west until they came to the Forest Curran. Here they relied on the cover of trees and the control that Grandfather had over their steeds, to weave their way northward, not stopping until they had reached the Pinnacles of Pons."

What a drama I was envisioning, and what bravery! "Is your grandfather still alive today?" I asked.

"Sadly no, but Grandmother is. She lives with us at our farm on the outskirts of Carrickbeg. In fact, the survivors and descendants of all those palace refugees still live on the Pinnacles of Pons."

"Do you have any recent knowledge about the state of things at the royal grounds today?" Rhue asked, pushing for useful intelligence specific to our mission.

"The doors to the old palace have been sealed with that distorted alchemy compound, the outer walls hexed by a spell. As far as I know, no one has been inside it for years."

"Is it impenetrable?" she asked.

"I have not tried to enter myself, but it is reputed to be so."

"Is 'The Golden Palace' guarded with barrier magic as well?" Rhue almost gagged as she voiced the name of that gilded monstrosity.

"No it is guarded, rather sloppily in my opinion, by the roughest drunkards on the planet. But if caught in the grounds you are gilded without hesitation."

"And if you are not caught?" Rhue asked.

"I myself have entered the palace on numerous occasions to do a little pilfering. If you know the way, you can access it easily."

Rhue shot me a significant glance, which was caught in its transmission by Keane as well.

"Why? Are you interested in breaching the palace?" he asked.

Rhue exchanged looks with me again. Why not, I thought, we would never do this on our own. I nodded my assent.

"Yes." she answered.

"Which palace?" he asked.

"Both."

Chapter 31: Mrs. Sweeney Recalls

"Both? The two palaces — old and new? You're going to breach and enter? Whatever for?"

"It is a necessary first step." Rhue answered cautiously. "Beyond that, I am not at liberty to say. But trust me when I tell you that we are your friends, and that our intentions are honourable."

Keane sat back in his chair to consider. "You told the children a bedtime story this evening," he said, "that sent them to their beds a little easier. Tell me … are you the 'fire breathing dragon' in that tale, or the 'red knights'?"

"What do you think?" Rhue asked.

He looked at her … then at me … then to the Elders, who had been listening without comment. "You are … the red knights."

The Elders nodded their agreement.

*****

I awoke at noon cocooned in soft sheets on one of the lodge's comfortable sofas, to discover that Rhue had already dressed and gone. I guessed where and I didn't worry. Instead I rolled over and slept for another delicious hour. I awoke a second time to the simple domestic sounds of dishes being washed and put away. That sense of normality felt wonderful. Better than wonderful — hopeful.

I snagged a piece of toast and a mug of coffee, and made my way outside to sit on the spacious veranda. Zee and her parents were waiting for me, with more breakfast tidbits on offer.

From my position on the veranda I witnessed the bustle of everyday life in Carrickbeg. The produce stalls were open for business and people were lined up for such items as bread, milk, fresh fruits and vegetables. It seemed that a barter system was in place — I saw no money change hands. It was more a matter of people exchanging one product for another. If only this would work on a grand scale, I mused. But certainly it did work in Carrickbeg.

"How long have you been up?" I asked Zee.

"I rose this morning at five a.m. to help with the dewing of the flowers." Zee answered.

"The dewing …?"

"… of the flowers, yes. Your on-Earth world has humid air which cools in the nighttime and leaves moisture in the morning on the plantings. Under the surface, in Nethermost, this dewing must be done by artificial means — by fairies, to be precise."

"Ooo! You have my full attention. More please."

"To dew the trees, grasses, grains, vegetables, and flowers, we fairies use our gift of intangibility. We wet ourselves thoroughly with water collected from underground springs. Then we literally run transparently *through* everything on every surface where plants grow, field and dale alike, shaking the water from our clothing as we go. It is hard work, but the fun can be found. This morning felt quite nostalgic. It's been years since I have helped my family with the morning chores."

I shut my eyes and tried to imagine an army of transparent fairies cavorting through flowers and grasses each morning, completing this essential job in such a carefree way. I could be content with a life like this, I mused.

"I assume my sister is off somewhere with Keane?" I asked.

"Yes, they are touring the farms and the meadows. You should join them; it is really quite beautiful." Zee led me along a path to the edge of the settlement where the view opened up into an explosion of pure paradise. The colour of day in this land was somehow different — like the pinkish tones of an early dawn without the glare of a fireball sun — which made the sky the first thing I noticed. The effect was created by a single shaft of light shining down, energizing the vitreous crystal ceiling and further diffused by large crystal boulders scattered about the fields.

"What's that?" I asked Zee, pointing to the beam of light.

"That is Light Shaft M," she explained matter of factly. "It is one of twenty-six skylights that provide sunlight to the realm. While we are north of The Capitol, we are also central to the continent, meaning that as much land exists to the west of us as to the east. "M" is halfway through the alphabet. Our skylight is halfway across the continent."

"Very neat," I replied, turning my attention now to the view beneath the sky. My sister and Keane were streaking across the meadowlands on small horses with long manes and tails. They resembled Icelandic horses and I wondered if they had been transported here in centuries past. The meadow before me was charged with daisies, lilies, buttercups, poppies, phlox and cornflowers — and a myriad of flowers I could not identify. Far beyond I could just make out hedgerows surrounding grain fields, pastures of mountain goats and a few long horned cattle. When Rhue saw me standing at the edge of the lea, she steered her horse in my direction.

"Good morning Cait! Is this not grand?" she shouted. "Keane is a whisperer too like his grandfather. Just look at him ride!" It did my heart good to witness my sister following her bliss. I wished her many more such days in life — just not at this precise moment. Meanwhile, I had to play the role of wet blanket.

"Should we talk about our day perhaps Rhue?" That brought her back with a crash. She stopped her horse and dismounted.

"Of course, dearest," she answered sheepishly. "But I wasn't being quite as frivolous as it seems. Keane has volunteered the use of his horses to travel to The Capitol, with himself as guide. I think we should take him up on his offer. What do you think?"

"I had that same thought last night when I realized how useful he would be to our mission, not only for finding a sneaky route into the city, but also into the two palaces. The horses are a nice bonus though."

She looked delighted and called Keane over to share the news. When he had dismounted, I broached a subject I'd been saving from the night before. "You mentioned that your grandmother still lived with you Keane. Is she well?"

"Very well, although she misses Grandfather. Why do you ask?"

"We have a picture that I hope you will let us show her." I didn't know if she was the friend that Zee was thinking of or not, but his grandmother's history with the royal children was interesting, and perhaps useful.

"A photograph? Of a person?"

"No, it's odder than that. It's a weird shot of a portion of a canvas, painted by one of our seers. By Ambassador Sinead, in fact."

That impressed him. "You know the Ambassador? My Grandfather spoke of her a lot, in the most glowing adjectives. May I see the photograph?"

I didn't see why not. It couldn't hurt, and it just might help. I took out the photo that I'd purloined from Rhue's satchel and handed it to him. He stared at it long and hard, perhaps searching for something to say.

"It is …"

"Weird?" I repeated.

"As you say. You think it will help to show this to Grandmother?"

"I believe so, yes."

"Then we shall."

*****

"I remember that wicked little boy," said Mrs. Sweeney, Keane's grandmother. "He was cute when he was a baby though. His sister Nicola would carry him on her hip around the palace with her everywhere she went. She adored him, and treated him like a little doll. He never grew very tall and that made him mad. And when he was old enough to realize that Nicola would inherit the throne and not he, that made him mad too. He had a kind of festering in his soul, that child. And he was smart — too smart some would say."

We were sitting in the front parlour of a modest farmhouse, simply furnished, but meticulously clean. Mrs. Sweeney sat by the window overlooking fields of goats to one side and a meadow of flowers to the other, looking quite content.

"May I show you a little portion of a painting dabbed by Ambassador Sinead?" I asked. She seemed of sound mind, despite the fact that she must have been in her late eighties by now. The alpine climate seemed to agree with her.

"Certainly … are you Cait or Rhue?"

"Cait," I confirmed, handing her the image.

"Well … that's odd …" she said. "What am I to make of that? Where's the rest of it?"

"I left it at home," I explained. "It wasn't a good idea to bring it."

"No, no," she muttered. "But if you had, would there have been a long desk with beakers and other lab equipment all over it, a clutter of library shelves, and an unmade bed?"

"I don't know about the bed," I said, "but the rest of it seems right. Do you know where this is?"

"Indeed! This is Peadar's bedroom suite, is it not?"

"That agrees with our findings."

"Oh look he's dropped his clothes on the floor like he did all his life. Never picked up after himself. I went through more maids than I care to remember, they were that disgusted with the smells as well as the messes. Especially the stink of those beakers, although he didn't use them much after he got his own lab."

"Can you tell from the clothes when this would have been?"

"Well, there's those terrible jeans he used to wear, but he wore jeans for years from the age of sixteen until the time of the coup."

That wasn't much help, so I pushed her further. "What about some of the other clothes? Can you recognize when he would have worn them?"

"Look there's his lab coat. That looks like the new one I gave him on his day of ascension. For some reason he liked it."

"Good … good," I coaxed her along. "So, he wore this after the age of nineteen then?"

"Yes, it would have been. He worked in his rooms while his parents were still alive and then when they died, his sister gave him his own chemistry lab, that ungrateful young whelp!"

"And did he wear this lab coat all the time?"

"Yes, he did. Even after he commuted back and forth to the lab."

My heart sunk. Now we had narrowed it only to somewhere between the age of nineteen and twenty-three years old. That was too wide a margin. We needed something more.

"I'm sorry I have to ask you to look at this again. Is there anything else about the clothes?" I shot a look of apology at Keane, who was beginning to frown now. But I needed something more, and I needed to take one more crack.

"I don't know!" Mrs. Sweeney was getting anxious now too. "The jeans, the lab coat, the satchel … wait … that satchel …"

"Yes, yes!" This was getting exciting now. We all leaned in to catch her every word.

"He started carrying that satchel with him everywhere he went after he got the laboratory. For two years, he would take it with him in the morning and bring it back again at night."

Great. Still this only narrowed it down to two years before that fateful day when he betrayed his sister.

"But there's something about that satchel. Something ..." She stopped and looked out the window while we waited for the 'something' to come to her. "Ah! … It's empty!" she declared like she had just cracked the code — which indeed she had just about. "That satchel was bulging in the mornings when he went to work and bulging in the evenings when he came home. But here in this painting it's flat. He did this night and day for two years, I'm certain. Why was the satchel empty at night?"

Why indeed? My heart sang. That was what we wanted to find and photograph — the contents of the satchel. If it was secret information he was working on, it would be most current just before his rebellion. We needed to search the room where a younger version of our great uncle lay sleeping, and we would need to get in and get out, without disturbing his rest.

We gave Mrs. Sweeney a huge hug and five gold coins 'for your retirement', thanking her son and daughter-in-law as we left. The air outside smelled fresher somehow, or perhaps I was breathing easier.

We were just on the edge of our return path to Carrickbeg when Keane's mother shouted from the front door, "She's remembered something ..."

Back in the room we stood calmly, not daring to break Mrs. Sweeney's concentration. "There was an odd thing that happened," she recalled, "it was two days before Peadar moved into his new residence — so five days it would have been before the coup. His maid at the time, Daisy it was, came to me all upset because of something she had done — in all innocence — but it made him madder than she'd ever seen him. 'A rage' is how she described it.

"Daisy was changing his sheets, as he'd already gone for the day. That was the rule: after Peadar left in the morning, the staff were to go in and clean up. She was stripping the bed, as you do, and she ran across a journal beneath the top mattress newer the pillow ... thick, handwritten it was, with funny symbols and numbers and such. She took a wee peek, and was putting it back when Peadar returned, and he saw her. He shouted at her something fierce and slapped her face hard ... told her to get out. So she did, but she looked back through the crack in the door before she left ... and saw him shove that book into his satchel, muttering, "Can't lose it now ... not when I've finally cracked it!"

I gasped and jumped to my feet, throwing my arms about Mrs. Sweeney again, nearly hugging the stuffing out of her this time. Rhue reached for Keane and gave him a spin. This was it! We had the time, the location, the object in question ...

Set the time travel dial for a few hours before Daisy found that journal under the mattress — and earned herself a good slap for doing so!

Chapter 32: A Glimpse of Paradise

The village seamstress fussed about our clothing, making a case for a change in disguise. She was of the opinion that we should dress like mountain folk, and she had set out a wardrobe for our consideration. Rhue was already convinced by her argument that, dressed as mountain folk, we would blend in better.

I was the dissenter. "Sad to say we cannot — for three very good reasons. One is that we want to look dirty and ugly, so that we will not stand out and are in fact avoided. Your clothes are far too beautiful, mistress."

"But we can make ourselves look dowdy still," Rhue added in support of her argument.

I looked at Rhue's hopeful expression and sighed. Was she allowing herself to become smitten with Keane, after denouncing the idea of romance in her pledge of loyalty to our mission? Was she loathe to let him see her in her old hag disguise? Where was that warrior I needed by my side? "Perhaps," I replied, looking pointedly at Rhue. "But there's the second more critical reason, and I'm surprised you didn't think of this Rhue. If we are caught, as we may well be, and are identified as mountain folk, Peadar will show no mercy to *all* the inhabitants of the Pinnacles of Pons. He *will* exact his revenge. And the third reason, of course, is the painting. These are the disguises in the painting!"

"You are right, Cait," Rhue said sheepishly, "I hadn't thought of that."

"If you like Rhue, *I* will be mother this time. *You* can be the kid."

*****

We set off in the late afternoon, looking quite disgusting. I had even managed to persuade Keane to wear his hair loose, in greasy strands, and to put on filthy garments. Even the horses were made to look like nags. I was taking no chances, and now that Rhue was thinking sensibly again, neither was she.

Keane had given Rhue and I good strong horses, while Zee was to ride with us each in turn. Keane's stallion was the tallest and most spirited. When well groomed he was white with a pale grey mane, although all that was hard to see now, smudged as he was with stove blacking. Rhue's horse was a dapple grey with a matching mane that she had braided and knotted badly, then had rubbed pie crust into his coat to simulate mange. My mare was a chestnut, more a like pony than a horse in size, but quite peppy nonetheless. I added teasels and burrs to her blond mane and tail, and apologized to her for the indignity.

The horses seemed comfortable on the steep slopes and picked their way slowly downward, following Keane's lead, until we had reached the base of the Carrickbeg Pinnacle. From there, Keane led us north through the foothills of four more pinnacles. He then turned east into the Forest Curran, no doubt taking the same path in reverse that his grandfather had chosen forty years before. Our journey was dark, our path gnarled with roots, making our progress slow, but happily uneventful, and we kept plodding well into the night. After hours of single file riding, avoiding low hanging branches, I was sore, exhausted and begged Keane to stop. He dismounted and gave us each a long draught of water to which he added a dollop of his grandmother's 'cure'.

"What does it cure?" I asked.

"The ague, the rheumatism … and saddle sores."

"Well, that's ambitious," I said, but I took a swig of it anyway in the hopes that something in it might do the trick.

"I was wanting to go as far as Termon tonight," Keane explained, "but we can search for someplace nearby, if you wish."

"What is Termon, and what makes it a good stopping point?" Rhue asked. Now that we were on the road again, she was all business — all warrior.

"Termon is a sanctuary and a favourite escape of Her Grace Fianna, in her day. Apparently she would teleport to such locations to recharge her spirits and commune with nature when things got frantic with her royal duties. I happened upon it several years ago, as I was exploring the Forest Curran. I identified it as one of her getaways after finding a cache of books, bearing her name, tucked into a crevice in an ancient elm tree. I have since created a small shelter there to store the books. This is where I stay when I'm in these parts."

"Cait, how are you feeling now?" Rhue asked. Surprisingly, I did feel better. Good old Grandma Sweeney. Plus the idea of being able to pay homage to my ancestor was an attractive one.

"I'm good," I chirruped. "I could go farther."

Keane looked pleased, and led us through more tiresome thickets and whipping leafage for another two hours. It was midnight before he stopped and dismounted. By now Zee had fallen asleep in my arms, so he took her from me and set her on his own saddle while we unpacked. He suggested the lowest light setting on our wands for safety's sake. "*Fiat lux — minima*" we called out, now knowing how to adjust the light levels. In the blue/green glow we could barely see what he was doing, but I did manage to catch him opening a hatch in the ground near the big old elm. He disappeared into a dark opening beneath, returning minutes later to announce, "You may enter now. I will bring the fairy."

The air below was stale — a space only adequate for the desperate traveller. It had earthen walls and a ceiling so low that you couldn't stand straight. Tree roots dangled from its low ceiling like tatty beaded curtains. Stacked into a wooden crate were musty blankets and pelts. It was a bachelor pad in the rough. Before we entered, he had laid out some skins to serve as bedding. Onto one of these, he placed Zee.

"You may raise the lights now. We cannot be seen from above."

"*Maxima*."

While Rhue and I pulled bits of food we had brought with us into a meal, Keane saw to the horses. Upon his return, we dined on cold meats, cheeses, and bread fresh from the Carrickbeg market that morning.

"We have travelled roughly forty kilometres today," Keane reported, "and are now twenty from the outskirts of The Capitol — about two hours' ride tomorrow. We must leave our beasts there, however, for I will not risk losing them by taking them into the city.

"It's another five kilometres on foot before we reach the palaces. Because of the need for stealth on the city streets under curfew, I must allot an hour for that trek. So, that's three hours' travel altogether. How long will you be in the palaces?"

"We have absolutely no idea, Keane," Rhue confessed, "but you can rest assured we won't dawdle."

"I only ask because it will be problematic to be caught in the city after daybreak."

*****

Our final travel day was spent in the 'Garden of Eden', to use a common metaphor. But Termon was indeed idyllic in the light of day. It was a small clearing enclosed by a thickness of trees, with grasses and wildflowers encircling a pond fed by a tiny waterfall. Keane was already in the water, frolicking.

"Hey," I called out, "don't do that! You'll get clean!"

"Don't worry, I brought along stove black to reapply the soot. Come in and join."

It was too alluring to resist. Rhue and I stripped off to our skivvies, tied up our filthy locks and waded in. As I stroked through these still waters, my mind took me back to the previous summer and my carefree day trips, when my biggest worry had been the long drive home at the end of a beach adventure. A few short months ago life had been so simple, boring even. The weight of the world was not yet on my shoulders — or *our* shoulders — as I shared this burden with my sister. It did not seem possible, yet all my sensibilities screamed its truth.

I picked through the trail mix, saving more raisins for Zee, for whenever she awoke. While I was musing by the pool, Keane brought a wooden box from the hovel and placed it between Rhue and me, looking very pleased with himself. "Please open it," he bowed. It contained six perfectly preserved volumes of tooled leather books which, when we explored their inside covers, were all signed in a childish scrawl: "*This book belongs to Fianna. If found please return to the palace, and I will give you a pretty token.*" The significance of this made me shiver, and my hand trembled a bit as I focussed on the smallest one. *The Language Of Flowers* it was called, with hand painted illustrations of flowers native to Nethermost.

Keane could not possibly have known the significance of this find — to my sister and me especially — because we had not yet divulged our royal connections to him, or to any of the citizens of Carrickbeg. Only Zee knew the truth, and she was not telling.

I spent an hour at least pouring over my great-grandmother's books, completely losing myself in their artistry and historical significance.

Nethermost Regained

They were priceless I knew, and really belonged to the people. When Nethermost was free again, I was determined to build a museum to house such treasures. It could go a long way to restoring the nation's pride, and to paving the road to cultural recovery.

It was almost noon when Zee finally stirred, looking quite flushed I thought. I didn't know what a fairy looked like when she was sickly, but something about her seemed wrong. Although she put aside all such suggestions, she didn't attack her raisins with any enthusiasm. I decided to keep a close watch.

Loath though we were to leave this glimpse of paradise, we hitched up our steeds and were off by early afternoon. Three hours to the city border would get us there, with time to spare before twilight, to allow us an opportunity to strategize and execute this last leg of our journey.

*****

While Rhue and I looked over the sketch Grandpa Fergus had made of the old palace, Keane whispered final instructions to his horses. Grandpa had marked Peadar's suite in red. It was on the top floor of the three storey complex, east side of the building, last room that overlooked the stable yard. Grandpa had marked the secret door's general whereabouts on the east side as well, also not far from the stables. More than that he did not know. Studying his not to scale map made us recall our rings and we pulled them from the hidden pockets we had sewn into our hems before leaving Nethermost Gate. Now was the time to place them on our fingers.

"Rhue," I asked, "did you get some instruction on the flame throwing thingy — like how to go about doing it?"

"I asked Shin. She said it was like most of these talents — intent is everything. If I intend to kill, I am to envision the enemy dead before pointing my hand in his direction. If I intend to maim, I must picture a specific injury before wielding the torch. What did you discover about teleportation?"

"Intent here also seems important. But in this case, the focus is on the details of the destination. You have to see it in your mind."

250

We looked at the rings and tried to fit them together once more, as we had done many times in the past to determine how they fit, concluding again that they didn't. We had to hope that inspiration would come if we needed to use them — and I was now sure that we would.

We didn't bother much with the city maps, although we had studied them and kept them tucked in our waistbands. But Keane seemed sure of his route, and we had come to trust his guidance. We tried to get Zee to stay with the horses, but she insisted on coming despite the fact that she was clearly getting worse. She was persuaded to take another dose of Grandma Sweeney's cure though. It seemed to be holding back the worst of her mounting symptoms.

It seems impossible, but nonetheless true, that our walk through the city was relatively uneventful, except for one minor incident with a dog walker, who chastised us for being out past curfew. We shot back that we ourselves were looking for a guardsman to report that a dog walker was out past *her* curfew. She'd scarpered before we'd even finished our implied threat.

Now we stood at the back of the old palace buried in bramble. Keane had taken us through the thick undergrowth that clawed at our ankles and whipped our faces, until we were standing at the back of this derelict seat of power, broken down stables behind us, erstwhile palace before. We had determined already that our intangibility wouldn't penetrate its walls from the outside while Peadar's perimeter spell was still in place. We needed to find the secret door instead. So while Zee stood guard behind a gargoyle over the tradesmen's entrance, we began a scan of its walls by running our hands over the surfaces to discover any differences.

Keane looked on perplexed. "Do you really think you will gain access, where everyone else has failed?"

"Yes," we whispered in unison. The solution, once we found it, was entirely logical, therefore completely unexpected. It lay in a series of friezes depicting the two Swayers at their coronation. The stone mason had carved their images in *bas relief* panels, raised from a flat background like a cameo in a ring. As I stood back and studied the scenes, I twigged onto it finally on the middle panel which showed the Swayers exchanging the rings — except the rings they were exchanging were not in *bas relief*, but *intaglio*, indented rather than raised. I placed my ring finger in front of the impression in Fianna's hand and could see that the positive rise of my ring fit into the negative depression in the panel precisely. Rhue did the same over Canice's.

"Well," she said, with a wink, "shall we?"

"I think we shall," I smiled, trying to control my elation. "One … two … three." At the exact same moment, we pushed our rings into their intended depressions, and the panel slid aside with a slight exhalation as the perimeter spell also released. At my shoulder, Zee whispered softly, "The building is sad. Hark how it sighs."

Keane's double take was delightful. He jumped forward with enthusiasm, as did Zee, to follow us through, but Rhue put out a hand to hold them back.

"Your help will be critical at The Golden Palace, my dears, but for this part of the mission, it must be just Cait and me. There are too many ghosts to disturb, and this destiny cannot be shared."

Keane

Chapter 33: Stealth Ops

"I'm assuming that Peadar's perimeter spell kept folks out, not in," Rhue commented as we crept along the befouled corridors of the east wing. The place had been ransacked — only broken or useless bits left as garbage. I was trying to imagine the opulence of bygone years, as we walked about the empty, stale smelling spaces in the twilight which penetrated softly through cracked and broken windows.

"Only one way to be sure," I said, putting my hand through a wall and pulling it out again. "Do you see any signs of life?"

"I see mouse 'raisins' … no footprints in the dust, if that's what you mean."

We crept cautiously along the full length of the hall before finding our route to the upper rooms. Even the neglect of decades couldn't disguise the grandeur of that marble staircase and the elegance of its spiral rise. One could easily imagine a young lady standing nervously on its top step in her first ballgown pausing to strike an alluring pose, her hand lightly caressing the hand carved bannister, her open toed shoes peeking out from under yards of chiffon. I felt the glide of the fabric as she descended, head held high, heart pounding in anticipation of her suitor's arm waiting on the bottom step to lead her into the debutante ball.

In contrast, we crept up these stairs like thieves, keeping our bodies low to the ground and our backs to the wall until we reached the topmost floor. In the half darkness, the corridor was faintly lit by squares of twilight in each open doorway. The few bedrooms we peeked into betrayed the aftermath of a brutal pilfering, breakage mixed with dust and cobwebs. We easily identified our target — the last room to the east, and stood outside its open door holding our collective breaths. It seemed the thing to do before stepping onto the stage of the most frightening performance of one's life. Rhue and I held hands and walked through together.

We confirmed the space was Peadar's by the shattered test tubes on the floor, and the remnants of books flung off broken shelves. We paced the suite trying to imagine how it would have looked forty years before — where the desk would have been, the arm chair and the ornamental carpet, and most importantly, where Peadar's old bed would have stood. The remnants of the test tubes identified the first room as the sitting room and boyhood lab. The second room had evidence of scuff marks on the floor to testify that large pieces of furniture had been dragged — a dresser perhaps, *or a bed*. In any case the scratches confirmed this as the likeliest place for us to search — forty years before.

"Okay, let's look at it methodically," I reasoned, "Where should we be standing when we transport? How will we remove the journal and get it photographed — especially from under the nose of our slumbering villain in the making?"

Rhue was all business now. I was pitching to her strengths. This was a military operation. "Let's shut this door and stand just inside when we transport," she suggested. "Then when we arrive in the past, we will be in shadow, out of the direct line of sight of the bedroom and its occupant; out of sight of anyone lurking outside in the corridor as well. I'm reasonably good at sliding unseen and unheard along the ground, so I will retrieve the journal from between the mattresses, resisting the urge to use father's birthday gift to slit the bastard's throat. It is likely that he was dyspeptic from too much drink and wild living back then, as now. I'm only guessing from Aunt Moira's description. That may be the real challenge — his restlessness."

"Right," I agreed, happy to leave the stealthiness to my sister. "That leaves the question of how to photograph it without making a noise, or waking him up. There's bound to be pages and pages of the stuff, and we've got to get it all."

Then, just like that, it came to me. How easy it is when you look at it a certain way. "We don't photograph it *in the past*," I exclaimed. "We take it with us to photograph it *in the present!* Then we return the original to the past when we're good and ready — no time elapsed from his perspective, no interference with the timeline."

We *imagined* ourselves five nights before the coup, at the midnight hour, standing just inside his doorway, and successfully travelled to the *when* we wanted to be, landing in the exact same location. While I remained by the door on watch, Rhue dropped to the floor and slid along like she was finding her way through a room protected by laser beams. It was ten minutes before I saw her again — with the ledger tucked into her shirt.

We stood on our marks, this time with Rhue holding the journal tightly and exhaling slowly to recover her nerves from the shock of her success. I held onto her arm to follow her into the present.

After weeks of planning, the actual task was all too simple to perform. Rhue laid the journal on the floor, after sweeping the glass aside, while I closed the tattered window curtains. Then she opened the journal to the first page and held it flat. *"Fiat lux,"* I commanded of my wand, and started taking snaps — two shots of each page, with that extra few seconds to ensure a good focus. It took twenty minutes, with Rhue holding and me snapping.

As I was tucking the camera into my bag again and securing it in the inside pocket, Rhue announced that 'Stage Two' would be hers and she grabbed the journal and disappeared. I hadn't had time to even scratch my head or do a victory dance, before she'd returned, proclaiming "job done."

"What?"

"I put the journal back. Job done."

"Just like that?"

"Well, no not just like that. It was harder returning it, than taking it in the first place, because he kept rolling over. He's got really bad breath by the way. I'm thinking tooth decay. But fortunately he stayed asleep. His *vile* journal is under his *vile* mattress, and I would like to go now … please. I feel dirty, all over."

*****

"You want to go where now?" Keane whispered, making the most of negative body language to emphasize his disapproval.

"To the dungeon," Rhue mouthed.

"Impossible!"

"Do you want to help or not?" Rhue was beginning to look peeved.

Keane scowled and hesitated, so she continued. "Just take us to the new palace and point us in the general direction of the cells. We must get in," she added, "We need to see Nicola — and hopefully our mother."

"What? Your mother? Nicola … your mother?" As Keane raised his voice slightly, Zee placed a tiny hand over his mouth.

"No, of course not. Do the math. She's our grandmother. Nora is our mother."

"Little Nora?"

"Yes. Will you help or not?"

"You could have trusted me with this knowledge beforehand," he chided.

"Would *you* have trusted a stranger with such vital information, after one day's acquaintance?" she returned. In hindsight, we could have handled that whole situation much better. But we both had trust issues, Rhue especially, and she wasn't going to let any man betray her again.

Keane led us past the bramble of the old grounds into the more tame gardens of the new, forcing us to creep along on our hands and knees through the outside hedges until we were even with the back of the residence and level with the servants' entrance. Here was one lone watchman, dozing in a chair, too old and too fat to cause anyone trouble. As we crossed the lawn, we walked right past him. Zee pulled a bottle from her little purse to put two drops of a clear liquid into his beer, giving me an exaggerated wink. That fairy had a large dollop of fearlessness about her!

We were jimmying the lock on the servants' door, when we felt the first rumble, nothing compared to the force of the earthquake a few days before, but still significant for what it meant — that the damage to the realm continued. The old dude awoke and stood sleepily to attention, forcing his eyes open like he'd always been on the alert. Moments later, I understood why.

 A larger than life character who could only have been Peadar, dressed in what looked like an old coronation cloak over satin undergarments, fat and bald from years of debauchery, raced across the lawn in a terrifying rage. He made a beeline for a short descent of steps and entered a dark doorway, followed by two lowlifes with strange looking guns.

Rhue turned to me, looking intense, "This could well be the break we need, Cait. Peadar will be heading for the dungeon right now to cast his wrath upon Nicola and Nora. He will blame them for what he will see as a dereliction of duty — for allowing another tremor to emerge."

She whispered to Keane and Zee. "No arguments now you two, no time to debate. Stay here on guard and wait. Cait and I must do this now. It is our duty."

It was the way she doled out her instructions that made us all comply without question — forcefully — unchallengeable. She pulled me along the gilded wall and fixed her sites on the doorway Peadar had just entered. We initiated our transparency a metre to the right of his door, and entered the wall in pursuit of Peadar. His shouting provided us with direction. Inside the wall, we inched through the stone, wooden struts and the gilding, honing in on the increased sound of his voice, until we knew we were nearly on top of him, the noise was that loud. It was like listening to a radio with the volume cranked up full, imagining the visual that went with it.

"If this continent crumbles, dear sister, it is you to blame," his voice bellowed at his invisible victim.

"I am doing my best," came the weary reply.

"Not good enough!" he shouted back.

"Don't you dare touch a hair on her head!" another female voice raised in reply. "You think you have power over your sister, but in truth she has power over you. She alone is saving this world. She alone is supporting your wanton lifestyle. If she dies, so does the nation. So do you!"

Rhue and I squeezed each other's hands. Our Mom. How brave!… and what an inspiration! She'd certainly stopped the rantings of her evil uncle. He blustered a few more garbled threats, as his footsteps and his voice faded away.

We waited a full five minutes after the noise ceased before daring to move. Finally I risked all — fulfilling a lifetime of anticipation. "Nora?" I whispered.

I could hear a rustling of bedclothes. Then silence again.

"Nora," I repeated in a normal tone.

"Oh heavens, am I dreaming?"

"Mother?" I said this time.

"Mother?" the shaky voice questioned. "Whose mother?"

I could bear it no longer, and stepped through the wall, Rhue holding onto my dress. "I am looking for my mother, Nora O'Quinn," I blubbed, no longer even trying to hold back my emotions. "My name is Cait. I am your daughter. And this," I raised my wand on its dim setting, "this is my sister, Rhue."

The woman before me gasped, her eyes still blinking as she adjusted to the sudden light; bloodshot eyes they were, their sockets smudged; a woman clearly overstretched with fatigue. But beauty was hiding within, beneath that white pallor and limp hair; and something else besides — strength, courage, defiance — those admirable features I saw in my sister. I witnessed her tears arrive as the full impact of the moment hit her. She grabbed for us both at once and pulled us to her. I was falling apart myself, and I had known we were coming. But we must have been a complete surprise to her, a shock after twenty years in a prison cell with one lone companion. Welcome or not, we were not what she expected.

I turned to her companion, my grandmother Nicola, who was lying on a bed barely conscious, looking confused at the two women who had emerged from the wall to invade her dark solitude. She was old beyond her years, and frail, almost transparent herself there was so little of her. I ached to see her suffer so.

"Are there any guards present?" This was the soldier in Rhue, with a very sensible question.

"The guards are down the hall on the other side of that thick door. They never come in and, in any case, they're usually drunk by this time each evening,"

With this assurance, we raised the light levels to see Nicola and Nora in a proper light. They were in their nightclothes, as expected, but had a wardrobe and a dresser for clothes in their bedroom sized cell. There were matching twin beds, two easy chairs, and a table with two chairs where they took their meals. The only luxury item I suppose was a few books on some shelves between the beds, and a discrete lidded chamber pot under one of them. All enclosed behind gilded bars — just like those sketched out in Shin's painting.

I turned to Nora. "Mother, I'm so sorry but we haven't come to rescue you …"

"Of course not, you can't," she replied, "but you have come to help. You are concerned about the earthquakes, I dare say. Are they being felt above ground as well?"

"Yes. We have been sent to bring you aid in fighting the damage, and in keeping Grandmother healthy."

"Thank you. It is almost enough just to have met you. I have dreamed of you nightly since the day I crossed the border. Although I do not regret coming to my mother's assistance, I'm so sorry I left you. I hope you understand."

I looked at Nicola who was sleeping again, now slumped in Rhue's embrace. I understood — it was no easier for any of us — but I did understand.

"How is Michael? Your father … is he alive? The last I saw of him, he seemed to be getting a good bashing from a vicious monster. Did he survive it? While your infant faces were the stuff of my sweet dreams all these years, my final remembrance of him receiving a beating has been my constant nightmare."

"He is alive," Rhue informed her, "and he sends his love, though certainly not his despair. He gets a bit cranky as he blocks out the difficult memories, but he is strong, Mother, so strong. He heads up the Resistance now. He has promised us a day of reckoning. Mother, please believe there will be … a day of reckoning!" she pleaded.

"I do dearest. Oh I hardly fathom that these strong women are my babies! My heart is full, my dreams replete."

"One other needs to be remembered to you," I added, sitting beside her and taking her hand. "Ol'Ben sends his love especially."

"Ol'Ben? Do you mean Grandpa Ben?" she asked, a swathe of delight pinking her cheeks. "He is still alive? He would be so old …."

"Old, but well — and living outside Nethermost Gate. He is my friend, my confidante and my dearest companion."

"How wonderful! Would that I could see him again," Nora replied, with a trace of nostalgia.

"You will … if we have anything to do with it … you will," I assured her. "But mother, we must not stay long and we have gifts for you. Useful tools, I hope."

I gave her the medicines from Moran — the very powders and potions she was lacking, she confirmed. She glanced over the small vials and envelopes, catching her breath in delight. "These will go along way in restoring my patient. Please thank Dr. Moran."

"Darragh, a stone mason, also sends a tool for you that he hopes will be equally helpful. He sends this along." I removed the ring that I had pinned inside my blouse. "He sends his balancing ring for you to wear. He means you to use it to assist Nicola — to help her keep order and balance over a land in disarray. It is his own talent ring, Mother, freely given, as an addendum to your own healing talent. You need to merge this with the ring you currently wear, by placing them together on the same finger. Oh Mother, you should have heard the nobility in his voice, and seen the strain on his face as he forced it from his own finger. He asked me to present it to you with his highest respect."

"But how can that be?" My mother looked amazed. "It will diminish him utterly. How can he sacrifice so much?"

"When I asked him, he said, and I quote, 'It is a disability I am willing to endure … for the greater good'."

"For the greater good," she echoed. "Let us hope I do him proud. Please tell him I am grateful … and humbled."

"There is another who has perhaps sacrificed too much," Rhue added, thinking of Zee now. "A fairy who has led us into Nethermost and used her contacts to get us here safely. She is ill now, although she will not admit it."

"What has she being doing that is out of the ordinary?"

Rhue described our journey in brief, knowing that we needed to be off very soon. She covered our entry into Nethermost, our time at Carrickbeg, our journey through the Forest Curran, and closed with a frank description of our task in the old palace.

By the time she had finished, Mother was nodding her head. "She is weakened by that long trek through the rocks, girls. Fairies are not designed for such enormous crossings. I noticed a powder here sent by Dr. Moran which should restore her to strength. She is so tiny that I can surely spare enough for her cure. But she will be months in the healing. And she must not cross that border — never walk through rock again. She would not survive — as I suspect she knows herself."

I repacked my satchel and went over to hug my grandmother who was cradled in Rhue's arms. It was time to depart. For our safety's sake, and theirs.

"Rhue," she added, "I'm thinking back to your description of your activities at the old palace tonight …"

"Yes," she acknowledged, "I think we may have acquired the formula for Peadar's alchemy experiments and maybe even a blueprint for his gilding gun."

"I know you are right," she agreed. "but make sure you read through all those pages, because I think they may just contain the *antidotes* for his wicked formulas as well. He would not risk any damage to himself, if he did not have the cure."

*****

"You were gone for nearly an hour!" Keane urgently whispered to Rhue. "I was just about to come in after you."

"I apologize … sort of," she retorted, "but we got what we wanted, and gave what was needed. It was a complete success." She looked pleased. I was thankful too, and overwhelmed with emotion, feelings I'd file for now to relive and examine at my leisure.

"Then let us leave quickly. I worry about our schedule," Keane said, still cross with her.

I swear we were using as much caution as we did when we came in, but this time our luck had run out. As we reached the final hedgerow on our hands and knees, a voice rang out above us. "Stop! On your feet!"

With no other option but to obey, we stood up and faced our doom. It was Donal Fadden, looking like a professional soldier, but also one of Peadar's henchmen, in a crisp new black uniform, packing a gilding gun. "You are all trespassers and curfew breakers, and who knows what you've stolen." He paced in front of us now, delivering what was no doubt intended to be our execution speech. As he turned about, he faced my sister directly. "What! Rhue?" he sputtered, completely flummoxed. "How are you here?"

Thinking fast on her feet, Rhue turned this same question back on him. "Donal? How are you here? I thought you were out on a special ops from Nethermost Gate."

Donal narrowed his eyes and studied her face. "No … you … didn't. You knew I was gone, and you knew it was me that stole your painting."

"Did you?" she answered, toying with him now. "I did wonder whether it was gone or simply misplaced. Did you notice it gone, sister?"

Now Donal turned his attention on me. "Cait … of course. I never liked you. And that boyfriend of yours … what's his name."

"I always thought well of you," I replied, stalling for time while trying to conjure up an idea.

"Sure you did. Well I've told Peadar all about you two — the hope of the hopeless. That's what they think isn't it? And who's with you here? Oh! Little Zee. Well, when you need muscle power, bring a fairy. And who's this guy? Ooo, now he does look dangerous! The new boyfriend? We can't have that!" He went for his gilding gun as Keane flew at him and wrestled him to the ground. Donal easily slipped through his grasp, having the intangibility talent that would give him the advantage no matter what Keane might try to do.

"Right … I'm *really* going to enjoy this," he sneered. Becoming solid again, he grabbed again for his gun and pointed it directly at Keane.

An explosion rent the air, as a thunderbolt shot across the short gap between us and hit its mark. Donal fell to the lawn, immobile. Rhue pulled her arm back and rubbed the finger on which Canice's ring sat, now spent of its final burst of power.

"Is he dead?" I asked to no one in particular. Keane ran over to him and checked his pulse. "No," he reported. "Not dead, but certainly deeply unconscious. Let's get out of here quickly."

Instead of moving straight away, I went up to Rhue. "Not dead, Rhue? It's all about *intent* right? What was your intent? Not kill him … but what?"

She looked me straight in the eye. "No, Cait, I didn't intend to kill, as you well know. In the end, I couldn't bring myself to do it. But I think I succeeded in my intent — which was to befuddle his brain and scramble his thoughts. He may be alive, but he won't have anything useful to tell. That will slow things down a bit, don't you think? As his boss wonders about how one of his soldiers could be wandering incoherently about the rose garden."

I smiled at her, then added, "and without his gilding gun too. He'll be in big trouble," I picked up his weapon and shoved it into my backpack.

We raced through that last hedgerow, just as another small rumble shook the ground. I'd like to think that tremor was my mother's doing this time, to provide a distraction for our escape. But in any case, the guards were certainly not looking for intruders at all as they ran to their emergency stations at the new palace. It wasn't surprising that no one was patrolling the old palace, but it was fortuitous. We nipped through those grounds sharpish and without further detection.

Before we hit the city streets, Rhue stopped us, making us wait while she held me close in an embrace. "What's that for?" I asked. "A victory hug?"

"Yes, of course," she said. "Congratulations dearest. You are a warrior now … But, it is also goodbye."

"What? Where are you going?"

"Nowhere. But you are."

"No, I'm not. Why would I do that?" I asked. She had me completely floored. I couldn't follow.

"Even those dumb guards will suspect something when they find Donal like that. They will increase their watch. And if we try to make our way back to the gate on foot, they will be waiting for us. So you must go now, Cait. You must teleport with the camera and the gilding gun. Get to the gate straight away, before they can react. You have Fianna's ring — use it!"

Use Fianna's ring? Did I dare? "But what about you?" I asked.

"I'm going back to Carrickbeg with Zee and Keane. We will organize a resistance movement within the realm. We will have a better chance of success this way, come the day of reckoning, don't you see?"

"You planned this all along, didn't you? Planned to stay, and send me home."

"Maybe not all along, but it was a scenario I had considered. Now it is the only possible scenario. We cannot take Zee back with us, as you know, so please entrust her medicine to me. I sense real strength in those mountain folk, Cait. I trust them. Let me build an army here to add to father's forces."

"Go, Cait," Keane added his voice to hers now. "We will meet again in battle."

"Goodbye, Cait," added little Zee, tweaking my nose in her cheeky fairy way.

It was the strategically sensible thing, I knew. Then why did I feel like I was deserting them? Into what dangers were they heading? I looked at Rhue one last time, and nodded.

I pictured myself at the rendezvous point east of the main gate, that spot Zee insisted I memorize. In my head I faced the stone wall — saw to my right some kiosks and a boundary fence, saw to my left the tangle of dead wood we'd hidden behind when we first landed. I looked forward again and saw my own footsteps by the wall. I took in a load of air, closed my eyes, experiencing a wave of nausea engulfing me and a rushing sensation in my ears.

'Hold your breath and don't move until you come to a complete stop', my aunt had said.

Fianna's & Canice's Rings

Chapter 34: Debriefing

I was grateful for all the pull ups Loo had made me do in my training, as I scaled the rock wall to reach that tiny ledge, our secret bypass through Nethermost Gate. That endurance training, along with a few nubbins in the rock, launched my inaugural voyage as a climber. The obliging pitted surface provided enough cracks and crevasses for my three metre climb. But that final push onto that 'jut in the rock', as Zee described it, was hard to negotiate, and required a combination of guts and brute strength.

Once aboard, I willed myself transparent, turned in place, and stepped forward, sweeping the curtain of rock aside in my mind. I didn't even stop to consider the nightmare that lay in wait. Maybe I should have, because for the next grim fifteen minutes, I fought back feelings of emptiness and despair that would have brought most of creature kind to its knees. Deprived of sight, beleaguered by the battering of the past day, I ploughed through the grasping sludge of the hostile passageway that demanded nothing less than perfect recall to navigate, and mental acuity to traverse.

When I finally pushed through to the inner sanctum behind the lower gate, I sagged like limp lettuce, gasping even for the stale air of that tomb. "*Fiat lux, maxima*" I breathed to my wand, now my only companion. Bright light made the space slightly more bearable. I didn't even consider the creepy crawly infestation as I leaned my back up against that damp wall and closed my eyes. I must have slept, though for how long I'm unclear and it didn't matter much. But after that nap, I had energy enough to considered the logistics of my long trek to the upper gate — scaling the staircase three times the height of the CN Tower.

My strategy was to divide the task into three. One CN Tower equivalent, then pause for a drink and a rest. Another CN Tower equivalent, another drink and a rest. I anticipated that the third CN Tower would be the toughest because, by then, my thighs would be on fire and my knees jelly. But the pay off at the end would be sweet. I downed an entire bottle of water with the rest of the trail mix, and I revved my courage to begin.

I never intend to relive those agonizing hours again, not even for this account. To this day I think twice about taking the stairs. But this I do rewind — often and with pride. I was proud that I made it back to Nethermost Gate, proud that I brought back the bounty we'd snagged, proud of my full membership in the most noble of families and a continent well worth risking it all for.

*****

"Rhue?" Through my stupefied fog, I could hear a familiar voice calling out.

"I told you, it's not Rhue, it's Cait." Another familiar voice.

"She's in the clothes I sent Rhue out in, so it's Rhue," argued the first voice.

"I saw how she looked at me, and I know that's Cait."

I opened one eye and smiled woozily at those blurry but beloved faces. "Loo's right Aunt Moira," I croaked, "It's a wise mother who knows her own daughter."

Aunt Moira rushed over to the bed where I lay in the critical care wing of Hub Medical. I was still grimy and foul smelling from my travels. "Oh Cait, you called me Mother," she blubbed.

"I did … and I've just come from meeting my other mother a few short hours ago," I said. "I've decided I love you both."

The medical team shooed all the relatives from the room while they went to work on me. I knew I was well enough, but they needed convincing. I also knew I was going to be accepting all offers to lessen my discomfort and hasten the cure — pain meds, muscle relaxers, whizz bang potions, the lot. Just so long as I could grab a long soak in a bathtub first.

But I was fine — I was home.

They made me stay at The Hub for a couple of days, but I didn't mind. I had so many visitors, it was like holding court. The first person I needed to see was my father. I wanted him to know about Nora, his wife, wanted to bring her to life in his mind as she was today, to experience her through my heart.

"She has worried all these years about you Father," I said. "She thought you were dead, and she was living with that constant heartache." I recounted every delicious sentence of our conversation, every memory I had of her face, the warmth of her hands, her expressions, her courage, her touch. I assured him that although she and Nicola lived a bare existence, they were not completely deprived, that she seemed to have as much control over Peadar as he had over them. He dared not do them harm.

With every detail, I could see my father's posture lighten. It aroused his passion, making him all the more intent on forging ahead with his preparations. He had already removed the camera and gilding gun from my bag and had entrusted them to the care of the Magic

Council. They would be working 24/7 until they deciphered the formulas, taking special note of Nora's hint about antidotes.

While I cherished the opportunity to describe my visit with my mother, I held back on my update about Rhue until I couldn't put it off any longer. It was these details that filled me with anxiety. I told Father about the border crossing, the trip through the Pinnacles of Pons, about meeting its inhabitants and about Rhue's affinity with their lifestyle. I praised her strong leadership on the mission and outlined her intent to mount a militia of her own to assist our rebellion from the inside. Finally … reluctantly, I related my surprise at her insistence that I return on my own. Clearly I hadn't yet reconciled myself to our separation, and was seeking his reaction.

"My dear girl, your strategy was flawless, your partnership superb. Don't fret about Rhue. She was born for this. I only wish I had thought of it myself."

*****

I knew I could trust Loo to give me a no frills interpretation of the truth.

"So," I began, taking advantage of a rare moment when we'd been left alone. "I'm fuzzy on details about my arrival."

"I was there at the gate when you fell through, Cait. That's why I knew it was you."

"A bit of a coincidence, don't you think."

"Well, I kind of never left after you'd gone. I felt the need for some open air and solitude for a spell, so I pitched a tent, borrowed some camping gear from Michael, and took a little break by the gate."

"As you do …" I laughed.

"Yeah. That's how come I was there to catch you. I could hear you before I could see you. Hear all this panting you know, and not in a good way. So I ran up to that boulder, setting off a bunch of alarm buzzers as I did. They don't like it when you get too close.

"Anyway, there you were, kind of falling through the rock. You only got halfway through when you collapsed. I had to pull you the rest of the way. I was worried in case you solidified inside that boulder."

"Thanks for that visual." I said, grateful to know he hadn't changed in the least.

"Sure. So, after I pulled you through, I held on pretty tight and that's when I saw those eyes shining through. You and your sister may be identical, Cait, but there's a difference in how you see me. So I knew it was you, though Moira tried to shout me down about it."

I smiled recalling their bizarre argument that had brought me back to consciousness.

"How's Ol'Ben?" I asked.

"A bit shaky still to be honest, and he won't leave Aileen's side for long. She's an inpatient here too by the way."

"She hasn't recovered?"

"Well, she's kind of taking her time. Just as well, cuz P49 is still in a real state."

"Oh right. I'd forgotten about the clean up."

"I should have helped out more. I just got ..."

"Distracted?"

"Yeah. Sorry about that. Anyway, they've made a lot of progress as far as I can see. The main tunnels have been repaired. It's just the individual bio pods that are still in a mess. Folks have been bunking in at that tennis dome — or, you know, camping in the open."

*****

"I can see from the fact that you are openly wearing Fianna's ring, that you found an opportunity to use it," Grandma Aileen said, holding my bejewelled hand in hers."

"I should have taken it off again," I said, "I guess I forgot."

"No need for secrets about it now, my dear. Did Rhue use Canice's too?"

"In a most dramatic way. It saved our lives, no doubt. Saved us from an unpleasant gilding."

"My!" she enthused, "that pleases me no end. I must tell your grandfather. He will be happy, and relieved ... Cait, do you mind if I try something with you? Do you trust me, I wonder? Would you allow me to read your mind while you contemplate the images of your adventures? I ask for a couple of reasons. One is to experience your challenges, triumphs and pain — especially the pain, which is halved in the sharing. The second, and just as important, would be so that I can use my modest drawing skills to sketch details of your quest to share with others, things that might become useful to our war preparations. We have your oral account, which I am certain is reliable, but I know you wouldn't have been taking pictures like a tourist, or filming it for a movie. My sketches may allow us to see something you may not have thought to report."

This sounded like a wonderful idea. It gave me a chance to unload therapeutically, and it gave my grandmother an enhanced role in the fight. I had no doubt it would aid in her healing as well. We scheduled the first of our sessions for the next morning, the day of my discharge from Hub Medical.

*****

Shin visited on day two as well, in the early evening after the bustle of the day was over. She came in on her own and sat by the bed while I napped, startling me when I awoke.

"Do you feel like you're missing an appendage — without your sister, I mean." She never began a conversation conventionally, always one for surprises. But in that first sentence, she voiced the very crux of the matter, and got right to the point.

I sat up on the bed crossed legged and looked at her intently. "Have you brought me something?" I asked, both suspicious and excited at the same time.

She gave me one of her enigmatic smiles. "I have." She hobbled to the end of the bed, pulled out a brown paper package she'd left leaning against the footboard, and placed it in my lap. I tore off the paper, all expectation. It was a painting of course, a prevision, a prediction of what would be. It was Rhue on her dapple grey horse, dressed all in leathers, with a tooled breastplate. She wore her hair wild like mine now, her face was determined and vibrant. In one hand she held the horse's reins, in the other she brandished a handsome sword. By her side, riding his fancy white steed, was Keane in similar garb. The bond between them was obvious, their determination mutual. In the painting's action loop she was flourishing the sword, while he looked intent upon her with admiration in his eyes.

"Best gift ever," I acknowledged with a throaty voice. I had determined that from now on I would hold back on tears, but this was certainly testing my conviction. So Rhue gets her army, and her man. 'A better time for love', eh Rhue?, I thought. Nonsense.

"I kept a close watch on that dirty laundry painting while you were gone, Cait. It stopped moving at 9:02 p.m. on the fourth night of your absence. Am I close?"

"Well, I didn't check my watch Shin, but I'd say you were exact," I laughed.

She leaned back, cozied herself as much as one can in a straight backed chair and smirked, "Right then. Tell all. I love a good story."

*****

"I've got a surprise for you," Ol'Ben announced as he drove through the doorway on his new scooter with Mánús by his side. This was the second time I'd gotten to see him since my return less than two days before. The first time, I was far too groggy for conversation.

"I got you a room next to mine in that Relatives Support Apartments thingy here at The Hub, just until they fix up our home, that is. I'm going to escort you there myself after your session with Aileen this morning. The room's a bit lacking in character, but full marks for comfort," he added.

"And I've got a surprise for you old man."

"Don't toy with me Cait. Did you see her? Is Nora alright?"

"I did see her … and she's fine. A bit fatigued, but healthy ... and she can't wait to see you."

"She can't?" he said, holding his top lip between two fingers, willing it to stop it quivering.

"Nope … though she was surprised you were still alive."

"Well, of course … aren't we all?"

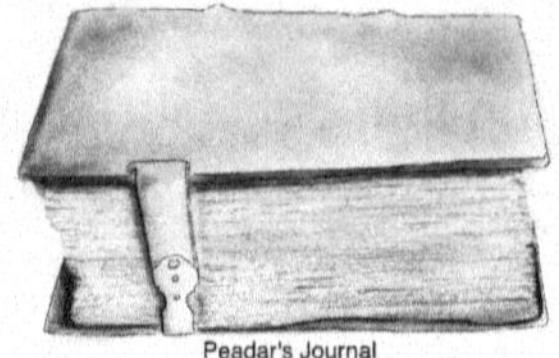
Peadar's Journal

Chapter 35: A Closer Look

"I want these sessions to be pleasant for us both, so let's agree to have fun above all. When you're completely relaxed is when the best recollections will flow."

Grandma Aileen had reserved us a therapy room at The Hub and had set the stage, so to speak, for maximum results. Towards this end, she had the uncomfortable wooden chairs replaced with soft furnishings, including two chaise lounges placed close together centrally with a small accent table between, a pitcher of lemon water and two glasses. I leaned back on my chaise, while she held one of my hands in her left one, a stick of graphite in her right, and a sketch book on her lap.

"We're going to go through this in slow motion so you can pay better attention to the images you were absorbing as you walked past them on your actual journey. I may even get you to stop altogether at times, when I see something I want to sketch, or when I want you to pay closer attention." Her instructions made perfect sense; I also understood her intent. She not only wanted me to see the particulars so we could add to our overall intelligence, but she wanted me to revisit the scarier bits, this time with herself as my companion. She meant for me to be able to stare down those fears that had enervated me in order to limit their power to frighten.

In our first session, for instance, we focussed only on the long staircase down to the inner gate and the grim passage through the rock wall that had robbed me of all sight and sapped my strength in the crossing.

She stopped me for a particularly long time in that anteroom before the lower gate, guiding my observations … "Okay, let's stop here to examine what they used to make this gate impassable. What are the hinges like?"

"It's hard to see them in detail because there's gobs of stuff all over them, like Spackle, thick and lumpy. It think it's supposed to be welding, and maybe it was golden once but it's changed somehow. It looks a bit flaky in places, and some of it is broken off. I would have said weathered, but it can't be that cuz there's only humidity and stale air in this chamber."

"Look at the latch of the gate. Has it been secured in the same way as the hinges?"

"Yes, but the erosion is more obvious here. The iron in the gate is standing up just fine, but the welding is more porous and dull looking."

"Do you see a perimeter spell? That is, do you notice a bright blue aura around the frame when you squint your eyes?"

"I see a dull glow surrounding the threshold, but it's almost too faint to make out."

As Aileen took me step by step through the architecture of this border entrance, I began to see it in a new light. I felt like an engineer examining the integrity of a building, finding fault with the design and construction materials. It made me realize that there *were* weaknesses that could be exploited to provide a possible route through to Nethermost for everyone, if we could just reverse engineer the alchemy that might not be standing up to time.

Before we ended the session, Aileen accompanied me through that breath stealing dark passageway again. "This time Cait, when you translate through the rock, I want you to close your eyes before you enter in order to deny its heavy density and utter darkness any power over you. That way you are controlling what you see and your reactions, instead of letting the rock take your sight and sap your strength. Let's use a metaphor to make this even less daunting. Pretend you are feeling your way to the bathroom at night. You know the way so well, you're not even going to take the time to turn on the lights."

I did as she suggested — closed my eyes and mentally began counting the paces — four hundred forward keeping to a straight line, turn left then ten more. But now in my head it was a long hallway to the bathroom, instead of a soulless drift into oblivion. I didn't feel heavy or dragged down. So it had been as much panic as physics that had weighed me down when we walked through that rock passage. I was unfettering that particular terror — it was a victory of sorts.

By the end of this session Aileen had made two accurate sketches …
- o the top of the staircase with its inadequate lighting and endless drop, pointing out the need for better lighting along the entire descent, with perhaps a hover stairlift, and
- o an inside view of the lower gate showcasing flaws in its design, opportunities to destroy the alchemy in order to stage a breach.

The bonus for me was the return of my fortitude. I felt liberated, and I could not wait for session two.

I've said it before — brilliant woman!

*****

Nethermost Regained

I was having lunch at Dr. Coffee Klatch with Loo, as I liked to do to break up our busy days, when I suddenly blurted out, "Do you think I've changed Loo? I mean am I more easily frightened now?"

He stopped mid sip to consider. "Well, that's two questions Cait, with two different answers. Have you changed? Yes, but then so have I. You're not the girl from Alta who was content to work at The General Store. You'll never be that girl again. You're stronger now, more worldly and open to adventure, with a strong sense of family. You've opened up your heart a lot too.

"But do I think you're more frightened after your mission? No, but I do think you're sadder. Look, you had a lot of shocking things happen to you that would have frightened the bejesus out of anyone. That's normal. What do they say about courage? That it's the willingness to act even though you want to crap your pants at the very thought of it? … I'm paraphrasing here."

I laughed long and hard at that one. He did have a way with words. I loved his unique mind. Loved him. "You've changed a lot too," I added. " You are even stronger, if possible, more focussed … and open. I can't believe how accepting you are of this bizarre new direction in our lives. You even seem happy."

"Guess I am. I think I stumbled onto my higher purpose by a stroke of dumb luck, and found that it fits me just fine. No, we're both better off now — except for that, you know, 'life and death' battle still to come." He stopped to stare at me for a few moments, until I started to feel a bit under scrutiny, like an open book that was his to read.

"Nope, the only thing bothering me right now is your sadness, Cait. And I know why. You still can't forgive yourself for leaving Rhue behind. But it had little to do with you. You didn't abandon her, and she didn't abandon you. Your paths just forked in the road, that's all. You found that your destinies differed. I bet Rhue's as happy as Larry right now ... becoming the General of her own army."

He was right, as usual.

I learned about the draft of the Nethermost reservists at that lunch. Loo had been called to serve in the motor pool — a semi military position, I guess. They were taking him up on his offer to work on his tunnel launch modifications with a team of mechanics. He wanted me to know he'd be away for a while.

"I'm going to set up a little chop shop with Larch and some of the Gate mechanics to do some jiggery pokery with the transporters," he explained. "We got the designs finalized, and have acquired some cheap materials. Now we just need a large enough space to do the customizing; so we're going to do it at the terminus where we met Aspen and Larch all those months ago. Apparently it's known as Ballaghmore which literally means 'big passage'. It'll be even bigger soon. There will be five lines running into that terminus in no time. One thousand reservists expected in all. We've got to be ready for them. I'm to stay with Aspen and Larch for a while. Aspen's a whiz with the needle it seems, and the roofs I designed for the launchers will be made from canvas, for budgetary reasons — meaning we haven't got one. Aspen and a bunch of her elf friends are going to get an assembly line going. Should be good."

I was happy for Loo — sad for me. I would miss him while he was away.

*****

Aunt Moira was moving in. She had had her own apartment at the Gate for years, but had given it up to be used for housing reservists. Since we were overhauling P49 anyway, for earthquake reasons, we had the dwarf masons cut another room into the rock for her. I loved it. For one thing, I had my second mother with me now, and I had missed her no nonsense attitude towards life. She simplified things, whereas I tended to tangle them.

Another reason I liked having Aunt Moira nearby was because she could keep me updated on the latest from campaign headquarters, since she was in the thick of it there.

Things really started heating up by early summer, and not because of the weather, although that was lovely too. The community began to bustle. The list of things to be done was daunting, nearly endless. Everyone was of one mind and one purpose, determined to be part of the solution. By late June, Aunt Moira was reporting real progress on the militia front.

"We've got the schedule worked out for bringing the reservists into Nethermost Gate. It's been a logistical nightmare. It's no small matter to increase a community of twenty-five hundred by fifty percent almost overnight. How do we house them, feed them, train them?

"Since it's summer we're able to house a lot of them outdoors. I found an absolute bargain on canvas pavilions at a hole in the road town north of Vancouver. Then almost every Gate citizen is taking billets into their homes, so that about covers it for lodging. We'll be fine, as long as we stage the invasion before mid September, when the evenings start getting nippy again."

I was curious. "So who are these folks who are coming in, Aunt Moira. Loo called it a *draft*. Does that mean that they have no option but to come?"

"Well, we're calling it a draft, because we're activating the pip tags of all citizens under the age of fifty. But we're not insisting that they come. Some have rebuilt their lives on-Earth by now, are married, have kids. We understand that. The callout comes with an RSVP, and NO is a possible answer."

I liked that idea, that respect of free will. It also meant that those who did arrive were keen to do a good job and didn't need to be given the incentive. When the first of the recruits arrived at the end of June, Father's role kicked into high gear. He set up training camps with classes running from four a.m. until midnight. Each soldier was self directed, but was expected to attend five hours of training per day — callisthenics, target practice, track, and fencing, and then select one fighting style from a choice of judo, jujitsu or karate.

Those who weren't physically strong were assigned a host of other duties with catering, field coordination or supplies acquisition. There was more work than there were workers.

*****

After my first debriefing with Aileen, she and I had suspected a flaw in Peadar's alchemy, beginning with the damage at the gate. When my memories of The Golden Palace reinforced these observations, we were convinced of its implications, but hesitated to race off half cocked. We needed a forum to test drive our notions, before taking them out for a serious spin.

This called for a family dinner. If our smart relatives were convinced, then it would be right to pass our intel to the appropriate scientists and strategists. By dessert time, Aileen was laying out her drawings before Grandpa Fergus, Michael, Aunt Moira and Ol'Ben, with an explanation about how she had harvested the images.

"I know you think my talent is less than scientific and is therefore more useful to the helping professions," she began, "but Cait and I have been very meticulous, even scientific, in preparing these sketches. Seeing these images in her mind's eye, I could argue, is more accurate than her verbal reports, because they contain, one might say, raw footage."

"I agree," I added, "Grandma has also been scrubbing the emotions from what I witnessed to get to the pure facts. Look at this drawing of the lower gate, Father. See how the welding is beginning to wear? It was fused just twenty years ago after Nora escaped, remember? At that time, it was tested from this side and found to be impenetrable. Peadar's alchemy compound was made with a super magic and resisted anything we could throw at it. And at the same time it was reinforced with a magic perimeter spell to increase this protection. All notions about piercing the border were abandoned. No one would suspect that it would change over time, so we haven't tested its strength in some years. A few weeks ago, it looked like this," I said, pointing to the drawing. "That's odd, don't you think? Wouldn't that indicate a weakness in their security now?"

Michel grabbed the drawing and held it up to the light. "So, is it flaky, or porous or what?"

"From what I could tell from the images in Cait's mind, 'or what' is the best answer." Aileen explained. "It could be metal fatigue of a sort. Or it could mean the power of alchemy breaks down over time, that it has a shelf life. Perhaps Peadar's super magic evaporates over time and the alchemized gold reverts back to the cheap metal that was used to transmogrify it in the first place."

"Well … this is impressive work, ladies," Grandpa Fergus was on his feet now, pacing about the room. "We can get this material tested tomorrow. We will remove our boulder temporarily and have engineers get down those stairs to take samples. If Peadar's formula is flawed, perhaps we can find a way to speed up its degradation. With the gates unsecured, we can breach the barricade!" He started dancing a little jig.

"But Cait's got concerns, don't you dear heart." Ol'Ben could always read me like a book. While most people watched the main performance onstage, Ol'Ben was watching the minor drama at the edges. And there were edges about me now.

"You're right Ol'Ben. I am worried. Don't get me wrong, this news is huge. It's giving us an unexpected advantage, an entry point for our forces and war machines. That's exciting … But don't you see there's danger here too?"

"What do you mean, dearie," Aunt Moira stroked my hand in comfort. "There's plenty of danger ahead for Peadar, but where's the danger for us?"

"Okay," I was searching within the logic of my argument to find my footing. "If the seal on this gate is crumbling and Peadar's alchemy formula is failing, then it's happening all over Nethermost. It's happening at the Palace."

"Hurrah!" cried Father, "the king is dead, or at least his palace is falling apart."

"Yes, but as I understand it, he built that monstrosity as a monument to his greed with a combination of pure gold, alchemized gold and weaponized gold. And now he is faced with a huge dilemma— the alchemized gold part is breaking down. What is he going to do?"

"He's going to repair and replace the bad gold. He's going to replace it with pure gold," said Aileen, visibly paling as she hopped on this loopy ride with me.

"Precisely," I turned and pitched the rest of my argument straight to her. "And how will Peadar be collecting this pure gold replacement, Grandma Aileen?"

"By over fracking on a massive scale!" she replied, staring at me in horror, "My goodness, the earthquakes — he's doing it already, isn't he?"

"Yes, likely for months. What happens if Nethermost's foundation becomes utterly mineral depleted?"

"Something much worse than earthquakes," Father muttered, looking quite ashen.

"We're almost out of time," I croaked, "… so is Nethermost … so is the world."

Nethermost Regained

Chapter 36: We Have The Technology

Something was different about Shin — and she wanted me to know.

"Cait!" she called out after me, as I rushed past her at The Intersect with an implied, rather than an actual, greeting. "Hold back can you!" I was running late for my date with Loo. I hadn't seen him in weeks and I was chomping at the bit to compare notes. When I saw Shin approaching the five tunnel corner at The Intersect, rather than risk disappointing Loo, I half considered nipping into the reception area of Hub Medical to avoid her altogether.

But when she called out again, I halted my step, and adjusted my attitude. She always deserved my respect, and I chided myself for this lapse in civility. She plunked herself in front of me, arms and legs akimbo, with a smug look on her face, and teased, "Do you notice anything different about me?"

I squinted my eyes and gave her the once over. "You're happy, which is odd because there's not all that much to rejoice in these days." But there was something else, perhaps too obvious to see.

"Here's a hint," she said with a wink. She did a brief two step right there on the cobbles, ending in a low bow.

"Hang on," I said, astounded, "Where's your shillelagh?"

"I've donated it to someone who needs it."

"You don't need it?"

She hitched up her trousers to show me her legs. The left one was pasty white, as usual. The right was … pasty white, and *that* was unusual.

"Where's the gold?"

*****

Nethermost Regained

Grandma and Grandpa O'Quinn had issued me with another formal invitation. I was guessing my two choices of reply was either 'as you wish' or 'I'd be honoured.' Nothing short of compliance was expected. But they sweetened the deal by inviting Loo as well.

I called the rendezvous where we were to meet the *inner sanctum*, but it was really the largest council chamber used by all seven governing councils — Elders, Magicians, Infrastructure, Defence, Finance, Science, and Medical. Being part of any meeting in this chamber was instructive, if a bit daunting. But being *summoned* to appear in front of any or all of these groups was like being called to the principal's office. So my knees were knocking just a tad as I entered the room — to applause with champagne no less. When I looked back at Loo, there he was, glass in hand, joining in — and I twigged. For some reason, this hoopla was for me!

By the numbers standing with charged glasses, I guessed that all seven councils were present. Grandpa Fergus was already dead centre to make the toast — one of his guilty pleasures.

"Cait O'Quinn, daughter to Nora and Michael O'Quinn, granddaughter to Nicola, our only rightful Swayer and her Consort Riley McCauley, great …"

"Really Fergus," Grandma Aileen interjected, "it doesn't require this much ceremony."

"Hush woman, she's proud of her pedigree. … great granddaughter of Benjamin and Nora McCauley, and Her Grace Fianna and His Canice …" he started to cough and sputter.

"You see," Grandma Aileen wrestled the reins from him, as usual. "Cait, we just wanted to thank you for all you've done both for our Gate community and for Nethermost proper."

A few mumbles from council members "Hear, hear!" "Well done!" "Brave soldier!"

Grandma continued, undeterred. "Your wisdom has guided your impeccable choice of talents. Your bravery has lead you over a hostile continent to discover and return with lifesaving intelligence. You have exceeded all expectation in helping us to find solutions for

the greatest peril this world has ever known. For this, we salute you."
They all raised their glasses and drank the contents.

A toast response was called for, and mine was simple but heartfelt. I
was no longer hiding in the shadows of insecurity. "I thank you for
this distinction. If I've learned anything since I've been here, it's that
circumstance can make the hero. I have been touched by the nobility
of everyone living in exile — the bravest and most resourceful people
I will ever meet. And so thank *you!*" I said, grabbing a glass from a
tray. "I salute *you.*" I drank my glass half off, and then added, while I
still had the stage. "I also toast my sister Rhue O'Quinn, my partner
in crime and easily the best part of me."

While those present were calling out "to Rhue!" Aunt Moira slipped in
behind me and whispered, "Well done my girl … proud of you."

Grandpa Fergus who had recovered his voice, stepped forward
again, looking all puffed up and ready to pop. "Cait, Loo, members of
the seven councils … I have been unable to sleep for days in
anticipation of the reports prepared by members of these councils. I
call first upon Dr. Cox to present the findings of the Science Council."

Dr. Cox, a wiry little man with wild grey hair and stained lab coat that
looked like he slept in it regularly, shuffled through the crowd to the
front, calling for his assistants to join him. Although on first
impression he lacked stage presence, the passion in his voice told
another tale.

"Thank you Elder O'Quinn. As you all know, in mid May our friend
and compatriot Cait O'Quinn photographed the secret contents of
Peadar's journal. The contents of that volume outlined the
Apparatchik's formulas and his manufacturing processes for turning
base metals into gold. There were a multitude of applications for this
alchemized material, from building materials to currency, from home
décor to jewelry. Because he duped us all into granting him his
abominable talent, he could also add a magical twist to these
products and create vile weapons of destruction."

At this point, Dr. Cox nodded to one of his assistants who pulled the
gilding gun from a box. He laid it on the conference table. There were
murmurs and gasps from members who had never seen it before.

"This is a gilding gun, or gilder, created by that demon." Cox picked it up and moved around the room with it for all to see. "It is relatively simple in design. In fact it works on the same principle as traditional electroplating, only in this case the objects being plated are living beings. The gun combines, in one directed beam, alchemized gold vapour, with electrical voltage and a triggering device. When it hits its target, it encases them in a thin shell of alchemized gold. Having tested this weapon, we now know that it in fact does not kill, rather it places its victims into stasis." There were sighs of relief at this last piece of information.

"I have shown you the sample weapon retrieved by Miss O'Quinn on her mission… and the Science Council thanks her — for this!" He pointed again to the weapon. "And for this copy." He nodded to another assistant, who pulled out another weapon and laid it beside the first. "And for these additional copies." He nodded to all his assistants, who laid out twenty more gilding guns. If he was looking for a profound reaction, he was not disappointed. The members began to comment loudly, words of shock, as well as praise.

"If we had more time and more materials," he added, "we could make many such weapons." Dr. Cox stood down and gave the floor back to Grandpa Fergus, who began to clap loudly. Everyone joined in, while Cox and his team took their bows.

Grandpa resumed his chair duties. "The excitement doesn't end there," he raised his voice slightly to quiet the body of advisors. "I now call upon the Council of Medicine, and its leader Dr. Moran, for the results of its diligent research.

Dr. Moran now stood in front of the councillors. "The task of analyzing some of the other formulas was given to the Medical Council. It was the specific job of the Medical Council to understand the formula Peadar used to create the poisonous application of liquid gold with which he tips his swords, axes, knives and arrows. While we are relieved that the gilding guns put victims into suspended animation, the grim truth remains that the poison tips of his weapons actually *kill* — slowly and painfully.

"But, council members," added Moran "there is a silver lining to this cloud. Within the pages of Peadar's journal was an antidote. Apparently the Apparatchik didn't dare risk his own life if there was any chance that he could accidentally poison himself. I am happy to say," and here Moran opened his clenched palm, "that this small vial contains enough antidote to cure a hundred afflicted creatures — and that we have been able to replicate as much as we need." The applause this time was loud and immediate. Councillors rushed forward to take Moran by the hand, congratulate him and his staff, while sneaking a peek at the vial.

My father took his father's place as convenor. He allowed the chaos to continue for several minutes, before calling the meeting to order again with his loud, commanding tone.

"Gentlefolk, this meeting is not over. Please take your seats." It was difficult for many to refocus. The information that had been presented so far was astonishing, and clearly some were celebrating already.

"Gentlefolk!" Father called out again. When he finally restored the room to quiet, he proceeded. "You have been excited no doubt by the news of Cox and Moran that we now have effective weapons and countermeasures for much of the technology that Peadar developed forty years ago to usurp the monarchy and place himself in power. Yet there is more … and I would ask that you possess your souls with patience while we explain.

"My mother and daughter have made a discovery that is exciting and enervating at once. This intelligence was not revealed by Peadar's journal. Indeed we believe it was not known to Peadar himself, until relatively recently."

Father pulled from his pocket what looked like grey putty, all dried and crumbly. The councillors craned their necks to see what it was, but clearly they were none the wiser from the view. "There is no such thing as alchemy!" He announced clearly and forcefully. "Do you see this dirt upon the table? Do you have any idea what this is?" When no one offered an explanation, he continued. "Nineteen years ago, this crap was alchemized gold that was welded to the border gates, then fortified by a magic barrier by Peadar to seal the border and to keep us out. Even if we could have mounted a defence back then, we could not have pierced the inner boundary gate. We were stuck in a holding pattern.

"But Cait and Aileen have discovered the weakness in Peadar's so called alchemy — and it is simply this. Peadar did not discover a way to turn base metal into gold — at least not permanently. His formula has a half life of less than twenty years. Indeed, now that we have his formula, we have been able to reverse engineer it to make the degradation of his phoney gold happen within hours.

"After forty years, we must assume that the fake materials holding The Golden Palace together are surely causing it to crumble about Peadar's ears! Certainly we know the boundary gates to Nethermost are no longer secure. Our kidnapped continent is ready to be rescued."

Cheers arose from the chamber, but my father quelled them yet again. "Now that we possess our own formula for reversing his alchemy, all Peadar's fake gold can be broken down. This same formula will also work on awakening the victims of his gilding guns. As illustration, you may be able to persuade Sinead to show you her erstwhile golden leg, which only this morning received this accelerated treatment."

Shin strutted before them, and displayed her healed leg, as she had done with me. This time the applause was more than he could control. He shouted over the roar. "We can now breach the gate! We can now free our gilded citizens!" The cheers and applause rose to a fever pitch as Father lost control of the room.

But I knew that the end of the story was still not told, and I was beyond concerned that we would never get to the critical bottom line for this group of rowdies. I jumped onto the table and started to stomp my feet like a petulant child. This both shocked the crowd and grabbed their attention. "You need to stop now!" I shouted, "This meeting is not over yet!"

"It's over for Peadar," someone laughed from the back.

"No!" I shouted back at him angrily. Finally I had their attention. For a group of smart people, they sure were acting dumb. "By now, Peadar knows that his formula is bogus too. When I saw him a few weeks ago, he looked like a wild man. He is desperate — and desperate people do desperate things.

"We have every reason to suppose that he is taking out his fury on Nethermost and its citizens. I am certain that his usual over mining has been revved to a fever pitch as he tries to replace his fool's gold with the real thing. It certainly explains the recent earthquakes that can no longer be balanced with conventional magic. Even the combination of Nicola and Nora's balancing talents will not be able to hold back full continental collapse for much longer."

I turned to Father, "I know you have been considering this for a couple of weeks now. I hope I do right by laying it out plainly for everyone. There's really only one question that needs answering now … When do we bust through the gate to regain Nethermost?"

"Next Tuesday. Please the heavens, we will be in time."

Gilding Gun

Chapter 37: Busting Through

The argument had been percolating in my brain for two days. After dinner Saturday night, I pitched it simply. "I want to come with you to Nethermost, Father."

"Yes, of course you do."

What was that, sarcasm? I'd prepared a list of counter arguments but didn't know which one to trot out. Was his response permission or refusal? "Is that *of course* I would want to come, or *of course* I am coming?"

He glanced up, took in my look of confusion, and remained straight faced. Then he erupted with laughter, "Cait, I've never met better officer material than you. You are an excellent strategist and an even better analyst. Of course you will be coming, as my second in command if you agree. I was only waiting for you to volunteer." It was just what I wanted, yet the very idea gave me the collywobbles. Was this the emotional push and pull that Loo claimed defined courage?

"On one condition," he added. Oh, here it is, I thought, the impossible corollary. "Loo comes along as your body guard. I'm relying on your brains, not on your brawn."

*****

From then on, we seldom left each other's side. Most of the major players, in fact, were bunking in at P49, as things kept cropping up that needed 'doing'. We worried constantly about the wisdom of a Tuesday deadline. But then, it could be argued, one would never feel completely ready for such a life and death challenge. Although we were rushed off our feet, I still made time to go with Shin to her studio, when she slipped me an urgent nod.

"When you took pity on a stray dog last February, did you ever think it would all come to this?" she laughed, as she escorted me into her back room. "I certainly didn't, and I'm supposed to be a seer. Speaking of which …" she added, "I have one more painting for you."

She pulled the drape off a canvas, still wet on her easel. "My fingers got me up last night and forced me to paint this image," she explained. "What do you think?"

The moving scene before me was set in a vast receiving hall, heavily burdened with elaborate gilded fretwork, wainscoting, a vaulted ceiling, with marble polished floors, and an overabundance of statuary — all in gold and gold tones, except for a narrow red receiving runner which bifurcated the chamber and stopped short of a centrally placed throne. "That's Canice's throne from the olden days," Shin explained, "but that's not the throne room I remember."

"It's Peadar's throne room, I'm sure," I shuddered, "Look how distastefully it is decorated. It screams Golden Palace to me."

"Do you recognize the people in the scene?" she asked. "This fellow was in another canvas I painted. And is this you he's beside?"

It was easy to identify the suspects. Amongst a crowd of characters, I noted some smudges that could represent Michael, Loo, and me far off in the background. But the *fellow* to whom Shin pointed was Keane, who was mid canvas and to the left of the throne, standing next to Rhue who brandished a red stained sword in her right hand. Rhue's attention seemed drawn to the right of the throne, where Peadar was holding Nora by the throat with one hand, a gilding gun in the other pointed directly at Rhue, with Nicola slumped at his feet. The six second action loop focussed on the movement of Peadar's trigger finger, which was on the point of depressing the lever. This scene screeched danger.

"That's Keane Sweeney," I explained, forcing myself to stay professionally on task. "I'd say that's Rhue standing next to him, not me, just as he was in your other painting. I imagine I'm one of those tiny blobs in the crowd, along with paint blobs of Michael, Loo, and Mánús."

"Ah, yes," Shin nodded. She slid her finger to the right of centre canvas. "Is that who I think it is?" she asked, pointing to the fat, dissolute Peadar.

"If you think it's Peadar, you would be right. And he's using Nora as his shield, the coward, and Nicola as his footstool apparently, the brute." The sight of that moving splotch of paint in the shape of the gilding gun trigger was making my heart seize with terror.

"Yes," Shin mused, frowning at the scene. "He used to be such a good looking boy, did Peadar. How vile he is now! But this action is suggestive — and rather worrying, isn't it? However, you know what they say, 'forewarned is forearmed.'"

I studied it a few minutes longer. "That's some picture, Shin. Very instructive."

*****

"I've found the greatest uniforms dearie," Aunt Moira announced on Saturday morning, three days before our sortie. "I picked them up in China at a fabulous price." She pulled out a sample to show me, from a stack of boxes. It was black leather, both jacket and trousers, fitted at the waist and tucked into high black boots — no Hell's Angels decal, but they had that biker's gear look about them. "They're fierce looking don't you think? And they say leather is practical in case you fall off your bike — protects you from road rash. But look, here's the best bit — a reinforced lining — won't stop bullets, but guaranteed to stop a sword or an arrow. Then matching helmets of course. They're cute, right?"

"Very," I laughed, so glad that my aunt could still amuse me, even in the most dire times.

"These will be for the Legion Commanders, your father, your grandfather and you. Yours is custom made to fit to your sweet curves. I couldn't get one in Mánús' size unfortunately, so he'll have to wear khaki like the foot soldiers but we'll give him some epaulets and a nice helmet. Oh, and I got one for myself. I couldn't resist."

Aunt Moira's job in fact, was an important one. She would use Aileen's drawings to teleport to Carrickbeg, as soon as the border gates opened, to meet up and coordinate with Rhue. Plus, she and her fellow teleporters would be providing us with updates on troop movement throughout the campaign.

*****

Nethermost Regained

Monday night had been frantic; still I carved out some time to take my leave of those remaining behind. It made me recall the wartime documentaries I'd been forced to watch in school — footage I'd viewed dispassionately back then. But now I was that soldier being waved off by loved ones, possibly never to return.

"I refuse to worry about you and Rhue," Grandma Aileen observed, clutching me tightly nonetheless. "It's Fergus I worry about. He's not used to flying. Please watch out for him Cait. But you two girls are wonders and what do they say 'wonders never cease'? — although I don't suppose that was the original meaning. I'm blithering now! Oh dear!" She paused to settle her nerves, then added more calmly, "There's nothing more I can give you then — except my love."

Ol'Ben was becoming far too used to people walking out of his life, so I began by promising faithfully to return, even though we both knew that there were no guarantees. He got all quiet, like he does when he's overcome with feeling. He had always been a better listener than an orator. Instead he gave me another souvenir from his past. "This is the helmet I wore in the big war. I came back with my head still on, so I guess you could say it was lucky. Don't take it off once the fighting begins. And Cait … bring your mother home this time, what-what?" The thing looked stupid on my head, but I wore it instead of one of Aunt Moira's cute helmets — for obvious reasons.

Shin's farewell was the most unique. "I pulled you into all this, so I don't know if I should be saying thank you, or sorry. Let's save that discussion for another day. Because there will be another day, Cait. The painting foresees it. And I shall be watching my canvas with baited breath."

Before I left her, she hit me with one last zinger, "I've been sensing vibrations in the ground of late. We're going to place The Gate on earthquake alert, crossing our fingers and toes. I suggest you be flexible with your plans."

*****

By Tuesday afternoon, we were flying low over the sparkling rose/grey asphalt, heading along Surfaced Road 36, the most direct route into The Capitol. I was buckled onto the rumble seat of a black and chrome hover bike, holding fast to Loo. Father and Mánús rode

296

tandem on another black and chrome in the lane adjacent, as we led a ragtag convoy of warriors, seasoned professionals and new recruits alike, on second hand and ancient hover bikes, pulling hover sleds carrying more troops and supplies.

We travelled openly this time. In fact, we were counting on a certain amount of 'shock and awe' to cower Peadar's undisciplined henchmen, whose loyalty to him I estimated at less than an inch deep. Instead, we set a leisurely pace, just fast enough to reach the settlement of Rathfergus by twilight. Although we hadn't booked reservations, so to speak, we were counting on the cooperation of the citizens of this small fort, located forty kilometres west of The Capitol, to offer us space to camp for the night. This was the birthplace of Grandpa Fergus, and he was confident that he still had connections there who remained true loyalists.

*****

It hadn't been the easiest business to get us this far to be honest. Father's announcement in front of the seven councils the previous Thursday had sent us into a tailspin, allowing a mere five days to launch.

The work of the dwarf masons took top honours. They began the overhaul of the gate and its staircase that very afternoon. It was a job that should have taken months, not hours, but a team of fifty stone masons and mechanical engineers achieved the impossible. Working twenty-four hours a day right up until late Monday night, they installed track lighting along the full flight of five thousand steps. They then repaired and widened the staircase in places and converted it into a wind powered floating conveyor belt that rested over top of the stairs. It had several speed settings from two to ten kilometres per hour, and could convey creatures three abreast, or accommodate a single seat vehicle. On top of all this, there was the additional challenge of finishing on the quiet, so as not to alert our enemy.

Our plans to breach were straightforward, relying primarily on timing. At six a.m. Tuesday morning, a technical team was in and out of the lower anti chamber in no time at all to apply accelerant to the welds on the inner gate. They returned a few hours later to lay timed explosive charges — sufficiently strong to loosen the rock blocking the lower gate, but not strong enough to blow the inside passage.

The first wave of fifty soldiers rushed through the opening, once the fallout of the blast had settled. They easily eliminated the few border guards, who they outnumbered by a factor of four.

Next came the master machines built by Loo and the boys at the Ballaghmore Chop Shop. They had disassembled a number of hover sleds into small sections to fit on the rolling belt, to be reassembled on the lower side.

Our force of twelve hundred soldiers systematically piled on and rode the belt, in small teams, in order to transport everyone along the one kilometre drop to the continent. By the time I reached the lower gate with the last of these warriors, it was four hours later, and most of the walking legions had already left. Five units had been sent out ahead of the main legion to diverse regions of the continent, about four hundred foot soldiers to each legion, under the leadership of well trained sub commanders, in order to secure the smaller settlements. They were armed with weapons designed for hand to hand combat — knives, swords, axes and long bows. While the campaign would certainly involve a fight for their lives, and for quality of life, it would never involve mass extermination or opening fire on a grand scale on either crowds of innocents or on enemy soldiers.

We long ago considered, and rejected, the idea of using explosive assault weapons or weapons of mass destruction, like those used on Earth's surface for centuries. The use of such weaponry in an enclosed environment with a crystallized sky roof was just folly. Sky collapse would eliminate the continent in seconds. Besides, this kind of warfare was both too easy and too hard. It took out entire populations impersonally, and in the blink of an eye. No matter how desperate we were, our goal would never be to destroy so utterly and so dispassionately. We intended to look our enemy in the eye before deciding whether he should live or die.

The most lethal weapon we had, the most lethal one we wanted, was the gilding gun — three per legion. With this weapon, we were fighting fire with fire. We knew this weapon incarcerated only, removing a threat until such time when we could administer the antidote. We wanted our continent restored, not destroyed — its lands and its citizenry made whole again.

The main legion, the sixth, was the largest one, led by Commander Michael, with me as second in command. It was a mobile unit with the toughest job, and needed speed on its side to accomplish its grand ambition. It was therefore better equipped — with the bikes and sleds, and with the largest number of gilders. After all, it was our job to subdue and secure The Capitol and to scoop out the cancer within. This primary target was the crux of our campaign. We strategized that if we could wrest The Capitol from the grips of its illegitimate tyrant, the rest of the continent would fall into line.

We arrived at our rest stop at eight p.m. after being on the road since noon. The people of Rathfergus were no doubt nervous, but Grandpa Fergus had flown ahead to prepare them and to calm the worst of their fears. We did not expect, nor did we receive a warm welcome. Rathfergus folks wanted as little to do with us as possible, but neither did they interfere, and even brought their animals in from the fields for the evening, to allow us the use of their pastures for our tents and campfires. We had brought meal packages enough for three days. If we were still on the continent on day four, we would need to forage for ourselves.

By ten o'clock that evening we were ready for our final briefing. The incursion into The Capitol was scheduled for six the next evening.

How could we know then that all our best laid plans would blow up in an instant?

Chapter 38: Rhue's Army

The teleporters' reports were encouraging. The legions so far had met with little resistance in the provinces. There was one incident relayed back from the border town of Trylare where a gun toting guardsman recklessly opened fire with his gilder on a phalanx of dwarf foot soldiers, and was gilded for his troubles in return. Upon witnessing that incident, the remaining ruffians of Trylare laid down their weapons and the entire community surrendered, most of them bowing down in gratitude to their captors.

The remaining reports were less interesting, but just as encouraging.

Except Aunt Moira's account, that is. She had turned up in Carrickbeg to find it nearly deserted — only children, the infirm, and the elderly were holding the fort. Zee, who had been confined to barracks as she recovered from her illness, provided Aunt Moira with the salient details.

"She described a community united in its resistance to the Apparatchik," Aunt Moira began. "They were so weary of living in fear and confinement, Zee explained, that they welcomed a dollop of danger. Their plans began in earnest two days after your return to Nethermost Gate.

"It turns out, Cait, that on the evening when you and your sister snuck into the two palaces, you teleported away just in time. According to Zee, they were descended upon by three more guardsmen moments after you left. Thank goodness you escaped when you did."

"What happened to them — to Rhue, Keane and Zee?" I asked, feeling moist with panic.

"What happened was that our two trained warriors thought fast on their feet. If the guardsmen had been aware of your real mission, they'd have come in far more forcefully, and in greater numbers. But they hadn't yet discovered Donal Fadden's unconscious body, and their order to halt was for a simple curfew violation. Still they intended to do our heroes harm, and had their gilders at the ready.

"That's when Keane, Rhue — and Zee actually — sprang into action. As one of the guardsmen raised his weapon, Zee flew straight into his face, tweaked his nose and poked a fist in his eye. This was all the distraction Rhue and Keane needed. Suddenly Rhue had the small dirk in her hand, her birthday gift from you, Michael. She slashed away at the one Zee had taken on, slitting the wrist of his gun hand, and forcing him to drop his weapon. At the same moment, Keane delivered a kick to the head of a second oaf, just as he was reaching for his gilding gun, sending it flying high. That guy dropped and was out for the count.

"While Rhue continued her battle with the biggest galoot, Keane took on the runt of the pack, who was scarpering away at speed. Keane's arrow took him out when he was half a block away. Meanwhile, Rhue was finishing off the big fellow, who according to Zee was just as low on intelligence as he was high in bulk. He tried several times to charge her. Each time she swerved, edging him closer and closer to the palace's stone wall, until finally he put an end to himself. His last charge, and her last swerve, ended with him careening into the wall and knocking himself out good and proper. With one dead guardsmen and two unconscious ones, they had to exit the city immediately, so they bound and hid the bodies at the edge of the Old Palace grounds, grabbed the three gilding guns, and made a dash for it."

I could imagine Zee's elaborate dramatization as she related this story to Aunt Moira. She would have had Aunt Moira in a sweat by the end of it, just as Aunt Moira's translation had frothed me up. But despite the danger and the drama, it made me more certain that the decisions we made on that white knuckled evening were both right and timely; also that my sister was indeed a force to be reckoned with.

"When Rhue returned to Carrickbeg with Keane and Zee, she was welcomed back as a hero," Aunt Moira relayed. "She briefed Keane on as much of the plan as she dared, only omitting a few details, such as the bit about the book of formulas. But she let him and the Elders in on the fact that Nora was indeed the mother of twin daughters who had now entered Nethermost to right a great wrong. She confirmed that Nora and Nicola had been held prisoner in the bowels of The Golden Palace for years. Because there was little choice, she risked telling them that an invasion from The Gate was in the works, and that she hoped to mount an army inside Nethermost to strengthen the thrust of this invasion, once it came.

"She couldn't have been more pleased with the overwhelming response. In no time, fairy scouts went out to recruit mountain folk from all thirteen pinnacles. Upwards of five hundred magicians and humans responded to the call from the Pinnacles alone.

"Rhue and Keane limited their numbers to those living on the Pinnacles, for the purpose of manageability mostly, and to limit any risk of sabotage from without. Although, to a creature, they all took a loyalty oath, they were nonetheless chomping at the bit to include their fathers, their sisters, their cousins, and their uncles living in far reaching regions.

"Rhue managed their enthusiasm by giving them a voice on where to expand the campaign, once the invasion began. She established and trained four units in all that would span out to other communities of magical folks once the invasion began, in order to exploit the strength of everyone's talents. Then they stood poised, awaiting a call to action."

As Aunt Moira relayed all this detail, I couldn't help my mind from wandering to the bigger picture. I considered the threat that our underworld problems presented to the entire planet, and I reflected on how typical it would be for on-Earth citizens to argue amongst themselves, rather than to respond to such a crisis. Would they cooperate, I wondered, if they realized the seriousness of this threat? Was there *any* worldwide catastrophe that would convince on-Earth population groups to cooperate with each other when faced with the possible ruination of our planet? Or would they continue to argue amongst themselves while their continents crumbled? We certainly could not let this happen to Nethermost — either for ourselves or for the rest of the planet.

My thoughts now veered to something I read in Shakespeare's play *A Midsummer Night's Dream,* a classic I had studied in eleventh grade English Lit. class. In this madcap tragicomedy, the fairy Puck sports with star crossed lovers who wildly dash about the forest at night, confounded by truth and love. There is a famous aside in the last act when the humans are at their most hopeless, and the fairy Puck removes to the side of the stage, mocking frail humanity to his amused audience, 'What fools we mortals be!'

When I snapped out of my reverie, Aunt Moira was coming to the main point of her tale — the fact that by the time she had teleported into Carrickbeg, she had found its streets empty. According to Zee, the rest of its citizens were already on the move, having been forewarned of our invasion by their fairy scouts.

"I had to think fast on my feet," she continued. "It was wonderful to know that they were making their way to The Capitol already, but I'd had no opportunity to deliver your instructions before their departure. So I had no choice but to pursue. I set my sights on the drawing my mother had completed of the Forest Curran — what a boon those sketches have been. I teleported there, hoping to at least be in the vicinity of their company.

"My first stop was a disappointment — no one there. But there were fresh hoof marks on the forest floor. So I followed by tele-sprinting, a rather unconventional method of teleporting. Tele-sprinting has become quite disreputable in recent years, ever since a few bad apples used it to cheat in sports. But with tele-sprinting, one moves forward only as far as the eye can see with each hop. I put it to good use today for tracking Rhue's army. Even with this advantage, it took me more than two hours to find them — and I felt quite bilious in the end."

She took another swig of fizzy water at the very memory of it. "Rhue looked amazing Cait. She was so confident, so strong riding that dapple grey mare. And the muscles she had! My goodness, they rivalled those of her first officer Keane Sweeney. Isn't he dishy, by the way? Now don't look cross, Michael, a girl can dream."

"In any case, I had a few moments with Rhue alone before they pressed on. She now knows that her role in our foray will be to move her troops in through the back door, while we come in through the front. She will make straight for the dungeon to remove Nora and Nicola to safety. Set your clocks to the switch of twilight tomorrow evening folks. It all happens then."

*****

Loo caught up with me while I was on my own by one of the campfires, staring into its dying embers. "Hey, don't run away like that. Michael will string me up by my little parts if I lose you. He can be a scary guy sometimes."

"Sorry, I needed a moment with my thoughts. When I take things minute by minute, it kind of makes sense. It's when I allow myself a look at the whole that it begins to unravel and becomes overwhelming."

"Don't think too much. That's my way of coping, although it doesn't always work. I have the opposite tendency. I shelve too much of my crap for a rainy day. Then it starts to pour ..."

"How about now, as you are about to go into battle?" I asked.

"It's not so much about the battle to be honest," he explained, more to the fire than to me. "Tomorrow we fight because it's the right thing to do. It's more a matter of *need* than *want*. There's no choice to be made. No, I get bogged down in regret about things not done — and a few bad choices I've made."

"Like what?"

"Like holding a grudge against my Dad all these years. I carry that load like a big old barbell about my neck. These last few months have certainly shown me how foolish I've been. He was just a guy, after all, drowning in grief and self pity, unable to care for himself, let alone for a kid. Do you know what I'm going to do right after this wraps up?"

"No idea."

"I'm going back to the village to find my old man. In my heart I'll be saying, 'I understand and I forgive you'. What I'll actually be telling him is the simple truth — that I love him. I'm letting go of this pain, as the shrinks say. It's not me anymore."

"Sounds great," I said, dreamily, snuggling into his arms. I had missed their warmth and security, and I damn well wasn't going to leave them until morning.

"Cait," Loo whispered, as I was nodding off. "What are you gonna do at the end?"

"Dunno," I mumbled dreamily.

But I did — I knew.

Chapter 39: Force Majeure

Six o'clock Wednesday evening and we stood on a hill outside The Capitol taking in the entire panorama. Its skyline was smaller than that of the average on-Earth city. Not only was there less urban sprawl, but its population had shrunk after the coup. I could even identify a number of buildings from my hilltop viewpoint that looked unoccupied, even derelict. But it was the seat of power, the place where the royal family resided and from which the body politic ruled, and so The Capitol qualified as a city despite its small size. Indeed, it was the only city sized settlement on the entire continent.

Between our legion and Rhue's army of mountain folk, we were less than a thousand strong. Even with all of our weapons and training, we were well outnumbered and out powered. It was going to take a lot of fancy footwork, and one giant miracle, to manage this victory. But Peadar had less at his disposal forty years earlier, when evil had triumphed over good, greed over philanthropy.

Despite the fact that I had walked a few of its streets once before, I didn't know this city at all. But many of our soldiers did, and I wondered what they felt as they stood and stared at its skyline now. Were they consumed with memories, or were they plotting the best approach to take to the city centre? I daresay a little of each.

Now at the beginning of twilight, what I saw beneath me was a sleepy settlement caged up under the restrictions of a nightly curfew, unaware of its destiny, unaware of the visitor at its door. What I saw were rows of grey houses, perched along twisty, gravel topped lanes, with dull grey outcroppings of rock pathetically landscaping their bare gardens. I saw windows with black shutters, closed for the night, and a captive, dull population locked up while their masters slept.

"Do you see Palace Park in the centre, Cait?" Grandpa Fergus pointed directly ahead. "And that's the gilded monstrosity, The Golden Palace, there to the south. That elegant building to the north is our historic palace. But you've been there before, of course."

Twilight made it difficult to catch much detail, although I did note that the gilded monstrosity was glowing a bit in the crepuscular light.

"Yes, but my views were mostly closeup," I replied, "and even then, it was mostly the insides of the buildings that remember. I never did get the long perspective. This skyline view is rather good."

As we watched together, the horizon began to shiver and heave. For a moment I wondered if the waviness was a mirage, but then the ground beneath us began to vibrate — just as the wise Shin had feared. Within two minutes we had begun to lose our footing and dropped to our knees. "Everyone out of the vehicles! Stay low over open ground," Commander Michael shouted. "Let's not get crushed by things toppling on us."

An enormous boom accompanied the appalling commotion — buildings were rippling and collapsing; boulders were popping; the earth groaned mournfully as it tore apart and gaped. When I looked up again, I witnessed the shocking eruption of an enormous roaring fountain of gold lava shooting fifty metres high, splashing over people and buildings alike. After that initial burst, the arc of its spray slumped to ten metres, but burbled heavily and persistently. The impurities in the lava issued sparks which danced over the walls of The Golden Palace, causing it to twinkle hideously and unnaturally in the gloaming.

The Commander turned to the company and barked, "Brave soldiers, we are compelled to change hats. We are no longer an army of warriors. We must become an emergency force of rescuers. Captains, direct your teams to initiate Plan B! Start at the outskirts and work your way around the edges to the city centre, rescuing as many lives as possible. Teams, obey your captains, and may destiny favour the brave!"

The legion dispersed into small pockets of first responders, each unit finding its own path down the hill into the city. The front runners hadn't even reached the lower levels when the first aftershock hit, throwing many to the ground once more, and tearing a new fissure into the face of the hillside. As its maw widened, it sucked in one of our number. He was instantly lost deep inside a sheer wall of burning rock, beyond rescue. The remainder of his team had no choice but to carry on as before to rescue a helpless population, many of which had been buried in rubble which moments before been their homes.

It was no longer about a conflict of politics and power, about who's right or who's wrong. It was now a question of who could be rescued and how. This was a race for survival, as basic as breathing in and out.

Loo and I formed a team with Mánús and Darragh. Those two could pull down doors and walls that to most would have been unmovable, had it not been for the engineering expertise of a dwarf, and the sheer brawn of a Canomorph. Loo was no slouch either, pulling out bodies by sheer brute strength and bringing them to me for assessment and treatment. Even with my limited first aid skills, I could still make a tourniquet, immobilize a broken leg, staunch a wound, calm a nerve and scream for a medic. We made our way through the tangle of houses along broken battlefields that had once been streets, all the while inching towards the city centre and the palace gates.

Four hours of crisis control drew us close to the team of Commander Michael and Aunt Moira, in their rescue efforts a few streets to our north. Seeing them again reminded me of the original intention of our mission and niggled at me about an opportunity about to be lost. While patching up the wounds of the superficially injured, triaging those needing surgical attention, and praying for the souls of the dying, I was again remembering the bigger picture.

When I realized that we had arrived outside Palace Park — or what was left of it — I took it as a sign. Much of The Golden Palace was now in ruins. Its faulty building materials had succumbed to the unnatural disaster. I sought out the Commander two blocks away and pulled him aside, holding onto his arm to command his attention.

"Commander Michael!" I shouted, using his military moniker. "We need to finish our mission, Sir!"

"No, we need to focus on saving lives!" he returned.

"No sir, with all due respect. This is precisely the right time to pursue the Apparatchik."

"No, final word," he shouted over his shoulder, and began tossing debris from the doorway of another crushed home.

"Father," I cried in frustration, "you brought me along for a reason. You wanted me to use my brain. Well my brain is speaking up and it's the only one talking sense here. So calm down and listen … Sir."

Loo froze in place, drew in a sharp breath, watching silently as my father/commander and I had it out. "You have six hundred men out saving the city, Sir. Trust that they will continue to do their jobs bravely. You won't find any of Peadar's guardsmen left on the streets. Those sad excuses for lawmakers have already raced off with their tails between their legs. There won't be many at the palace either. With all its crumbling joists and supports, that monstrosity is in ruins and many will have run to save their own puny butts. We will never find Peadar more vulnerable. We must move against him, Sir … this instant!"

He got very quiet and contemplative. I knew when to apply the brakes and did so now, waiting in stiff warrior pose, fingers crossed behind my back. "You are right. Of course you are," he sighed. "It's just … just … the enormity of it all."

"Yes," I agreed, "and wouldn't you say that neither the continent nor the planet could take another such 'enormity'? We can't let this happen … ever again. Peadar's abuses must be blocked now! We must make it stop," and added in hushed tones, "or die trying."

"How shall we proceed?" He was looking to me now for orders, overwhelmed as he was with misery.

"I'd say through the front door. Let's not stand on ceremony. I'd also recommend my team to you, Sir — that's Darragh, Mánús, Loo and me. Under your leadership, we'd be magic."

"Good thought."

So in the end, our army of five walked calmly up The Palace Way. Commander Michael and Loo with gilders looped in their belts had the look of new palace recruits. Mánús, in his faithful dog's body now, tagged along like a pet on four legs beside Darragh, who pretended to be assessing the architectural damage of the building. I gave myself an especially interesting cover story — that of a dopey tour guide with a vacuous grin, spewing forth a lot of nonsense about the palace as we walked. A plausible back story, I thought, and it did get us through the broken gate, guarded by a vacuous idiot who was not much more than a kid. We walked straight up the crumbling golden steps, and into the front door, without so much as a by your leave.

"Where's the throne room do you suppose?" I asked the others, after we found ourselves alone, scanning the shambles of the entry hall.

"Why the throne room?" The Commander and my Father both wanted to know.

"Shin painted me a picture."

"Oh? … You might have said."

*****

We didn't need a map in the end. Peadar's loud rantings provided direction enough. But as we power walked the length of that long corridor, we were halted by those ever tiresome words, "Stop or I'll shoot!"

We stopped instantly, lifting our hands in the air. I whispered, "Turn clockwise on three. One … two …" On three, we turned slowly in unison. "Reporting for duty Sir!" I called out with exaggerated deference to the galoot in front of me.

"Badge number?" He barked.

He looked as dumb as a sponge, so I fudged it audaciously. "Five, six, seven, one, two, three … Sir!" I was counting on my forceful demeanour to carry some weight with this bozo.

"Right then … these your prisoners?"

"No sir, new recruits and a property inspector. Lousy night to break them in. Am I right?" I guffawed and turned to leave, directing the others to do the same.

It almost worked. "Hang on … just a second. There's always a letter in a guards' badge number. What's the letter?"

"Q … Sir!" It was the first letter to pop into my head. Blame my last name.

"Right … where does it come in the order."

"In the middle … Sir," I was guessing again.

"Right," he confirmed. I thought he was nodding us on, so I spun around again. "Hang on …" he continued.

"Yes Sir!"

"We don't use the letter 'Q'. Peadar don't like that letter."

"Plan B," I cued my companions. We turned … one final time …

Commander Michael had his gun out before the guard had his completely drawn, and he gilded him with one quick zap. The telltale clatter of his gun hitting the floor must have alerted others, because we were soon descended upon by a dozen more — six with gilders, six without. Darragh picked up the first guard's gun and opened fire at each and everything, letting loose Rambo style — a little frenetic I thought, as he missed as many as he hit. He really should stick to his axe, I thought.

Loo placed himself in front of me, and took out three more who were approaching from the front door, guns drawn and ready to fire. With his video game experience, his aim was deadly efficient. While Loo continued to defend my front, I sensed an approach from the rear — a thug with an axe bearing down on me. I pulled out my sword to challenge, mentally chanting to myself — 'step two, three, … thrust, back two, three … parry', hoping to bluff through this fight long enough for one of my team mates to notice and take him out for me. Clearly he had targeted me as the lame duck of the gang and was enjoying wearing me down. I was nearly out of dance moves when his axe bore down hard and shattered my blade.

I was grabbing for my dirk when Mánús came flying in from nowhere in full werewolf mode, aimed at the neck of my axeman. The bastard swung his poisoned tipped blade wildly, connecting with Mánús' ankle, as he sank his teeth into the creep's throat. While avoiding further blows from the flailing weapon, Mánús' grip tightened, his jaw crunching deeper until I heard the neck snap and the axeman lay limp on the floor, Mánús straddling his dormant body, blood and froth dripping from his tongue and oozing from his ankle.

That left one final villain for the Commander. This guy was a big bruiser, and no mistake. He deliberately threw his gun to the ground and challenged Commander Michael to hand to hand combat. Big miscalculation! I had seen my father in action, and the possibility of being in the same building as his estranged wife gave him that extra incentive. With what I can only describe as a ballet leap and karate kick combo, the Commander launched himself at the guardsman with a blow to the head, and while still airborne, completed one revolution, kicking the guy in the groin on the way down. The oaf moaned and grabbed his crotch, but the Commander showed no mercy, pummelling him with his bare fists until he slid to the floor unconscious.

He kept the up beating until Loo stayed his fists and cautioned him forcefully, "Let's not stick around waiting for any more of these bastards Sir."

As if to illustrate Loo's suggestion, our attention was redirected to the end of the long hallway, from where hideous howls were emanating both loudly and furiously. "That's Peadar," I said. "No doubt about it."

We followed the dreadful sounds to the last archway, but before we could cross the threshold, our steps were halted by a horrific sight — it was Shin's painting in the making — my worst nightmare! Peadar had Nora by the throat between his thumb and forefinger, going nose to nose with her, rage issuing from his fetid, foaming lips, "I said get it under control … now! Make her do it or I swear I will kill her this time!" He booted the prone body of Nicola for emphasis.

"I won't! Not any more. It's out of control and beyond our capabilities. Do it yourself, you brute!" Nora returned. "Besides she's comatose, can't you see that? I can't wake her up."

I could feel Commander Michael tensing beside me and whispered, "Not yet Soldier … Father. Let's do this the smart way."

At that moment Rhue and Keane bounded in, breathless and sweaty. Distracted from previous swordplay they pitched forward, bloody weapons still brandished, barely applying the brakes before ploughing into the throne. "Mother," Rhue squeaked, before she could stop her mouth.

Peadar wheeled about to face the newcomers, squeezing my mother's neck even tighter. "Mother?" he mocked. "Who is this Nora? One of your sprogs? You are, aren't you? So, where's your sister?"

He pulled out his gilding gun and aimed it at Rhue. "I said, where's your sister?"

I was keeping watch over his trigger finger and could see it moving towards the lever. This was the climax in Shin's moving painting. This was my moment to write history and I knew it. I only hoped I didn't screw it up. "I'm here, Uncle Peadar," I said, as nonchalantly as I could muster. I advanced towards the throne with a stupid grin on my face.

"Which one are you," he growled at me, taking his hand off the trigger for the moment, shifting his aim from Rhue to me.

"I'm Cait. I'm the pretty one," I joked, trying to diffuse the heat in his voice.

"The pretty one eh? You're the joker more like."

"Sure, that's me too. So, we've got a bit of a situation don't you think?" I tried. "We should call in some balancing experts — get a grip on this fountain of goop that's drenching the city… waste of good gold, am I right? Maybe get some dwarf architects in … fix the place up a bit. What do you say?"

He did hesitate, but only for a few seconds. The years of excess and debauchery had pickled his brain and all logical thought seemed beyond him. He was out for revenge, not for solutions. He narrowed his eyes at me, then back to my sister. "No … I don't think so," he spat. "Tell you what though. I think your Mom will be more motivated to get Nicola to balance this earthquake if I kill one of you right now and keep the other hostage. Which one will it be Nora? The pretty one or the warrior?"

"No!" she screamed frantically. He had her then and he knew it. He finally had her defiance in check. Threatening her life was one thing, but threatening the lives of her daughters …

"Brother?" Nicola called up from the floor. "Brother, is that you?" Her voice was barely more than a whisper. She sat up, and focussed solely on him, smiling vaguely. Then she tried to pull herself up, using his leg as a crutch. She stroked his velvet leggings, cooing and whispering, like a doting mother to a baby.

By her fawning and giggling, she could well have been mad, but I suspected that she was acting a role. After years under his thumb, she must have been practiced in managing his insanity. "Look, we're in one of the great rooms, brother! We love great rooms. Remember all the hiding places we used to explore in the old palace? Those paintings with the eyes that opened from behind so you could watch over everything from inside the walls? We would sneak behind a painting and watch those silly Elders doing their lawmaking in their huge council chamber …"

She had his full attention now. He let his gun hand drop. "And that old fart Needham ..." Peadar smirked, caught up in the memory. "Remember that glass eye of his? He'd pull it out of its socket in the middle of a chambers session to polish it … just to throw off the discussion." He was laughing hard now, relaxing his grip on Nora's throat.

"We were such naughty children," Nicola added, pulling herself up even higher onto his thigh. *What is she doing?* I wondered. Then I noticed the dagger hanging loosely from Peadar's belt. My heart seized and I held my breath.

"Where have you been brother?" Nicola continued. "I've missed you."

This was a step in the wrong direction. "You left me sister!" he accused her. Ignoring Nora entirely now, he dropped down and grabbed Nicola by the shoulders, pulling her up to full height. I could see her hand gripping the knife handle now. The tension was unbearable.

"How can you say that Peadar? I never left. Remember all those love gifts I gave you? I built you a big laboratory for all your stinky experiments. I let you build your own house ..."

"You *let* me?" His voice was edgier now — I could sense the agitation resurfacing. "*Let* me? Isn't that the point Nicola? First you desert me by marrying that vile on-Earther. Then you replace me by bearing his child. Then Mommy and Daddy leave us and put you in charge! For the rest of my life, I would need your *permission* and that would never do!"

"That wasn't my doing, brother. That was the law of succession."

This was too close to the truth for Peadar. He turned his attention back to his gun hand and, without warning, aimed and shot a stream of gilding straight at Rhue. He would have hit her too, had Mánús not put himself between that stream of bastardized gold and Rhue's body. He was instantly gilded and fell to the floor, still in his werewolf form.

This provided sufficient distraction for Nicola to rise to full strength. "No!" she screamed. In one slick motion, she yanked the knife from its casing, and thrust it into Peadar's fat belly — again, again, again — until he fell to the floor writhing.

"Sister? ... Sister why? ... I love you."

Nicola wrenched the gilder from his slackened hand and pointed it in his face. "Why?" she laughed hysterically, "Because you're a mad dog, and you need putting down." She pulled the trigger — again, again, again — covering his body with a thick layer of gold. Dropping to her knees, she sobbed mournfully. In the few seconds that it took for Nora to reach her side, Nicola had slumped against Peadar's grotesque form, lifeless.

Loo rushed to Mánús with the antidote, applying it liberally over every inch of his body. But in all our preparations, we had never considered another consequence — that beneath this alchemized gilding was a small wound previously poisoned by that axe dipped with Peadar's lethal concoction. We were so quick to move forward in our rescue attempts that none of us had thought to apply the antidote right away to the nick Mánús had sustained from the deadly axe blade. Sealed beneath the layer of gold, Mánús' blood now became host to a rare confluence of the two dastardly agents, and a deadly combination of evil technologies. The fake gilding fused with the poisoned gold to render our medicines useless. The damage was done. Our friend was beyond help. ... It was an outcome we hadn't considered.

Chapter 40: The Burden of Victory

It pains me to review the aftermath, yet it is essential to do so. We need to acknowledge the messes that we make. We need to clean them up. While we rejoiced in our victory for five minutes, rehabilitating an entire continent and its people took years.

*****

It was through unassuaged tears that I finally bore witness to my own brass ring moment, however, to what had really brought me here in the first place — the sight of my parents' first embrace. For them it was two decades, for me my entire life. I couldn't begin to imagine a love that could endure such wretchedness. Rhue and I held onto each other with no apologies for staring unabashedly, for invading the privacy of this intimate reunion. We had lost something too, after all.

Their joy was mingled with sadness of course, and after holding her husband in an enduring embrace, after swathing her babies with mother love, my mother retreated into her mental 'safe place' far away from us all. The loss of her own mother after so much effort to keep her safe for so many years seemed too high a price for her daughter, even though in the end it had been Nicola's decision to make the ultimate sacrifice — for the greater good.

As Father lifted Nicola's body from the floor and bore her gently away, Mother followed mutely, continuing to hold that withered little hand and to stroke that careworn head. From his nod in my direction, I knew the Commander was handing over the reins of command to me now. His duty was clear — it would require the full commitment of his time and compassion to make this right for his wife — whatever and whenever that would be.

*****

I sat on the floor with Mánús, postured in strength and nobility even in death. Did he know when he was wounded while saving my life, did he realize when he shielded my sister, that he would be risking all? My guess was that, while he didn't comprehend the precise price to be paid, he would have acted the same had it been made more clear.

He had pledged himself to our service, had honoured it fully. What was it that Shin had said at our birthday party?

"This is Mánús' gift to you both. He means to pledge his life in all its forms for your protection. It may well be the most valuable gift you will receive today — or ever for that matter."

*****

Peadar was dead, gilded, and best forgotten. Before allowing the evidence of him to be removed, I paused for a few moments to study his golden remains, and the irony was not lost on me. This was an empty man, consumed with jealousy and greed. To fill his own abyss, he relied as many do, upon the acquisition of wealth. But in his case, he bypassed excess and soared into obsession, the consequences be hanged. Yet here he was in death — a mere nugget of gold. What had he really wanted to fill that void with anyway? Respect? Love? Companionship? In the end, those were the very things he lacked.

*****

I asked Keane and his military force to incarcerate the palace staff, remove the dead, then evacuate the premises, condemning it as a death trap. I also instructed him to revive the miraculously unscathed old palace, giving him the use of the two regal rings that my sister and I still wore, to find his way in. He promised a cleanup of the building within the day, and planned to use furnishings pilfered from the golden ruins to begin the refurbishment of its empty rooms. It would serve as our temporary command post — an infirmary for the seriously ill, a dormitory for the homeless, and a sundry of emergency services to support our earthquake recovery.

Then I asked Rhue, Darragh and Loo to follow me back into the wreckage of the city, where the lives of its citizens still remained in great jeopardy. I hunted down Aunt Moira and Grandpa Fergus. After briefing them on the outcome of our confrontation with Peadar, we discussed our individual roles over the next few days.

Grandpa Fergus and Loo would work as a team — Grandpa to fly back to the border to brief those on the home front, to gather supplies and volunteers of every kind; Loo to enlist troops as drivers for our vehicles, along with other transport he could repurpose from the wreckage, to create a supply line from The Gate to The Capitol.

As a first priority, Darragh would supervise his fellow dwarf masons to use their combined balancing talents to stem the flow of the lava. Once the geological crisis had been contained, he would identify leaders from amongst the builders, masons, and engineers to begin the clean up and the rebuild.

Rhue would manage the troops previously deployed to the settlements in all the provinces to ensure that order was being restored within the realm as a whole.

Aunt Moira and I would oversee and coordinate all other logistical support, identifying leaders, assigning jobs, with the aim of caring for the wounded, housing the homeless and burying the dead.

Recovery seemed endless, the assignments hopelessly inadequate. But they would do as a starting point. It would take months to heal the land, years to heal ourselves. We had no idea what we were doing precisely — how could we — but our intentions were honourable and our focus was forward moving.

How would we rebuild Nethermost? How do you restore an entire realm?

Chapter 41: In Hindsight

"What happened was foolishness, and entirely my fault." That was Rhue's overture to our long anticipated reunion. I was getting used to conversations in Nethermost that began with 'a riddle, wrapped in a mystery, inside an enigma', as Churchill so cleverly painted.

"Is this the beginning or the end of some sort of confession?" I asked nonchalantly. I was certain that Rhue was being unnecessarily self reproving. "And is it one particular foolishness you had in mind, or do you have a list? I mean, it's been awhile, so … " I stopped with the teasing when I got an eyeful of her deeply puckered brow and pouty lips. I sighed, "Come here, you goof!" and threw my arms about her neck, kissing both cheeks, joyful to see her after so many weeks apart.

Although I had had that brief glimpse of her on Nethermost's restoration day, Rhue and her army of mountain folk had been treading the continent ever since, bringing outlying criminals to justice and establishing recovery services in the smaller communities. I was only able to keep track of her whereabouts from Aunt Moira's and Grandpa's Fergus' surveillance reports. Last I heard, she and her crew were still on roundup duty. Yet here she was sneaking up on me again — like she did on that very first day. How long ago that seemed now, although in truth it was barely four months. How odd, I thought, that some days I couldn't remember life before her, never a time when she was not a part of me.

Now standing before me, she looked wild and wonderful! Still the warrior in her leathers and armour — but even more vibrant, more toned, less cinched up! I knew there must be a thrilling story behind such a transformation, and I was going to force it from her by fair means or foul.

"You asked us to remove Nicola and Nora from harm's way," she explained, with chagrin. "Not only did we fail to do so, but we blundered into the throne room without caution, causing unnecessary damage."

"Oh … that …"

Nethermost Regained

*****

Rhue had tracked me down at Dr. Coffee Klatch at the end of what was turning out to be a very long day. I was nursing a cup of froth at my favourite table, while Loo and Ol'Ben were down at P49 packing up the last dregs of our stuff. Loo and I had travelled back to The Gate that morning in a borrowed hover roadster to collect Ol'Ben and our worldly possessions. Although we planned to return to The Capitol that evening, the notion of a same day return trip was beginning to look overly optimistic.

Loo was keen to show me all the changes he had made already to the boundary gate. It had been just two weeks since Nethermost had been regained, the borders reopened. But Loo had already been working with the stone masons and the mechanics from the gate community, on 'another thingamajig'. This giant sized gadget involved widening, strengthening and speeding up the wind powered beltway between the lower continent and the upper deck. Loo was already referring to it as 'The Slide'. Now a small vehicle could drive up onto a platform below, shut down its engine and be conveyed upwards along the belt at about 15 kph, to then drive off through the open gate on the upside — all in five minutes or less. For the first time in its forty year history, Nethermost Gate was going to need a parking lot!

Our first priority on arrival was Ol'Ben, of course. He was installed temporarily in the Relatives Support Apartments at The Hub again. Aileen had been called away to The Capitol to operate a trauma centre, post earthquake. With no one at P49 for company, my old guy needed a bit of help, for his meals in particular, but also for the company and to have access to the daily news from Nethermost. I could imagine him waiting on every scrap of information that trickled through, concerning family especially, and being frustrated that he could not contribute to the massive cleanup underway.

Loo and I surprised him as he was pouring over some books about Nethermost in his tiny room. The relief on his ancient face told it all. It took a while to calm him down, he was so delighted to see us. He grilled us for ages, insisting on hearing every detail in our own words, even though much of it was known to him already.

But all that was forgotten as soon as Loo put this suggestion to him. "I got this apartment of sorts at the palace, Ol'Ben — a real fixer upper, but it has good bones … It's not as cool as your old place yet, but it could be. You and I could do a lot to the place. So, what do you think? It's rent free, and you'll like the neighbours."

"Live underground … with you?" Ol'Ben asked.

"Well, sure, but except for the sparkly sky you'd hardly know it was underground. Plus the weather's always great. The city is a real tip right now cuz of the earthquakes, but the rebuild is coming along just fine. And you'll be right in the thick of things. Cait will be there. And the rest of the O'Quinns …"

"Would I have to act like a royal? You know, it being a palace and all?"

"Are you considering turning this down, old man?" Loo was astonished.

Ol'Ben laughed and slapped his knee. "Of course, I'm coming! That's where my family lives. It's a bit grand for me, but one makes sacrifices."

He giggled all the way along the tunnel to P49. After three hours of folding and boxing, Loo suggested that he and Ol'Ben could collect the final bits and pack the car themselves and that I should take some time for myself. I grabbed at the chance to pay my farewells both to friends and to favourite haunts, especially around The Hub. I ended up camping out at Dr. Coffee Klatch a couple of hours later, awaiting my friends' return, which is where Rhue suddenly popped up behind my right shoulder. I was sitting there thinking about her too, willing her to be with me again. I'm not saying I manifested her though. I may believe in magic, but I'm not crazy.

*****

"That night when we breached both palaces, Cait, was when the war to regain Nethermost actually began," Rhue contended, when I finally got her settled beside me with her favourite brew. "I understand you've heard account of our skirmish with the palace guards. That was the first battle really.

"Fighting off those degenerates showed Keane and me how well suited in combat we were. Of course, it helped that Peadar's henchmen were ill trained and out of shape. The only thing in their favour were their gilding guns — which were so poorly defended that they were sort of ripe on the vine for the plucking. The downside of course was that in taking down three guards, we would alert Peadar to the threat.

"From that moment on, we had to assume that we were in combat mode. Our intent was to form and train a fighting force, then lay low and await the starting pistol from Nethermost Gate. I had fairy scouts busy 24/7 bringing us news of any changes both at The Capitol and at The Gate.

"But I was astonished at how little Peadar reacted to the incident with the guardsmen. While he did increase the numbers of surveillance patrols, they were sent everywhere willy nilly without obvious coordination or purpose. We ducked a few more random patrols ourselves over the next weeks. But there was little evidence that Peadar was really engaging his troops or planning to go to war. To the contrary, from what the fairies relayed, I got the sense that Peadar was more overwrought and quick to tantrum with his immediate subordinates — beating his household staff more frequently, gilding more innocents in the immediate neighbourhood — rather than organizing and preparing for an outside attack."

"I think these tantrums may have been caused by him finally acknowledging that his alchemy was failing," I explained to Rhue. "The Golden Palace was quite literally falling about his ears. He was desperate for a solution; so desperate that he stepped up his gold fracking business to unreasonable heights, with more serious quakes and ruptures as a consequence; the worst one being that massive eruption which preceded our entrance into the city.

"Add to all this, the fiction of the painting that we sent in with Donal to befuddle him and make him paranoid about betrayal amongst his own ranks. He likely lost all sense of perspective and in the end feared his own henchmen."

"That explains a lot," Rhue agreed. "But allow me to relay to my account, because I have been rehearsing this for two weeks. As you have no doubt been informed, after Keane and I returned to Carrickbeg, we turned that idyllic community into military headquarters for a strange collection of fighters.

"I adored life for those six weeks on the Pinnacles of Pons, Cait, despite the advent of war. Everything about Carrickbeg and its citizens astonishes me. Amazing folks these mountaineers! It is humbling to realize how much magic per square inch abides on those Pinnacles, yet how little the folks themselves rely upon it. For them, magic is not the short cut through old fashioned hard work. All that they have, they have earned through good honest toil.

"I felt this strength of character daily while I prepared them for combat. They wouldn't be counting on hocus-pocus alone in a fight, and they would engage their enemy with farm implements if need be. There was a great deal of interest in being part of this resistance movement throughout the Pinnacles. Humans and magicians alike had felt downtrodden from years of virtual house arrest, which restricted them essentially to the confines of their hills. In truth, the hardest part was limiting recruitment numbers, as I could not train them all.

"I had to divide my troops into those to precision train on the serious weapons for our attack on The Capitol, and those who could better serve as ambassadors of peace, to rove the small hill communities to the north after the civil war began. It was indeed these satellite troops that captured the few stray henchmen hiding out in the mountains, after the cowards fled The Capitol. This same collection of mismatched soldiers have restored hope and vigour to the smallest of settlements in the days post Restoration, and use their magical talents wisely even today to aid the wounded and the traumatized.

"But it is specifically our role in the assault on The Capitol that I need to explain, Cait. Aunt Moira tracked us down with orders to rescue our mother and grandmother. She gave us a good supply of the inventions you fashioned from Peadar's journal notes, including the antidotes to the poison tips of our enemy's weapons and to the human electroplating. We were clear in our task, determined to succeed … yet …"

"Yet, the earthquake utterly changed the game plan," I finished her sentence for her.

"Yes … thank you." Rhue looked slightly easier now.

"We were all flying by the seats of our pants at that point!" I assured her. She sat back in her chair, sipping her coffee, silent in her own thoughts.

"But you want me to understand what happened," I prompted. "You want to explain how you and Keane stumbled into that throne room, blood dripping from your swords!" This story would be worth the price of admission. This is what I had been waiting two weeks to learn.

"What happened …" Rhue repeated, shaking her head and sighing, "… so much happened, the worst of which was blowback … from unfinished business.

"We were halfway to Palace Park, when the quake struck. Our original plan was to get into the dungeons before news of your frontal assault had even reached the Apparatchik. We fully intended to have Nora and Nicola halfway to Termon by the time you stormed the palace in earnest.

"Then the earth ripped open. The sheer breadth of the suffering, Cait! People were dying, needing our immediate help. The magical talents of my troops clicked in as they moved rock and wall, found bodies, rescued the reachable, healed who they could, and held back further quakes as best as their talents allowed. We knew it would take days to reach everyone, even with magical assistance.

"Yet still I focused on my orders. I selected myself, Keane and our two strongest dwarf warriors, Munch and Mayhem, to push ahead to The Golden Palace, leaving my second lieutenant in charge of the rescue teams in their house by house search and rescue. Our race to the palace grounds was held back somewhat by the sheer amount of debris blocking our way. Perhaps it was in part due to the sheer scope of this chaos … In any case, mistakes were made.

"I think the guards we first encountered were actually running away from the palace, but once they saw us, they engaged. Only one guard had a gilder, but Mayhem and Munch were furnished with gilders themselves, and he was easily removed. The others, ten in all, were armed with long swords and massive axes, presumably poison tipped. We fought valiantly and better than they — four against ten. It took time, but by the end of it, they were all either dead or trussed up and left in Peadar's once tidy rose gardens. I treated our nicks and scratches sustained at the hands of those foul weapons with antidote, and we pushed ahead.

" … On to the dungeons of the new palace, though it was no surprise to find the cells empty. So we set out to scour the palace room by room in search of Peadar's prisoners, with Keane as our experienced guide. There were so many rooms to search on the ground floor alone. We took all precaution, Cait. It was pure reversal of fortune that led that first guard to us. We weren't aware of him, until Mayhem was run through from behind by his foul sword. Mayhem's death cry alerted yet more security. Another skirmish ensued, more guards were neutralized, more wounds for us, more antidote absorbed.

"I heard the shouts from the throne room when I was at my weakest, feeling overwhelmed by exhaustion. I turned quickly — too carelessly — towards the sound of Peadar's roar, and found myself nose to nose with Donal Fadden, my old fencing instructor and worst boyfriend ever. He had recovered from the zapping I'd given him weeks before and was sporting for revenge. Nor was he alone. Three more swordsmen backed up his muscle and weaponry. But it was clear that Donal was targeting me. While his seconds kept my comrades occupied, he alone descended upon me.

"It was a interesting dilemma, the combat between the fencing instructor and his best pupil, made more compelling by the fact that we both had the transparency talent. While we could each avoid the force of a blow by becoming transparent, neither of us could deliver an assault without becoming solid again. Donal was initially surprised by my talent, but soon began to enjoy the challenge. He knew he had the advantage. I had been weakened by my wounds and hours of battle. He was fresh, bloodthirsty and intent on revenge. He taunted me smugly throughout our sword dance, waiting for me to make just one mistake, but I kept my concentration until my teeth ached from clenching as I focused and struggled.

"But Donal was unaware of my one advantage. He was ignorant of my second talent. He'd seen the transparency, he'd experienced the thunder blast. He suspected nothing of the time travel. So while we engaged in our fatiguing swordplay, I was also planning a new *beginning* to this encounter. Before I succumbed to exhaustion, I time travelled back to moments before his ambush began and positioned myself behind a pillar. Watching him sneak up this time on my two remaining comrades Keane and Munch, I knew I had just one chance to defeat him and his entourage. But I was about to do the unthinkable. Furthermore, I would need to alter the timeline for an instant to change the plot — a clear violation of the rules of time travel. And, it would require a ruthlessness beyond the bounds of warfare, as described in those books you had me read, Cait. In peacetime, it would be labelled downright murder … Just as Shin described, I certainly felt that this use of my talent would indeed take a piece of my soul."

"Fortune favours the brave?" I suggested, lamely.

"But was it bravery, survival instinct … or cowardice?" she sighed. "In any case … When Donal and his colleagues approached, after my time reset, he charged Keane and Munch, being unaware of my presence of course. I couldn't wait an instant, couldn't allow him to play his transparency card again. I had to strike before he could land a first blow on my comrades.

"I took my sword in both hands and raced up behind him. Swinging as hard as I could, I took aim at his neck and beheaded him cleanly in one stroke. His comrades scattered in an instant. I reeled, appalled by my own actions. I staggered, stumbled, got up, staggered again, while Keane lunged forward to catch me, full of confusion at the time shift.

"Then I caught sight of the blood dripping from my sword. The blood of my enemy, yes, but the blood of a sometime friend. I pitched forward into real time again, aimless in my blind hysteria, and falling, unbeknownst to me, through the wide arches of the throne room, with a befuddled Keane in pursuit, trying to make sense of it all. I was stopped only by the sight of my mother."

"Of course … your love for our absent mother … your natural reaction in seeing her peril," I whispered.

"My foolishness was to call her name. My foolishness exposed us both to Peadar's weapon. My foolishness caused Mánús' death."

"No," I confessed, "My foolishness … in not treating Mánús' wound, however small, with the antidote instantly. He had saved my life moments before, but we were also foolishly distracted by Peadar's roar and ran forward without thinking any more of the nick to his ankle. That was what caused his death."

We sat together, miserable in our victory. We had done our duty. We had played our parts in saving a continent. But we had made mistakes … and had paid an enormous price.

"Peadar's foolishness," I whispered at long last. "Let's not tussle for a share of the blame."

Chapter 42: A Perfect Place to Begin

"I don't know how to begin again, Cait."

That raw statement was the most expression I'd heard from my mother since her rescue three weeks before. She and Father had been staying at the palace, in a suite prepared especially for them, away from the chaos of the earthquake relief effort.

Mother seldom came out of their suite of rooms and Father faithfully stayed by her side. Except for a few visits from Rhue Begin me, no one else had been granted an audience. But each time I called on her, I sensed more and more her desire to free herself from her mental bondage.

Nethermost Regained

After Shin showed me another of her recent moving canvases, I proposed a next step to Father and although he had his concerns, he agreed to let me try. Early one morning while the city still slept, I arranged for my parents and me to sneak away from the palace in a hover car driven by Loo. Although Mother was nervous to step outdoors, she was willing to leave in the stillness of daybreak, and her curiosity about the secret adventure I suggested gave me hope. Loo took a short cut through the city to reach the edge of the Forrest Curran.

We arrived at the rendezvous point just as dawn was switching on, to be greeted by Rhue, Keane and his string of Icelandic horses. We left the car there and mounted our steeds — Keane and Rhue leading the party, Mother and me riding behind, Father and Loo at our backs.

The horses seemed to know their way and demanded little of us, except to keep our seats. Although Mother seemed uneasy at first, eventually she relaxed and began looking about with just the teeniest touch of interest. When she finally spoke, she revealed her innermost fear. "I'm a doctor, Cait, but I don't know how to heal myself."

I had been trying to imagine her psychic pain all these weeks, finding that impossible. "Perhaps begin with enjoying the moment," I suggested, "Baby steps … what-what?"

"That phrase is familiar," she replied, "where have I heard that before?"

"Perhaps it will come to you, as we go along," I suggested, a hint of excitement entering my voice. "Trust that these ponies are taking us on a beautiful journey."

"I am certainly curious, but it's been years since I was even outside."

I began second guessing myself. Was my plan too complex, its staging too elaborate? I tried to prepare her for our destination. "When Father and Aunt Moira were trying to fill in the blanks for me, on all that I had missed growing up, they stuffed me to bursting with stories about family."

"I'd forgotten about your childhood, my dear. You must have felt a bit caged yourself."

"Yes … well … I imagine I enjoyed my captivity more than you did yours, and my jailer was rather lovely." I brought us back on track. "While I was being caught up on the family stories, I was especially intrigued by the tales about Fianna and Canice."

"I remember them, you know," Mother replied, now fully engaged in our discussion. "My grandparents … I do remember. I recall the splendour of their costumes, the mystery of their regal duties. I was very young and couldn't understand why they were so popular with strangers. I guess I felt a bit jealous. I loved it when I got their personal attention — especially at the end of the day, when Grandma Fianna and Grandpa Canice would come to tuck me up with a bedtime story — she reading the words, he acting out the pictures. It was magical!"

I watched my mother's face pink up as she recalled these good memories, and it gave me the confidence to continue. "Do you remember Grandma Fianna's talent?"

"She teleported like Moira."

"That's right! She used her talent to get closer to her subjects. I have heard from others how important this intimate connection became to her subjects, what hope she instilled in them at their lowest moments."

"I envy her that. I fear I'm so lacking in such skills anymore."

"I wouldn't worry, Mother. I suspect that you are more like Fianna than you realize. In any case, Fianna had a few secrets …"

"Did she? How intriguing!"

"Indeed!" I was getting exhilarated now. We were nearing our destination. "As much as she loved her duties, she longed for the occasional escape on her own, and was in the habit of teleporting to one of her own little paradises to recharge her batteries."

"Hmmm! How delicious!" Mother was enjoying the image I was sketching; my anticipation was mounting. I prayed that I had got this right.

Our horses plodded on silently a few minutes more until we came to an opening in the trees, and I knew we were drawing near. Mother took note, with more than a little curiosity now.

There it was — the big reveal! Paradise, or rather Termon reimagined. The very sight made me giddy. My friends and family had done it proud. They had spent the night before setting the scene. The trimmings had Aunt Moira's touch — flower petals dotted the path leading to the water, orchids floating on its surface, jouncing in the drizzle of the waterfall, a scent of jasmine in the air. At the bijou shoreline, a wooden folding table had been set, laden with food dainties that could only have been the handiwork of Shin. A freshly brewed teapot leaked steam into the still air, and my mother's hand selected companion sat at the table.

"Oh … my!" She breathed, as Father lifted her from her horse.

"I like to call it Fee's Paradise, but others call it Termon," I explained, leading her carefully along the uneven path. With each step, my mother got more excited; with each step, lighter of heart; until she reached the verge of the pond, and the well staged tea party.

There sat Ol'Ben in his best cardigan and chinos, beaming with expectation, leaking sappiness. "Grandpa? … Grandpa!" He stood up and pulled her slight body into his — a brass ring moment for them both.

We backed off and hid out at the base of the elm, drenching our shirt sleeves with tears, while Mother and Ol'Ben focussed solely on each other, weeping a great deal, then sharing tales of a simpler time. It was so endearing to watch Ol'Ben work his special brand of magic on his long lost granddaughter. The love between them overspilled, infecting us all — Loo cleaved to me, Keane held fast to Rhue — Father was bewitched and bursting with joy.

After an hour of their visit had elapsed, I nodded to Keane. I could bear it no longer — I had one additional secret. Keane handed me the wooden box from its hiding spot, and I proudly presented it to my mother, then watched as she opened and identified its contents. She inspected each book with delight, until she got to the final one: <u>A Child's Companion in Nethermost Verse</u>, illustrated edition.

"Cait! This is it! My bedtime stories! Can anything be so wonderful!"

She read nostalgically from it aloud to Ol'Ben and Father, while we naughty children stripped down to our altogethers, splashing in the clear water to wash away weeks of drudgery, and to purify our spirits. It wasn't long before we were joined by my parents as well, innocent as the day they were born, revelling in our water play, equaling our enthusiasm.

I pushed through the sprays of water to get to my mother, swooped her up and asked through tears of joy, "Are you having a good time Mother?"

"You've taken me back to the innocence of childhood, Cait. This is the perfect place to begin."

*****

Every morning dawned exactly the same in Nethermost. It would take a while to get used to that. But this day was very special. You could feel excitement in the air. The ceremony was set to begin at noon and everyone was all aflutter. Nethermost hadn't been this joyous in decades, and it was bringing out the best in us all.

The palace was looking much better these days. Order had been restored to its corridors as the emergency services were gradually returned to their community locations. So many lives had been lost that day; so many more had been saved. Even more lives were restored weeks later when Peadar's cache of electroplated citizens was discovered. It was life affirming to witness the reunions of family members — fathers, mothers, brothers, sisters and friends who, gilded years before, were suddenly restored to life after decades of being stacked in a closet. It must have been strange for children to be reunited with parents who still looked young, while they themselves had aged forty years. But it was all about redemption now in a land badly scarred by deprivation and terror.

This morning I felt light headed and giddy as I walked about sneaking a closeup view of the decorations for the big event — the bouquets of freesia, the boughs of ivy, the white fairy lights and pink balloons. Not to mention those exciting magical flourishes secretly lying in wait to come to life at the close of the ceremony — special effects courtesy of Nethermost's six species of magicians. Tables had been set with precision and elegance for the reception, the kitchens were bursting with the finest of food and drink. Pink carpet runners had been laid along the full length of the palatial hallway and beyond — all the way along its outdoor walkway to the dais.

I ran into Grandma and Grandpa O'Quinn on my stroll. They'd obviously had the same thought — to prime their excitement for the day ahead. This morning our greeting had that smoothness of love and familiarity I had so craved from the beginning.

"How goes the new job?" I asked Grandma Aileen.

"It's been great coming out of retirement," she enthused, "but I'm using mental muscles that had atrophied, so it can be exhausting as well. Mind you, I'm not complaining. People are being so strong, so committed to finding their bliss again."

"And you Grandpa Fergus? Are the Elders behaving themselves? No dastardly plots for world domination?"

He laughed. "No, not quite, although I am developing new skills. Your man and I have been working on plans to better connect the continent with the surface. That's exciting, and keeps me young."

In the garden I found a buffet already laden with continental breakfast — one of the better inventions of the upper world, I think. I poured myself a coffee, slipped a pastry onto the saucer, and joined my beloved on the terrace, planting one of my sweetest kisses smack on his mouth before sitting beside him on the low stone wall. "I remember this view from the night of our break in," I observed, "You could barely see the walls then, let alone the garden. The weeds and grasses were a metre high."

"Yeah?" Loo muttered vaguely — never a good sign.

"Alright, what's this about?"

"Nothing … everything."

"Well, at least we're narrowing it down."

"I guess it's about today … and tomorrow."

"Loosing me completely now."

"Okay, I'll start again. I'm not as smart as you …"

"Not true … but go on."

"And I'm not royalty."

"What! We are entering silly town now. I'm not royalty either. I was raised in the same village, went to the same schools as you ..."

"Yes, but your family …"

"… are wonderful right?"

"Right! … but also royal."

"Do they treat you any differently. If so I'll knock some heads together!"

"No of course not. I love them all, although I have my favourites."

"Ol'Ben?"

" … Cait, I love you, that's not news is it?"

"And I love you. 'Done deal', as you would say."

"Be serious, Cait! I love you … and I want someone to give me … permission … to love you forever."

"Just as well, because I'm going to marry you. And you have *my* permission to love me forever."

"Yes?"

"Yes!" I moved onto his lap and plastered that gorgeous face of his with kisses. I cherished this man, and I intended to keep him close. "Now, let's get this wedding started."

✶✶✶✶✶

As I walked that long pink carpet in my gorgeous gown, I tried to switch into slow motion in order to savour each moment, to mentally record it so I could replay it in my heart forever. This first grand celebration seemed a foretaste of decades to come, when love of family and country would become one and the same.

I noticed my mother sitting near the front, looking lovely and peaceful, waiting for my father to join her after his official duties. Shin, glorious in her usual taffeta, a triumph of colour and flounce. Aunt Moira — was that a Parisian design? Had it been a bargain she couldn't resist? Grandma Aileen holding onto Ol'Ben, both beaming pridefully. Another bucket list check mark for him. Another gorgeous but slightly risqué creation for her.

I was almost to the dais now, where Grandpa Fergus was standing in his ceremonial robes, fully primed to conduct the proceedings. There was Loo standing up with Keane to the right of centre, watching the processional arrive, looking so uncomfortable in that tux. I managed to reach my mark without falling over, and waited for all the players to shift into position. The music trailed away — the ceremony began.

"Repeat after me," boomed Grandpa Fergus. "I, Rhue"

"I, Rhue ..."

"Take you, Keane ..."

"Take you Keane ..."

"As my husband..."

"As my husband ..."

Epilogue

We arrive in Alta early to be in plenty of time for the ceremony. John and Mary Smith, who still operate The General Store, will be waiting by the front door. At 7:30 a.m. sharp, they will open up. I'm not sure how many will even remember Ol'Ben. It's been ten years, so I don't know what the turnout will be like.

Riley and Benny are hyper excited. They've never been 'up top' before and can't believe what they're seeing. The sun is especially shocking to them. I'm worried about their skin and eyes in this harsh climate, so I slather them with lotion and make them wear sunglasses.

We are here to lay Ol'Ben's ashes to rest — or at least half of them. The other half lies beside his friend Mánús in the palace gardens. But this half will be buried with my great-grandmother Nora McCauley, Ol'Ben's wife of forty years. It is my duty, and my pleasure, to honour his final wishes — a fitting tribute to a life lived honourably to the age of one hundred and three!

My husband Loo joins me on this journey. Between the two of us, we can just about keep the boys corralled — our twins, Riley and Benjamin, named for ancestors we choose to remember. They're just four, so we have to watch them carefully in case they lick all the cream off their skin or drop their glasses as they bounce about.

*****

I am not a Queen — or a Swayer as we like to call it back home. But I am a Regent, along with my sister, advisor to Her Grace Nora. Rhue and I like to lighten Mother's duties, to allow her and my father time to live their lives, to make up for those stolen years.

When Loo and I finally married, it was even more glorious than Rhue and Keane's wedding — or so I'm always teasing my sister. The best thing about our wedding was that Loo's father attended, and he's been back several times since.

His son, and my husband, is Minister of Transportation now, although he hates that title. "I'm Loo," he begins, when addressing a crowd.

Nethermost Regained

He's come a long way since the tunnel pod days — since the store.
He's established a rapid transit system throughout the continent with
a seamless link to Nethermost Gate and the upside. It's clean, fast,
energy efficient, with more than a touch of magic. So proud of that
man!

Shin has retired; she tells me she's thinking of taking up painting —
the little scamp! My father is now Ambassador and has forged new
trade relations, increased supply lines, and has translated this into a
renewed prosperity for the realm. He leaves all matters military to
Rhue and Keane these days, who keep their workforce sharp, the
palace protected, and do their best to keep their rowdy daughters in
line.

Grandma and Grandpa O'Quinn claim to be semi-retired, but are
always on the go. They've opened that museum I envisioned long
ago, to collect and preserve those memories and artifacts unique to
our culture. That's what makes Nethermost a society rather than a
loose connection of disparate people. That's what makes their jobs
about the most important on the continent.

Aunt Moira is enjoying co-ownership of me as one of my Moms, and
travels for pleasure now that she has some free time. She still
dresses me, rather well I think, with bargains she finds worldwide.
And, although she never lacks for companionship, she's not the
marrying kind.

We do our best to keep intelligence about Nethermost somewhat
contained. There are lots of bad habits in the upper world that we'd
like to avoid. Our location especially is a closely kept secret, and with
millions of acres of unexplored Canadian forest to search through,
we're unlikely to be found.

*****

Loo grabs my hand and lets the boys skip ahead, along the newly
poured sidewalks on Queen. Once we turn onto Main, we will be
there. I'm nervous, to be honest. I want The General Store to look
just the same. I want to preserve the memories I have of when it was
just Ol'Ben, Loo and me.

We turn the corner — thankfully the old store does look the same —
except that there's this huge crowd out front.

343

Nethermost Regained

— **Acknowledgements** —

My Thanks

… to Paul McElhone
for the wonderfully generous foreword

… to Judy Duffin
for her excellent proofreading skills

… to Judith Dyck
Elizabeth Duern
my early readers

… to Barbara Plank
Cyndi Richards Jamieson
Brenda Barr Worsnop
supportive friends

****

... but mostly I thank my husband Ian who took this
ride with me, step by awkward step

"Being deeply loved by someone gives you strength,
while loving someone deeply gives you courage."
(Lao Tzu)

— About the Author —

"My education in fantasy writing comes from an M.A. from McMaster University, Canada, with a thesis specialty in the fairy tale. As an artist, I have had formal training from Sheridan School of Fine Arts, and have operated my own fine art business for more than twenty-five years."

NANCY GUILD BENDALL writes, paints and sculpts from her studio at the edge of a small village near Toronto Canada, looking all the while for fairies at the top of her garden.

Other books by this author …

<u>The Nights and Times of Ned Clery</u>. Toronto, Canada: Meade House Press, 2014.

<u>The StarKeeper's Daughter — And The Closely Kept Secret</u>. Toronto, Canada: Meade House Press, 2016.